The enemy vehicles raced away across the desert

"Take it easy, Congressman," Bolan said without turning to look at him. "I think this might be over."

A sudden glare of blue light erupted from the floor. Flames covered Morrow, who was still strapped to the toppled chair. Bolan cursed and tossed the subgun aside to reach for a bedroll. Yet the fire consumed the man before the Executioner could attempt to smother the blaze.

The heat was like a blast furnace and drove Bolan out the door, his vision impaired by the bright light. Half-blind and dazed by the heat wave, he was lucky the enemy hadn't left someone behind to hide in ambush. He would have been an easy target.

"What the hell is going on?" he demanded in angry frustration.

There was no one left alive to reply.

D1530230

*Other titles available in
this series:*

DON PENDLETON's
MACK BOLAN®
FLAMES OF WRATH

A GOLD EAGLE BOOK FROM
W⊕RLDWIDE®

TORONTO • NEW YORK • LONDON
AMSTERDAM • PARIS • SYDNEY • HAMBURG
STOCKHOLM • ATHENS • TOKYO • MILAN
MADRID • WARSAW • BUDAPEST • AUCKLAND

If you purchased this book without a cover you should be aware
that this book is stolen property. It was reported as "unsold and
destroyed" to the publisher, and neither the author nor the
publisher has received any payment for this "stripped book."

First edition April 1997

ISBN 0-373-61453-5

Special thanks and acknowledgment to
Bill Fieldhouse for his contribution to this work.

FLAMES OF WRATH

Copyright © 1997 by Worldwide Library.

All rights reserved. Except for use in any review, the
reproduction or utilization of this work in whole or in part
in any form by any electronic, mechanical or other means,
now known or hereafter invented, including xerography,
photocopying and recording, or in any information storage
or retrieval system, is forbidden without the written permission
of the publisher, Worldwide Library, 225 Duncan Mill Road,
Don Mills, Ontario, Canada M3B 3K9.

All characters in this book have no existence outside the
imagination of the author and have no relation whatsoever to
anyone bearing the same name or names. They are not even
distantly inspired by any individual known or unknown to the
author, and all incidents are pure invention.

® and TM are trademarks of the publisher. Trademarks indicated
with ® are registered in the United States Patent and Trademark
Office, the Canadian Trade Marks Office and in other countries.

Printed in U.S.A.

..."O Horror! he is here...Call the death eternally engendered in the corrupted humours of the vicious body itself—Spontaneous Combustion, and none other."
—*Bleak House*
by Charles Dickens

Sometimes natural phenomena and scientific technology merge. This may mean wonder drugs to heal the sick, power sources for communities or weapons of mass destruction. These are human innovations. They may be used for good or evil. Either way, humans are responsible for the results.

—Mack Bolan

magazine pouches, grenades, knives and garrotes

CHAPTER ONE

A full moon shone like a celestial spotlight, surrounded by a plethora of stars. Mack Bolan would have appreciated the astronomic display under different circumstances, as he'd rather approach a band of terrorists under cover of a dark, cloudy night. However, it couldn't be helped. Time was running out.

The Executioner glanced at the six soldiers under his command. He hadn't met them until a few hours prior to the beginning of the mission. They were members of the Israeli Independent Paratroop Battalion, and they had a well-deserved reputation for getting the job done. The Israelis moved well across the rocks and sand, with the skill and discipline associated with highly trained night fighters. Like Bolan, they wore black camouflage fatigues and desert combat boots, with black berets instead of their usual red airborne headgear.

Bolan carried an Uzi submachine gun for the occasion, as well as his Beretta 93-R, complete with attached sound suppressor, in a special shoulder holster. His .44 Magnum Desert Eagle rode in a hip holster, and his military webbing was festooned with magazine pouches, grenades, knives and garrotes.

The paratroopers were well armed. Four carried Galil assault rifles, and the two officers packed Uzis. All had side arms, grenades and blades.

The Israelis appeared to accept Bolan's authority and cooperated without complaint. They might have objected to service under an American's command, but the Executioner understood soldiers. Like everyone else, they wanted to be treated with respect. A good leader kept that in mind. The paratroopers were intelligent, skilled fighting men, and Bolan treated them in the manner they deserved.

While the caliber of the paratroopers pleased Bolan, he was less than happy about the other aspects of the mission. The job was simple. Terrorists held Walter Morrow captive and he had to be rescued. Morrow was a junior U.S. congressman who had gone to Israel to help negotiate new trade agreements on import-export goods. It had been a chance for Morrow to do some international grandstanding, and some genius in Washington had decided he would be a good choice for the task because he wasn't Jewish and would be regarded as neutral in matters of religion and politics of the Middle East.

The theory proved to be wrong. Morrow hadn't been in Israel twenty-four hours before he was kidnapped. His security was poor, and the abductors had had little trouble grabbing the congressman. They managed to take Morrow from Tel Aviv without being observed, but were less careful when they reached their base on the West Bank. Some goatherds in the area reportedly saw several armed men with a pale-faced prisoner clad in pajamas and apparently bound and gagged. The site was an old adobe brick dwelling used by a group believed to be members of Jinn 2000.

Considered a religious cult, Jinn 2000 had been under scrutiny since it began in 1994. Based on the alleged predictions of a Shiite mystic known as Omar, the sect started in Saudi Arabia. Cells appeared in several Islamic countries and seemed to attract more members wherever Jinn 2000 established a base.

The name came from Omar's best-known prediction. He had claimed Judgment Day would occur in the year 2000, and God would reward the followers of the true faith and punish the infidels. True believers would be avenging angels assigned to crush the enemies of God. The devotees would be transformed into jinn. Not cute genies that respond to a master with a lamp or bottle, but mighty spirits with almost limitless power for all eternity.

Jinn 2000 had been called an Islamic version of the Aum Shinri Kyo—Supreme Truth—movement in Japan, blamed for the infamous sarin gas attack on the Tokyo subway on March 20, 1995. However, such comparisons were often inaccurate, and there had been no evidence to suggest that Jinn 2000 would resort to terrorist tactics...until now.

The President of the United States had planned a visit to Israel, and he didn't want to cancel the trip due to the Morrow abduction, aware it would appear to be a sign of weakness and fear of the threat of terrorist actions. Yet the danger was very real, and only a fool would ignore that fact. The Man in the Oval Office had contacted Hal Brognola at Stony Man Farm. The big Fed called on his old friend for assistance.

Although the operation had sounded like something the Israelis could handle on their own, Mack Bolan agreed to participate. He had arrived in Tel Aviv, got his equipment through a CIA contact at the U.S. Embassy and discovered Mossad had already located the terrorist base where Morrow was most likely being held hostage. The Israeli Intelligence agency had called on a liaison agent with Aman, Israeli military Intelligence, to assemble a commando team to launch the rescue operation.

Major Ziyyon, the Aman liaison, wasn't happy when Mossad told him an American counterterrorist specialist wouldn't only join his team, but would be placed in command of the unit. Ziyyon complained about the politics involved and objected to CIA interference because Washington didn't trust the Israelis to handle the problem.

Bolan could sympathize with the major's point of view, but he had his job to do and that took priority over Ziyyon's indignation. Reluctantly the Aman officer briefed the American introduced as Michael Belasko on the details and introduced him to the paratroopers.

THE EXECUTIONER EXAMINED the adobe structure through the lenses of Starlite binoculars. He didn't need the night-vision optics due to the full moon, but the scope allowed him to observe the site from a distance. Two canvas-top trucks were parked by the building, and three men, armed with AK-47 assault rifles, stood guard. A few others lounged about outside, perhaps to avoid the heat inside the structure.

The structure was large enough to house a dozen or more persons, depending on what level of comfort they desired. A canvas lean-to, which Bolan took to be the latrine, stood about twenty yards from the building. Several mounds of sandbags had been placed around the area to provide cover in case the base was attacked.

The Executioner knew better than to regard an enemy site as easy, but it did appear to be a fairly standard bivouac. He doubted there was a basement, so Congressman Morrow would most likely be held in a room or improvised cell area away from a door or window to discourage an escape attempt. However, Bolan couldn't guess how the terrorists would respond when the raid began. He didn't even know their motivation for kidnapping Morrow.

Mossad claimed the Jinn 2000 sect to be fanatics, but Bolan knew this to be a term people applied too quickly to religious groups other than their own. No one had been able to provide him with enough information to determine if the kidnappers would be more apt to throw down their weapons and surrender or fight to the last man and kill the hostage without hesitation. He didn't know if the site could have been rigged with explosives, or if the members of the sect were the type to die for the cause. The Executioner had encountered a great number of terrorists of various nationalities, with extremist beliefs and twisted dogma. Many were homicidal, yet most weren't truly suicidal.

The Executioner and the paratroopers had discussed strategy in advance, and what they saw through binoculars didn't suggest any reason to change it. The plan was simple. Bolan and two volunteers would stealthfully approach the base while the other commandos would take cover approximately one hundred yards beyond the bivouac perimeter. They would provide backup with the long-range Galil rifles. Bolan and the men with him intended to take out one or more sentries to reach a side window. With luck they would locate Morrow immediately.

If they found the hostage, the trio would try to take out any guards. If Morrow wasn't visible from the window, they would have to deal with the terrorists they encountered and hastily enter the building. Either way the sound of gunfire would signal the paratroopers outside to take out the enemy and lob grenades at the vehicles. The move would distract the sect members and give Bolan and his companions a better chance to get Morrow out of the building alive.

The commandos maintained radio silence as they advanced, but two NCOs carried transceivers and could contact Major Ziyyon, who waited at the nearby village of Abu Gosh with a company of troops and a heavily armed gunship. If anything went wrong, they could call in reinforcements.

Bolan and the paratroopers continued to approach the enemy base. All the Israelis understood English, some better than others, but communication was limited to hand gestures as the riflemen moved into position, selecting boulders and ridges for cover. The big American signaled to the remaining pair that it was time to advance. As silent as three serpents, they crept toward the base.

The Executioner studied the area from the cover of a rockpile approximately fifty yards from the heart of the small compound. He didn't like what he saw. A metal cylinder extended above the tailgate of one of the trucks. The muzzle seemed to be made of glass or transparent plastic, cone shaped with a dish mounted to the metal frame. Bolan wasn't certain what this object was, but he suspected it might be a motion detector or body-heat sensor. The kidnappers weren't as low-tech as they seemed.

The big American rolled on his side, his body angled to make the most of the rocky cover. He searched for the two Israelis who followed him, then raised an open palm and pushed it forward in a universal gesture to stop. The paratroopers saw the signal and came to a halt.

Then they burst into flames, blue fire exploding across their backs. No sparks warned of danger; no projectile had been launched at the pair. The hungry blaze seemed to jet up from the ground to consume them. It struck so quickly that neither man screamed before being engulfed. A white-hot core burned in the center of each blaze as the bodies convulsed on the ground. Ammunition cooked off with loud popping sounds similar to a string of firecrackers during a Chinese New Year celebration.

The stench of burned cloth and charred flesh assaulted Bolan's nostrils. The fire crackled across the blackened bones of what had been living men only scant seconds before the mysterious flames appeared. The Executioner stared at the blaze as it continued to devour the remains.

A terrorist gunman pointed at the blue flames with the barrel of his Kalashnikov as he spoke to his comrades. Some observed the ghastly scene in silence. Others cheered with joy, thrilled by what they saw.

Galil rifles snarled, and two terrorists toppled to the ground. The cheers came to an abrupt halt. The enemy scrambled for the cover of sandbags or bolted for shelter near the house, some taking aim and returning fire with their AK-47s. Bolan resisted the impulse to use his Uzi and attempted to creep closer, his heart hammering in his chest. He didn't know how the two paratroopers had been reduced to ashes before his eyes, but he risked the same fate.

It was possible that some sort of network of gas pipes had been set up around the perimeter of the camp, utilizing pressure plates to trigger concentrated jets of intense flame from spouts under a layer of sand. Perhaps the terrorists used a new kind of laser that transmitted an invisible beam, directed to a target determined by a body-heat sensor.

Other theories nagged Bolan as he moved closer. He tried to dismiss such speculation, aware it could only distract him in a dangerous situation. He had to concentrate on the terrorists in the base. However they managed to turn two men into human torches, they had missed Bolan and apparently didn't realize he was a threat. The Executioner intended to use that to the best advantage and try to employ the element of surprise for all it was worth.

Screams erupted from the shadows. Bolan glanced over his shoulder and saw blue flames burst from the earth one hundred yards away. The other Israelis were being taken out by the mysterious fire. The Executioner's stomach knotted with anger, as he turned his attention back to the Jinn 2000 bivouac.

Two enemy gunmen stared back at him.

The pair had approached Bolan's position while the paratroopers burned. Their startled expressions revealed they hadn't expected to encounter anyone so close to the camp. Young and tough, the pair wore scruffy fatigues and carried Kalashnikovs.

One man recovered faster than his companion and

thrust his rifle toward Bolan. The Executioner had already raised his Uzi, immediately shifted the barrel and squeezed the trigger. A trio of 9 mm rounds spit from the subgun to tear into the Arab, puncturing the guy's solar plexus and drilling into his chest cavity. The impact hurled the man backward and slammed him to the ground, his unfired AK-47 still clenched in his fists.

Bolan swung his weapon toward the next man, but it was too late. His opponent had already let loose with his assault rifle. High-velocity slugs struck the Uzi, raising sparks along the steel frame, and the force of the 7.62 mm bullets sent the subgun spinning from the Executioner's hands.

The enemy gunman blinked with surprise when he discovered he had unintentionally shot the gun out of his enemy's grasp. A cruel smile appeared as he aimed his rifle at the warrior's chest. Bolan realized he couldn't draw a pistol and fire before his opponent could squeeze the trigger. The gunman stood more than three yards from him, too far to attempt a grab or kick.

The terrorist squeezed the trigger, but a hollow click mocked his effort. Smoke curled from the open port on the frame. The gunman had to have burned up most of his ammunition when he targeted the Israelis and fired his last few rounds at Bolan's Uzi. Startled and enraged, the terrorist charged with the empty AK-47.

The guy was quick, but Bolan saw the attack before he swung the rifle. The terrorist had adjusted his grip from the trigger guard to the top of the walnut stock, and his shoulder shifted to signal the direction of the stroke. The Executioner moved back and ducked to avoid the vicious swipe, the rifle butt missing his head by inches.

Bolan snared his opponent's wrist above the fist clenched to the AK stock, pulled to increase the terrorist's momentum and yanked the guy off balance. As the man dropped to the ground, the Executioner chopped him twice across the nape with the callused edge of his hand. Convinced the terrorist was stunned, Bolan grabbed the AK-47 with both hands, then drove the buttstock at his adversary's temple, making sure the man would stay down. He dropped the assault rifle and unleathered the Desert Eagle.

A voice shouted out in Arabic. It was a dialect Bolan didn't recognize, but the tone suggested he could expect more trouble. Two terrorists rushed toward him, but the warrior raised the big pistol and opened fire before either gunner could take aim. A .44 Magnum round stabbed into the closer man's chest, his sternum exploding as the high-velocity slug slammed him backward two yards. The body hit the ground and twitched before lying still.

The Executioner sprinted for the first line of sandbags, swinging his weapon toward the second gunman, who dropped to a crouch and triggered his AK-47. Bullets slashed air near Bolan, close enough for a stray round to tug the sleeve of his jacket. Yet none scored a hit or even grazed him.

A projectile drilled the terrorist through the lower stomach and pancreas. As the man doubled up in agony, Bolan fired another round into the top of the opponent's bowed head, effectively taking him out of play.

Figures darted about the camp in frantic confusion,

none noticing Bolan as he stayed low along the sandbags and made his way to the house.

There was still a chance Congressman Morrow could be alive, and the Executioner hoped to get the hostage out before the enemy tried to spirit him away in a vehicle. The warrior ran some quick numbers through his head. He reckoned there were between a dozen and fifteen terrorists at the site. Nearly half had already been taken out, which left at least six opponents and perhaps as many as nine. A lot for one man to deal with, but he had faced worse odds.

Bolan reached the house and slipped to the rear, hidden from the view of the terrorists. He returned the Desert Eagle to its hip holster and drew his Beretta 93-R from shoulder leather. He made certain the sound suppressor was in place before he thumbed the selector switch from safety to semiauto. The big man carefully moved to the first window and peered inside. He discovered an untidy room, cluttered with bedrolls, bags of gear, a couple kerosene lanterns and a small field desk. There was no sign of Morrow or any of the terrorists.

The Executioner headed for the next window, looked in and recognized Congressman Morrow from photographs, although the man appeared very different in pictures taken on Capitol Hill. He wore torn and soiled pajamas instead of an expensive suit. The usual red necktie that looked good on TV had been replaced with a cloth gag, and the man was bound to a metal folding chair by several strands of thick wire. He was bruised and bloodied, but still alive. A medallion hung from his neck from a leather thong. Probably the image of a saint or good-luck piece, Bolan guessed.

·

A single Jinn 2000 gunner stood guard by the hostage. The terrorist's back was to the window, as the man's attention was fixed on a door at the other side of the room. Neither glass nor wire screen blocked Bolan as he thrust the Beretta through the window. He aimed and triggered the 93-R, a muffled report the only sound from the muzzle. A scarlet spider appeared at the back of the gunman's skull, and he slumped to the floor in a lifeless heap.

Bolan climbed through the window and stepped onto the earthen floor. Morrow stared at him and began to wiggle in his chair, shaking his head wildly in an effort to work loose his gag. The soldier moved beside him and held the Beretta to his lips as a signal for Morrow to be quiet.

"Sorry," he whispered, tipping over the chair to dump it and the captive to the floor. The congressman grunted through his gag. Bolan imagined Morrow cursed him at that moment, unaware he had been placed on the floor to take him out of the line of fire.

Truck engines growled to life outside the building. The Jinn 2000 extremists were ready to flee the base, but they would want to take their prize with them.

The soldier plucked an M-26 grenade from his belt and yanked the pin. He planned to discourage the enemy, and a fragmentation blast was a good way to do it. Bolan lobbed the metal egg through the gap at the open door, and seconds later an explosion rocked the building. Dirt and some bloodied debris spewed across the threshold.

Bolan grabbed another grenade and moved to the corpse, prying a PPSh-41 subgun from lifeless fingers. The Russian chopper was obsolete by modern combat standards, but it provided Bolan with more firepower. With a blow-back system that kicked out close to 900 rounds per minute, the PPSh-41 could still do some serious damage. Bolan recalled the standard magazine held 25 rounds of 7.62 mm ammo, which could help even the odds that waited outside.

However, as dust cleared from the doorway, Bolan saw both trucks were making a hasty retreat from the area, speeding into the desert.

"Take it easy, Congressman," Bolan told Morrow without turning to look at him. "I think this might be over."

A sudden glare of bright blue light drew his attention to the floor. Flames covered Morrow, who was still strapped to the chair. Bolan cursed and tossed the subgun aside to reach for a bedroll. Yet the fire had consumed Morrow before Bolan could attempt to smother the blaze with the blanket. The intense white core warned that such an effort would be futile anyway. More flames erupted as the dead terrorist was consumed by the brilliant blue light.

The heat was like a blast furnace and drove Bolan out the door. His vision was impaired by the bright light. Half-blind and dazed by the blast of heat, he was lucky the enemy hadn't left someone to hide in ambush. He would have been an easy target.

"What the hell is going on?" he asked in angry frustration.

There was no one left to reply.

CHAPTER TWO

Major Gideon Ziyyon stared down at the ashes. A charred boot at one end of the pile was all that suggested the ashes had formerly been a human. He picked up the Uzi subgun beside the mound, frowning as he blew some ashes from the steel frame.

"You claim this is all that remains of my paratroopers?" he demanded. "Congressman Morrow, the terrorists...all reduced to ashes?"

"Some of the terrorists escaped in the trucks," Bolan replied. "If you called in an air search, we might be able to catch them."

The major and his troops had arrived by helicopter and trucks a few minutes after Bolan's battle with the Jinn 2000 gunmen. They had been startled and confused by what they found. The Israelis were even more amazed by the Executioner's explanation of what happened.

"I think you can tell us where they went, Belasko," Ziyyon declared, "or whatever your real name is. We'll find that out, as well as everything else you know."

Bolan met the major's hard gaze without blinking. He was aware the paratroopers watched him like a flock of hungry hawks, ready to descend on the

American at the first provocation. Most of them probably understood English to some degree, and all could appreciate the tone of Ziyyon's voice and his hostile manner.

"I know it's hard to imagine men bursting into flame without warning or any evidence of pyrotechnics," Bolan replied, "but that's what happened. You figure I'm responsible for this? Tell me how you think I managed to cremate sixteen or seventeen men and arrange their ashes at different positions?"

"We don't know these ashes were people," Ziyyon replied. "All we have is your word about what happened. Why should we believe a goy from the United States? Because you got authority over us due to CIA influence with Mossad? Supposedly your President even asked our prime minister to cooperate in this matter. I knew there was something suspicious about this mess from the start."

"What sort of paranoid conspiracy theory are you working on, Major?" Bolan asked. "Instead of wasting time here, we should be trying to cut off the terrorists who ran into the desert. Whatever they used to make humans burst into flames is probably in one of those vehicles."

"But you have no idea how they did this?" Ziyyon replied. "You actually saw the six men I assigned to you burn to death, and then Congressman Morrow caught fire, as well. You even claim the bodies of the Arab terrorists you supposedly killed also burned up. How many did you claim you took out all by yourself? Seven or eight?"

"Five," Bolan answered. "I don't know how many the grenade took out. Two. Maybe three. All the dead men were burned into ash piles as the trucks fled the area.''

"Yet, somehow you weren't affected," the major remarked. "Why didn't you catch fire, Belasko? Maybe because you're such an invincible American hero you're immune. I'm surprised you didn't chase after those speeding trucks and turn them over with your superhuman strength. Too bad you didn't have a magic cape so you could fly and swoop down on those villains before they got away."

"I don't know why I wasn't affected by what burned those men," Bolan stated. "I don't know how they did this. It was no ordinary blaze. That much I do know. Even the bones were reduced to ash in a matter of seconds. Looked like the center of the fire was actually inside the bodies of the victims."

"This story sounds more absurd with every sentence you utter. I wonder about this congressman. What made him so special? Why did you get such high authority to find him? What did Morrow know? What was he doing in Israel? Perhaps he was connected to something your government didn't want us to know about. Could it be you were sent to silence Morrow and had to take out any witnesses...Arab or Israeli?"

Bolan was surprised by Ziyyon's accusation. The major seemed to resent the Executioner's status as a foreigner placed in charge of the operation to find Morrow, a status that gave the warrior authority over Ziyyon and his commandos. The big American wasn't going to get the officer to back off by saying anything that would make him angrier.

"Look, Major," he began, "I'd find this story

pretty hard to believe myself if I hadn't seen it with my own eyes. Why don't we get some planes in the desert with surveillance gear and try to nail the terrorists? Then you can see about having the ashes analyzed to determine if they really are human remains and how this was done.''

"You're trying to distract us, Belasko, send us on a wild-goose chase. We're supposed to chase after these alleged Jinn 2000 fanatics in the desert and let you sneak back to Tel Aviv and the U.S. Embassy. Then we can't touch you. Diplomatic immunity.''

"I intend to go with you to hunt down the enemy.''

"You think I would allow a serpent among my men again?'' Ziyyon asked. "Lieutenant Hevron! Sergeant Jaffe! Take Mr. Michael Belasko's weapons. If he tries to resist, shoot him.''

Two soldiers approached Bolan. Others brought the buttstocks of their weapons to their shoulders, fingers on triggers. They kept the barrels of Galils and Uzis high, but clearly they were ready to point and fire if necessary. Ziyyon said something in rapid Hebrew. Bolan raised his hands to shoulder level as his pistols, grenades, knives and other weapons were confiscated.

"You are under arrest, Belasko,'' Ziyyon declared. "By my authority as a field-grade officer in the Israeli military, I charge you with suspicion of murder and espionage against the state of Israel. That makes everything nice and legal and official. You do understand the charges, Belasko?''

"I understand what you said,'' Bolan replied. "I'm not so sure why you're doing it.''

"It'll be made clear to you later," Ziyyon assured him.

A stocky man with a bulldog face snapped a pair of handcuffs on Bolan's wrists. The Executioner noticed he wore three bar-shaped chevrons with a leaf emblem in the center, which meant his rank was staff sergeant. Bolan's hands were cuffed in front instead of behind his back. The departure from standard procedure for arrest seemed odd to Bolan. Jaffe didn't appear to be a careless man, and Bolan was sure Ziyyon would have upbraided the man had he objected.

Hevron was thin, with hollow cheeks, a long jaw and dark, sad eyes. Two black bars on the collar of his fatigues labeled his rank as a lieutenant in the Israeli military, and he held Bolan's .44 Magnum Desert Eagle. Hevron and Jaffe escorted Bolan to a Land Rover while Ziyyon addressed the rest of his men. The Executioner was shoved into the back of the vehicle. Hevron sat beside him and jammed the pistol in his ribs while Jaffe slid behind the steering wheel.

"Where are we going?" Bolan asked in halting Hebrew.

"We understand English," Hevron stated. "You're going where we take you. There's nothing you can do about it, so just shut up and don't give us any trouble."

Ziyyon approached the vehicle. "You'll be pleased to know I'm leading the rest of my troops in an effort to track down those phantom Jinn 2000 terrorists you spoke of," he announced. "I'll leave a few men to guard this site until a team can be sent to study the evidence here."

"Great," Bolan said dryly. "You plan to tell your superiors you decided to disobey orders that put me in charge and placed me under arrest?"

"I'll mention that to them," Ziyyon assured him, "but I intend to give Lieutenant Hevron and Sergeant Jaffe a chance to interrogate you. They just need to take you somewhere private to talk to you without being disturbed."

"You've already heard the truth, so there won't be anything gained by having them try to beat it out of me. If you have a personal problem with me, Ziyyon, you ought to take it up with me yourself. One-on-one."

"I'd like that," Ziyyon said. "I'd like to break your neck right now, but that'll have to wait. Don't try anything stupid, Belasko. They'll shoot you if you try to escape."

"But they won't shoot me in front of witnesses," Bolan commented. "I'm not sure why you're doing this, Ziyyon, but you'll regret it."

"I doubt that."

The major leaned close to Hevron and whispered something in Hebrew. Then Jaffe started the Land Rover, and the vehicle headed into the desert toward Abu Gosh.

Bolan guessed his keepers had no intention of delivering him to the village alive. He understood now why Jaffe had cuffed his hands in front of him instead of behind his back...with the rest of the paratrooper company for witnesses. It would be hard to justify killing a prisoner for trying to escape if his hands were manacled behind his back. To claim Bolan grabbed a weapon and had to be shot would be more acceptable if his hands were cuffed in front.

Hevron and Jaffe weren't taking him to be interrogated; they planned to kill him.

The Executioner didn't ask the pair if his assumption was correct. That would only make them alert and suspicious. Hevron kept the muzzle of the pistol jammed in Bolan's side as they traveled beyond the sight of the men at the terrorist base.

As the vehicle traveled into the desert, they seemed surrounded by a sea of sand and rocks. There was no sign of another living thing. Bolan figured time was running out, and he would have to make his move soon.

Hevron unbuttoned a shirt pocket and removed a pack of cigarettes. He shook a cigarette loose and caught the end with his lips. It dangled from his mouth as he slipped the pack back into the shirt pocket. He still held the pistol on Bolan with one hand as he searched his own pockets with the other.

"Need a light?" Bolan asked.

"I'll manage," Hevron answered. "There's nothing personal about this, Belasko. Whatever you did back there was probably in the service of your country. Maybe you had to get rid of Morrow. Maybe you even told the truth about everybody burning up in some mysterious manner."

"But you and Sergeant Jaffe will still do me because Major Ziyyon wants it done."

"'Do' you?" the lieutenant asked, unfamiliar with the term. "We obey our commander's orders, and if a mistake is done it will be due to his bad judgment. We will not be to blame for being good soldiers."

"That's a comfort," Bolan said dryly.

Hevron finally produced a book of matches. He opened it and fumbled with the paper matches awkwardly with one hand as he tried to strike one with his thumb. Frustrated, he glanced at the matches. It wasn't a big distraction, but it was the best Bolan could hope for.

The Executioner suddenly shifted in his seat and rammed both manacled hands against Hevron's fist, shoving the Desert Eagle aside as the Israeli pulled the trigger. The .44 roared, the muzzle-flash flaring near Bolan's knee, but the bullet punched through the backrest to the front seat. Jaffe cried out in alarm. The sergeant was fortunate the Land Rover had a right-hand driver's seat, or the Magnum slug would have burrowed into his back.

Bolan gripped the barrel and frame of the Desert Eagle with both hands as he shoved Hevron against the wall of the Land Rover. He twisted with strength fueled by desperation and determination. Hevron's free hand swung a clumsy overhand punch, his knuckles striking Bolan above the right temple. His skull throbbed from the blow, but the pain only increased his pressure on the pistol. Bone cracked, and Hevron howled as his index finger broke, trapped inside the trigger guard of the weapon as Bolan gave it a final twist.

Jaffe stomped the brake, and the vehicle came to an abrupt halt. The Executioner was propelled forward, across the backrest of the front seat. The Desert Eagle flew from his grasp, and he raised his cuffed hands to protect his head and face from impact with the dashboard. His back hit the front-seat cushion next to Jaffe.

The NCO rasped something in Hebrew and clawed at his side arm. The attempted draw was awkward due to his seated position, and the steering wheel blocked his arm. Bolan braced himself with his elbows and left foot as he swung his right leg. His boot slammed into Jaffe's face, blood gushing from the sergeant's nose and mouth.

Hevron rose from the back seat, left hand clasped to his broken index finger. The officer appeared dazed. He glanced down at Bolan in the front seat, apparently surprised to find the Executioner was still in the vehicle. Bolan swiftly jammed his right fist into his left palm and thrust a powerful elbow to the point of Hevron's chin. The blow snapped the lieutenant's head back. His eyes closed, and he slumped unconscious in the back seat.

Jaffe groaned and mopped a hand across his bloodied face. Bolan didn't give him a chance to recover. He clasped his hands together and swung as if he wielded an ax. Steel links of a cuff hit Jaffe behind the ear, and the man crumpled in a senseless heap by the steering wheel.

Bolan opened the door and shoved the unconscious NCO from the vehicle. He slid beside Jaffe and took the guy's side arm, which was a Desert Eagle. Not a surprise, since the pistol was manufactured by Israeli Military Industries. Jaffe's Eagle was a .357 Magnum instead of the .44 the Executioner favored, but the basic design was the same. He thrust the handgun in his belt and searched the sergeant's pockets.

"Bingo," he said aloud when he found the handcuff keys.

The Executioner unlocked the manacles from his wrists, then moved to the rear of the Land Rover. Hevron moaned as he started to regain his senses, which Bolan prevented with a fist to the officer's battered jaw. He dragged Hevron from the vehicle and hauled him to where Jaffe lay. The big American snapped one handcuff bracelet around Hevron's wrist and the other to Jaffe.

He then helped himself to the paratroopers' gear. Since he had no extra magazines for his .44 Desert Eagle, he took the other .357 Magnum Desert Eagle pistol from Hevron and collected four spare magazines from their combined ammo pouches. Bolan also confiscated a two-way radio unit, a combat knife—similar to a Ka-bar—and a smaller dagger-style boot knife. Both Israelis carried canteens and first-aid kits. He took only one of each.

"You guys don't deserve it, but I won't leave you without water or first aid in the desert."

He also found some shekel notes. Bolan didn't know if he would need the money, but decided to take it just in case.

Bolan slid behind the steering wheel and started the engine. He found a map in the glove compartment, but it was printed in Hebrew, and he could barely understand any of it. He had less trouble with a compass. The needle pointed at a Hebrew letter that resembled a *Y* with a bent tail. North was the direction he planned to travel that night.

At that moment it was one of the few things the Executioner could be sure about.

CHAPTER THREE

Hal Brognola jammed the unlit cigar between his teeth and began to methodically chew while he watched images form on the wall monitor. The President of the United States appeared, five times larger than life. His dress shirt was open at the throat, his face tired and eyes ringed by bags from lack of sleep. The man in the Oval Office didn't try to present the polished public image familiar to the rest of the world. Brognola wasn't impressed by such trappings, and the President knew it.

The big Fed sat at the conference table of the War Room at Stony Man Farm. He looked even more haggard than the man on the screen. Indeed, if anyone had to deal with more pressure than the President of the United States, that person was Hal Brognola. Two days of stubble announced his inability to find time to shave. He had been getting by on naps on the office sofa and a lot of coffee since first hearing about the abduction of Congressman Morrow.

"Hello, Hal," the President greeted. "How are you today?"

"Probably about the same as you."

"I believe that. You know why I'm calling?"

"Got a pretty good idea," Brognola said. "Our

computer-telemetry intelligence is as good as any sources you may have heard from already.''

''Probably better,'' the President agreed.

''We try. Unfortunately the news from Israel isn't good. They carried out the raid on the Jinn 2000 group, but Morrow is dead. Apparently his body was burned to a crisp, along with half a dozen Israeli commandos working with Striker.''

''That's not quite the version I've heard,'' the President began. ''CIA and NSA say what really happened is questionable. An Israeli military Intelligence officer seems suspicious of our man's story that people just burst into flames. Our own experts doubt this could have happened. They say burning a human being in a crematorium requires heat at two thousand degrees Fahrenheit or higher for a period of two hours or more.''

''Yeah,'' Brognola said as he glanced at some data sheets on the table. ''We got that information, too. Even after a body is subjected to such intense heat for such a period of time, there are still bone fragments among the ashes at a crematorium. These are crushed into powder with a mortar and pestle.''

''How could a body be reduced to ashes in a few seconds?''

''There are claims this has happened before.''

''You mean so-called spontaneous human combustion?'' the President asked, and shook his head. ''I understand most experts regard that as a myth.''

''Well, the experts you've been in touch with might dismiss it,'' Brognola replied, ''but I'm not so sure they speak for the majority of the scientific community. What I do know is that Striker claimed those people burned up right before his eyes, and that's good enough for me to believe that's what happened.''

"I know you trust your people, and I know that Striker is your best man. Still, the Israelis are suspicious of his story. It didn't help them to believe in him when he jumped the men escorting him to an Aman base to make a full, detailed report about what happened. He assaulted two soldiers, took their weapons and left them to die in the desert while he escaped in a stolen vehicle."

"A couple of the paratroopers at the Jinn 2000 site apparently claimed their commander had placed Striker under arrest," Brognola argued. "So he might not have been on his way to make a 'report' as that Aman major claimed. By the way, those two soldiers 'left to die in the desert' had been given water and rations. If Striker wanted them dead, they'd be on an autopsy table now. He's a top-notch fighting man, not a sadist. Leaving somebody to suffer and die in the desert isn't his style."

"Okay," the President conceded, "Striker has never let us down, and I know he's a very honorable and decent individual, as well as a highly skilled, very experienced operative. Fact is, the Israelis aren't so sure. They think he might be responsible for whatever happened to Morrow and the missing paratroopers."

"They know what happened to them. They were reduced to piles of ashes. There were even charred human extremities found by some of the ashes. Some boots with feet still in them, a few hands or what was left of them...parts of fingers, according to the reports. A number of weapons and other gear were found by the ashes, as well. These were Israeli military hardware with serial numbers that matched the weapons issued to the troopers and Soviet-made arms probably used by the Jinn 2000. Tons of the stuff is in the Middle East, left over from the decades the USSR supported several Arab nations during the cold war. Black-market weapons still thrive in the region, and terrorists there never have any trouble getting their hands on such deadly hardware.''

"My advisers say that the pieces of human remains aren't proof. Feet and hands could have been amputated and left among the ashes to try to make the claim of spontaneous human combustion more believable.''

"Mr. President, how do these jackasses think Striker managed to do all this in the amount of time between hitting the terrorist base and the arrival of the Aman backup unit?''

"There's a theory he might have been working with the terrorists," the President replied, quickly adding, "I'm not saying I believe that story, but it's still being considered by my advisers and apparently by some people in Israeli Intelligence, as well.''

"They're wasting time trying to pin this on Striker instead of going after the terrorists. Why is anybody listening to this Aman major? He didn't even have the area ringed with troops to cut off the terrorists if they bolted, and he sure seemed to take his time before he sent out a search team and called in air surveillance to try to locate the enemy who fled the scene in two trucks. They got away because of that guy.''

"That hasn't gone unnoticed by my advisers, either," the Man assured Brognola. "Still, the Israelis tend to believe one of their own rather than a foreigner. The officer has been in their army for a lot of years and got promoted to his high rank in Aman military Intelligence because they trusted him and believed in his loyalty, as well as his ability.''

"I seem to recall a lot of people in the Colonial army thought Benedict Arnold was a great officer at one time, too.''

"It's a bit premature to suggest the Israeli major is a traitor. He's probably suspicious and somewhat resentful of Striker's status and puzzled by what happened.''

"Whatever his problem is, he's still screwing up our mission," Brognola insisted. "Striker is out there somewhere on his own with Aman and Mossad agents looking for him. He can't carry out his assignment under these circumstances.''

"We'll see what we can do from here to help him. Meanwhile I'd better give this job to CIA and NSA. Striker is pretty much out of the picture now, Hal.''

"This is the sort of assignment Stony Man is better suited for than either CIA or NSA," Brognola insisted. "A small unit of specialists can accomplish more in the Middle East than those big, clumsy Intel outfits. The Company and NSA spend more time trying to spy on each other and bitching about who should have authority than actually doing their work in the field in that part of the world. The Middle East is a place where human intelligence is still more important than the high-tech data collected by spy satellites and other fancy systems. That's why they've got such a poor record in the Middle East. Stony Man is still your best bet.''

"I'd usually agree with you, Hal, but I've got a trip planned in less than a week. Some of my advisers want me to call it off due to the Morrow abduction. I might be tempted to follow their advice if this trip wasn't so important. This will be the biggest effort for a widespread peace agreement between Israel and various Arab nations. It's our best hope for a lasting peace in the Middle East, but it's high risk, as well. We all know what happened to Prime Minister Rabin and President Sadat.''

''It could happen to you, too, Mr. President.''

''I'm not eager to risk assassination, but I can't tell the leaders involved in the Middle East peace efforts they should continue to take that risk without showing them I'm willing to do the same. It's not macho grandstanding, Hal. I have to do this to show we really care about peace.''

''Putting your life on the line?'' Brognola asked. ''That's what we're supposed to do, Mr. President. Not you.''

''Mine is on the line more often than you might think. If Stony Man can handle some sort of damage control on this mission and take care of the terrorists before I go to Israel, I'll be very pleased. Even if you don't, I'm still going.''

''We don't shut down an operation until it's finished,'' the big Fed replied. ''I appreciate your situation, and we'll do everything we can to protect you and complete this mission.''

''I'd probably have more confidence if Striker wasn't in so much trouble himself. Frankly you don't even know for certain if he's still alive.''

''I don't have any reason to believe he's dead,'' Brognola said, ''and he sure as hell isn't an easy man to kill.''

AARON KURTZMAN ROLLED from the elevator car to the War Room. Still known as "The Bear," although confined to a wheelchair for life due to a bullet in the spine, Kurtzman was the Stony Man head of computer operations. John "Cowboy" Kissinger was already seated next to Brognola by the conference table, and the weapons expert nodded in greeting as Kurtzman parked his chair and placed a stack of printout sheets on the table.

"How's the President today?" he asked.

"Not too happy," Brognola answered, "but he's still stubborn about going to Israel. I take it you haven't heard from Striker?"

"I would have told you if I had," Kurtzman assured him. "Mack would have to get to a computer system with communications capacity or some other type of international transceiver device. That might not be so easy if he's still somewhere in the West Bank with Mossad and Aman hunting him. The good news is we've been monitoring the Israeli Intel systems, and they haven't reported Striker's capture or…his death."

"Nobody is better at staying alive than the Executioner," Brognola remarked. "I'm as concerned about him as any of the rest of you, but our main concern has to be the mission. The safety of the President is now a primary concern, as well as the potential danger of whatever kind of weapon Jinn 2000 has that can seem to make people spontaneously combust."

"Well," Kissinger began with a sigh, "I can't help you much there. Fire as a weapon isn't new. Thousands of years ago, the Romans used a type of flamethrower that sprayed burning oil. Fire has been used in twentieth-century warfare in the form of Molotov cocktails to napalm. They're all vicious...even by the brutal standards of war. Yet none of these methods literally burns a body to a pile of ashes. Closest thing I can think of would probably be white phosphorus. That stuff will burn muscle, bone and just about everything else.''

"Yeah," Brognola said, "but WP has to be used as an incendiary device such as a bomb or a projectile. From Striker's description, they used something different. Some kind of invisible ray or wavelength that caused those men to burst into flames.''

"Spontaneous human combustion isn't my field,'' Kissinger admitted. "Maybe they used some sort of laser cannon, but I'm not familiar with any concentrated-light weapon that would cause that reaction.''

"I did some research on the subject with our computers," Kurtzman announced as he reached for his data sheets. "There have been claims of spontaneous human combustion—or SHC—for at least three hundred years. Some people even think SHC might be the source of ancient stories of sinners being struck down by lightning bolts in the Bible and countless tales from mythology throughout the world.''

"Most myths are based on some degree of truth," Brognola mused. "What do they think might be the cause of SHC?''

"A popular belief in the past has been that SHC is linked to chronic alcoholism," Kurtzman began, consulting his notes. "A medical report in 1673 claimed an alcoholic in Paris was reduced to a pile of ash with only a skull and some digital bones left to identify the remains as human. As if this story isn't weird enough, the guy supposedly burned up on a straw bed that was only singed by the fire.''

''A fire hot enough to cremate a man's body didn't burn the straw he was on?'' Kissinger asked with surprise. ''How the hell is that supposed to happen?''

''That's a question that comes up again and again with SHC cases,'' Kurtzman stated. ''Most of the stories claim there were combustible materials near the victims that didn't burn with the flames that consumed human flesh, muscle and bone. A sixty-year-old woman in 1744 allegedly burned up in front of her horrified daughter in Lipswich, England. The fire didn't ignite a screen or kid's clothing nearby. A story from St. Petersburg, Florida, in 1951 reported a sixty-seven-year-old woman died in a mysterious fire that reduced her body to ashes with only a few pieces of bone and a skull shrunk to about one-third its size by the heat. Candles in the room, twelve feet from the remains, melted, but stacks of paper only inches from the fire hadn't burned. There was a similar story about a sixty-eight-year-old woman in West Philadelphia in 1957. She burned up, but newspapers about two feet from what was left of her were virtually untouched.''

Kurtzman glanced over his printout sheets as he spoke and selected a fax copy of a black-and-white photograph, which he handed to Brognola. The big Fed grimaced when he examined the picture of a charred human leg, apparently burned off at the knee, foot encased in a slipper. It jutted from a lump of dark ashes and a vertical arrangement of metal rods or pipes.

''That's probably the best-known photograph of an alleged SHC case,'' Kurtzman explained. ''It's what was left of an elderly physician named Dr. J. Irving Bentley. He died in a mysterious fire at his home in Pennsylvania in 1966. That thing by the ashes was Bentley's walker. The rubber tips on it didn't melt, although the fire that consumed the guy's body was estimated to be close to three thousand degrees.''

Kissinger studied the picture and remarked, ''Sure burned down more than a victim of a flamethrower or even WP. They have any idea what causes this to happen?''

''There are several theories. Some say the body is somehow 'cooked' down to ashes. Food can be cooked in an oven down to ashes, and the theory suggests the human body somehow fuels a fire to produce this phenomenon. Now, there have been lab experiments with raw pork wrapped in cloth to simulate a human body. The fat in the pork will burn in a localized manner, sort of like a candle. This would explain why combustible materials nearby may not be burned, while the body burns itself out...cooked in its own fat.''

''So a person falls asleep with a cigarette or whatever and winds up really well-done?'' Kissinger asked. ''I guess that's possible if circumstances are right, but you said one victim supposedly burned while her daughter watched it happen. It would take a body a long time to roast down to ashes.''

''Yeah. It doesn't say here how long the daughter watched her mother burn, but it suggests this happened pretty fast. Actually a fireman who responded to a report of smoke coming from a home claims he saw blue flames literally appear from inside a man's abdomen, like the fire had occurred within the victim's body. A case of SHC in Ontario, reported in

1828, claimed the victim stood fully erect and burned in full view of witnesses. Maybe a lot of SHC stories are just accidental fires that somehow burn hotter than usual for whatever reason. And believe it or not, one theory suggests SHC may occur inside human beings due to gas actually manufactured by the body. In a British medical journal, a doctor claimed blue flame ignited from the belly of a patient during surgery. It scared the hell out of the operating team, but the patient wasn't badly burned in this case. Apparently the cause was hydrogen and methane gas, naturally produced by the patient and sparked by metal instruments during the operation.''

"So they really don't know what causes this spontaneous human combustion or even if it's for real," Kissinger said.

"Right," Kurtzman answered. "Apparently it's a pretty rare phenomenon if it even exists."

"When was the most recent case believed to be SHC?" Brognola asked.

"Some people think the death of George Mott, in Ticonderoga, New York, in 1986 might have been SHC. Mott was a nonsmoker and a fireman who was said to be very conscious of fire hazards. Yet he burned to death in his cabin in the woods. His body was reduced to ashes with just some bone fragments found, but his mattress was also burned, as were floorboards under it. Maybe it was an accident, but the heat had to be very intense. A TV set melted, and Mott's guns were charred. Still, the cabin didn't burn down. Nobody really knows for sure. That could be said about nearly all the reported cases of spontaneous human combustion.''

"Yeah," Brognola declared, "but Mack Bolan

says he saw men burst into flame, and that means somebody has found a way to create SHC or something very similar. Even if it didn't exist before, it does now.''

''And that power is in the hands of a bunch of terrorist fanatics,'' Kissinger said grimly. ''We don't know where they are or how they do it, but Bolan is missing and the President plans to make a trip to the SHC killers' stalking ground.''

''That's what we have to deal with,'' Brognola agreed. ''So let's figure out what the hell to do about it.''

CHAPTER FOUR

Solomon Golomb shuffled to the stone steps of a white brick house, his shoulders slumped as he carried a canvas sack filled with groceries. A white beard framed his thin face, and a yarmulke covered the top of his bald pate. Golomb wore loose-fitting cotton shirt and trousers, with a prayer shawl draped across his neck.

He checked the thin wire attached to a hinge near the doorpost. It hadn't been disturbed. Satisfied, he reached for the keys in his pocket.

"Shalom, Solomon," a voice greeted him.

Golomb moved his hand from the pocket to the hem of his shirt as he turned, lowering the bag to conceal the hand. He peered through the lenses of his dark glasses to see a tall, muscular figure appear by the side of the house. The man wore a gray-and-black blanket, his head poking through a hole in the improvised poncho. A straw hat with a wide brim shielded his face from the afternoon sun, but Golomb recognized the dark, rugged features and cool blue eyes.

"Still carry that Walther .380?" Mack Bolan asked.

"When you get to be my age," Golomb replied,

"you don't like to carry anything too heavy. How are you, Michael?"

"Well, I've got some problems. You might not want to get involved."

"I'll decide that after you tell me what this is about," Golomb said. "Come in. You look like you could use something cool to drink."

He followed Golomb into the house. As the old man took the groceries to the kitchen, Bolan pulled the draperies closed. He glanced at the comfortable sofa and chairs in the front room. A library of leather-bound books covered one wall. English, French and Arabic were represented, as well as Hebrew publications. A menorah stood beside an ornate ark on a small altar. Golomb carried two glasses of iced tea to a coffee table and invited Bolan to have a seat.

"You still attached to Mossad?" Bolan asked.

"Not really," Golomb answered. "I'm retired. I still have some connections, but I'm not in the trade anymore. I put in a lot of years, Michael."

"I need your help to cross the border into Egypt and get to Cairo as soon as possible," Bolan explained. "This has to be done as covertly as possible. Even Mossad and Aman can't know about it. We've helped each other in the past. I hope I can count on you again."

"They're hunting you?" Golomb asked with a frown. "I never expected you to carry out a mission against my country. You must realize I won't help anyone trying to harm Israel."

"I'll tell you the truth, but a clever lie would probably be easier to believe."

"I spent most of my adult life being a professional

liar and dealing with other liars even more skilled than myself,'' the former Mossad agent replied. ''You tell me what happened, and I'll decide if you're lying or not.''

The Executioner explained the events during the effort to rescue Congressman Morrow from the Jinn 2000 terrorists. He described the fiery deaths of the Israeli commandos and Morrow and the uncanny cremations of the slain enemies. He also told how Major Ziyyon refused to listen to his story, assuming he was involved in the ''disappearance'' of Morrow and the paratroopers and placing him under arrest.

Golomb listened in silence, not interrupting even when told about the lethal blue flames that struck without warning. The veteran Israeli agent seemed fascinated, but his expression didn't reveal whether he believed the American or simply found the tale to be a fantastic fabrication by a desperate fugitive.

''You say the two men ordered to take you away in the Land Rover were Ziyyon's henchmen?'' Golomb asked. ''You think they intended to kill you and claim you tried to escape?''

''That's right.''

''But you didn't kill them?''

''I didn't have to. They were still breathing when I left them in the desert with water and supplies.''

''Under the circumstances I'd say you were very generous,'' Golomb remarked. ''You managed to drive from Abu Gosh to Gaza?''

''Not exactly Abu Gosh. But I abandoned the Land Rover when I approached the first town that looked big enough to have some form of transportation to and from the coast. I also figured I'd have a better chance of finding someone who spoke English. The tallest building in the town was a mosque. When I spotted the crescent moon on the steeple, I started to put together a story for the locals. Told them I was a tourist from the States who came to visit some family on my mother's side.''

"Of course your mother was an Arab," Golomb remarked.

"That's what I told them," Bolan confirmed. "Then I said my car broke down in the desert and I needed to get to Ramla to look for my uncle. Some farmers had to make a delivery of dates to Tel Aviv, so they didn't mind giving me a ride in their truck. I wanted to avoid Tel Aviv, for obvious reasons, so I got off outside the city limits. I managed to get to another town, a little place near Rehovot. This one had a synagogue, but no mosques or churches.''

"So you became an American Jew who got stranded on foot.''

"Not just stranded," the Executioner explained. "I'd been robbed by a gang of young Arabs who took my car, supplies and all my money except what I had hidden in a boot. The locals were very sympathetic and refused to take any payment to give me a ride to the Gaza Strip, where I told them the rest of my tour group was located. Then I just had to hope you were still living here and you'd be willing to help me.''

"Quite a story. The claim you saw men burst into flames is particularly remarkable. You ever hear of spontaneous human combustion?''

"I read a magazine article about it once, but never really thought much about it until now. I don't know it really applies in this case, Solomon. What I saw wasn't any type of natural or even supernatural phenomenon. The Jinn 2000 terrorists made those bodies catch fire. I don't know what sort of weapon they have or how it works, but I'm sure they made it happen.''

"Why didn't they use it on you?" the Israeli asked with a raised eyebrow.

"I don't know," the Executioner admitted. "I've been trying to figure that out. At first I guessed the paratroopers must have triggered some sort of heat or motion detectors that I had managed to avoid. That would explain how they targeted victims even if it didn't answer how the flames are produced inside a human being. But Morrow burned in the same room with me. So did the bodies of two dead terrorists. They didn't use heat or motion detectors to find targets, or I would have gone up in flames, too.''

"No wonder Major Ziyyon is suspicious," Golomb remarked. "If I didn't know you, although I really don't know who you are, where you came from or the other details that are usually part of such a claim, I'd find your story hard to believe. Still, Ziyyon must be something of a fanatic himself to want you dead before they could even attempt to establish what happened. Of course, that 'eye for an eye' philosophy is very popular here in Israel. Maybe he was convinced you helped the terrorists kill his men and he didn't want the CIA to spirit you out of the country before you could face justice in a courtroom in Tel Aviv.''

"I'm not sure what Ziyyon's motives were. Right now I need to contact my people back in the States, and I can't do that as long as I'm in Israel. Mossad or Aman will nail me if I go back to Tel Aviv or any other major city.''

"They'll track you down anywhere else you go," Golomb warned. "They may not come to the Gaza Strip today, but they'll come. You're not safe here and you won't be safe in Cairo. I know that from my own experience."

"I realize that, but I can't go after Jinn 2000 and stop them from using whatever weapon they have while I'm on the run from Israeli Intelligence. I can't get them to call off this manhunt, but my people in the States might be able to do it."

"Well, Michael," the Israeli began with a sigh, "I guess I'm getting more religious as I get older. God isn't directly handling justice or governing nations on earth at this time. So it is up to men to do the best they can. They don't always do a very good job, but each of us can do whatever possible on an individual level. Major Ziyyon might have decided you're guilty, but I don't believe that. It is my duty to help you, as your friend and as a patriot to Israel and the causes we both hold sacred."

"Thanks, Solomon," the Executioner replied. "I have some money, but I'm not sure if it'll be enough to cover the cost of a forged passport."

"I can forge a passport for you," Golomb stated. "I can do it in Hebrew, English, French or Arabic and include the proper document seals. That's no problem. What we need is the best way to get you into Egypt without Mossad's knowledge. You need something they won't be looking for."

"What do you suggest?" Bolan asked.

Golomb smiled and said, "A wife."

THE BATTERED old Volkswagen rolled along the narrow road between rows of small adobe-brick dwellings. Larger, much older buildings stood in the distance, beyond the community-housing area. Some of these structures dated back to the sixth century when the city of Gaza was ruled by the Byzantine Empire.

Golomb drove the VW, apparently undisturbed by the smoke that rose from the rear of the vehicle and the frequent backfires and sputtering from the exhaust pipe. Tape covered a long crack in the windshield, and a back window had been replaced with cardboard. The car had no seat belts, but it seemed incapable of speed greater than fifty miles per hour.

"Is this thing going to make it to Cairo?"

"It'll get you to Egypt," the Israeli replied. "You'll have to put in oil every couple hours or so."

"Who do you intend to play the role of my wife?"

"You remember Abraham Shapiro?" Golomb asked. "American Jew who moved to Israel in the early eighties?"

"Electronics and communications expert," Bolan said with a nod. "He wasn't Mossad, but he worked for them sometimes. I thought he planned to move to Jerusalem."

"He did," Golomb confirmed. "Abe also died two years ago. Massive heart attack. I hear it was quick."

The Executioner guessed Golomb had mentioned Shapiro as small talk and an update about a man Bolan had known briefly years ago.

"Abe was a good man," Bolan said, not sure what else to say.

"You might recall he was a widower and he had a daughter named Sarah," Golomb continued. "She liked you. What you Americans call a 'crush,' right?"

"I remember her. You're not thinking of having Sarah play the part of my wife, are you?"

The Israeli shrugged and said, "She's smart, you know. Sarah speaks Arabic, as well as Hebrew and English. She's also been to Egypt many times. Did research for an archaeological magazine in the States."

"She's a kid."

"Not anymore,' Golomb replied. "You knew Sarah seven or eight years ago. She's in her mid-twenties now."

"But she's not trained for this sort of thing, Solomon. Mossad and Aman probably have agents posted along the border. You know a lot of them get trigger-happy, especially when they're assigned a cowboy job."

"Cowboy? You mean like Gary Cooper?"

"I mean like an assassination assignment that's carried out quickly, with little planning or care."

"Sarah is smart and she's careful," Golomb insisted. "You only speak a smattering of Arabic, and your Hebrew is even worse. I don't think you're very familiar with Egypt, and you'll have a hard time getting to Cairo on your own. I can't go with you. A lot of people in Mossad know me. In fact they may have already learned you and I worked together in the past. Are you using a different cover name than 'Michael Belasko' this time?"

"No," the Executioner admitted. "Same name. I didn't expect to find myself in this position during this mission."

"That means you've got to get out of Gaza as fast as possible," Golomb said. "Personally I suggest you head straight for the U.S. Embassy when you get to Cairo. That's regarded as American soil. Even Mossad won't want to go after you then and risk an international incident.''

"To be honest," Bolan began, "I'm sort of playing this by ear. My entire mission has gone in a direction nobody could have guessed. I'm trying to handle a situation I sure didn't expect, but I'm not just concerned with my own survival. Jinn 2000 has a terrible weapon, and I'm sure they plan to use it against more people in the future.''

Golomb stopped the VW as a pair of shepherds drove a small flock of sheep across the road. The engine stalled and refused to start for almost five minutes, which didn't inspire Bolan with confidence about using the car for transportation to Cairo.

At last they arrived at a small dwelling at the edge of the Gaza city limits. They left the VW and walked to the front of the house. Golomb knocked, and the door soon opened.

Sarah Shapiro had certainly changed since Bolan last saw her. He had recalled a bright, pretty teenager from the past. The young woman at the doorway had developed a slender, athletic figure. Full breasts strained the fabric of her white bush shirt. Shapely legs and thighs with superb muscle tone extended from a pair of high-cut shorts. Her long black hair was in a ponytail. High cheekbones stood above a wide mouth with full lips.

The woman's dark eyes widened with surprise when she saw Bolan beside Golomb.

"Hello, Sarah," the old man began. "I hope we didn't come at a bad time.''

"I was just reviewing an article on a dig near Ca-

pernaum,'' the woman replied, her gaze fixed on Bolan. ''You're Michael, aren't you?''

''Glad you remember him,'' the Israeli said. ''We
came to ask you a favor.''

''Of course,'' Shapiro agreed. ''Come in and we'll
talk.''

''I think you should know right now,'' Bolan
stated, ''that even talking to me could be dangerous,
Sarah.''

She smiled and said, ''Please come in, Michael.''

CHAPTER FIVE

Hafez Buraydah stood in the center of the room, back straight and arms at his sides in the military position of attention. He faced a platform with a long table. Three men sat behind the table, their expressions stern and eyes hard. A black-and-green flag was mounted on the wall behind the trio, bearing a white Islamic crescent symbol and a gold-scimitar emblem with "God" printed in Arabic above the sword.

"You received no orders to abduct this American politician," Jadallah al-Qatrun stated. "That action was, in fact, a serious violation of the mission we gave you."

Qatrun sat erect in his chair, broad shoulders back and firm chin raised. His face was almost square, the muscles around his jaw tense and his mouth turned down at the corners from an almost perpetual frown. The man's dark eyes seemed to stare through Buraydah to drill into his mind and thoughts.

A military officer in his native Libya, Qatrun had commanded an elite unit of special-forces commandos. He still wore a khaki uniform, but without a symbol of rank or crest insignia. However, he generally wore a side arm and sheathed knife. His Makarov pistol lay on the table in front of him within easy reach if needed.

"The opportunity presented itself," Buraydah replied, his voice strained by the stress of the inquest. "Morrow was such an easy target. His security seemed so poor, I felt Morrow had been delivered to us as a gift from God."

"Idiot!" Qabus an-Sabkhat roared. "What makes you think you are qualified to interpret the will of God?"

Clad in a traditional white sleeveless robe, Sabkhat also wore a dress shirt and suit trousers tailor-made in London. He was an example of a modern Arab thrust into the latter part of the twentieth century and still linked to the culture of his ancestors. Light flashed along the expensive gold Swiss watch on his wrist. His black hair had been professionally styled at a French salon in Abu Dhabi.

Sabkhat's handsome features and obvious wealth made him very attractive to women, but he regarded them as a minor diversion. Other passions dominated Sabkhat's interests. He glared at Buraydah as if he wanted to strangle the Palestinian.

"We're all Jinn 2000," Buraydah stated. "Does that mean our actions and goals are predetermined by God? Do we not serve his will? I simply responded as I believed he wished me to."

"That was a grave mistake," Abdel al-Barrah stated, shaking his head with dismay. "You obviously did not read the signs correctly. You should have contacted us before taking any action on your own."

Barrah spoke in an even, gentle tone. His manner always seemed in control, and he presented an image of intelligence and culture. In fact the bearded Saudi Arabian was a nuclear physicist, once considered to be one of the most gifted researchers working in the field of nuclear fusion. However, Barrah's efforts had shifted another direction when he became an advocate of the Jinn 2000 movement.

"One thing we did learn from this incident," the scientist commented, "was that the machine worked in actual field combat. The Israelis and the American burst into flames and were reduced to ashes just as we predicted."

"That is a small comfort considering the potential cost of this incident," Sabkhat insisted. "Our agents were supposed to remain in place, recruiting more members to build the strength of our organization and to wait for the moment when your SHC device could be used to accomplish an unexpected and effective blow against the enemies of Islam. This moron has jeopardized our plans."

"He thought he was obeying a message from God," Barrah said in lame defense of Buraydah's actions.

"He may have succeeded in using the SHC weapon against our enemies," Qatrun began, "but the Israelis had previously considered Jinn 2000 to be a relatively harmless, if odd sect of Muslim dreamers. Kidnapping Morrow drew their attention and caused the Jews to send a team to rescue the congressman."

"And the Israelis died in glorious flames, as well as the politician from the United States," Barrah stated. "Our sources have confirmed this."

"But," Sabkhat said, "our intelligence also stated that a mysterious commando from America managed to penetrate Buraydah's base and killed more than half his men and forced this fool to run for his life. He had enough sense to use the device to burn the bodies, but it would not have happened if he had not made such a rash and stupid error. Now we've lost several good men and possibly alerted the Americans and Mossad to danger that they never would have guessed existed before. The U.S. President may cancel his plan to attend the peace conference."

"According to our most recent information," Barrah began, "Mossad and Aman believe the American commando is involved in the disappearance of the Israeli paratroopers and Congressman Morrow. They are not even convinced the ashes left are human, although I imagine they'll assume the remains of some feet and hands will be ample evidence this is not a complete hoax."

"Qabus is right," the Libyan officer stated as he reached for the Makarov on the table. "Buraydah's mistake might have ruined our plans. Besides, he did disobey a direct order from this committee, and we represent the command center of Jinn 2000. An example must be made."

"No!" Buraydah shouted.

He raised his arms and held his hands out as if to fend off Qatrun's bullets. The Libyan didn't argue and simply squeezed the trigger. The bullet struck Buraydah in the chest, and the Palestinian cried out, clasping a hand to his ribs and staggering backward several steps.

"Missed the heart," Qatrun complained. "He shouldn't have moved. Stand still! It'll be over faster if you—"

Buraydah bolted for the door. The Libyan gripped

his Makarov in both hands and tracked his target
with the front sight of the pistol. He allowed Buraydah to reach for the doorknob and fired the next
shot. A bloodied hole burst beneath the Palestinian's
left shoulder blade. He stumbled forward, slammed
his face into the door and slumped to the floor.

"That's better," Qatrun commented with satisfaction.

"Good shot," Sabkhat stated his approval.

Barrah's face became pale, and he covered his
mouth with a hand. The Saudi looked away from the
corpse. "I thought you intended to take him outside
if we agreed to execute him, Jadallah."

"I'll take him outside now and let the others see
his body," Qatrun replied. "He can't serve as an
example if they don't see what happens to anyone
who disobeys us, Abdel."

Barrah's stomach settled, and he glared at his companions. "I did not agree he should be killed. You
should have waited until we discussed it."

"There was nothing left to discuss," Sabkhat said,
his tone suggesting he was bored with the subject.
"Jadallah and I agreed he deserved to die. A majority
opinion on such a trivial matter is all that was required by this committee to determine his fate."

"I must accept part of the blame," Qatrun told
them. "I approved of Buraydah as an officer in command of a unit to transfer an SHC weapon to Israel
and remain to assist the main cell already in place."

"You shouldn't blame yourself," Sabkhat told
him. "No one could have guessed he would prove
to be such a fool."

"I should have seen it in him," Qatrun insisted.
The Libyan rose from his chair and crossed the room.

He paused by the door to grab Buraydah's ankle, then dragged the corpse across the threshold. Only a red puddle remained to mark where the man had been killed.

"Perhaps we should all pray and ask for strength and guidance," Barrah remarked.

"The holy men will announce time for afternoon prayer in a matter of minutes," Sabkhat replied.

He gave lip service to the Jinn 2000 dogma, but Sabkhat didn't really have any faith in God. Despite his secret agnostic views, Sabkhat had joined Jinn 2000 to study it from within. He was amazed to discover many intelligent and well-educated individuals belonged to the sect.

Abdel al-Barrah was the most remarkable example of a great paradox Sabkhat encountered. The man was a brilliant scientist and one of the leaders in the study of nuclear fusion in the entire world, yet he truly believed the doctrine of Jinn 2000. When he'd stumbled upon the method to cause spontaneous human combustion, Barrah was convinced this was a message from God and that the device had been delivered to him as a means to help wipe out the world's infidels.

Sabkhat didn't believe Jinn 2000 could actually kill them all. He wouldn't have wanted that anyway. He spent much of his time with non-Muslims in Europe and the United States. He had done a great deal of international banking and trade with them and wouldn't wish to see that end. Besides, Jinn 2000 regarded most Muslims outside their own sect to be infidels on the same level with Jews, Christians, Buddhists, Hindus and the rest. Even the majority of the Shiites were considered "enemies of God."

Yet Sabkhat did believe Barrah's weapon could make Jinn 2000 the most powerful force in the Middle East. He thought they had the potential to finally unite all the Arab nations. Sabkhat had even designed the flag to be the banner for this new Arab empire. Among his areas of expertise, Sabkhat was a student of world history. He believed the greatest weakness of the Arab people had been ancient tribal conflicts and a clannish desire to maintain control of territory. Divided, fighting among themselves, Arabs would always be a number of small, weak nations instead of a large, strong one.

In the twelfth century Genghis Khan had united the Mongol tribes and established one of the greatest empires in history. The Mongols conquered most of Asia and much of Europe. Sabkhat believed this was proof of the glory a unified Arab nation could accomplish. Not that he would favor a military campaign to conquer the world. Sabkhat felt force and the threat of force would be necessary to form the union and hold back enemies who might oppose them, but the expansion of power should consist of increased international trade and financial influence.

Sabkhat was a banking executive in the United Arab Emirates. He knew the power of commodities, money, credit and petroleum. He had participated in BCCI before evidence of international corruption, gunrunning, drug trafficking and covert financing of "black-bag operations" of various Intelligence agencies came to public attention. To control finance and trade was better than trying to occupy territory. Sabkhat believed he could create a successful international network without making the same mistakes as BCCI.

His ability as a banker had gained him his rank as one of the three ringleaders of Jinn 2000. Sabkhat had transferred funds from money-laundering operations for Turkish and Afghan heroin trafficking. He had raised more money by drawing in contributions for bogus charities that claimed to assist starving masses in Africa or earthquake victims in India and Japan. These only existed on paper, but the money wired to Sabkhat's numbered bank account was real enough. He transferred the funds and closed the accounts for these charities before Interpol or any other investigative organization could track down the source.

Sabkhat was the money man for Jinn 2000. His obvious skills as an insider in high finance impressed members on every social level. The advantages of having such a man working for the sect were obvious. His shrewd, manipulative mind proved an even greater asset than the cult followers expected, and Sabkhat soon rose in authority among the conspirators until he was one of the planners of the conspiracy itself.

Abdel al-Barrah's qualifications as a leader were basically the fact he had invented the SHC machine and his strong, genuine commitment to Jinn 2000. Despite his intelligence and education, Barrah was still incredibly naive and usually easy for Sabkhat to manipulate.

Jadallah al-Qatrun was the military strategist and enforcement commander of the trio. A veteran soldier, he was neither stupid nor naive...unless one included his belief in the prophecies of Omar, a Shiite dervish, and Jinn 2000. Sabkhat had to be more careful with the Libyan. Qatrun was a fanatic, but he still retained a hard, suspicious edge and a practical side that wouldn't easily be molded to suit Sabkhat.

That wasn't really a problem for the banker. His goals weren't much different from those of Qatrun. Sabkhat had no illusions about his lack of military expertise, and he needed Qatrun to command the troops anyway. Barrah might be viewed by the majority of Jinn 2000 as a special messenger from God who gave them the unique weapon that could smite opponents with fire and brimstone. Fine with Sabkhat. He would rather be a power behind the figurative throne.

Cheers outside the room drew Sabkhat and Barrah to the door. They discovered Qatrun had dragged the body of Buraydah outside for the rest of the Jinn 2000 followers to see what happened to anyone who jeopardized their mission. That might not have pleased the crowd, but the spectators were favorably impressed when Qatrun removed his own shirt and raised a flail. The instrument resembled a cat-o'-nine-tails with three lengths of chain instead of leather straps.

Qatrun announced he accepted part of the blame for what happened in Israel because he had selected Buraydah to command troops at the West Bank. He raised the flail and called for God to forgive him and grant him guidance and wisdom. Qatrun expressed his sincerity by whipping the chains across his well-muscled back. Metal struck skin again and again as the man repeated his prayer.

This declaration of faith inspired the followers. Many began to flog themselves with chains or sticks. Sabkhat observed the display of self-punishment with amazement. The fanatics—Qatrun included—seemed delighted with their actions. They smiled as they beat themselves, drawing blood in their frenzy.

"Their devotion is beautiful to behold," Barrah remarked, "is it not, Qabus?"

Sabkhat noticed Barrah was no more eager to rush outside and join the others in this masochistic orgy than he was, but the banker simply nodded in solemn agreement.

CHAPTER SIX

"Where the hell is Katz?" Hal Brognola demanded as he reached for a cigar in his shirt pocket. "We need him in Israel."

"Katz is in Labrador. I haven't been able to establish contact with him so far," Kurtzman replied.

"Labrador?" The big Fed unwrapped the cigar and jammed one end into a corner of his mouth. "What's he doing in Canada?"

"Taking a three-day vacation. He told us about it last week, remember?"

"I wouldn't be asking you if I did," Brognola groused.

"Well, you know Katz has always had an interest in archaeology. He got a chance to head up north to take part in an Inuit excavation."

"He picked a hell of a time to go on a holiday."

"I haven't been able to get in touch with him due to atmospheric conditions in the area. Meteorological telemetry confirms aurora borealis activity over the Labrador area. Northern lights can interfere with satellite communications."

"Keep trying," Brognola urged as he gnawed the cigar in his teeth. "Any word on Striker?"

"Not yet. He hasn't been in contact yet, but Mossad hasn't caught up with him, either. I did manage to tap into a forensic lab at Mossad HQ. They analyzed the ashes found at the Jinn 2000 base. The traces of carbon, calcium, nitrogen and so forth confirm the remains were almost certainly human. Other elements may have been from metal gun frames, literally melted into the victim by the heat. There is also evidence of chemicals that may have formed explosives. If this is accurate, the targets actually burned so rapidly grenades didn't get a chance to detonate because the fuses melted in a second or two. Maybe some cartridges blew, but even most of the ammunition was probably destroyed before it could go off.''

"That's incredible. Sounds like this supports the SHC story. Isn't Mossad looking at this data and reconsidering their search-and-destroy manhunt? This seems to be pretty good evidence Striker told the truth.''

"Mossad is convinced the ashes are human, but they still doubt Mack's version of what happened. Apparently their scientists are also skeptical of stories about SHC and suspect this may be some kind of slick effort to cover up what really happened. I can't be sure what Mossad is really doing because my only source is what they're recording in their computers at this time. The Israelis may be less skeptical than they appear, but they still take an official position that views spontaneous human combustion as improbable.''

"So they'd rather believe the theory that Aman major came up with?''

"I don't know how much influence the guy has,'' Kurtzman began as he reached for a printout sheet, "but he's a field-grade officer and the Israelis tend to believe their own. I did manage to get some more info on him. His name is Gideon Ziyyon. He came from a well-to-do family of Egyptian Jews who migrated to Israel in the early fifties. Ziyyon scored high on IQ tests and speaks three languages fluently. Of course, military service in Israel is mandatory, but Ziyyon was considered ideal officer material. He impressed just about all his superiors and eventually landed his current rank and position in Agaf Modiin, Israeli military Intelligence, better known as Aman."

"Nice for him," Brognola muttered. "Not so good for us under the circumstances. How about CIA or NSA at the U.S. Embassy in Tel Aviv? We can get them to try to influence Mossad and have the hit squads called off before they have an unnecessary confrontation with Mack Bolan."

"Mossad isn't going to care what CIA or NSA wants at this point, Hal. Ziyyon and some others in Mossad and Aman think this whole mess is some sort of weird conspiracy with CIA covertly supporting the Jinn 2000. After all, they figure Striker is probably with the Company, and they believe he's involved in the disappearance of all those paratroopers and Congressman Morrow."

"Why the hell would CIA back a bunch of fanatics who are pretty much anti-American, anti-Jewish, anti-Christian, anti-Israel and anti just about everything else, including most Muslims not members of the Jinn 2000 sect?"

"I haven't been able to acquire any information that might directly answer that question or even allow me to extrapolate in a knowledgeable manner," Kurtzman stated.

"So just take a guess," the big Fed urged.

"Well, U.S. involvement in Middle East affairs has generally revolved around strategic interests, petroleum, banking or shipping routes. The Israelis may suspect the Company might support and manipulate an outfit like Jinn 2000 as part of a scheme to influence one or more of those interests. An extremist cult isn't likely to get much support from any government or major religious group, so Jinn 2000 could theoretically be used to urge Israelis or Arabs to alter politics in a manner that would better suit U.S. interests."

"You've got to be pretty suspicious to buy into an idea like that," Brognola commented, "but everybody in the Middle East tends to be paranoid. They've got good reason to be distrustful."

"Don't we all?" Kurtzman said with a shrug.

"Okay, let's say Mossad thinks CIA may be involved in this twisted conspiracy. Why would they think the Company would have Morrow kidnapped?"

"Maybe because they think Morrow found out what they were up to," Kurtzman suggested. "A U.S. congressman abroad would probably spend time at the embassy, right? Everybody knows CIA operates some of their activities right out of our embassies. Most other Intel outfits throughout the world do the same. They might figure Morrow had the opportunity to stumble on something, and the Company had Jinn 2000 grab him. Could be they think the terrorists kidnapped Morrow without approval and Striker was sent in to help terminate all involved, Morrow included. Hell, I'm just trying to guess what they might be thinking. Obviously they don't trust Uncle Sam for some reason."

"Mossad isn't stupid, and eventually they'll realize how absurd all this crap is," Brognola said. "But by then some of their agents may catch up with Striker. He won't kill them unless he has to, but they may not leave him any other option."

"They may take him out, Hal," Kurtzman replied grimly. "I know Mack is the best, but Mossad are damn good, too, and it's their turf. Nobody is indestructible, not even Mack Bolan. If Mossad wants somebody badly enough, they usually get him."

"The fastest route out of Israel from the West Bank is to head to the Gaza Strip, then across the border into Egypt. If he can manage to get out, he might try to contact CIA at our embassy in Cairo and try to reach us."

"Yeah. Striker knows a couple people who might help him, but even if he reaches Cairo he won't be far enough to avoid Mossad if they're still after him."

"I know that, too," Brognola assured him. "Damn it, we need Katz."

Lights flashed on a screen on a wall above the console. A code number and word appeared to request access. Kurtzman reached for a keyboard and punched in a response. The computer requested a password. Yellow letters on the green screen printed "Ambage." The computer acknowledged this as correct. Kurtzman punched some more keys to remove the final block to access for the caller.

"Ambage?" Brognola commented. "That's a password?"

"Not very likely anybody would guess it and gain

access to our system," Kurtzman explained. "*Ambage* is an archaic word with about three meanings. Can you guess who came up with it? It's the sort of word a master linguist would like."

Brognola knew whom Kurtzman referred to before colors and shapes appeared on the screen. These materialized to display the face of a man in the later years of middle age. Intelligent eyes and the calm expression suggested he was a gentle man with an intellectual mind and a kind personality. All of this applied to Yakov Katzenelenbogen. Yet he was also one of the most experienced operatives in the dangerous world of espionage and antiterrorism.

Katz wore an arctic parka, the fur hood slung back from his head. The wall behind him appeared to be metal, most likely a temporary dwelling at the excavation site in Canada. He had contacted Stony Man Farm with the use of a special high-tech laptop computer designed for field operations.

"I received a signal on my pager," he explained. "Couldn't reach you until now due to static by the borealis."

"Sorry to disturb you on vacation," Brognola began. "If you've been following the news, you can probably guess why we needed to get in touch with you."

"Well, I haven't been listening to the news for the past three days," Katz explained. "Too much to do at the site."

"Then you don't know what happened in Israel," Brognola said.

The big Fed explained the situation. Katz listened and frowned when he heard about the spontaneous human combustion and Bolan's plight.

"Okay," Brognola continued. "Yakov, you understand why we need you. Since you were formerly with Mossad, your influence will be greater than anybody else from the Farm. Of course, you also speak Hebrew and Arab, which can be a real advantage in the Middle East."

"I'll be on the next plane out," Katz assured him. "Do you plan to send Phoenix Force to back up Bolan?"

"They're wrapping up another mission, but we'll send them in as soon as possible."

"I'll be glad to act as an adviser and help any way I can."

"Great," Brognola said. "I just hope Striker is okay and we're not already too late to help him."

"He's certainly not an easy man to kill," Katz remarked. "If anybody can survive a dangerous situation, Bolan can."

"That's what I keep telling myself," Brognola replied. "Take care and get back soon."

They signed off, and lights blinked to signal another call. Kurtzman turned his chair to work the keyboard as a different code number and password appeared on the screen. Brognola knew the Stony Man personnel had different passwords that changed from mission to mission. "Duck Hunt" appeared on the screen. Kurtzman seemed to recognize the password and prepared to allow access to the main frame.

"Who is it? Striker?"

"Nope," Kurtzman answered. "It's the President."

"Oh, hell," Brognola muttered.

CHAPTER SEVEN

Sarah Shapiro wasn't a kid anymore, Mack Bolan thought as he sat beside her in the front seat of the decrepit Volkswagen. He was half-sprawled in his seat, head on a pillow. A felt hat with a wide brim, a pair of tinted glasses and a black beard, streaked with gray, served as a disguise. A blanket was draped across his torso and legs.

He was supposed to pretend to be asleep, but Bolan found it difficult to keep his eyes closed next to Shapiro. The profile of her lovely face extended to a graceful neck and a generous display of cleavage. Her white blouse was open, knotted below the breasts to expose a slender bare waist. She wore a short denim skirt, hemline high on her shapely thighs.

The car approached a roadblock manned by several soldiers. All Bolan had to do was stay where he was and play the role of a sleeping, sick, middle-aged man. Sarah would do all the talking. She would show the soldiers the forged passports and ask them not to disturb her "husband," who was sound asleep due to medication to slow his heart rate because he suffered from dangerously high blood pressure.

Hopefully the soldiers wouldn't be suspicious, and

they would be too distracted by Shapiro's beauty to pay much attention to Bolan. The vehicle came to a halt, and a pair of soldiers approached. Bolan closed his eyes and waited. He heard the woman and the troops converse in Hebrew. He understood only a few words, but the tone sounded pleasant and conversational. Soon the VW rolled forward with a belch from the exhaust pipe. A loud backfire startled Bolan, but he resisted the urge to reach for the .357 Magnum Desert Eagle concealed under the seat.

"Stay down," Shapiro urged. "They're still watching us."

Moments later she spoke again. "No one can see us now. You ought to take that blanket off while you can. It must be uncomfortable in this heat."

Bolan raised his head to scan the surrounding area. Shapiro hadn't exaggerated. No other vehicles or people were visible, and the soldier's range of vision was at least four miles in all directions. The road extended through a landscape as remote and lonely as any he had ever seen.

"Not much smoke from the engine," Bolan commented as he looked out the rear window. "Maybe this car is in better shape than I thought."

"We can put some oil in just in case," Shapiro announced. "Better do it now before we reach the border to Egypt."

She pulled the car to the shoulder of the road and put the gearshift in neutral. The woman used a foot to push her handbag onto the gas pedal, discovering the weight would keep the engine idling fast enough to prevent it from stalling as it tended to do at a full stop. Bolan glanced at his companion and her provocative attire.

"You plan to dress like that when we enter Egypt?" he asked. "It might not be a wise fashion statement in an Arab country."

"I knew I should have packed my veil," she said with a laugh. "Actually I intend to adjust this blouse to be more conservative and I'll put on a long skirt when we reach Egypt. Will that be better?"

"By their standards, yeah."

ABDEL AL-BARRAH examined the machine and was pleased by what he found. The photovoltaic cells hadn't been damaged during use in the field. The hard plastic barrel was barely scratched. Barrah used a wrench to loosen the bolts and removed the barrel to study the electromagnetic transmission system.

Jadallah al-Qatrun watched the Saudi scientist. He had no idea what Barrah was doing or the functions of the various parts of the contraption. The Libyan soldier had only a vague idea how the device caused spontaneous human combustion. The technology was impressive, but it wasn't his field of expertise. He didn't have to know the exact chemical composition of gunpowder to use bullets or the names of every metal alloy used to make good-quality steel.

Yet Qatrun worried about the fact only Barrah really understood the machine and how it worked. The Saudi alone could handle maintenance or repairs on the SHC cannon. Barrah had another name for the device: a microfusion organic-nuclei transmitter. Qatrun wasn't sure what that meant, either. He did know the system depended on the Saudi physicist. The weapon wasn't complicated to use, but its design and method of function remained a mystery for all but Barrah.

Perhaps Qatrun didn't need to know such things. He was a strategist and battlefield commander, not an artillery gunner or a maintenance mechanic. However, an effective military needed troops with such skills. True, Jinn 2000 was a small army indeed. The members involved with their plot numbered no larger than a battalion. They had only two SHC cannons, but more would have to be built, and trained personnel would have to take care of them.

Qatrun was also concerned about Barrah going into the field, exposed to dangers the scientist didn't seem to appreciate. The Saudi had to do this to inspect the SHC device used in the West Bank. Because Barrah had unique knowledge, they couldn't afford to lose him. The others were expendable—even Qatrun himself or Sabkhat, who had remained at the main base. The banker from the United Arab Emirates probably considered himself as irreplaceable, but Qatrun didn't share this belief. Sabkhat supplied money and he had many grand ideas. These were the dreams of a politician or a tycoon. Sabkhat understood money and banking, but he knew nothing about combat. The banker talked about eliminating people as if deleting evidence from a computer after one of his financial swindles.

What did the banker know about soldiers? Sabkhat's kind had no loyalty to anything except their own greed. They dealt in lies and manipulation. A commander had to earn the trust and loyalty of his troops. Soldiers had to work together, believe in one another and the goals they were expected to risk their lives to reach. Qatrun regarded soldiers as the most noble of men. He had more respect for enemy soldiers—even infidels—than for civilians. The Libyan believed the greatest proof of a soldier's dedication was his willingness to kill fellow soldiers.

Sabkhat was useful, but still expendable. Qatrun didn't really trust the banker and doubted Sabkhat's sincerity. The slick money man was a thief, accustomed to stealing from his clients and taking advantage of those who believed he was trying to help them or serve a worthy cause that was really a hoax to get their money. How could such a man be a true Muslim let alone embrace a jihad movement such as Jinn 2000? Nonetheless, the man had been valuable to their cause. If Qatrun decided he intended to betray them, the Libyan could solve that problem with a bullet or a blade.

However, Barrah was different. He had invented the SHC cannon. Qatrun believed the man had been chosen for this to help Jinn 2000 fulfill the predictions of Omar the prophet. The scientist had to be protected in case God decided to use him as a messenger again.

Two dozen Jinn 2000 followers formed a semicircle around Qatrun and Barrah. They treated the pair with respect, even awe. Four of the men present had been at the site in the West Bank and witnessed the SHC cannon in action. They knew the claims of its fearsome power to be true, and Barrah was the man who had brought the weapon into existence. They also knew Qatrun had personally executed Buraydah for the unauthorized abduction of Congressman Morrow. This was a leader who didn't expect others to handle the undesirable duties. The fact they had come to the base in enemy territory proved their courage.

"It's in excellent condition," Barrah announced as

he reassembled the barrel section. "No damage caused in transport or during its use against the Israelis. The battery is fully charged. I was worried about using the solar cells for electrical power, but the system works fine."

"Good," Qatrun replied with a nod. "At least something positive came from Buraydah's idiot mistake. I'm going to make certain nothing like this happens again. I'll stay here and personally supervise the operation."

"Then I should stay to make sure there are no problems with the SHC cannon...as you call it."

"We can't afford to lose you, Abdel."

"If there is a malfunction or damage to the device," Barrah replied, "you can't afford not to have me here."

"Apparently the President of the United States still intends to arrive for the meeting with the Jewish prime minister and the traitors willing to betray the Arab people to please world powers that favor Israel," Qatrun stated. "That means we have to be concerned with the combined security forces of all the countries involved. The risk is very high, my friend."

"Perhaps," Barrah agreed, "but we serve the will of God. We will triumph as long as we keep our faith and act as God commanded through the great prophet Omar."

"Too bad he's not here to lead this mission," Qatrun remarked, "instead of us."

"Would you really want to miss this opportunity to strike such a vital blow for the jihad?" Barrah asked.

"I can give you a better answer after this is over," the Libyan replied.

CHAPTER EIGHT

"You can tell the President that next time he can tell the bloody Chinese to take care of their own bleedin' messes," David McCarter declared, his cockney accent more pronounced than usual due to anger. "Patch me through to the White House. I'll tell him myself."

Hal Brognola groaned and shook his head. He looked at the computer screen and the image of McCarter. The Briton's foxlike face was flushed, and he jabbed the air with an unlit Player's cigarette held between thumb and forefinger.

With everything else to deal with, Brognola didn't need a demonstration of McCarter's famous temper. Actually the Briton had achieved much greater control of his anger and a tongue that tended to be sharp and caustic. Obviously he was aggravated by the circumstances of his current mission.

"David," Brognola began, "I hate to disappoint you, but you're not going to talk to the President. What happened with the mission in China to get you so worked up?"

"You sent us here to take care of the Red Tide terrorists, who allegedly presented a threat to American and European tourists, businessmen and possibly diplomats," the Briton began, his tone already more calm. "They killed Gary Neville, that nice young man from the upper-middle-class family in Maryland."

"Yeah," Brognola said, "go on."

"Well, they gunned down Neville here in the Shan province, outside Motuo. Not a lot of tourists go out of their way to pay visits to Motuo. Seemed a little odd to us until we found out Gary had really come to China to be a mule for one of the Triads operating in the Shan area."

"You mean he was a heroin smuggler?"

"That's the product Triad deals in," McCarter confirmed. "Although the Golden Triangle is known for producing opium poppies, Shan Province is still one of the major areas for opium, although the dope is transported out of China to other countries. Turns out SAD was sitting on evidence that proved Neville was going to smuggle out ten to fifteen kilos to a Triad outfit in Singapore."

"SAD is the Chinese Intelligence service?"

"Social Affairs Department," McCarter confirmed. "Sounds like they arrange picnics and square dances. SAD didn't want us to know what Neville was up to because the Chinese government likes to pretend it doesn't have any organized crime here, and all that nasty business with the Triads and heroin syndicates is done by anti-Communist renegades who left the country long ago."

"So Red Tide isn't a terrorist group?"

"Depends on what you call terrorists," the Briton replied. "Red Tide is definitely involved in the drug trade, but it's also made up of Maoist extremists. Sort of a variation of the old Red Guard who still think

Chairman Mao's little red book is the scripture for the People's Revolution. They're anti-West, anti-American and anti-democratic reforms. They're sort of an embarrassment for Beijing. After all, this country is still a Communist nation, but they want to be on good terms with the West in general and America in particular. Hard for the government to condemn Red Tide for being too enthusiastic about communism.''

"The Chinese government has made a lot of progress along the lines of economic and social reforms," Brognola stated. "I know the slaughter at Tiananmen Square was a major setback, and mainland China still has a long way to go in the area of human rights—"

"But they still have most-favored-nation trade status with Washington," McCarter muttered. "That'll teach them to violate human rights and use slave labor to produce more goods to be sold to consumers at low prices in the United States."

"We don't make foreign policy," the big Fed stated. "We have our job and we do it. You're the unit commander of Phoenix Force. What do you plan to do about Red Tide?"

McCarter looked at the cigarette in his hand as if he weren't sure what it was. He shrugged, stuck it in his mouth and reached in a pocket for a lighter before answering.

"We decided to take them down. Attention was placed on these blokes because Neville got himself killed. Can't get all that choked up about a dope smuggler's death, but Red Tide has killed a number of innocent people in Shan Province, poor Chinese farmers who happened to be in the wrong place at the wrong time.''

"Stony Man isn't in the revenge business, and we can't go around carrying out justice for all the world's victims," Brognola insisted. "Might be tempting, but there are just too many of them."

"I'm aware of that," McCarter stated. "I mention it because it proves Red Tide is ruthless enough to attempt to carry out plans to help the Triad transport more heroin to the U.S. and Western Europe. They made a mistake with Neville, thinking he was a DEA agent when they killed him. That means they're ready and willing to target Drug Enforcement Administration personnel and Interpol operatives here in China. That's why we're getting ready to pay them a visit.''

"Looks like you're ready now," the big Fed remarked.

"We're moving out in a few minutes. Got the location on the Red Tide base, local guides to help us get there and a couple SAD agents to get in our way.''

"I'm sure you can handle it," Brognola said, "but don't get overconfident. Red Tide may not be as big or sophisticated as most of the opponents Phoenix Force has dealt with in the past, but they're dangerous. Actually I didn't contact you about this mission. As soon as you finish work there, we need you to head to Israel.''

"Israel?" McCarter asked with surprise.

"You heard about the kidnapping," the big Fed began. "Officially Morrow's still considered missing, but we have a reliable source that claims he's dead and his body was reduced to ashes.''

"Reliable source?" McCarter asked in a skeptical tone.

"Striker," Brognola replied.

The Briton puffed his cigarette and said, "That's good enough for me. Must be bloody serious if Striker needs our help."

"It's serious," Brognola confirmed. "We're also calling in your old unit commander for this."

"I thought Katz was on vacation. Checking out an Inuit burial ground or something like that."

"He was," Brognola said, "but we need his expertise and his connections with Mossad. It's a hell of a mess, David. We'll explain it to you later. You take care of what's on your plate before we give you the second helping."

"I can hardly wait," McCarter replied.

AKIRA TOKAIDO SAT at his post in the Stony Man computer center. The young Japanese-American watched the wall screens as he worked a keyboard, columns of binary numerals appearing. The code was quickly translated, and Tokaido stared at rows of Hebrew writing. The computerized translation system produced the information in English two seconds later.

Tokaido smiled as he bobbed his head to the beat of the music from the earphones, his portable CD player cranking out an Aerosmith hit popular a few years earlier. He enjoyed his work. Computers were fast and fancy, and each generation improved. The gestation period for a new generation of computers became shorter and shorter. Major innovations used to take decades, but now improvement in cybernetics occurred within a matter of months.

Such rapid change frightened some people. The high-tech world left them scratching their heads and wondering how they would manage in the twenty-first century when the latter part of the twentieth left them bewildered. Tokaido didn't have that problem. He had been familiar with computers since childhood. They were no more sinister to him than a television set or an automobile. He loved working with them and with others who embraced the cybernetic century of the future.

Tokaido also liked tapping into top secret government systems and stealing information. He was a hacker with White House approval, an outlaw with a keyboard and permission to use his skill in a way few could get away with. It was a great job, and he was very good at it.

However, what he got from the Mossad mainframe proved to be another letdown. Still no word on Michael Belasko or the mysterious SHC deaths in Israel. He accepted the disappointment and began to search for access to another system. A flashing light on the console drew his attention to a special transceiver unit. It was a telephone call, though the line was to a number in Maryland and patched through to Stony Man Farm. It couldn't be traced to Stony Man, but nor could the phone in Maryland be considered a truly secure line.

Tokaido removed his CD earphones and grabbed the handset to the transceiver. Agents in the field rarely used this line. They did so only when they couldn't make contact with the special laptop computer units used by Stony Man personnel in the field. He picked up and spoke into the mouthpiece.

"Hello," he said.

"This is Ulysses," a familiar voice announced. "Sorry it took a while to call. Had a few problems come up, and I've been kind of busy."

"Yeah," Tokaido replied, startled by the call. "Figured that. You okay? Not sick or anything?"

"Physically I'm fine," Bolan assured him. "I'm sort of stressed out by how business turned out here in Greece. Headed back to Athens to try to get things straightened out."

"Athens?" the young computer expert said, confused by the remark.

He glanced at the transceiver's digital display. The place of origin of the call was Cairo, Egypt. Tokaido felt foolish he hadn't guessed the Executioner claimed to be in a different city and country. He knew the line in Maryland wasn't secure and probably had to use a phone in Cairo that was also risky.

Aaron Kurtzman rolled his wheelchair toward Tokaido, obviously intrigued by who might be on the phone.

Tokaido plucked a pen from his pocket and quickly wrote "Striker" on a notepad by the console. He showed it to his boss as he said, "It's Ulysses."

Kurtzman nodded, aware Bolan was using an improvised cover name. He took the phone from Tokaido.

"Hello, Ulysses," he began. "This is Ursus. You get lost on your way back from the Trojan War?"

"Something like that," Bolan replied. "I'm not sure if there was a horse involved this time. Think you can get a representative to me here in Athens? I plan to be at the Great Aqueduct. Damn thing still works. Handles water just fine. I could meet with a representative at the Hesperus Tavern by the Aqueduct.''

"We'll see to it, Ulysses. Anything else?"

"My time on the phone is about up. Expensive to use a pay phone this way. Maybe I can make the next one collect?"

"Sure thing," Kurtzman assured him. "Take care, Ulysses."

"You too, Ursus. By the way, I'll be at the Hesperus Tavern about noon. Tell the guy you send I'll be in summer white, with a brown briefcase. Usual outfit for this hot weather."

"Okay," Kurtzman replied as he jotted down Bolan's message. "Talk to you later."

He hung up and looked at the notepad. Tokaido sighed.

"You called yourself Ursus?" Tokaido asked.

"It means 'Bear,'" Kurtzman explained. "Now, we have to figure out what the rest of this stuff means. He mentioned a Great Aqueduct. The Romans did occupy Egypt at one time and may have built aqueducts, but I doubt that's what he means."

"So something like an aqueduct or maybe just the opposite?" the younger man guessed.

"He said 'the damn thing still works,'" Kurtzman remarked. "Striker must mean the Aswân High Dam. The biggest and best-known in Egypt."

"What about the Hesperus Tavern?" Tokaido asked.

"I'm not sure. Run the word *hesperus* in the computer and get a general meaning."

Tokaido followed instructions and put the question to the machines. The answer came quickly.

"It's an Old Greek term," he stated. "Refers to

'west' or 'western,' especially to the west sky at evening when the sun sets. Hesperus is a name for the Evening Star...."

"Okay," Kurtzman said. "So we got an idea. I doubt the tavern is really a tavern. They have a few in Egypt, but Islamic countries frown on alcohol because it is forbidden in the Koran. It's probably a coffee- or teahouse."

"What's this stuff about summer whites and a brown briefcase?" Tokaido asked as he looked over the notes.

"You ever known Bolan to wear summer whites? He's a former Special Forces sergeant. To an Army vet the summer uniform is khaki. That's what he'll wear. The briefcase remark was just to make him sound more like a businessman in case anyone listened on the line. He might have a duffel bag, but I doubt he'll have a briefcase."

"And the representative he wants to meet him at noon must be a CIA, NSA or whatever kind of operative Stony Man can send."

"Yeah," Kurtzman remarked as he punched some keys to access a chart of international time zones on the screen. "I thought so. There is an hour difference between Athens and Cairo. So the 'representative' should probably arrive at eleven o'clock."

"Pretty slick," Tokaido said. "Of course, Mack has survived out there so long because he's smart, as well as tough. It's a relief to know he's still alive."

"He's not out of danger yet," Kurtzman commented. "Mossad is still hunting Striker. They may have even tapped into the phone call. Maybe the reference to Athens will throw them off. Depends on what sort of method they use and whether they have a cable line tap or a radio scan. We figured this out pretty quick, but we know Striker so we had an advantage. That doesn't mean Mossad won't be able to put the pieces of the puzzle together if they get suspicious of the call.''

"Let's hope they don't," the younger man said. He glanced at Kurtzman's notes again. "Why is 'Trojan horse' here?"

"When I asked 'Ulysses' if he got lost on his way from the Trojan War, he said he wasn't sure if there was a horse. I think that means he suspects an enemy in disguise may have been among the Israeli agents at the West Bank, but he's not sure. Of course, he doesn't know we've already considered that same possibility."

"That military intelligence officer?"

"Major Ziyyon. He might be overeager and too quick to kill for his country...or he might have some other reason. That's something else we have to worry about."

"Like a gang of crazy terrorists with the power to make people spontaneously combust isn't bad enough?" Tokaido asked.

"Sometimes you get more than you need, Akira," Kurtzman replied with a shrug.

CHAPTER NINE

The roar of rushing water was a strange contrast to the desert terrain. Mist rose from the concrete walls of the Aswân High Dam. The moisture caused a pleasant cool breeze over the immediate area of the dam. A number of businesses had taken advantage of this quasioasis setting, one of which was the Evening Star Coffeehouse.

Mack Bolan sat in the shade of a canopy over a table outside the coffeehouse. The place tried to present a sidewalk-café atmosphere. The Evening Star was only vaguely similar to cafés Bolan had visited in Paris, but he was comfortable as he sipped his second cup of coffee and waited for the person he hoped to meet there.

The Executioner had had to speak to Aaron Kurtzman in a cryptic manner during his phone call to the Stony Man phone line in Maryland. Yet he was confident the Bear would figure out what he meant. Bolan was less certain Stony Man would be able to get CIA or NSA to cooperate on short notice. He also had to consider the possibility Mossad may have tapped into the call and deciphered his meaning.

The small black duffel bag by his feet contained one of the two .357 Magnum Desert Eagle pistols he had taken from Lieutenant Hevron and Sergeant Jaffe when he escaped from the West Bank. Bolan didn't want to use a powerful handgun in an area populated by civilians and tourists. A fair number of both were present by the Aswân Dam. Egyptian laborers from oil fields and petrochemical factories visited the area for a cool spot for a break from work. The appeal to tourists was more difficult for Bolan to understand. In a land with the fabulous pyramids, the Great Sphinx and the catacombs of Alexandria, it seemed odd anyone would go out of their way to see a dam that wasn't particularly different from any that could be found almost anywhere else in the world.

Watching for friend or foe, he peered through a pair of dark glasses as people strolled by. Bolan's gaze fell on a figure dressed in khaki shirt and pants similar to his own attire. The guy appeared to be about forty, burdened by a spare tire around his middle that suggested he was basically a desk jockey. Bolan guessed the man would have been more comfortable in a single-breasted suit, white shirt and striped tie, the unofficial uniform of U.S. Intel agents.

The closer the man got, the more certain Bolan became he was a government agent from the U.S. Embassy in Cairo. The guy was remarkably pale for a person living in Egypt. Damp spots under his arms revealed a man accustomed to working in an air-conditioned office. He carried an aluminum case that appeared to be the right size for a portable typewriter or a laptop computer. Bolan decided to introduce himself. He rose from his chair, slung the duffel across his shoulder and approached the man.

"Hey," he began, "didn't we meet briefly on that plane flight from Washington, D.C., to Athens?"

The man frowned and slid his glasses down his nose to study Bolan with bloodshot hazel eyes. "Ulysses?" he asked.

"Yeah."

"You can call me Harry Coburn. I'm tempted to use 'Hercules' or 'Zeus,' but I guess I'll go with the name on my U.S. Embassy ID."

"Pleased to meet you, Coburn," Bolan said, offering his hand.

Coburn shook it, saying, "I'm not so sure I want to be too close to you. Mossad is still hunting you, Ulysses. Or should I call you Belasko?"

"Not as long as Mossad's looking for me," Bolan replied. "Guess I'll go by 'Ulysses' for a while longer."

"Well, you got a better chance of getting past Scylla and Charybdis than Israeli agents in the Middle East."

"I managed to get to Egypt."

"Don't push your luck," Coburn warned. "Better have your odyssey end at the U.S. Embassy. You can hide in the trunk of my car, and I'll take you there."

"You're working out of the embassy," the soldier said, "so you're probably CIA. National Security Agency gathers most of their Intel in the Middle East from SIGINT satellites."

"I'm with the Company," Coburn answered, "and we use satellite Intel, too. You coming to the embassy or not?"

"Not yet. Mossad will expect me to head for the embassy. I might be able to get in, but I won't be able to get out so easily. I don't want to have to hide in the embassy. I still need to be mobile, and I can't be if I'm boxed in the embassy."

"You can't if you're boxed in a coffin, either."

"I'll try not to get killed," Bolan assured the CIA agent, "but I've got things to do. Is that case you're carrying for me?"

"Yeah," Coburn answered. "It's a pretty fancy high-tech machine. Special telecommunications laptop model. I hope you know how to use it, because I'm not sure."

"I think I can manage."

"I was told to give you anything else you might need," the Company man said. "They figured you could use some money. You'll find twenty grand in the case. Half is in American dollars and the other half is in pound notes…Egyptian, not British."

"Thanks."

"A diplomatic pouch will deliver some weapons and gear for you, as well," Coburn added. "You need anything else before it arrives?"

"I'll let you know. I'm not sure what my next move will be or what I'll need. Somebody helped me get out of Israel. You can take her to the embassy."

"Her?" Coburn asked with a raised eyebrow.

"She's the daughter of a man who helped me out a long time ago. The guy was an American, but became an Israeli citizen and worked for Mossad. She's still a U.S. citizen and has a right to seek sanctuary at the embassy."

"If her old man was Mossad, you were taking a risk by getting her to help you."

"Not that big a risk," the Executioner assured him. "And she took a big risk to help me. I want her in a safe place, Coburn. Okay?"

"Okay," the CIA man agreed. "Where is she?"

"I'll send her to the embassy. There's a chance

you might have been followed, too. You head back to Cairo. Mossad won't bother you if you're alone. The woman will ask for you when she gets to the embassy. You appreciate how important security is for this matter?''

"Whoever you work for has White House authority," Coburn replied. "You're not with the Company or NSA, are you?''

"Don't worry about that," Bolan assured him. "I'll be in touch.''

"Yeah," the CIA officer said with a sigh. "I can hardly wait.''

MACK BOLAN DIDN'T go back to Cairo with Coburn. He stayed by the curio stores and diners in the Aswân area for an hour to be certain the CIA man hadn't unintentionally led Mossad agents to him. Satisfied, he approached the driver of a small tour bus who had delivered half a dozen Americans to the site. As Bolan suspected, the man spoke English and he was willing to listen to the stranger's story that he was stranded at the dam because his motorcycle had broken down a few miles away. Bolan also guessed the guy hadn't made much money that day with such a small number of passengers, and he eagerly agreed to take the soldier back to Cairo for fifty U.S. dollars.

The Executioner walked through the busy streets of the Egyptian capital. A combination of cultures, architecture and beliefs appeared on every corner. Modern office buildings and apartment complexes towered above sidewalk market stands with peddlers who sold everything from fresh fish and fruits to jewelry and hand-woven clothing. The great domes and minarets of mosques were visible from almost every angle, yet the steeples of Coptic churches weren't uncommon.

Most of the people appeared to be Hamitic Arabs, an ethnic order of northern Africans who varied greatly in appearance and pigment, yet most were considered Caucasoid by anthropologists who considered such matters important. Other Egyptians were of Greek, Italian and Turkish descent. Many wore Western attire, while others wore Arab headgear and Berber desert garb.

Although hundreds of people moved through the streets on foot, the number of cars, trucks and buses was comparatively low. Traffic was slow due to the flow of pedestrians who seemed to have the right of way in the narrow cobblestoned streets. Some of these streets were more than four hundred years old, constructed by the Turks when Egypt was part of the Ottoman Empire. This was especially true of Cairo's Old Quarter.

Bolan's destination was a small hotel located on the edge of the New Quarter, and as he approached the building, he noticed a man seated on a bench who seemed to be ignoring the cries of the muezzins, calling people to evening prayer. He held a newspaper open in his hands, yet didn't appear to have much interest in the contents. Although the majority of Egyptians were Sunni Muslims, others might not acknowledge the call to prayer and Bolan realized the man on the bench might be a tourist. He wore a lightweight jacket, straw hat and sunglasses. The soldier guessed he wasn't an Arab, and he was suspicious as to why the guy was posted in front of the hotel.

The Executioner used parked vehicles and an open-air market stand to conceal his progress as he avoided the view of the man on the bench to make his way to a small parking lot at the rear of the hotel. He spotted the battered old VW bug and a dark four-door sedan with a man in the driver's seat. Bolan crept toward the vehicle.

He paused by the rear of the sedan to place the computer case on the ground. Bolan slipped his hand inside the duffel bag as he moved alongside the car. The man in the front seat didn't notice him until he stood by the window.

"Shalom," he announced.

The man's head turned, his eyes widening as he reached inside his jacket. Bolan produced the .357 Desert Eagle from the duffel and pointed it at the man's startled face.

"Put your hands on the windshield, palms flat on the glass. *Ha-keem a-ta may-vin?*"

The guy nodded and raised his hands. Suddenly he thrust one arm out the window to try to shove Bolan's gun aside while the other hand dipped into the jacket. The Executioner swung the Desert Eagle away from the groping hand and hammered the barrel across the man's wrist. The Israeli yelped in pain but still tried to draw his own weapon.

Bolan jabbed his gun hand through the open window. The heavy steel barrel of the pistol slammed into the man's chin, and his head recoiled from the blow. The soldier slugged his opponent across the forearm to prevent him from drawing his piece and quickly opened the car door. He drove a hard fist to the man's solar plexus to knock the wind out of him. The Executioner charged inside, jammed the barrel of the pistol under the man's jawline and applied pressure to his carotid artery. The guy didn't have much fight left and quickly passed out.

The Executioner frisked the unconscious man and found a silenced .22-caliber Beretta in a shoulder holster. Many Mossad teams used small-caliber handguns, especially if they intended to take a target alive. It was easier to restrain an opponent if one put a couple of .22 slugs in a thigh or biceps first. Bolan also found a pair of handcuffs and a Nova stun gun on the guy.

He didn't find a passport, but Bolan knew the man was an Israeli agent. In addition to the gear he carried, the guy comprehended what Bolan said in English and Hebrew when the soldier had asked if he'd understood.

Mossad had caught up with him. The .22 and the stun gun suggested they wanted to capture him, but the Executioner knew they would rather kill him than let him get away. He was also familiar with standard procedure for Mossad field operations. The Israelis tended to use groups of six or more agents for this sort of assignment. If they considered Bolan dangerous and resourceful, Mossad probably sent a dozen.

He could have tried to quietly slip away, but he didn't intend to abandon Sarah Shapiro. If Mossad wanted him badly enough, some of their agents might be willing to try to use any means possible to persuade the woman to tell them where to find him.

He cuffed the unconscious Mossad agent's hands behind his back. Bolan found a roll of electrical tape in the glove compartment and used it to bind the man's ankles together and strapped a length of tape across his mouth. He took the keys from the ignition and slipped them in his pocket. He put the tape and the Nova stun gun in his duffel bag before he left the car and headed for the back door to the hotel.

The Executioner eased the door open a crack and peered inside. A man dressed in gray slacks, a white shirt and a tan jacket stood under a ceiling fan in the hallway. He held the jacket open to try to absorb the weak breeze from the fan. Bolan clearly saw the leather strap and the butt of a pistol holstered under the man's arm.

Time wasn't in Bolan's favor, so he decided to act quickly and play it by ear. He pushed open the door and stepped across the threshold, the Desert Eagle pistol pointed at the surprised man in the hall. The door suddenly slammed into Bolan with punishing force. He staggered toward the man, knocked off balance by the unexpected blow.

He realized he had made a potentially fatal mistake. In his haste Bolan had failed to check the hall to be sure the guy was alone. A second agent had been hidden behind the door and used it as a weapon. His partner lunged at Bolan and reached for the pistol. The Executioner could have shot him point-blank in the face, but held his fire. Hesitation was another potentially fatal mistake, but Bolan didn't want to kill the Mossad agents. They weren't his enemy.

The first Israeli gripped Bolan's wrist and began to twist it to force him to drop the pistol. The second agent charged from the door. Stocky and muscular, the guy swung an overhand right toward the Executioner's face. Bolan's free arm rose to block the attack, his forearm slamming the burly Israeli's inner wrist to deflect the punch.

The soldier delivered a short, hard chop to the

bridge of his attacker's nose, crimson oozing from a nostril as the Israeli stumbled, dazed by the blow.

The first agent still held Bolan's other arm with both hands. The big American shoved his wrist against the guy's thumbs, the weakest part of the grip, and abruptly broke the hold.

The Israeli gasped, surprised his mark had freed himself so easily. Bolan didn't give him a chance to recover, quickly grabbing one of the man's hands. He dug his fingers into the base of the Israeli's thumb and jammed his own thumb into the back of the guy's hand, between the lowest knuckles of the middle and ring fingers.

He twisted the captive hand, and the man groaned in pain. Bolan held the guy as his other hand streaked out and snared his second opponent's hand, gripping the stocky agent's index and middle finger and bending them backward. The guy yelped as a finger joint popped loose.

Bolan knew the Israelis would try to break free. They would know better than to try to pull away. Instead, the men would attempt to either use their free hands to try to break the holds or strike out at Bolan. Either way they would close in. He pulled and increased their momentum, then swept his arms across one another, ducked his head and weaved backward to move clear of the Israelis as the pair crashed into each other.

The aikido technique caught the agents off guard and left them stunned and disoriented. Bolan swiftly slashed the edge of his hand across the side of the larger man's thick neck. The Israeli collapsed to the floor in front of his astonished partner. The remaining agent lashed out a leg in a karate front kick aimed for Bolan's groin. The soldier dodged the foot and slammed the heel of a palm to the guy's sternum. The blow sent the man off balance and backward into a wall. As his back slapped the hard surface, Bolan hit him in the side of the jaw with a solid right cross. The agent slumped into a corner and quietly slid to the floor.

The pair wouldn't remain unconscious for long, and there was little time to spare. Bolan retrieved his Desert Eagle and quickly frisked the Israelis. He took their guns, handcuffs and the keys for the manacles. He cuffed their right wrists together and moved into the hall, toward a stairwell.

Footsteps on the wooden stairs announced that someone was descending the risers. Bolan thrust his Eagle in his belt in favor of one of the silenced .22 Berettas taken from the Mossad agents. He waited by the side of the stairs, crouched out of view as a man rushed to the bottom, a pistol in hand. It was enough proof for the Executioner. He thumbed the catch from safety to fire and took aim. The silencer coughed, and the man cried out as a .22 round burrowed into his thigh. As the Israeli fell to the floor, Bolan rushed forward and kicked the gun from his hand before he could try to use it. Another kick behind the fallen man's ear put him into dreamland.

Bolan quickly handcuffed the guy to the handrail and headed upstairs, reaching the third floor without incident. He peered over the top riser and saw a beefy figure stationed in front of the door to room 33. Although the man was dressed in civilian clothing, Bolan recognized Sergeant Jaffe.

The big American had spotted the Aman NCO, but Jaffe didn't see him until he rose at the head of the stairs, muzzle of the silenced pistol pointed at the startled Israeli's belly.

"Small world, isn't it?" Bolan stated.

Jaffe's hand jerked toward his jacket but stopped short. He realized he couldn't hope to draw his weapon before Bolan could shoot him. The NCO raised his hands to shoulder level as the Executioner stepped closer.

"You're probably carrying a pair of handcuffs," Bolan said. "Use your left hand to get them. No sudden moves. If I have half a reason to kill you, I will. I already spared your life once. Don't push your luck, Sergeant."

"Bastard," Jaffe growled.

However, he obeyed the instructions. Bolan told him to snap a manacle of a handcuff to a wrist, then ordered him to face a wall, keep his hands on it and get to his knees. He was then to put his hands behind his back.

"How many of your buddies are in the room with the woman?" Bolan asked as he cuffed the Israeli's wrists together.

"Only one."

"Really?" Bolan took the roll of tape from his duffel bag. "If I find two guys in there, I'll come back and shoot you in a leg. If I find three, I'll put a bullet in both legs."

"Two men!" Jaffe quickly replied. "Lieutenant Hevron and a Mossad agent. I don't remember his name."

"That's okay," Bolan assured him as he used a length of tape to bind Jaffe's ankles together. "I don't plan on making any introductions. Where are the keys to your cuffs?"

"Left pants pocket," Jaffe said with a sigh. "You're not going to kill me?"

Bolan took a ring of keys that included one for handcuffs, as well as car keys. He also found Jaffe's pistol, a .380-caliber Heckler & Koch with a sound suppressor.

"Probably not," Bolan replied. "Stay down, stay quiet and stay out of the way if you want to stay alive."

He strapped some tape across the NCO's mouth and left him kneeling on the floor. Bolan stuffed the .380 in his belt and grabbed his duffel bag. It was getting heavy from the gear he was taking from the Israelis. Silenced .22 in hand, Bolan moved to the door, stood by the frame and carefully turned the knob. The door wasn't locked. He hit it with a hard kick. The door swung open and slammed into a wall. He didn't intend to be ambushed by another Mossad lurking behind a door.

Lieutenant Hevron and another man stood in the center of the hotel room. Both had removed their jackets, and weapons holstered under their arms were clearly visible. They stared at Bolan and the black muzzle of the sound suppressor.

Sarah Shapiro sat on the edge of the bed behind the pair. She still wore the shorts and undershirt she had on when Bolan had left for the meeting in Aswân, but she also had a bruise on her cheek.

"You guys looking for me?" the Executioner asked, a hard edge in his voice. "Here I am. If you both go for your guns at the same time, maybe I'll kill one of you. Probably get you both, but you might manage to take me with you if you're fast enough."

Hevron's right index finger was wrapped and

splinted. He wouldn't be able to use his pistol quickly. The Mossad agent with the lieutenant didn't seem eager to accept Bolan's challenge, either. Both raised their hands in surrender.

"Hands on the wall, feet apart," Bolan ordered. "You know the routine."

"I am so glad you're here," Shapiro declared as she jumped from the bed.

"Somebody is going to wish I hadn't shown up," he replied. "You guys shouldn't have hit her. She couldn't tell you where I went because she didn't know."

"Only one of them hit me. The other man made him stop."

"Which one?" Bolan asked.

Shapiro stepped behind the two Israelis, who still faced the wall in a spread-eagle stance. She swung a foot between Hevron's splayed legs and smashed the instep into the lieutenant's groin. The man moaned as his knees buckled, and he started to slide down the wall.

"Keep your hands flat on the wall," Bolan ordered. "Both of you."

Bolan jammed the muzzle of the silenced .22 against the Mossad agent's back, just above the buttocks. The Israeli realized the American could shoot his tailbone with the twitch of a finger. The guy didn't move as the Executioner confiscated the agent's pistol and handcuffs.

The soldier glanced at Hevron as he handcuffed the Mossad man's hands behind his back. Hevron must have assumed Bolan was distracted by the chore, because suddenly he pushed away from the wall, reaching for the gun in shoulder leather. The

Executioner swiftly turned the .22 toward the lieutenant and triggered the weapon. The pistol chugged discreetly, and Hevron cried out as a diminutive bullet pierced an arm above the elbow. The Aman officer clutched his wounded biceps and dropped to his knees.

"You keep making the wrong choices, Lieutenant," Bolan commented.

He turned to Shapiro. "We're leaving as soon as I can secure these two. Grab your handbag and whatever you can stuff into it because we've got to move fast."

CHAPTER TEN

Shapiro packed as much as she could into her handbag as Bolan finished gagging the two Israelis with electrical tape. They were already handcuffed and their ankles bound with tape.

"You ever had any training in firearms?" Bolan asked.

She shook her head.

"Then you shouldn't carry one." He found the Nova stun gun among the Mossad weapons in the bag. "Take this instead. Know how it works?"

"Stick the electrodes into a person and press the button," Shapiro replied with a nod. "I used to carry one when I worked nights in Miami."

"Let's hope you won't need it," Bolan said as he led the way to the open door.

The soldier stood at the threshold and glanced at the hallway. He didn't see Sergeant Jaffe until the NCO lunged from the doorway. The man's wrists were still handcuffed, but he had managed to slide them over his legs and feet to put his hands in front of him. The sergeant had also peeled the tape from his ankles, although his mouth was still covered by a thick black strip.

His doubled fists swung like an ax, aimed at Bolan's head. The big American raised the duffel bag to block the attack, so Jaffe's hands pounded the canvas and the numerous metal objects inside it. Bolan swung the .22 pistol in his fist, hammering the butt under his adversary's rib cage. The Israeli uttered a muffled groan and staggered into a wall.

Bolan used the heavy duffel to knock Jaffe's arms aside and deliver another pistol stroke. The gun butt hit the man in the side of the jaw and dumped him on the floor in a dazed heap. The Executioner jogged to the stairs, Shapiro close behind. His boots pounded the risers as he peered down at two figures at the foot of the stairwell. A man in a white jacket and cloth hat was about to unlock the handcuffs that held another Israeli trapped to the handrail.

The man in white looked up as Bolan charged down the stairs. He reached inside his jacket as the Executioner jumped over the last four or five risers and slammed into him, feetfirst. The impact knocked the man to the floor with Bolan on top of him. The soldier tucked his chin to his chest as he tumbled to the floor in a shoulder roll to break his fall, his body continuing into a wall.

The agent in white lay stunned by the powerful blow to his chest. Shapiro reached the foot of the stairs and knelt by the fallen man. She jammed the electrodes of the Nova into his battered chest and hit him with a jolt of nonlethal electricity. The man's body convulsed from the charge and lay still, drained of energy. Bolan got to his feet and glanced about for more opponents. The man cuffed to the rail growled something in Hebrew, but could do nothing while restrained and hobbled by a .22 bullet in his leg.

"Back door!" Bolan told his companion.

He once again took the lead. The two agents Bolan had encountered when he first entered the building had regained consciousness, but were still seated on the floor. Handcuffed together, they were groggy and confused as Bolan and Shapiro approached. The Executioner pointed the .22 at the pair and convinced them to stay down while he and the woman headed for the exit. Voices shouted from the other end of the hallway, by the lobby of the hotel.

The pair raced outside to the parking lot. Bolan headed for the sedan, reaching into a pocket and withdrawing some keys.

"We'll take this car," he announced. "It's got to be in better shape and faster than the VW."

"I'll drive," Shapiro said. "I know the city."

"Okay," Bolan agreed. "Just a minute. I left a guy in the car."

The woman had already reached the vehicle and looked inside the window at the driver's side. She opened the door and grabbed the Israeli sprawled on the front seat. The guy was still bound and gagged. She dragged him from the vehicle as Bolan approached.

"Take the keys," Bolan said. "I've got to get something." He rushed to the rear of the vehicle and scooped up the computer case he had left under the rig, then headed for the passenger side of the sedan as two figures appeared from the side of the hotel.

"These keys don't work!" Shapiro shouted.

"Damn," Bolan rasped, aware he had to have given her the keys he took from Sergeant Jaffe.

The two men by the hotel had spotted Bolan, one of them pointing at the Executioner as the other pulled a silenced pistol from his jacket. The Executioner thrust his arm forward and aimed low before he squeezed off two shots. The sound suppressor muted the reports, but both .22 rounds struck pavement near the feet of the Israelis. Startled, the agents jumped for cover along the side of the building.

Bolan yanked open the car door and hastily stuffed the duffel bag and computer case into the back seat. He fired two more rounds at the ground near the Israelis' position to keep them at bay as he fished in a pocket for the other set of keys.

"I don't know how to hot-wire a car, Michael," Shapiro said with frustration.

"Try these," he urged as he handed her the keys.

As the soldier slid next to her and closed the door, Shapiro inserted the key, turned it and the engine growled to life. Bolan set the Beretta by his feet and drew the .357 Desert Eagle, the sedan lurching forward. The Israelis bolted from the hotel. One fired a pistol at the sedan as the other dashed for an old Ford parked at the edge of the lot.

Metal struck metal along the side of the vehicle. Bolan knew that a sound suppressor reduced the accuracy and the velocity of a bullet. Luckily the rounds didn't have enough energy to pierce the metal skin. However, luck could swing either way.

The Executioner aimed his Desert Eagle and squeezed the trigger, but the sedan swerved abruptly to the right and the bullet struck the Ford's windshield. Bolan glimpsed a crack in the glass. He also noticed the Israelis had dropped to the floorboards, surprised and alarmed by the unexpected thunderous report of the Magnum pistol.

He glanced out the rear window. A Mossad agent

tried to close the hood to the Ford. Bolan's shot had
to have punctured the radiator and either smashed the
latch to the hood or damaged the engine. Either way
it would slow the Israelis. He and Shapiro had one
of the Mossad cars, as well as the keys for another
taken from Jaffe. Bolan didn't know how many more
vehicles they might have or how many agents would
be able to continue to stalk him.

The sedan rolled onto the street and headed for the
New Quarter, Shapiro realizing the car would have
too much trouble with the narrow pathways and numerous open-air markets of the Old Quarter. Headlights appeared in the rear window, and Bolan suspected that Mossad could be in pursuit.

Shapiro increased speed as the sedan's headlights
revealed a clear path ahead. Bolan noticed the car
behind them kept pace, as well. His concern that
Mossad was still after them was suddenly confirmed.
A figure on the front passenger side poked a weapon
out the window and pointed it at the sedan. Even in
dim light Bolan recognized the short barrel and elevated sights with a top cocking knob. No more .22
pistols for the Israeli team; the gunner was armed
with an Uzi.

A burst of full-auto 9 mm slugs raked the sedan,
bullets slamming into the bodywork. Glass shattered
from the rear window, and a stray round burrowed
into the dashboard. Shapiro cried out as metal split
and sparked scant inches from her elbow, but she
didn't panic and kept the car under control.

Bolan crawled over the backrest and tumbled into
the back seat. Glass crunched around him, and pain
lanced his left hand, telling him he had been cut.

"Pull to the left as far as possible!" Bolan shouted

to be heard above the hailstorm of metal on metal. "Make a harder target for the shooter!"

A lull in the action gave Bolan a split second to glance at the Israelis' vehicle, a medium-sized American-made car. He could only guess at the model or year, but the rig was probably as fast or faster than the sedan. Still reluctant to kill Mossad agents, the soldier thrust the barrel of the Desert Eagle through the shattered rear window.

He lowered the aim and fired a shot into the grille at the radiator. The vehicle didn't slow, and the Uzi snarled once more. Bolan ducked his head as more glass burst from a side window to the back seat. At least one parabellum round tore into the seat fabric beside him.

He raised his head and glanced outside the windows, spotting a narrow side street with a fish market on one corner and a building that resembled a small warehouse across from it. He didn't understand the sign in Arabic above the structure, but he did notice a stack of wooden kegs by the curb. The barrels formed a pyramid roughly three yards high. Bolan shook off some glass fragments and turned to a side window.

"Go right!" he told Sarah. "Turn onto that side street!"

She followed his instructions, the sedan heading between the buildings with the Mossad vehicle close behind. Bolan quickly fired two rounds at the kegs at the base of the pyramid. The powerful .357 Magnum slugs split wood, and two containers burst apart. Dozens of iron roofing nails poured from the shattered barrels. The rest of the stack teetered off balance on the damaged foundation.

The sedan sped on as the Israelis' car drove into the path of the kegs, wood and iron crashing across the hood and windshield. The vehicle swerved out of control, hopped the curb and slammed nose first into a streetlight. The car was out of action, the hood bent and dented, the windshield cracked. Water poured from the ruptured radiator.

"That did it," Bolan announced. "Nice work, Sarah."

"Any idea what we do now?" she asked.

"Head for the U.S. Embassy. Take it easy, but try to avoid the police. They'll be headed toward the shooting, but they probably won't notice this car is shot up unless we do something to draw attention to it. If they stop us, just show your passport and demand to go to the embassy. We might even get an escort."

"So we're going to seek sanctuary at the embassy," Shapiro said in a tone of relief. "What changed your mind?"

"You're getting sanctuary," Bolan explained. "It's already been arranged. Just go in and ask to speak with a security chief named Coburn. He'll look after you."

"I'm not going in without you."

"You need to get to safety," the soldier insisted. "You could have been killed tonight, Sarah. I don't want to put you in any more danger. I couldn't have come this far without you, but now I finish this mission without you."

"Michael..." she said, her voice almost pleading.

"You've been great, Sarah. It may not be easy to wait until this is over, but that's what you have to do."

"You won't just take off without seeing me again?" she asked.

"No, I won't," Bolan promised.

He didn't add that he would see her again...if he survived the mission.

CHAPTER ELEVEN

"Long time no interface," Hal Brognola said to the image on the wall screen in the Stony Man War Room. "Good to see you, Striker. For a while there we were afraid we might have lost you."

"I've had a few people trying to end my career," Bolan stated. "I had to be careful what I said on the phone with the Bear, but the Company man's remarks suggested you must have gotten some information by tapping into Israeli Intel computers in Tel Aviv."

"Yeah," Brognola confirmed. "You can probably guess they're not real happy with you. Especially a Major Ziyyon."

"I'm not too happy with him, either," Bolan commented. "That goes for his henchmen Lieutenant Hevron and Sergeant Jaffe."

"Those are the two guys who tried to escort you out of the West Bank?"

"They didn't intend to take me out unless I was ready for a body bag, Hal," Bolan replied. "That's why I had to make a break out in the desert."

"You sure they planned to kill you?"

"Yeah," Bolan stated. "I think they planned to try again today. The Mossad agents with them probably intended to take me alive, but I'm sure those two would have tried—"

"What are you talking about?" Brognola asked with surprise. "You mean the Israelis tried to nail you in Cairo?"

"About a dozen of them. Didn't really get a chance to count them for sure. Cairo police are probably investigating the incident now. Hevron is going to be laid up for a while. Probably Jaffe and a couple of the Mossad agents, as well."

"Well," Brognola began, "I sent Katz to Tel Aviv. He should be arriving tomorrow. If anybody can get Mossad off your back, Katz is the man. And Phoenix Force has wrapped up business in China. I'm sending them to help back you up."

"I'll be glad to have them in my corner, but I'm not sure what they'll be able to do at this point. Jinn 2000 has one hell of a weapon, Hal."

"Spontaneous human combustion?"

"I saw those men go up in flames. Israeli paratroopers, Congressman Morrow and even the bodies of the dead terrorists. I think I got a glimpse of the device they used, but I can only guess how the thing works."

"Why didn't this SHC contraption work on you?"

"I've been trying to figure that out ever since it happened," Bolan answered. "I don't know. If it worked by escalating human body heat to some incredible level, I should have burned with the others. If dead bodies burned, I certainly would have if it increased heat levels."

"The Bear came up with a bunch of theories of how SHC might occur. They all sounded pretty weird to me. I did some research, and the only one that seemed at all plausible was the idea a person might fall asleep, maybe pass out drunk, set himself or herself on fire somehow and then cook down to ashes by roasting in body fat. Sort of like tallow in a candle.''

''I don't know about the people who died in mysterious fires believed to be spontaneous human combustion,'' Bolan admitted, ''but a person burning up in their own body fat would seem to take a long time. What I saw happened fast. Victims were reduced to piles of ashes in a few seconds. I hope it happened so fast they didn't feel much pain.''

''If it happened as fast as you said, they probably didn't feel much of anything except a hell of a lot of fear,'' the big Fed commented. ''It has to be terrifying to realize you're on fire. I wish we knew why you seem to be immune to this SHC stuff. The President still plans to come to the Middle East in support of peace talks.''

''Noble effort, but poor timing.''

''I don't think he's going to back down. He believes this is too important to wait until the situation is safer. The Middle East is never really safe for anyone.''

''I'm not so sure any place is anymore,'' Bolan replied, ''but most of the time a person doesn't have to worry about being burned to death by an invisible ray, force field or whatever the enemy uses. Maybe you should try to convince the President to delay the trip until we can find out what's going on and deal with the Jinn 2000 terrorists.''

''The Man has a lot of faith in our ability to take care of emergencies,'' Brognola said. ''That's what happens when somebody gets used to expecting us to deliver miracles.''

"Tell him we're flesh-and-blood mortal human beings and he can't count on us to perform the impossible.''

"Okay," the big Fed agreed. "What do we do in the meantime?''

"Try to perform the impossible," Bolan told him.

"Might be able to help you do that. The Egyptian Criminal Investigation Division has been watching the branch of Jinn 2000 in their country with a lot of concern and suspicion. No wonder, because violent fanatics of Islamic splinter groups are believed responsible for the assassination of Sadat and at least two of the attempts on Mubarak. CID computers have recorded a lot of detailed information about meetings by Jinn 2000, including sermons with political overtones, rituals of various types that aren't generally found in the Muslim faith and descriptions of leaders. Some of these have been positively identified by photos and even fingerprints.''

"They have an agent working undercover within Jinn 2000," Bolan guessed.

"That's what we figure, too," Brognola answered. "We're trying to get some trust and cooperation with the Egyptians on this. Of course, they're concerned about the peace talks, and they've been supportive. If Sadat hadn't gone to Jerusalem in 1977 to offer peace proposals with Israel, there probably wouldn't be any peace talks in the Middle East today.''

"You think you can convince the Egyptians to hook me up with their undercover agent?''

"We'll see what we can do, Striker," Brognola

assured him. "You're not calling from the embassy. Found a safehouse?"

"I don't know how safe it is with Mossad stalking me. I'll probably have to move around a lot, but I'll stay in touch."

"Watch your ass. We'll do what we can at this end, but we expect you to stay alive."

"I'll try not to disappoint you," Bolan replied.

DIRECTOR GELLER GLARED at the figure on the threshold to his office. The top officer of Mossad wasn't in a good mood, and the visitor didn't improve his attitude. Major Ziyyon seemed aware of that. He closed the door and assumed a stiff military "attention" stance.

"Major Ziyyon, Aman, reporting."

"I know who you are and why you're here," Geller replied. "I also got a report about what happened in Cairo. Your two Aman operatives are in a hospital. So are four Mossad agents. Four others were picked up by the police and are being held by Egyptian authorities. This is quite an embarrassment, Major. Fortunately our ambassador has been able to convince the Egyptians that stupid, sloppy mess wasn't an act of espionage against their government. We basically told the truth and explained that an overzealous, possibly unbalanced field-grade officer in Aman was responsible."

Ziyyon's eyes were fixed on the blue-and-white Israeli flag on the wall behind Geller's desk. He seemed to concentrate solely on the Star of David in the center of the banner. The major's expression didn't reveal any emotion at Geller's verbal jabs. He remained at attention, aware the man hadn't told him to relax because the Mossad director wanted him to be uncomfortable, forced to stand quietly and endure a tongue-lashing.

"I spoke with your commanding officer, and he's not pleased with your actions, either, Major," Geller continued. "Your behavior has been extreme, to say the least. You've overstepped your authority. Aman is unhappy with you, and we at Mossad are even more upset with this business."

"If the director will be good enough to allow me to speak?" Ziyyon began, attention still fixed on the flag.

"At ease, Major," Geller replied. "Go ahead and speak."

"This American agent or mercenary or whatever he is," Ziyyon began, "was involved in the deaths of several Israeli soldiers and U.S. Congressman Morrow. His flight is further evidence of his guilt—"

"Major," the director said, cutting him off. "I know something about the man who calls himself Michael Belasko. He's carried out missions here in Israel and probably other parts of the Middle East in the past. I don't know who he really is, I don't know what organization he works for. I have never met the man, and I haven't even seen a photograph of him aside from a blurry copy of a passport photo. He has conducted his previous missions in a rather unorthodox manner, but he has always been successful and never acted against the interests of the state of Israel. It is difficult for me to believe this man would suddenly fall in with a group of fanatic terrorists."

"I can only say that we must be suspicious of any man who tells a bizarre fantasy about humans bursting into flame, yet his clothes aren't even scorched.

He has no explanation for how these people burned or why he was immune to the fire."

"The reports I've received have confirmed the ashes from that Jinn 2000 site were indeed human remains. They had been burned by some sort of incredible heat. How do you think Belasko and these terrorists managed to do this in such a short time? Did they have some kind of portable crematorium able to produce heat levels of at least three thousand degrees?"

"I suspect they may have employed a very powerful acid compound," Ziyyon replied. "Perhaps something used to dissolve metals that is unfamiliar to the medical staff who evaluated the ashes. If you'll allow me to go to Cairo, I will personally supervise a team to capture Belasko and bring him back to be interrogated. If he is telling the truth, he'll have nothing to fear."

"That request is denied," Geller stated. "This has already gotten out of hand, and I won't allow you to make matters worse. Your commander and I agree that for now you are to be restricted to your living quarters and the immediate area of your housing complex. You are relieved of duties until we have a chance to conduct a detailed inquest."

"I'm under house arrest?"

"I said an inquest, not a court-martial, although that will be considered. For now you will be regarded as an officer in the Israeli military and expected to behave with honor and honesty. Forget about Cairo and Belasko. Also—"

A buzzer sounded by Geller's phone. He punched a key, and his secretary announced that Colonel Katzenelenbogen had arrived. Geller told her to send him in. The door opened, and a man of senior years entered. Katz's face appeared gentle, with more lines than Geller recalled. He still wore his iron gray hair cut short and favored tweeds even in warm weather. The hook at the end of his right sleeve was clearly visible. Katz had lost an arm decades earlier and wore a prosthesis attached to the stump at the elbow of the abbreviated limb.

"It's good to see you again, Mr. Director," he said. "How are you?"

"How am I?" Geller replied with raised eyebrows. "Things aren't going so well."

"Sorry to hear that," Katz said. "Maybe things will start to go better for you now."

"I've always considered you to be a mixed blessing, Yakov," Geller stated. "Major Ziyyon, this is Yakov Katzenelenbogen, formerly a colonel in the Israeli military and a retired officer of Mossad. He was one of our most experienced and gifted agents. If things had been a bit different, he probably would have wound up behind this desk instead of me."

"That's a great compliment, Mr. Director," Katz said, "but you exaggerate. I am curious as to why Major Ziyyon has caused so much trouble for Michael Belasko. You know he's a good friend of mine. You might recall we worked a mission in Israel a few years ago. I would think Belasko should have earned some trust and cooperation rather than the hostility he has experienced on his most recent trip."

"With respect to your age and distinguished service," Ziyyon began, "you are retired. Correct, Colonel?"

"I still have an interest in the welfare of my

friends, as well as situations that may be a threat to either Israel or the United States, Major.''

"I would like to talk to you privately, Yakov," Geller urged. "We'll talk again later, Major. Goodbye."

Ziyyon nodded and left the office. Geller opened a desk drawer and got out a pack of Camel cigarettes. He shook one loose and offered it to Katz.

"No, thank you," Katz replied. "I'm trying to quit. After I retired, I found my stress level dropped considerably. I have been able to cut down after all these years."

"Something for me to look forward to," Geller remarked as he placed the cigarette in his own mouth. "So you really are retired, Yakov? According to our sources at customs, you're even traveling under your own name. That must be strange after so many years of intrigue."

"It's not so bad," Katz assured him. "I'm sort of a senior statesman now. This is a diplomatic mission to see what can be done about this business with your organization attempting to kidnap or kill Belasko."

"You can contact him?" Geller asked.

"Perhaps."

The director lit his cigarette and inhaled deeply. "Tell him the manhunt has been called off. Mossad and Aman are no longer looking for him. No Israeli will be a problem for him…at least at this time. We still have an investigation in progress concerning the events at the West Bank."

"Good," Katz replied. "What about Ziyyon?"

"His movements are restricted, and he won't be a problem, either."

"Is he under investigation?"

"Not exactly. We plan an inquest. Ziyyon has a pretty impressive record until now. This whole business seems out of character with his previous service."

"I don't trust him, and I suggest you don't, either," Katz insisted. "How about the plans for the peace talks? What precautions are being taken to protect all involved from a possible threat of the enemy's SHC device?"

"We don't know there is such a device," Geller said with a sigh. "Scientists contacted seem to feel the stories about so-called spontaneous human combustion are nonsense. If it is real, I'm not sure what special security methods could be used to protect anyone from such a threat."

"If Belasko says it's real," Katz insisted, "it's real. Instead of arguing about this, we should concentrate on stopping the terrorists and their strange technology."

"I thought Belasko was your concern," Geller remarked. "Let us handle this, Yakov. You're retired. Remember?"

"True," Katz replied with a smile, "but I still want to stay involved. It's important for a man to find something to do after he retires so he doesn't get bored and inactive."

"Bored and inactive?" the director asked, one eyebrow cocked in disbelief. "I have never met a man with a wider range of interests or ability in so many fields than you, Yakov. Visit some museums and see the sights in the cities and at historical areas. You've always been interested in archaeology. You have time to pursue those studies now. You read and write five or six languages fluently. You could write a book in Hebrew or English and translate it into French, Arabic and German.''

"Right now I have something else that has to take top priority. We have a very serious situation on our hands, and it'll get worse if we don't deal with it. Better accept all the help you can get, Mr. Director.''

"You're right," Geller admitted. "That's an annoying trait, Yakov. You always seem to be right about everything.''

"I've certainly made plenty of mistakes," Katz assured him. "At my age one can look back at all the things one did wrong and wish they could be changed. I try not to do that. The worst things are the regrets about what you wish you had done, not the ones you did. Anyway, I'll be in touch.''

"I know," Geller replied. "Not so easy for me to say this, but I actually am glad you're here, Yakov.''

"Oh," Katz said with a laugh, "I knew that all along.''

CHAPTER TWELVE

Nadia sprawled on the mattress beneath satin sheets, watching Qabus an-Sabkhat strolling naked across the bedroom. He was in good shape for a banker, she thought, muscles toned by regular exercise. Sabkhat worked out more to relieve stress than for physical fitness. The woman wondered if he used sex for a similar reason.

"Thank you," Sabkhat told her as he slipped into a robe. "That was excellent, Nadia."

"Bringing you pleasure is pleasure for me, as well," she replied. "You had a lot of energy tonight."

"It's been a while since I've been with you. Chastity may be considered a virtue by some, but I've never found celibacy to bring me anything except more frustration."

Nadia laughed. "You expect me to believe you haven't been with any other woman since you left the United Arab Emirates?"

"You may not believe me," Sabkhat said, "but it's the truth. Frankly the Jinn 2000 are terrible prudes. We're not supposed to have sex with anyone except our wives. Not many of the members of Jinn 2000 are married, but they all plan to get wives after we crush the infidels. They figure they'll be able to have the four-wives limit from the Koran. Obviously they don't realize how expensive you women can be.''

"Some of us more than others," Nadia replied with a shrug. "So you really haven't been with another woman? Not even your wife?"

"My wife and I haven't done much together for a long time. The relationship is a business arrangement more than a marriage. She plays her role by pretending to be a wife and mother. That means she has servants take care of the house and the children while she goes shopping and enjoys social gatherings of rich, shallow women like herself.''

"Have you ever thought she might be enjoying the company of other men, as well?" Nadia asked.

"Perhaps," Sabkhat replied. "I really don't care. She and I have no passion together. If she finds it with someone else, good for her. I have.''

Nadia laughed again and drew her knees up to her breasts as she sat naked on the bed. Her body was well toned and sleek. Sabkhat still admired her beauty and sexual prowess. Of course, they met only a few times a year. Perhaps he would get tired of her if they were together more often. Yet he had known many women of different cultures and backgrounds. Sabkhat had been with blond Scandinavians, high-priced French prostitutes, Asian sex goddesses who treated men to pleasures by use of stroking pressure points and nerve centers more familiar to martial artists and practitioners of acupuncture than ladies of the evening.

None could compare with Nadia. He had met her in the UAE as a member of the secretarial pool at the bank. Originally from Morocco, Nadia had moved from country to country, trying to be an independent woman in countries that still regarded females as second-class citizens. She was intelligent, strong willed and not afraid to speak her mind. She soon came to mean more to him than he cared to admit...even to himself.

"Next you'll tell me you love me," she remarked.

"Would you want me to say that," he asked, "if that's how I really feel about you?"

"No," Nadia replied. "Love just means people feel they own each other. It means you have an obligation to the person who 'loves' you. No one can really be free if they love or allow themselves to be loved."

"I thought that would be your answer," Sabkhat said with a shrug. "Care for some brandy? It's been smuggled in from France."

"Breaking all the Islamic rules tonight?"

"Why not?" he replied. "Those rules are just restrictions to keep some people in line while others get ahead. Religion is a form of social control."

"That's a dangerous opinion to voice in Libya," Nadia commented. "Even more dangerous to say around members of Jinn 2000. They'd be very upset if they knew what a decadent atheist you really are."

Sabkhat unlocked a cabinet and produced a bottle from a compartment hidden behind a false panel. He poured brandy into two coffee cups as he spoke.

"Jinn 2000 has the potential to unite Arab and Islamic countries as a great world power. It will be risky. Blackmail always is. Yet if we can succeed, we'll be able to establish an economic base, financed and supported by the West. The biggest threat will be these jihad lunatics who think they'll be able to use the SHC device to destroy the infidels.''

"Isn't that what the whole sect is based on? The predictions of Omar, the whirling dervish who spun around and around until he vomited up nonsense about an impossible victory over the enemies of Islam?''

"Not Islam,'' Sabkhat told her. "Jinn 2000 has as much contempt for Sunni Muslims and every other Islamic sect as it has for the Christians, Jews and all the rest. Even the majority of Shiites will be out of luck, according to Jinn 2000. Still, fanatics have their uses. They'll take action when reasonable men would not dare do so. The trick will be to keep them from charging into self-destruction before I can manage to steer Jinn 2000 in a more logical direction.''

"How do you plan to do that?'' Nadia asked as she sipped some brandy. "Captain Qatrun killed a man right in front of you because he failed to follow orders. What do you think he'll do if he thinks you've turned against the goals of Jinn 2000?''

"I think Qatrun will have to be removed,'' Sabkhat replied. "Probably a few others, as well. We still need Barrah because he's the scientist who discovered the SHC device.''

"How can a brilliant man of science like Barrah believe in this Jinn 2000 insanity?'' Nadia asked.

"Many people who are very intelligent believe in all sorts of foolish things,'' Sabkhat replied. "Isaac Newton was certainly a brilliant physicist, but he believed in astrology and alchemy. Sir Arthur Conan Doyle, a British physician and author of the Sherlock Holmes detective stories, believed in spiritualism and séances. Doyle even claimed Houdini must have been able to turn himself into ectoplasm to be able to carry out some of his famous escapes.''

''I've known a number of smart people who believe in things like flying saucers and fortune-telling,'' Nadia agreed.

''Of course. I've done business with a banker in Hong Kong who is an expert in antique art, computer technology and speaks four languages. He also consults the *I Ching* by tossing coins to see what fate has planned for him. Most religious leaders are very intelligent and educated men, but they still endorse the superstitions and fables of their faith. Barrah's belief in Jinn 2000 isn't that unusual even if it seems foolish to us.''

''So you think you'll be able to threaten the governments of the United States and Israel with this spontaneous-human-combustion method and they'll agree to let you rule the world?''

''Not quite,'' Sabkhat said with a smile. ''If they're afraid of our ability to burn them to death, they'll agree to a few changes in foreign aid, banking agreements and trade. That's all. Then I'll have control of approximately one-third of the financial power in the world. They'll still run their own countries and deal with their stupid human masses, but I'll manipulate oil prices, international loans and interest rates, and influence commodities and monetary systems, as well. That, my dear Nadia, is conquest in the twenty-first century.''

''What about us?'' she asked. ''Or won't you need me anymore?''

''I'll need you more than ever,'' he assured her as he sat on the edge of the bed. ''You are my trusted ally and lover…I assume that term won't chase you off."

"Making love and being in love are two different things," she replied. "So I'll be the mistress of the most powerful and richest man in the world? Sounds good."

"It sure does," Sabkhat agreed, "but I'll have to get you out of here and back to the UAE. Right now I can't have Jinn 2000 know you're here."

"Sure you can trust the men who brought me here?"

"Kamel is loyal to me and knows he'll profit when I come to power," Sabkhat explained. "He'll be my security chief and one of my top advisers. People are most loyal when to do so benefits them."

"I hope you're right," she said.

Nadia recalled Kamel. A big man with a barrel chest and heavily muscled limbs, he was a formidable character. His eyes seemed dark and cold beneath thick black brows. A jagged white scar along his cheek appeared to be an old knife wound, and his hands were large and callused, perhaps from karate training. Kamel might be a valuable ally, but he would certainly be a dangerous enemy.

"I need to take care of a few matters before Qatrun and Barrah return," Sabkhat told her. "Let's make the most of what time we have left."

THE TUNNEL WAS LINED by ancient stone walls, and no one was quite sure how old the passages might be. Sabkhat had told Nadia the tunnels may have been built by the Romans when they ruled Libya.

"The Jinn 2000 cult members don't know about

these tunnels?'' she asked. ''Not even Captain Qat-run and Professor Barrah?''

''No talking,'' Kamel growled. ''Sound carries a long way in this place.''

She didn't speak again until they reached the end of the tunnel. Nadia breathed deeply, relieved to be free of the ancient walls. She gazed up at the night sky. She was clad in the costume of a Berber nomad, and the *brussa* shirt, turban and face scarf had been uncomfortable in the confined area and stale air within the passage. Miles of sand extended before her with dunes like hunchback shapes in the horizon. However, a truck was parked near the stone mouth of the tunnel. A face gazed from the canvas gap at the back of the vehicle, the grin on the man's face cruel and lustful. She didn't relish his company on the road.

''You are going with me, Kamel?'' she asked.

The big man didn't reply. He removed a copper medallion from a pocket and held the chain in his fists. Nadia recoiled when he raised it and approached.

''This is a gift from Mr. Sabkhat,'' Kamel declared. ''He asked me to give it to you before you set out to the desert.''

''A gift?'' she asked with surprise. ''Why didn't he give it to me? We were together all night.''

''It bears the face of the Prophet and the crescent of Islam,'' Kamel explained. ''He knows you do not believe in Muhammad, the Koran or God. Perhaps it would embarrass him to give it to you.''

''Why would he want me to wear it?''

''It will make your disguise more convincing if Libyan soldiers should stop the truck,'' Kamel stated.

"This way you will appear to be a good Muslim woman. Otherwise, they might mistake you for a traveling whore."

"I don't like your choice of words or your tone," she said with anger in her voice. "Just give it to me. I'll put it on myself."

"As you wish," Kamel replied.

Nadia slipped the chain over her head. She barely glanced at the medal, her attention fixed on Kamel and the grinning man at the rear of the vehicle. Fear rose inside her. Would Sabkhat's trusted flunkies dare rape his mistress? If so, would they leave her alive to tell what happened?

"You are his weakness," Kamel remarked as he shook his head. "Mr. Sabkhat should not have spoken so freely to you. No woman can be trusted to keep a still tongue, especially a slut without principles or religion."

"You were listening to our conversation!"

Nadia started to back away from Kamel, her eyes wide with shock and terror, her mouth open wide in astonishment. Kamel suddenly stepped forward and thrust out his arm. His big fist hit her hard on the point of the chin. Nadia's teeth clashed together, and her head snapped back from the unexpected blow. She uttered a groan and fell unconscious in the sand.

"Let's get this over with," Kamel told the man in the truck. "Do it, Muda."

"Why not have our way with her first, Kamel?" the man in the truck asked. "What difference will it make?"

"We're getting rid of this harlot because she is a threat to Sabkhat and to us," Kamel replied. "We're not rapists or murderers. She just has to be taken out of Sabkhat's life for his own good, as well as ours. Do it!''

Muda frowned with disappointment and sighed.

"Now!" Kamel insisted.

Muda shoved the barrel of the device through the gap in the canvas, pointing the transparent muzzle at the fallen woman. Blue flame ignited from her motionless form. Kamel looked away to avoid the brilliant white light at the core of the fire. He felt the blast-furnace heat rise from the ground and waited a few seconds before he turned his head to witness the streak of charred ashes in the sand.

"Weather reports say a strong wind will sweep across this area from the east tonight," Kamel commented. "Probably sandstorm conditions for desert travelers, they say. That will scatter her ashes all over the desert. It'll be as if she never existed.''

"She was a beauty," Muda commented. "Such a pity.''

"Pity is something we can't grant anyone who stands in our way, Muda," Kamel declared. "Let's go.''

CHAPTER THIRTEEN

The menu was written in Arabic with no English translations. Mack Bolan put it down as the waiter approached, notepad in hand.

"I'd like a cup of coffee," Bolan said.

"Coffee," the waiter replied with a nod. "Sir, like food?"

"Just coffee, okay?"

The waiter nodded and headed for the counter. The restaurant was small, pleasant and clean. The other customers appeared to be locals, not the sort of place that attracted many tourists. That was fine with the Executioner. If Mossad was still hunting him, they probably wouldn't look for him at the restaurant.

Bolan sat at a table near an exit, his back to a wall and one eye on the entrance. He was confident he couldn't be seen from a window. The duffel bag beside him contained one of the silenced .22 Beretta pistols he had confiscated from the Israeli agents, as well as a .357 Magnum Desert Eagle. He hoped he wouldn't need either weapon, but he couldn't afford to drop his guard.

The waiter had returned with the coffee, and Bolan raised the cup as a man entered the restaurant. A dark man of average height and build, he wore traditional *brussa* shirt with a pair of Levi's slacks. His black mustache and beard had been carefully trimmed, and a pair of dark glasses was perched just below the bridge of his hawkish nose. The guy spotted Bolan and headed for his table.

"Sorry I'm late," he announced as he extended a hand to the soldier. "Maybe you're early."

"It's okay either way," Bolan assured him. "Shall we discuss business over coffee?"

"I'll have breakfast," the man answered. "Omelets here are good. So is the bread and beans. You Americans don't usually eat beans for breakfast?"

"I've eaten lots of things for breakfast. Depends on where I am and what's available."

The stranger took a seat across from Bolan. The soldier noticed a bulge under the guy's shirt—likely a small-frame pistol.

"I'm calling myself Ulysses right now," Bolan explained.

"Call me Ahmed. My office told me to meet you, but I can't say I'm very comfortable about it. Do you want breakfast?"

Bolan nodded as the waiter headed for the table again. The Executioner noticed the two men seemed to know each other. They exchanged some sentences in Arabic, and the waiter departed.

"I appreciate your position," Bolan began, "but I need to find out more about Jinn 2000 and you know more than anyone else I can get in touch with."

"CID will be glad to cooperate with CIA when we finish our investigation, but I'm not so sure this is the time for it."

"I can help you, too," Bolan said. "Jinn 2000 has

a new special weapon. Have you encountered it yet?''

"A weapon?" the Egyptian asked with a frown.

"It can cause living human beings to burst into flame and burn into ashes in a few seconds. Spontaneous human combustion or something worse.''

"You're serious?" the CID man asked, stunned.

"I'm very serious. I've seen them use it.''

"Is that a fact? It is a remarkable claim. You personally witnessed this SHC device? This isn't just more Jinn 2000 propaganda about Judgment Day for the infidels?''

"It's true. I need information about the sect.''

The waiter returned with their food. Breakfast consisted of large omelets, fresh baked bread and fried, spiced beans. More coffee was poured, and the waiter left once more.

"I've been attending meetings of the Jinn 2000 branch set up a few kilometers outside of Cairo,'' Ahmed began. "They have prayers and read from the Koran, with a Shiite attitude. The local teacher rambles on about infidels, the Judgment and Omar's claim that the true believers who help destroy the enemy will be jinn with incredible magic powers. Recently he's been saying God will deliver a 'sword of fire' to slay the infidels.''

"That's an interesting expression," Bolan remarked.

"I had thought it was just another effort to stir the emotions of the Jinn 2000 followers with some colorful terms to encourage determination and a fighting spirit. I did consider the possibility it meant more than that because the teacher referred to the 'sword of fire' so often, but I guessed this might be rocket launchers or perhaps even a small nuclear device they planned to get their hands on. Spontaneous human combustion never entered my mind.''

"No reason it should have,'' Bolan replied. "How many followers are there in Egypt?''

"Most Egyptians are Sunni Muslims. Jinn 2000 is directed more toward Shiites, and only those with a violent extremist personality at that. We have more Christians than Shiites here. Even the Jewish population in Egypt might be larger than the number of Shiites. Most of the Jinn 2000 members I've encountered aren't Egyptians. We speak Arabic that falls into two major dialects—the North Nile Valley, or Cairo, dialect and the South Nile Valley dialect, which is also widely used in the Sudan. Many of the Jinn 2000 here speak a North African dialect more common to Algeria, Morocco or Libya. Some speak a Mediterranean dialect, which suggests they may be from Syria, Lebanon or Jordan.''

"So the Mediterranean dialect would probably be spoken by most Palestinians, as well?'' Bolan asked.

"That's right,'' Ahmed said with a nod. "Now, the teachers at the Jinn 2000 meetings speak what's often called classical Arabic. That's the dialect spoken in the Arabian Peninsula. Of course, that's where our language began. This includes Saudi Arabia, Kuwait, Yemen and Oman. The classical dialect is also spoken by many scholars of the Koran, as well as by nomads found throughout the Middle East and North Africa. You might compare it to so-called proper English among the upper-middle-class British.''

"Arabian Peninsula,'' Bolan remarked. "Would that include Iraq?''

"Actually the Iraqi dialect resembles the Mediterranean dialect more than the classical. Iraqi Arabic tends to use many expressions incorporated from Persian and Kurdish, just as our Cairo dialect has been influenced by Latin and, more recently, English. In Morocco and Algeria, Arabic has been 'corrupted' by French and so on. The important point is that Jinn 2000 members in Egypt are mostly outsiders, and the leaders certainly are.''

''Interesting,'' the soldier said. ''I'd like to check out one of these Jinn 2000 meetings myself. Only men attend, right?''

''No women or children allowed,'' Ahmed confirmed. ''But no infidels are welcome, either.''

''You're a Sunni Muslim. That makes you as much an infidel as I am, according to the doctrine of Jinn 2000.''

''But they don't know that.''

''We won't tell them I'm an infidel, either.''

''You're an American, and you don't speak Arabic well enough to order breakfast,'' Ahmed stated, amazed by the suggestion. ''How do you think you could possibly pass for an Arab?''

''What if I pretended to be mute or an imbecile?''

''The notion sounds like something an imbecile might come up with,'' Ahmed replied in a frustrated tone. ''You don't look like an Arab, sound like an Arab or move like an Arab. People have subtle mannerisms that reveal a great deal about their background and culture.''

''I'm aware of that. I've infiltrated enemy ranks in the past and pulled it off. You can coach me in certain gestures and actions. I've seen enough variety in the people on the streets of Cairo to realize Arabs look, dress and behave differently...just like everybody else does. Some Arabs are taller than me, their complexion is lighter than mine and their features aren't much different from mine."

"You're probably talking about people who are of Greek or Italian descent," Ahmed replied. "The majority of them are Christians. They'll be suspicious of you the moment they see you. It won't work, Ulysses. You even have blue eyes."

"So I'll wear a pair of brown contacts," Bolan replied. "You already think I'm a half-wit to make this suggestion. It shouldn't be too hard for me to convince other people by shuffling around with my head bowed, unable to understand what anyone says and occasionally grunting something in an unintelligible manner."

"It would be easier to believe you must be out of your mind if they could understand what you say," Ahmed commented, and shook his head with dismay. "I was told to cooperate with you. My superiors said you're supposed to be a superb field operative. Nobody seems to be quite sure what agency you're with or exactly what you are, but supposedly you're the best. No offense, but that's a little hard for me to believe at this moment."

"Maybe your opinion will change," the Executioner replied. "Frankly I'm not here to make friends. I have a mission to accomplish. Now *we* have a mission. Let's get on with it."

CHAPTER FOURTEEN

The drone of the engines vibrated through the hull of the C-130 transport. David McCarter placed the laptop computer on a folding bench along the wall of the plane. The British ace had never cared much for computers, but realized they were part of the tools of his trade. He wished the plane would remain steady and his fellow Phoenix Force commandos would shut up while he punched a series of numbers on the keyboard.

"How can you say the Chinese have a better drug policy than the United States?" Rafael Encizo demanded with an uncharacteristic edge in his voice. "We took out a gang of heroin smugglers in southern China about forty-eight hours ago, in case you forgot. They're growing fields of opium poppies, and you say they're doing a better job at fighting drug use?"

"Triad harvests opium in the Golden Triangle and China," Calvin James began. "I'm not arguing about that or defending their actions or the Chinese government for trying to pretend it doesn't go on. My point is drug abuse within mainland China is almost nonexistent. Poppies are grown and opium processed there, but the Triad has to sell the shit abroad to make a profit."

"They sell it all over the world," Gary Manning commented, "especially to the United States. They don't grow fields of opium poppies in the States. There wouldn't be heroin addiction in America if it wasn't being smuggled into the U.S. from China, the Golden Triangle, Afghanistan, Mexico and a bunch of other countries."

"Actually," T. J. Hawkins said, "during the War Between the States, a couple of the Southern states did grow poppies to produce opium as painkillers for the Confederacy."

"Thank you, Jefferson Davis," James said dryly. "Aside from that piece of history, opium and heroin have been imported, but we can't blame drug abuse in the United States on the fact they produce heroin and cocaine in other countries. Our problem is that we have so many Americans willing to buy and use the crap. None of you hate dope dealers more than I do. I lost a couple family members due to drugs and junkies. That doesn't change the fact the problem of drugs in America isn't going to be solved by going after the source in foreign countries."

"Will you blokes keep it down?" McCarter asked. "I'm trying to call the office."

"So what are the Communists doing that pleases you so much, Calvin?" Encizo asked, contempt in his tone.

"Oh, hell," James replied. "I'm not supporting communism, and you know it. I appreciate your personal reasons to despise communism, Rafe, but their policy on drug abuse isn't based on communism in China. The Japanese use a similar method, and they have a very low rate of drug abuse, as well. In both countries the emphasis is on the user. A person caught using drugs is sent to a clinic, similar to a mental hospital. No fun to go, and they make the junkies dry out. When they get released, the authorities make it clear they'll send them right back if they start using again. If they commit any crimes to buy their drugs, they'll have to go to prison when they get out of the clinic.''

McCarter cursed under his breath when the computer screen announced, ''Access denied.''

Aware he had punched in the wrong series of numbers, McCarter tried to ignore the argument among his teammates. The other Phoenix Force warriors failed to appreciate his plight as the heated conversation continued.

''There are clinics like that in Canada, the United States and other countries,'' Manning said. ''I'm not sure how successful they've been, Cal. Seems like you're always reading about some celebrity going into rehab for drug or alcohol abuse, and a lot of them are going back for the third, fourth and fifth time.''

''Those clinics aren't handled the same way,'' James insisted. ''Some of them are professional outfits with real medical personnel. Some are just plain crap. Most drug programs are run by counselors who aren't required to have any sort of training. A lot of them are ex-junkies themselves. Some of them aren't really 'ex,' either. Pretty miserable system when we have drug-rehab outfits that can actually be run by people still using drugs and sometimes selling dope, as well. Even worse, a lot of those programs are supported with taxpayers' money.''

''You make it sound like our war on drugs is all

screwed up," Hawkins said with a frown. "Personally I'd like to see some of the pushers executed."

"You think that would be a deterrent?" Manning asked. "A lot of the people involved in the narcotics trade are young gang members. They face death every day on the street from drive-by shootings and all the insanity that goes with that life-style. What makes you think they'll be worried about the possibility of going to the electric chair?"

Hawkins shrugged and replied, "Dead men don't sell drugs. Maybe it wouldn't be a deterrent, but it would sure stop the bastards you wasted from selling more poison to school kids and making more youngsters into criminals to support their dumb-ass habit."

"There will always be thousands more to take their place," James stated. "As long as there are poor kids growing up in slums who don't have any future and think the only way they'll ever get anything in life is if they've got a lot of money—"

"Bloody hell!" McCarter roared. "I did it wrong again!"

He backed away from the computer and glared at the screen that once more denied him access. The Briton folded his arms on his chest, his expression tense with anger and frustration. The others fell silent.

Manning worried that McCarter's hand was close to the Browning pistol holstered under his arm. "That's an expensive piece of equipment, David," the Canadian said. "You're not going to shoot it, are you?"

"No," the Briton replied, his voice tense. "I'm not going to shoot it, break it or anything of the sort."

"If you're having trouble with that machine, I'll give you a hand," Hawkins suggested. "Handling computers is second nature to me."

"Maybe I'm not a bleedin' computer whiz," McCarter answered, "but I can manage this if I can concentrate on what I'm doing. You blokes go on with your debate. I'll move to the sleeper cabin and use the outlet there."

"I didn't know our conversation was disturbing you," James said. "We can just stop. I don't think anybody is going to change his mind about the issue anyway."

"I'm rethinking my position," Manning stated. "Cal has some good points. Maybe we should consider the antidrug policies used in China and Japan. They seem to work better than what we've been doing in the West."

"So we should send drug addicts to a mental hospital and hope that works," Encizo commented with disgust. "Maybe they can use some of the medications the Soviets tried on patients at their asylums. The type that kill thousands of brain cells and break down a person's willpower. Maybe we can set up political prisons and labor camps in the future."

"Come on, Rafe," James replied. "That's got nothing to do with this...."

McCarter gathered up the laptop and headed for the cabin. The others began their discussion again as he entered the sleeper and set the computer on a bunk. He closed the door for privacy, then took a deep breath to relax before he plugged in the machine and worked the keyboard once more. Finally he gained access on the high-security line.

Colors and shapes formed on the screen. McCarter

took a pack of Player's cigarettes from his pocket and fired one up as Yakov Katzenelenbogen's face appeared. The Israeli warhorse seemed relaxed with a teacup in his left hand. Katz wore a bathrobe, the empty right sleeve pinned at the stump of the amputated limb.

"Hello, David," he greeted. "How did China go?"

"We pretty much did our job and left," the Briton replied. "Saw the Great Wall from the air, but didn't do much sight-seeing. We spent most of the time in some obscure places in a southern province that's not part of the tours. Business as usual. What's up on your end?"

"Right now I'm doing some diplomatic duties," Katz replied. "So far so good. Mossad has called off its manhunt, and Striker will have some more breathing space. Now he just has to worry about terrorists who can cause spontaneous human combustion."

"Bloody incredible. We'll be arriving in Israel in a few hours. I'm not quite sure what we're supposed to do when we get there."

"You'll just have to wait for Striker to decide when and if he needs you," Katz replied. "This is really his mission. You'll be called in to assist him when he has a better grasp of the situation."

"Still seems strange to be working without you in command of Phoenix Force," the Briton admitted. "Sometimes I wonder if you blokes made the right choice when you decided to put me in charge as unit commander."

"Hal and I agreed you were the best choice, and we even had the Bear run the idea through the computers. We have confidence in you, David. Five years ago you wouldn't be ready for command, but you are now.''

"I appreciate your support, but I still have some doubts, Yakov. Don't let the others know I said this. I'm trying to get them to believe in me, you know.''

"They do,'' Katz assured him. "They're good men, very brave, intelligent with a strong sense of independence, as well as the ability to function together as a team. Men like that wouldn't follow anyone they didn't believe in.''

"It was different when you were commander, Yakov. We all knew you were the smartest and most experienced member of Phoenix Force. We didn't doubt your qualifications, and we sort of looked up to you—''

"As a father figure?'' Katz asked with a smile. "I was also the oldest member of Phoenix Force. I just got too old to stay in the field. You have command now because you're best suited for the task, David. The others are highly skilled, experienced and very intelligent. I don't know Hawkins very well, but I have read his record and it's impressive.''

"Among other things, he's a computer and electronics expert. Sometimes I don't even understand what sort of high-tech stuff he's talking about. You know how smart the others are. Calvin, Gary and Rafael seem to know more than I do about a hell of a lot of things.''

"Of course,'' Katz said. "You know things they don't know. We didn't pick you because you're smarter, braver or more skilled than the others. You have a talent for strategy and tactics. You were always at your best in the battlefield. We used to wonder if you might be a little crazy because you were always willing to take the greatest risks. Yet you never acted in a foolhardy manner that would put the lives of your teammates in greater danger. Their lives were more important to you than your own.''

"I reckon my biggest concern is trying to keep it together when we're not in combat," McCarter confessed. "I almost lost my temper with my mates because they were arguing so much about how the bloody war on drugs should be handled, I couldn't concentrate on the computer."

"So you got away from them and made contact," Katz replied. "That's what you're supposed to do. They are going to have arguments and debates, including some about subjects that aren't related to your mission. Intelligent adults have different opinions. That's normal. I recall you used to get in some heated discussions about a variety of subjects. You're the commander of Phoenix Force, but that doesn't mean you try to control everything your men do or think. Just the opposite. Their individual abilities and personalities are resources you should use for the advantage of Phoenix Force as a whole."

"I realize that," the Briton assured him.

"Just watch your temper," Katz urged. "It doesn't inspire confidence if your men see you have a tantrum due to some minor setback or because you have to work with a bureaucratic case officer for an Intel agency who rubs you the wrong way."

"Hell," the Briton groaned. "The time I punched out that CIA bloke happened a long time ago."

"It shouldn't have happened at all," the Israeli reminded him, "but I think Confucius said a wise man learns from his mistakes and a fool does not."

"Can't afford to make many mistakes in this line of business," McCarter remarked. "Of course, you know that better than anyone. You must have made a lot of mistakes to learn to be so wise, Yakov."

"I've made some," Katz admitted, "but there are other ways to learn...such as by observing the mistakes of others."

"I'm not going to ask if you learned anything from me," McCarter said. "Better get back to work. I know you have a busy day of sight-seeing to take care of, too."

"Have a nice flight," Katz replied.

CHAPTER FIFTEEN

The Jinn 2000 branch outside Cairo was located at a green tent large enough for a medium-sized circus. Wooden towers had been constructed by the tent to serve as minarets, but the men with rifles stationed on the platforms at the summits of the towers obviously acted as sentries, not muezzin criers. Mack Bolan noticed their weapons resembled the old U.S. military M-2 carbine and guessed they were probably Egyptian-made Hakim rifles.

The Executioner had to take care not to appear too interested in the guards or anything else around him as he accompanied Ahmed to the canvas mosque. He had to play the role of a brain-damaged man, barely able to speak more than a few words in Arabic and capable of understanding even less. He hung his head low and raised it occasionally to glance about in a dazed manner. Bolan felt uncomfortable clad in an unfamiliar *abayeh* robe and *keffiyeh* headgear, scarf held in place by an *akal* band.

He shuffled beside Ahmed like a trained dog. Other men walked toward the tent, most wearing traditional Arab garb similar to Bolan's attire. Several carried firearms, and virtually all had a sheathed knife of one type or another. A few eyes turned to

Bolan, but none seemed to linger when they saw an individual who appeared to be mentally impaired.

Ahmed led Bolan to the mouth of the tent. Two burly figures stood at the entrance. They recognized Ahmed and greeted him in a formal, polite manner, but they regarded Bolan with an expression that seemed fueled by distaste more than distrust.

"Mi irra-gill da?" one of the doormen asked.

The Executioner knew he wondered who the stranger with Ahmed was and why was he there. Bolan couldn't follow the conversation with his limited grasp of Arabic, but he knew the story the CID operative would tell them. Ahmed explained that Bolan was his cousin Muhammad, an unfortunate victim of an accident while mining iron ore that left him in his present condition. He claimed Muhammad had suffered terrible head injuries that left him simpleminded, barely able to speak or hear and unable to understand most of what he could hear.

Ahmed declared his cousin to be a devout Shiite Muslim, and he believed Muhammad might have his mind and physical senses restored during the services at Jinn 2000. After all, anything was possible with the will of God. Bolan heard the Arabic word for "God" and took his cue.

"Allah akhbar!" he declared, speaking each word with a proper Cairo dialect.

He repeated "God is great" over and over like an Islamic mantra. This seemed to please the Jinn 2000 doormen. They spoke briefly with Ahmed, then stepped aside to offer access to the threshold.

Bolan and Ahmed entered the tent. At least forty Jinn 2000 followers had assembled for the services. They knelt on prayer rugs in a horseshoe formation, all faced east toward the Islamic holy city of Mecca. A dervish, clad in a green robe and turban, spun in circles before the congregation. He whirled faster and faster as another man read aloud from the Koran.

A mosque was considered a house of God by Muslims, and tradition required a person to remove his shoes as a sign of respect. Bolan and Ahmed placed their boots among the collection of footgear of the congregation. They carried prayer rugs to a vacant spot among the worshipers. Both men knelt and lowered their foreheads to the rug in the formal manner of Islamic prayer, humble and prostrate in the presence of God.

"There is but one God!" the congregation chanted in Arabic.

Bolan understood little of the reader's words from the Koran, but he recognized the names of prophets. Many prophets and stories in the Koran were virtually the same as those found in the Jewish Torah and Christian Bible. Abraham, Joseph, Moses, Solomon and many others were as important to Islam as they were to the Jewish and Christian religions.

Nothing about the service seemed disturbing or unusual to the Executioner. He had attended Islamic worship before, and the Jinn 2000 sect hadn't been much different. The dervish finally stopped whirling and dropped to his knees, head bowed and eyes closed.

The man started to speak, and Bolan glanced up, intrigued by the man's remarks. The dervish spoke about achieving success and added, "Fire! Fire!" The soldier couldn't understand the rapid string of Arabic that followed, but he noticed the crowd became more excited than it had been during the readings from the Koran.

The dervish shouted, *"Jihad! Hariah Allah!"*

Suddenly the congregation rose and chanted with the holy man in support of a "holy war" and "God's fire." Bolan was glad he was disguised as a mentally defective visitor because he was the only person not on his feet. Ahmed had also joined the frenzied cry. Bolan decided he should do likewise. It wasn't difficult for him to appear to be confused and disoriented under the circumstances.

Two figures clad in Berber garb appeared, scarves across their noses and mouths as if in preparation for a sandstorm. They wore thick gloves as they pushed a wooden cart by a long handle. The men behaved as if they didn't want to get any closer to the contents of the cart than absolutely necessary. Bolan saw why when he recognized the bulky, four-legged shape contained by the bars of an animal pen in the cart.

The hog was large and noisy. It squealed and snorted, snout jammed between the wood bars. Swine flesh was considered unclean by both Muslims and Jews. The men with the cart acted as if they were transporting toxic waste.

Voices expressed surprise and revulsion about the unexpected arrival of a pig at the mosque tent. The dervish waved at the congregation to urge them to be silent. He made a rapid-fire announcement that was too difficult for Bolan's limited grasp of Arabic. The dervish pointed at the cart as the two men near it retreated from the pen as if they expected the pig to explode.

The animal didn't blow up. Instead, it burst into blue flame. The crowd gasped in astonishment and terror. The hog barely managed a single squeal before the fire claimed it from stubby snout to curled tail. Bolan raised a hand to shield his eyes from the brilliant white core of the blaze. Ahmed grabbed his robe and yanked hard to try to get Bolan's attention. He uttered something in Arabic, apparently stunned by what he saw.

The soldier ignored his CID companion and scanned the area for the device he knew had to be responsible. Bolan looked at the canvas walls of the tent but couldn't locate the SHC weapon, which obviously worked what seemed to be spontaneous combustion on living flesh. He noticed two open folds in the tent and realized the device could be located outside the mosque.

Only a lump of ashes remained of the hog, the wooden cage barely scorched by the fierce flames. Only a trace of odor from the burned beast rose from the cart. The fire had to have been so fast and intense it cremated the victim too quickly and completely to leave much scent. The dervish shouted at the congregation, but Bolan didn't even try to understand what he said. The spontaneous-combustion machine was nearby, and that was all he needed to know.

"I SAW IT and I can still hardly believe it is real," Ahmed commented in a tense whisper as the two men knelt by a row of vehicles parked by the tent. "I thought you had to be crazy or at least exaggerating about what happened at the West Bank."

"Can we talk about this later?"

Bolan was busy adjusting the radar probe to the audioamplifier listening device that Coburn had provided. It was no larger than a pack of cigarettes, but it functioned in the same manner as the much larger rifle microphone. Basically it transmitted a radar radio wave onto a surface and received vibrations that produced sounds from the amplifier.

Unfortunately the pocket amplifier was a short-range device. They had to get close to the canvas mosque to eavesdrop on Jinn 2000.

Bolan and Ahmed had hidden in the area after the services and waited for the majority of participants to leave. Dozens departed the tent and the scene, either on foot or by vehicle. The remaining cars and trucks belonged to the hard-core members stationed at the mosque. The soldier could only guess how many terrorists were inside the tent.

Ahmed had previously explained what had been said during the service. Bolan hadn't been surprised to learn the dervish had spouted claims of visions that declared Jinn 2000 was going to strike down infidels with the fire of God. The hog had been sacrificed to show how God would destroy unclean beasts and unclean people who opposed the gospel according to Jinn 2000.

The demonstration had certainly amazed everyone present, especially the potential new recruits who attended the services. Shiite extremists, they believed the pig had burned due to supernatural power rather than a man-made device. Bolan could understand how the Jinn 2000 ranks could rapidly grow when word of this "magic" spread. The following would get bigger and more dangerous the longer the enemy carried out their deadly charade and a campaign of terror and murder.

Bolan and Ahmed had made their way to the row of vehicles to try to eavesdrop on the terrorists after the services. The guards atop the wooden minarets weren't very alert and appeared bored with their duty. Neither noticed two dark shapes among the shadows by the cars and trucks. Clad in black fatigues—previously hidden beneath their robes—the two men were virtually invisible to the sentries.

The soldier inserted an earphone into the eavesdropping device and handed the equipment to Ahmed. The terrorists would certainly converse in Arabic, so the CID officer was the logical choice to use the listening device. Bolan drew the .22 Beretta from his belt. He regretted not having a large-caliber, more powerful handgun, but he didn't want to risk hiding one of the big .357 Magnum Desert Eagles under the robe he had worn as a disguise.

He had prepared for a soft probe of the site, unaware the Jinn 2000 terrorists would have the SHC device in Cairo. The Executioner was tempted to slip inside the tent, capture the enemy weapon and one or two of the higher-ranked members of the extremist group. He wasn't equipped for such a raid, but he could always claim more firepower from the corpses of his opponents.

But the Executioner didn't know what kind of odds he might be up against, and he couldn't assume he was somehow immune to the SHC device. Nothing would be accomplished if he only managed to get himself and Ahmed killed. It was better to try to learn more about the site and the enemy in order to put together a better strategy.

Ahmed knelt by the tailgate of a battered pickup truck and stuck the radar probe around the edge to train the device on the tent. He frowned and shifted the listening device from side to side. Bolan realized the CID man was having trouble getting reception from the mosque.

Bolan glanced at his wristwatch—2357 hours, almost midnight. The guards in the tower would probably be relieved soon, he thought. The pair on duty had been at their post for about four hours. Unless the guard commander was a fool, he wouldn't leave his men perched atop the minarets any longer than four hours and expect them to do their job properly. The sentries would naturally get bored and weary, forced to stand on small wooden platforms and survey the ground below.

Voices from the mouth of the tent drew Bolan's attention. He carefully peered around the edge of the tailgate. Two men had emerged from the canvas shelter and headed for the vehicles. The soldier drew in a tense breath as he watched the pair approach. He held the .22 firmly in one hand and reached for the Ka-bar fighting knife in a sheath at the small of his back.

Ahmed hadn't noticed the threat, as he was preoccupied with the listening device. Bolan moved beside the CID officer and pushed him against the tailgate with a shoulder. Ahmed was confused and opened his mouth. Bolan held the blade of the fighting knife to his lips to signal for silence and canted his head in the direction of the advancing Jinn terrorists. The Executioner used the tip of the Ka-bar to point at Ahmed's chest, then gestured under the truck.

Although his expression indicated uncertainty about Bolan's decision, Ahmed reluctantly crawled between the rear tires and slithered under the vehicle. Bolan got on his belly and crawled to the car next to the truck. The fender was too low and he couldn't get under it. The Executioner employed the only method possible to hide. He stretched his body and pressed himself on the ground at the rear of the car. Like a serpent, he coiled around the tires and slid as much of his torso as possible under the fender. Bolan pressed the pistol high against his chest, the sound suppressor extended above a shoulder. He kept the knife low and waited.

The soldier didn't move as the voices drew closer. He heard footfalls only a few yards from where he lay. Bolan didn't know which vehicle the men would head for. If either of the rigs used to conceal Bolan or Ahmed was selected, there would be a problem. Would the truck or car pull forward or back up? The sentries on the towers would probably be watching simply because the moving vehicles and headlights below would give them something different to look at for a minute or two.

Bolan figured he would handle the situation when it unfolded. Until whatever happened actually occurred, his best strategy was simply to stay put and try to blend with the shadows.

Metal slammed on metal. Bolan didn't feel vibrations and knew the terrorists hadn't moved to the car where he was positioned. The sound didn't sound close enough to be the pickup, either. An engine growled, and a car near the soldier rolled forward. He waited for the vehicle to drive from the area and to be certain no other Jinn 2000 members were headed toward them.

Satisfied as much as circumstances allowed, Bolan carefully crawled back to the rear of the pickup and Ahmed. The CID agent wiggled **from u**nder the vehicle, listening device in one hand and a Walther PPK in the other. The Executioner signaled that it was time to go.

Ahmed eagerly nodded in agreement.

The pair crept along the shadows, away from the tent mosque. They slipped over a ridge and headed for the road. Ahmed had parked his car about three hundred yards from the tent, concealed behind a large billboard that advertised tours of the pyramids in five languages.

"That was about as close as I care to come to a confrontation with terrorists in the dark," Ahmed admitted. "I thought it was nerve-racking to go under cover before, but you've introduced me to a whole new level of fear."

"You're welcome," Bolan replied. "What did you hear from the listening device, Ahmed?"

"Several voices spoke. At least three dialects of Arabic, and most did not sound Egyptian. They discussed preparations for tomorrow night and congratulated one another about how well the services went tonight. They mentioned the fire of God several times."

"Did they mention where they have the machine or how the thing works?" Bolan asked.

"Not really," Ahmed replied, "but they did mention an engineer who is a messenger of God and a modern tool of his Will. They call him Professor Barrah."

"Barrah," the Executioner repeated the name, aware he had found out a vital bit of information...if the guy's name was genuine.

"They said he was perhaps the most important man in Jinn 2000 aside from the Imam himself."

"The Imam?" Bolan asked with a frown. "Isn't an Imam sort of an Islamic version of a saint?"

Ahmed adopted an expression of distaste and said, "I would not make a comparison of that sort."

"A saint is canonized by the church after death following an investigation to determine if he or she achieved a holy status in heaven. Is an Imam really that different?"

"The belief in the twelve Imams is basically a Shiite practice," Ahmed stated. "Of course, I'm a Sunni Muslim so I'm not certain how the Shiite view the Imam. They are twelve great and holy teachers, said to help and guide the faithful Shiite from Paradise."

"That's pretty much the same as heaven," Bolan asked, "isn't it?"

"I suppose there are similarities between the Imams and Paradise and Christian saints and heaven," Ahmed admitted. "I suspect the Imam the Jinn 2000 refer to is either a living person they regard as a holy man or they believe an Imam in Paradise is their personal champion."

They walked along the shoulder of the road, still favoring shadows until they reached the car. Ahmed fished the keys from a pocket and unlocked the door by the driver's side.

"Is Barrah there?" Bolan asked.

"Not now," Ahmed answered. "He left earlier this morning. However, a high-ranking leader of the Jinn 2000 is still at the tent. They referred to him as the captain. He spoke occasionally, and his dialect sounded as if he might be from Morocco, Algeria or perhaps Libya."

"Libya?" Bolan repeated with interest.

"Yes," the CID agent confirmed. "It's possible. You think that's the origin of this conspiracy, Ulysses?"

"I don't know," Bolan admitted. "Libya has been involved in state-sponsored terrorism in the past, but so have plenty of other countries, including Syria, Iraq and a couple others in the region. Hell, we can't rule out Iran although you didn't hear anyone speak Farsi. The Jinn 2000 movement is a Shiite offshoot and Iran is predominantly a Shiite Islamic nation."

Ahmed slid behind the steering wheel as Bolan got in the passenger seat beside him. The Egyptian took the listening device from a pocket and handed it to the Executioner before he started the engine. Bolan examined the piece of equipment and frowned.

"Where is the radar probe?" he asked.

"What?" Ahmed replied with surprise. "What probe?"

"The part I attached to it before I gave it to you back at the enemy camp," Bolan explained. "It's missing."

The CID officer searched his pockets and failed to find the part. He uttered a sigh and shook his head. "It must have come loose when I was crawling around under that bloody truck," Ahmed announced. "You think the terrorists will find it?"

"Maybe," Bolan said. "It's small and they might overlook it. Even if they find it, they might not guess what it is."

"Do we have to go back there tomorrow night?" Ahmed asked, his tone suggesting he was afraid he wouldn't like the answer.

"Yeah," the Executioner replied, "I think we have to."

CHAPTER SIXTEEN

"Barrah," Aaron Kurtzman said as he worked the keyboard to the computer console at his horseshoe-shaped cockpit. "No first name or nationality?"

"Striker said the CID guy with him just heard some of the Jinn 2000 members mention the name," Hal Brognola replied. "They said he was the engineer behind 'God's fire.' Figure he's some kind of scientist or inventor. Probably an Arab, but it's possible he's an Iranian or maybe even a Turk or an Afghan."

Kurtzman leaned back in his wheelchair and uttered a long sigh as he stared at the screen above the console. The name "Barrah" stared back at him as the computer waited for more information.

"That's a lot of 'maybes' and 'what-ifs' to work with," Kurtzman commented. "What kind of scientist am I supposed to be looking for? SHC researcher with a degree in mad-scientist weaponry?"

"Sounds like a good place to start."

"Great. Okay. We'll start with a general search of scientists named Barrah, especially those involved in research in the fields of pyrotechnics, thermodynamic developments and maybe kinetics with the use of some kind of wavelengths or ultraviolet light. Prob-

lem is, we don't really know what could cause
SHC.''

"The theories sure vary," the big Fed agreed. "I
just hope the bastards didn't really find a way to tap
into some way to attack the human aura or something
like that. You know, supernatural or supernormal
stuff isn't exactly our line."

"Don't let this hocus-pocus bull get to you,"
Kurtzman urged. "If there is such a thing as a human
aura, it's probably a type of electromagnetic energy
produced by the body. Really wouldn't be that remarkable if something like that exists. We know that
sort of energy comes from certain animals, plants and
even minerals. Most dramatic example is probably
the electric eel. No reason to believe this couldn't
happen with people."

"Humans produce body heat," Brognola said. "I
guess that wouldn't be so strange after all."

"Yeah. Besides, Striker saw some type of machine
at the West Bank. That means we're dealing with
some kind of technology, not fires started by a su-
perpowered psycho psychic with killer telekinesis
ability."

"I know," the big Fed replied. "I just don't like
being up against something we've never encountered
before. The idea of Striker or the President of the
United States getting burned alive makes me a little
nervous."

"That's not going to happen," Kurtzman replied
as he worked the keyboard. "I'll start with Arabs
named Barrah because Ahmed didn't hear anybody
speaking Farsi or Turkish or whatever. I know a lot
of devout Muslims learn Arabic because it's the language of Muhammad and the Koran, but it's still the

most likely place to start. I'm also going to try to find a guy named Barrah who is a gifted, perhaps brilliant scientist who has a history of extreme politics or religious-fanatic behavior. Especially if his co-workers and family haven't been able to get in touch with him recently.''

"Good idea," Brognola agreed. "This Barrah character had to be missing for a couple days at least. Maybe longer if he's been running with the Jinn 2000 cult for any length of time. You also need to check on another guy we know even less about. There's a high-muck-a-muck at the Cairo camp they call 'the captain.' Ahmed seems to have a good ear for dialects. Claims this guy might be from Libya, Morocco or Algeria.''

Kurtzman rolled his eyes and groaned. "You expect me to come up with something based on that?" he asked. "Come on, Hal. This won't help unless he's already on the list of known members of Jinn 2000 we've got on file.''

"You've gotten results with less information," the big Fed stated.

"Oh, yeah?" Kurtzman replied. "When?"

"Well, I'm sure you could have.''

"I'll see what I can do. Any word from Katz or Phoenix Force in Israel?''

"Nothing since Katz spoke with the Mossad director about calling off the manhunt on Striker. Turns out he had done it anyway. Phoenix arrived. Now they have to decide what to do next. That's Striker's call. If he wants them in Egypt, they'll move in for backup, but right now I think he'll have them stay put in Tel Aviv to help with security for the President's visit.''

"I'm sure they'll do the best they can," Kurtzman said, "but I don't know what they can do to protect the President from the SHC weapon when we don't know how it works and have only a vague idea what the device looks like. We can only guess what sort of effective range the thing has or how wide an area it can cover. Does it fire in bursts of energy or produce a steady wave of destruction?"

"All we've got right now are questions," Brognola declared with frustration in his tone. "Before you bring it up, I'm also aware of the fact we still don't know why the weapon didn't burn up Bolan along with the Israeli paratroopers, Congressman Morrow and the corpses of the terrorists at the Jinn 2000 site. We need some answers, Aaron. Striker finally has some leads for us to look into, and I'm counting on you to find something with the information he's given us."

"What do you think I'm doing at this keyboard?" the computer whiz asked gruffly. "Typing up my memoirs?"

"I know you'll come up with something for us," Brognola said. "I know it's not much to go on with just a name and some possibly related information."

"Let's just hope 'Barrah' isn't an alias," Kurtzman responded.

"You always know just what to say when I'm feeling worried and depressed," Brognola replied.

THE DIPLOMATIC POUCH reminded Mack Bolan of a body bag. The rubber bag was large enough to hold a human being. In fact such pouches had been used to smuggle people—willingly and otherwise—in and out of countries by governments that made the most of the diplomatic-immunity status of their embassies. Bolan had seen a lot of body bags and had personally placed more than one friend into one. He pushed some grim memories to the back of his mind in order to concentrate on the subject before him.

Harry Coburn had removed the official U.S. Embassy seal and lock. Bolan unzipped the bag, which contained special equipment from Stony Man Farm. The soldier was glad to see his familiar arsenal. Coburn whistled softly, amazed by the collection.

An M-16 assault rifle, complete with an M-203 grenade launcher attached to the underside of the barrel, was packed inside, along with one thousand rounds of 5.56 mm ammo. Ten cartridge-style grenade shells for the launcher were also included. An Uzi submachine gun was stored in a case, with spare magazines and a long silencer in a lid compartment.

The Executioner's pistols were included with the delivery. The Beretta 93-R was a welcome sight, as were the shoulder-stock attachment and sound suppressor. A .44 Magnum version of the Desert Eagle was sheathed in a leather holster, and plenty of 9 mm parabellum and .44 Magnum rounds had been included for the weapons. Additionally there was a compact Beretta .380 pistol, which could be easily concealed.

"Good God," Coburn commented. "How many guns do you figure you'll need for this mission?"

"Better to have too much firepower than not enough," the Executioner replied. "I still have some .22 Berettas, a couple .357 Magnum Desert Eagles and a .380 automatic confiscated from the Israelis."

"Ever think about becoming an international gunrunner if business dries up at...well, whatever it is you do?"

"I think I'll find something else if that day ever comes along, but thanks for the suggestion."

"By the way," the CIA agent said, "since the Israelis called off their manhunt for you, I guess you don't have to go by 'Ulysses' anymore. Michael Belasko probably isn't your real name, either."

"No," Bolan admitted, "but it might be less confusing when you speak with Sarah. How's she been?"

"She asks about you a lot," Coburn answered. "Makes me a little jealous. Mighty pretty woman."

Bolan continued to inspect the package. Several grenades had been sent. The M-26 fragmentation models were standard issue, and a trio of stun grenades had been included for special needs. Two CS tear-gas canisters and an M-17 protective mask were wrapped in a plastic poncho.

"How much of that stuff do you think you'll need?" the Company man asked.

"That'll depend on the enemy," the Executioner replied. "Who else is supposed to be at the peace conference besides our President?"

"Well, the Israeli prime minister will be there, of course, and the president of Egypt. The king of Jordan will probably attend, and possibly the king of Saudi Arabia and the emir from Kuwait, but they'll probably send representatives instead of coming in person. The prime minister of Bahrain plans to come, and possibly the sheikh who holds the same position in the United Arab Emirates. The sultan of Oman is sending a member of his royal family. Lebanon plans to send one of their top officials."

"Quite a gathering," Bolan commented.

"Never anything like it in the history of the Middle East," Coburn agreed. "Hell, nobody could have dreamed anything like this could happen even six years ago. The emir or the prime minister of Qatar may also attend. Come to think of it, he's the same guy. They even extended invitations to Syria and Yemen, but they haven't responded last I heard."

"So there'll be nine or ten high-ranking officials and leaders of countries the Jinn 2000 consider infidel nations," the Executioner remarked. "Christians, Muslims and Jews. It'll be a tempting target for fanatics who want to prove God is on their side."

"Needless to say, security is going to be tighter than a miser's fist. They were preparing to protect the conference from possible terrorist attacks even before this business with the Jinn 2000 occurred. There are always plenty of extremist groups operating in the Middle East under the best of circumstances."

"This part of the world does have more than its share of problems," the Executioner admitted. "Of course, every place seems to. Think you can get us a real long-range rifle microphone? I'd rather not have to get so close to the Jinn 2000 for eavesdropping after the service tonight."

"I can get you a laser mike," Coburn assured him. "You can listen in on conversations over a half a mile away if you can lock the laser beam on to a surface that will carry vibrations from sounds and voices inside the tent. People usually try to put the beam on a windowpane, but I guess that won't work in this case."

"No windows," Bolan confirmed. "The canvas

won't absorb sounds well enough. Might work on one of the support poles, but I'm not sure of that. Better go with the old-fashioned rifle mike.''

"That's low-tech, Belasko," the Company man said. "I don't even know if we have anything that outdated, but we might be able to throw something together."

"Have somebody do it who knows what he's throwing and how to make it work when it's together," the Executioner insisted. "A rifle mike isn't complicated. Basically just some aluminum rods clustered into multibarrels for a microphone and amplifier, but it still has to be assembled properly for it to work at all."

"That can be done," Coburn said. "We can probably get you a couple tin cans attached with a long string for communications, too."

"Sometimes the fancy high-tech devices don't work as well as their predecessors. A rifle mike covers a wider area than the concentrated laser beam. It doesn't have as great a range, and reception might not be as good, but it's better for eavesdropping on a structure such as the tent at the Jinn 2000 site."

"Okay," Coburn agreed with a shrug. "We'll take care of it. You and that CID operative plan to actually attend services tonight? I think it would be smarter and safer to cover the terrorists from a distance. Just listen in and take notes."

"They have the SHC device at that tent," Bolan replied. "I wasn't able to locate where they have it hidden last night, but I might be able to get a glimpse of it this time. Can't count on somebody being considerate enough to mention exactly where they have the thing. There's also supposed to be a commander of some importance at the camp. Maybe we can nail him or at least get a good look at him for identification."

"What do you think you'll do if you do find this SHC machine?" the CIA man asked. "How can you approach the device safely?"

"Someone has to operate it," Bolan replied with a shrug. "Maybe I'll just shoot the guy and take control of the machine myself."

"What about that team of special commandos in Israel? You don't intend to call them in to help with this?"

"Not yet," the soldier answered. "Right now I don't know enough about the SHC device to know what to do about it myself. Bad enough I'm risking Ahmed's life this way. No point putting anyone else's life in jeopardy until I know how to deal with the Jinn 2000 terrorists without getting our people turned into charred leftovers."

"Hope you don't wind up that way yourself."

"I'll try to avoid that, but I have to go back tonight. If the terrorists found the radar probe to that pocket eavesdropper you gave me yesterday, they might be planning to cut and run. If they do, I want to be on their tail as fast as possible."

"You'd better hope they don't guess what it is and they're not suspicious about the new guy who can't speak Arabic and pretends to be an idiot."

"Thanks for reminding me," the Executioner said dryly. "I almost forgot I have to worry about that."

CHAPTER SEVENTEEN

Lieutenant Hevron appeared to be miserable as he lay in a hospital bed, head propped on pillows, bandaged arm suspended in traction. His upper lip was marked by a line of stitches. Yakov Katzenelenbogen looked down at the disabled military Intel officer with a degree of sympathy.

Hevron stared at the prosthesis at the end of Katz's right sleeve, the metal hooks seeming to make the junior officer uncomfortable. Katz wondered how serious Hevron's injury might be and if his arm might have to be amputated.

"Heard you took a .22 slug through the biceps," Katz commented as he examined the splint around Hevron's upper arm. "Looks like a broken humerus. Probably some tissue damage to muscles. Hope the brachial artery wasn't cut. Of course, you probably would have died from internal bleeding if that had happened. If you have a pinched ulnar nerve, you may experience considerable pain."

"You're not here to cheer me up," Hevron remarked. "What do you want?"

"You and your friend Sergeant Jaffe had a run-in with a man known as Michael Belasko," Katz answered. "In fact you had two encounters with this man. You have no idea how lucky you are to still be alive, Lieutenant.''

"I'm not feeling so lucky right now, Mr...?"

"My name isn't important, but the reason I'm here is. You and Jaffe were acting on the orders of Major Ziyyon when you escorted Belasko across the desert at the West Bank. What did he tell you to do to Belasko?''

"You speak Hebrew very well, but I don't believe it is your first language. Where are you from?''

"Actually it is one of several languages I learned as a youth,'' Katz explained, "but I haven't used it in daily conversation very much for the past few years. And I've lived in so many different countries I don't know how to answer your question. Now, you can try to answer mine. Did you intend to take Belasko to Tel Aviv or kill him in the desert?''

"We had placed him under arrest. Of course we would have taken him to Tel Aviv for interrogation.''

"What if Ziyyon ordered you to kill him?''

"He did not give such an order.''

"Then why did you try to kill Belasko? You and Jaffe just decided to do that on your own? Ziyyon is sort of a zealot. He may even be proud of being one. You know the first Zealots were a militant sect from Judea in the first century opposed to the Roman occupation of Israel...still known as Palestine at the time.''

"You're a scholar,'' Hevron said with a sneer. "How impressive. What does a scholar know about soldiers and what we must do to protect the state of Israel?''

"What do you have to do, Lieutenant?''

"I don't think I care to talk to you any longer,''

the officer declared. "I was already tired and now I'm getting bored."

Katz smiled as he strolled to the foot of the bed and glanced at the chart that contained data about Hevron's condition. The lieutenant would probably recover, but he would never be the same according to the doctors.

"Ziyyon sent you after Belasko in Cairo, too," Katz commented. "You made two very serious mistakes when you found him. You went for a weapon and you slapped the woman with Belasko. One mistake earned you a bullet, and you were lucky the other didn't get you killed. I'd say you'll have a lack of mobility with that arm for the rest of your life."

"I know they called off the manhunt, but Belasko is still an enemy of the state," Hevron insisted. "Why did those paratroopers burn to death along with Morrow, but Belasko wasn't harmed?"

"The fact he survived doesn't make him a terrorist," Katz replied. "Ziyyon was very eager to get rid of him. Seems a little suspicious to me. Are you so sure your commander didn't want him dead for some reason aside from national security? That's a phrase that's been used countless times to justify brutality and bloodshed."

"Didn't I ask you to leave?" Hevron said gruffly.

"I will in a moment," Katz assured him. "You are aware most of the other members of your group in Cairo were also injured? Sergeant Jaffe has a skull fracture. One Mossad agent was shot in the leg, and a couple have broken bones. All of you could have been killed. Belasko was comparatively gentle because you were agents for Israel instead of terrorists."

"You talk as if you know this bastard personally."

"Do I?" Katz said with raised eyebrows. "Perhaps I do. You obviously do not. Major Ziyyon seems a bit too eager to have Belasko silenced. He's either a fanatic or a traitor."

"How dare you question his patriotism!" Hevron replied with outrage. "The major is a great man and a great soldier."

"Is that why you're willing to be his thug? His murderer? You'll suffer for the rest of your life because of his orders. Is this because you were serving the interests of your country or your commander's personal wishes? What was his motivation, Lieutenant?"

"Didn't you say you were going to leave?" Hevron asked.

"I may as well," Katz said with a sigh. "Apparently I'm wasting my time, as well as yours, Lieutenant. Goodbye."

Katz left the hospital room. His hopes hadn't been high that the conversation with the young officer would answer any nagging questions about Ziyyon one way or the other. He had learned Hevron and Jaffe were extremely loyal to the major, and their devotion suggested he had drummed some pretty extreme views into their heads.

The Israeli warhorse was surprised to see two familiar figures in the corridor. Calvin James and Gary Manning smiled when they saw their former unit commander. The tall African-American and the brawny Canadian greeted Katz warmly.

"I thought you were retired," James commented. "Here they've got you running around with us again."

"Not exactly with you," Katz replied. "I'm working as more of a liaison officer this time. How's David doing?"

"Better than I'd admit to him," Manning said with a grin. "Once in a while the old McCarter still bubbles up to the surface, but he's handling command pretty well. I almost hate to say it, but I think you and the Farm made the right choice after all."

The trio walked through the hallway and headed for the exit. They spoke quietly and made certain no passersby overheard their conversation.

"Hal wants to talk to you," James said. "That's why we came looking for you at the clinic. He said you didn't answer your pager."

"I'm semiretired," Katz commented. "I never did like those things anyway. Got out of the habit of carrying one, and I guess I've been avoiding doing it since I arrived in Israel."

"We have a van out front," Manning explained. "There's a laptop unit on board, and we can put you on-line with the Farm."

"Lucky me," Katz said with a sigh. "This high-tech world really is moving too fast for me, gentlemen. I remember a time when we still carried messages written in disappearing ink. Now you hit the Delete key on a computer."

"Still need people with good minds," James remarked. "That's why they called you back on duty for this job."

"I'm smart enough not to need my ego stroked," Katz replied, "but thanks anyway."

They emerged from the clinic and headed for a gray van in the parking lot. The trio climbed inside. Manning slid behind the steering wheel while James and Katz moved into the back of the vehicle. The Israeli veteran took a seat by a bench with a laptop computer set up.

Katz punched in the code numbers on the keyboard, accessing the ultrasecure Stony Man Farm satellite link. Hal Brognola appeared on the screen, and Katz recognized the computer-center equipment behind the big Fed. Apparently Brognola had been stationed at the Bear's domain to wait for Katz to contact him.

"I hear you've been trying to get in touch with me," the Israeli remarked.

"Damn right," Brognola replied gruffly. "And you haven't been easy to find. Batteries die in your pager?"

Katz shrugged and smiled. "I didn't take it with me."

"Well, I've got you now," Brognola said, aware there was no point arguing with the Israeli. "I need you for another special assignment that requires your unique talents and expertise."

"Really?" Katz commented. "What now?"

"Striker gave us a lead about a guy named Barrah who's involved with the Jinn 2000 sect. All we had was a last name and a claim Barrah was directly involved in bringing the Jinn 2000 what seems to be the SHC device. By the way, it works on pigs, as well as on people."

"Sometimes it's hard to tell the difference," Katz replied. "Did Striker actually see a pig burned up in some sort of demonstration or sacrifice?"

"Jinn 2000 showed some recruits that their claims about a divine sword of fire were genuine," Brognola explained. "So they spontaneously combusted a hog in a cage for the entertainment and education of an awestruck audience.''

"So they actually have this long-range crematorium machine in Cairo?" the Israeli asked with surprise.

"Apparently. We think Barrah may have helped build it. Thanks to Aaron, we have a pretty good idea who the guy is. It seems a certain Professor Barrah was doing some research in the field of nuclear fusion in Saudi Arabia about eight months ago, but he disappeared after a mishap during an experiment."

"Nuclear fusion?" Katz inquired with a frown.

"Yeah." Brognola glanced at a data sheet as he spoke. "I don't know much about this sort of thing, but apparently nuclear fusion creates energy by compressing light atomic elements such as hydrogen or oxygen. This is similar to the process that takes place on the sun to make solar energy."

Kurtzman rolled his wheelchair next to Brognola. "See, the sun is a star," the computer whiz began, "and all stars are gaseous. The density of these gases varies from a fraction of the density of air to billions of times thicker than water. The sun is an average-size star with average density."

"We don't need a whole course on astronomy, Aaron," Brognola groused.

"Point is," Kurtzman continued, "incredible pressure at the core of the sun—and most other stars—transforms hydrogen into helium. This produces enormous energy that keeps the surface gases at about eleven thousand degrees, but the center is charged to a heat level that's millions of degrees. If we could harness two pounds of energy produced by the sun turning hydrogen into helium, it would equal that of about twenty-five thousand tons of coal."

"Okay," Brognola cut in. "We're talking about the greatest energy source in the universe. Problem is, man hasn't been able to harness it yet. Our current form of nuclear power is fission, which requires tearing apart heavy elements like uranium through atom-smashing to produce a chain reaction. Maybe I'm not up on the exact technology, but fission energy is dangerous and hard to control. Three Mile Island and Chernobyl prove that."

"Of course," Kurtzman said, unwilling to remain silent during the explanation. "A nuclear weapon uses the fission principle. It's explosive and works well enough to cause mass destruction, but it sure leaves a lot to be desired as a safe, clean energy source. An atomic furnace that used fusion would be stable, easy to control and produce almost limitless energy."

"Actually," Katz said, "I've read some material about this subject. Enough to realize research and development of nuclear fusion hasn't been very successful. I understood fusion was still on the drawing board. A lot of theories, but not much else."

"About ten years ago there was a reported breakthrough in cold fusion," Kurtzman stated. "It turned out to be another disappointment. A big problem has been trying to produce the extraordinary levels of pressure and heat necessary to compress light elements and create energy. The task would require about ten to a hundred million degrees Fahrenheit."

"Producing that sort of heat must be a major problem," Calvin James commented, joining the conversation. "And what would be used to contain heat that intense? It would vaporize metal and just about anything else it got near.''

"So far the greatest heat anybody has been able to generate in fusion experiments is about one million degrees," Kurtzman explained. "You're right about containing the heat. Best method used so far seems to be to keep the heat from touching the walls of a vessel by using layers of microwaves. Barrah was involved in this effort in Saudi Arabia.''

"I didn't know the Saudis were involved in that sort of research," James admitted.

"They've been concerned about new energy sources just like everybody else," Brognola said. "The OPEC nations have become economic powers thanks to oil, but they know nothing lasts forever. Their oil reserves will eventually run out, and efforts are under way to replace the internal-combustion engines used in automobiles with other energy sources.''

"Hell," Kurtzman chimed in, "that technology has existed for almost a hundred years. Thomas Edison came up with a car that used an electrical battery that could be recharged at electrostations, but Henry Ford's gas guzzlers were more popular. Most people think there aren't any reliable electric cars, but there are already perfectly functional models available. Cars can run on solar energy, too. Not little go-carts. Nice big cars that do everything other cars do except spread air pollution and help make oil companies rich.''

"Thank you for the environmental commentary," Brognola said dryly. "Actually he has a point. The technology to use other energy sources does exist. The general public might not know it, but the auto industries do and the petroleum companies damn sure know. Big oil spills, like the *Exxon Valdez* incident, and the deliberate sabotage of oil fields in Kuwait show the risks to the environment. The OPEC nations know time could be running out for their gravy train. A number of them have already turned to international trading and banking as primary sources of finance that won't rely on oil."

"But the OPEC countries have learned how useful a major source of energy can be," Katz remarked, "so nuclear fusion is a subject worth looking into because of the tremendous potential."

"Exactly," Brognola stated. "Most work on nuclear fusion has been done by the United States, France, Great Britain and the former Soviet Union. Nuclear proliferation is a big concern, and it's even more serious since the end of the cold war. All the countries of the Middle East have been trying to get nuclear power. Of course, some have it already, and there's a lot of wringing of hands about the possibility of a guy like Saddam Hussein getting access to nuclear missiles in the future. Needless to say, there aren't a lot of nuclear physicists in the Arab world because there's a reluctance to train them abroad in a technology most of the rest of the world is paranoid about sharing with them."

"They'd like to keep the international nuclear club pretty much 'whites only,'" James commented. "The United States doesn't seem to worry much if Western Europe or Canada have nuclear power, but everybody seems to get real uptight when India or Pakistan gets such technology."

Brognola frowned at the African-American's implication and asked, "You think that's because of racist attitudes or because the governments of India and Pakistan have been a little unstable at times, Cal? You didn't mention China, but it has nuclear weapons and it's still a Communist country.''

"Yeah," James replied, "I noticed. We just got back from there, remember? I'll agree Uncle Sam has a reason to be suspicious of nuclear power under the control of some of the governments of the countries of the Third World, but I still think there's at least a touch of racism involved in some of those attitudes.''

"I can't really say I'm very comfortable with any government having access to nuclear weapons," Katz commented, "but reality has a way of making one uncomfortable for one reason or another. Back to Professor Barrah, though. I take it he is one of those rare nuclear physicists in Saudi Arabia involved in nuclear fusion?"

"Yeah," Brognola said, once more checking his notes. "Professor Abdel al-Barrah is one of the leading men in the field of fusion research and microwave technology used for heat containment.''

"And he's been missing since the mishap you mentioned," Katz said with a nod. "I assume this means you want me to go to Saudi Arabia and speak with someone about Barrah and his experiments.''

"You do speak fluent Arabic and you have contacts in Saudi Arabia, Yakov. We don't have any details about where Barrah is now. I'll fax you the file on the guy. His educational background is impressive, and apparently he's got a genius IQ. Barrah comes from a family that was more or less middle-class. Respectable people, although they probably found being Shiite Muslim a bit difficult at times in predominantly Sunni Muslim Saudi Arabia.''

"The Shiite religion has gotten a lot of negative publicity due to extremist factions," Katz remarked, "but most aren't fanatics."

"Well, Barrah seems to be," Brognola stated. "In 1979, when the Ayatollah took over Iran after the Shah left the country, a band of fanatics in Saudi Arabia seized the Grand Mosque in Mecca. Of course, they didn't hold it for very long. A group of sympathizers, mostly university students, planned a violent demonstration at the U.S. Embassy in Riyadh. Some were armed with pistols and homemade explosives. Barrah was among them."

"The Saudis are pretty strict when it comes to law and order," Katz remarked. "What happened?"

"The authorities caught the group before they could carry out the plan," Brognola explained. "The ringleaders and a couple others got stiff sentences, but Barrah claimed he didn't know about the weapons and believed the demonstration was supposed to be a nonviolent protest. He was a young student at the time, brilliant and already a candidate for advanced scientific research when he graduated. They let him go with a slap on the wrist. Barrah hasn't gotten in any trouble since, but it is included in his psychological profile that he has some extremist attitudes that could develop into problems."

"I'll go to Saudi Arabia and see what I can do," Katz said, "but I'm not sure what I can hope to accomplish that the Saudis haven't already done. For that matter, we haven't really been able to do much here in Tel Aviv that isn't already being done by Israeli security, CIA, NSA and various Arab Intel outfits to provide protection for the President and the

other VIPs scheduled to attend the peace conference.''

''We're still not sure what we're dealing with,''
Brognola said. ''We're all grasping at phantoms until
Striker comes up with some answers in Cairo. He
might have something for us within the next twelve
hours. I sure hope so, because the President is going
to be leaving soon on *Air Force One*.''

Deal Yourself In and Play

® GOLD EAGLE'S

ACTION POKER

Peel off this card and complete the hand on the next page

It can get you:

♠ Free books

♠ PLUS a free surprise gift

NO BLUFF! NO RISK! NO OBLIGATION TO BUY!

PLAY "ACTION POKER" AND GET...

★ 4 Hard-hitting, action-packed Gold Eagle novels — FREE
★ PLUS a surprise mystery gift — FREE

Peel off the card on the front of this brochure and stick it in the hand opposite. Then check the claim chart to see what we have for you — FREE BOOKS and a gift — ALL YOURS! ALL FREE! They're yours to keep even if you never buy another Gold Eagle novel!

THEN DEAL YOURSELF IN FOR MORE GUT-CHILLING ACTION AT DEEP SUBSCRIBER SAVINGS

1. Play Action Poker as instructed on the opposite page.
2. Send back the card and you'll get hot-off-the-press Gold Eagle books, never before published. These books have a total cover price of $18.50, but they are yours to keep absolutely free.
3. There's no catch. You're under no obligation to buy anything. We charge nothing — ZERO — for your first shipment. And you don't have to make any minimum number of purchases — not even one!
4. The fact is thousands of readers enjoy receiving books by mail from the Gold Eagle Reader Service. They like the convenience of home delivery…they like getting the best new novels before they're available in stores…and they think our discount prices are dynamite!
5. We hope that after receiving your free books you'll want to remain a subscriber. But the choice is yours — to continue or cancel, anytime at all! So why not take us up on our invitation, with no risk of any kind. You'll be glad you did!

AND THERE'S MORE!!!

• With every shipment you'll receive *AUTOMAG*, our exciting newsletter — FREE.

SO DON'T WAIT UNTIL YOUR FAVORITE TITLES HAVE BEEN SNAPPED UP! YOU GET CONVENIENT FREE DELIVERY RIGHT TO YOUR DOOR. AT DEEP DISCOUNTS. GIVE US A TRY!

© 1993 GOLD EAGLE

SURPRISE MYSTERY GIFT COULD BE YOURS <u>FREE</u> WHEN YOU PLAY ACTION POKER

DETACH AND MAIL TODAY

® GOLD EAGLE'S
ACTION POKER

Check below to see how many gifts you get

YES! I have placed my card in the hand above. Please send me all the gifts for which I qualify. I understand that I am under no obligation to purchase any books, as explained on the back and on the opposite page.

(U-M-B-03/97)   164 CIM A7DV

Name: _____

Address: _____

City: _____ State: _____

Zip Code: _____

Four aces get you 4 free books and a surprise mystery gift

Full House gets you 3 free books

Three-of-a-kind gets you 2 free books

Offer limited to one per household and not valid to present subscribers. All orders subject to approval.

PRINTED IN U.S.A.

THE GOLD EAGLE READER SERVICE: HERE'S HOW IT WORKS

Accepting free books places you under no obligation to buy anything. You may keep the books and gift and return the shipping statement marked "cancel". If you do not cancel, about a month later we will send you four additional novels and bill you just $15.80—that's a savings of 15% off the cover price of all four books! And there's no extra charge for shipping! You may cancel at any time, but if you choose to continue, then every other month we'll send you four more books, which you may either purchase at the discount price…or return to us and cancel your subscription.

*Terms and prices subject to change without notice. Sales tax applicable in N.Y.

If offer card is missing, write to: Gold Eagle Reader Service, 3010 Walden Ave., P.O. Box 1867, Buffalo, NY 14240-1867

BUSINESS REPLY MAIL

FIRST-CLASS MAIL   PERMIT NO. 717   BUFFALO, NY

POSTAGE WILL BE PAID BY ADDRESSEE

GOLD EAGLE READER SERVICE
3010 WALDEN AVE
PO BOX 1867
BUFFALO NY 14240-9952

NO POSTAGE
NECESSARY
IF MAILED
IN THE
UNITED STATES

CHAPTER EIGHTEEN

Ahmed glanced over his shoulder into the back seat of the Land Rover, seemingly concerned some tell-tale sign might alert an interested observer to the secret compartment under the seat. The Egyptian CID officer knew what was hidden there, and he didn't want the Jinn 2000 fanatics to find out.

"The road is in front of you, Ahmed," Bolan reminded him.

"How do you think we can explain the arsenal you've packed into this vehicle if the Jinn 2000 decide to search the Rover?"

"I won't say anything," the Executioner replied. "I'm your brain-damaged, almost deaf and virtually mute cousin."

Ahmed muttered something in Arabic that didn't really need to be translated.

"They won't search the vehicle unless they get suspicious," Bolan told him. "Let's not give them any reason to have doubts about us."

"You would have to bring a selection of weapons made in the United States and Israel," Ahmed complained.

"Berettas are Italian," Bolan said with a shrug. "If the vehicle worries you, park it far enough from the mosque to avoid being seen by the sentries on the minaret towers.''

Ahmed had turned his attention to the long stretch of unpaved road outside Cairo. He recognized an obscure ruins of ancient bricks, all that remained of a Roman structure built during the reign of the Caesars. Only portions of walls remained with no clue as to what the building might have been. The landmark signaled they were only four miles from the Jinn 2000 tent.

''This Rover does handle well,'' Ahmed commented. ''CIA gave this to you?''

''Yeah,'' Bolan answered. ''It has a souped-up engine, and the body has been lightly armored. The windshield is also bullet resistant.''

''Too bad it has an open top and no side windows. I think I would feel more protected if we had more cover.''

''It's not the best vehicle to have in a firefight,'' the soldier admitted, ''but that's not the idea. We're not expecting any trouble. This is just a little insurance in case something unexpected happens, Ahmed.''

''Everything has been unexpected for me since I met you,'' the CID officer remarked. ''Better start getting into character, Ulysses.''

Bolan had already placed dark contact lenses on his eyes. He adjusted the *keffiyeh* scarf around his head as the canvas mosque and wooden minarets appeared on the horizon.

More cars and trucks had assembled by the tent. The men on the towers appeared more alert, scanning the area with greater intensity than before. Bolan didn't like what he saw, but he knew the increased number of recruits at the mosque and concern for security also meant something important was going to happen at the site. Despite the possibility of greater risk, they couldn't turn back.

Ahmed parked the Land Rover, and they stepped from the vehicle and approached the entrance, aware of the gazes of the guards above. Two men met them at the threshold of the tent, one of whom had been on duty the night before. They spoke with each other before they addressed Bolan and Ahmed. A question was directed to Ahmed.

Bolan's Arabic was limited, but he was pretty sure Ahmed had replied, "Two weeks before." They had probably asked how long he had been attending the mosque services. A doorman pointed at Bolan and asked Ahmed another question.

"*Embare,*" the CID officer replied.

That meant "yesterday," Bolan thought, certain of the answer this time. The Jinn 2000 doormen wanted to know how long he had been among the recruits. There had to be a reason for this sudden interest. The men at the door finally allowed Bolan and Ahmed to enter, but directed them to a section of the tent separated by a canvas wall. The improvised corridor hadn't been there the night before.

Hard-faced men, weapons openly displayed, waited for them at the segregated area. The soldier and CID officer reluctantly approached. They were instructed to raise their arms and stand still. Some pantomime was provided for the sake of the "brain-damaged" Bolan.

They frisked the pair for weapons. The Jinn 2000 followers quickly found the .380 Beretta that Bolan had hidden in his robe, and Ahmed's Walther pistol.

They checked for ankle holsters, sleeve knives and other hidden weapons. Bolan continued to pretend to be mentally incapacitated, somewhat confused yet too dull to really be worried. Ahmed's expression openly revealed his concern and fear.

Men armed with AK-47 assault rifles watched the pair with grim faces, hands on pistol grips in case they needed to use the automatic weapons. Five others seemed to be in the same situation as Bolan and Ahmed. They knelt on the ground, hands atop their heads, guarded by a suspicious gunman. However, Bolan and Ahmed weren't told to join the five apparent captives. This special attention didn't make them feel more secure.

The Executioner wondered what had caused this action by Jinn 2000. The questions about how long they had attended the service suggested the terrorists wanted to separate the more recent members from the rest of the congregation. This might have been because the radar probe to the listening device had been discovered and the extremists assumed one or more of the new recruits had to be a spy.

That could mean they would be subjected to interrogation, probably with some physical abuse or even torture. The terrorists didn't seem to be particularly sophisticated, yet the fact they had the mysterious SHC device meant that appearances were deceptive. They might have someone skilled in the use of truth serums, or the terrorists might simply eliminate all doubt by executing everyone they suspected of being an enemy.

Bolan tried to keep his imagination from jumping to conclusions. The Jinn 2000 hardmen could have some other reason for their actions. Perhaps someone had had an argument and one of the new recruits had threatened the life of a senior member. It could be a test of loyalty or general intimidation to use fear as a tool for control among the sect. Such tactics were often used among cults, so-called elite paramilitary units and other groups.

A tall figure appeared at the opening in the canvas. His ramrod posture and even, confident stride suggested he was a military veteran, accustomed to command. The man wore a tan-leopard-pattern fatigue uniform, designed for desert terrain with colors to match sand, earth and indigenous plant life. The style was popular with many military forces in the Middle East, including Egypt, Iraq and Iran. He wore no insignia, but his manner labeled him an officer.

No one introduced Jadallah al-Qatrun, but Bolan guessed the man was the captain mentioned by the Jinn 2000 members. Qatrun swaggered closer, his features stern and his eyes critical as he studied the segregated group. Bolan offered a stupid grin when the reptilian gaze fell upon him.

The Executioner greeted him as if saying hello to a good friend.

Qatrun's mood didn't improve. He turned to the Jinn 2000 hardmen and spoke with them in Arabic too rapid for Bolan to follow. They showed the captain the .380 Beretta confiscated from the soldier. Qatrun frowned as he examined the pistol.

He might wonder why a supposedly mentally defective person, barely able to speak or hear, would carry a gun. Bolan and Ahmed had considered the possibility their weapons might be discovered, and they had prepared an explanation. Ahmed stepped forward to try to speak with Qatrun, but he was

stopped abruptly by a man who slammed the butt of
an AK-47 into the CID officer's gut.

Ahmed doubled over with a groan, dazed and
winded by the blow. He dropped to one knee and
gasped in an effort to regain his breath. Bolan managed to react in a puzzled manner and stayed calm,
although his survival instincts screamed for direct action.

Qatrun stepped around Ahmed and approached
Bolan. He snapped a sentence in curt Arabic that
Bolan didn't understand. The captain folded his arms
on his thick chest and growled another sentence. Bolan recognized the language spoken was Hebrew, but
he didn't understand Qatrun any better than he had
in Arabic.

"Are you really so stupid?" Qatrun asked in English.

Bolan concealed the fact he finally understood the
captain and attempted a weak smile and a nervous
shrug. Qatrun suddenly swung an arm in a backhand
sweep. His fist struck Bolan in the side of the face.
The Executioner began to counterattack, but altered
the response and simply raised his hands to ward off
another blow.

Qatrun drove a fist into his stomach. Bolan
moaned and staggered backward. The Jinn 2000
members seemed content to simply knock Ahmed to
his knees. The big American assumed the same position and hoped it would satisfy Qatrun. A boot to
the ribs proved otherwise. Bolan sprawled on his
back. He drew his legs up, knees bent and ankles
crossed to protect his testicles from another kick. The
soldier covered his head with his hands, chin tucked
into his chest and elbows close to his side.

"American CIA?" Qatrun demanded. "I kill you, Yankee pig!"

He delivered another kick to Bolan's side. The soldier resisted the urge to fight back, but figured he would have to act if Qatrun continued the assault. He would rather die fighting than lie on the ground and be stomped to death.

The captain ceased his attack and turned to Ahmed. The CID officer was hauled to his feet, flanked by two Jinn 2000 hardmen. Ahmed tried to answer Qatrun's questions, but the terrorist commander hit him in the solar plexus with a solid uppercut. The CID officer groaned as the men beside him grabbed his arms to hold him fast.

Qatrun took the .380 Beretta from one of his henchmen and thrust the muzzle under Ahmed's jaw as he spoke in Arabic that sounded hostile to the Executioner. Bolan guessed the captain wanted to know why an idiot was packing heat. Ahmed replied, teeth clenched due to the hard steel at his chin. He had to have given the previously prepared explanation.

Their story was shaky at best. Ahmed would claim that in his youth his cousin had formerly been a soldier in the Egyptian military and an exceptional marksman. Although robbed of most of his senses, the brain-damaged man still possessed ability with a firearm. Qatrun didn't seem convinced by the story as he ejected the magazine from the Beretta. One .380 round remained chambered in the spout.

The captain snapped some orders to his men. Someone brought forth a length of rope, and Ahmed's hands were tied behind his back. They hauled him to a wall of the tent away from the others and forced him to sit on the ground. A two-way radio was handed to Qatrun, and he spoke briefly into the mouthpiece. Bolan guessed he gave some instructions to the guards outside the tent, perhaps to inform them shots would be fired.

Qatrun turned to Bolan and gestured for him to rise. The Executioner reluctantly obeyed. He noticed Qatrun held the Beretta in one fist by the barrel and used his other hand to draw a Makarov pistol from a hip holster. A Jinn 2000 hardman grinned from ear to ear as he placed a clay pot, about twice the size of a coffee cup, on Ahmed's head. The CID officer rolled his eyes upward, as if trying to see the object perched atop his skull. He clenched his teeth and tried not to tremble.

Bolan guessed what the terrorists wanted him to do. Qatrun explained in Arabic, accompanied by elaborate gestures, before he handed the Beretta to the Executioner. They had conjured up a William Tell–style test for the "idiot's" alleged ability as a marksman. Bolan had the pistol with only one round and a target on Ahmed's head. Qatrun pointed the muzzle of his own Makarov at the side of Bolan's face in case he decided to try to use his one shot to take out his tormentor.

The Executioner would have preferred to put a bullet in the captain, but realized the futility of the notion. The only chance he and Ahmed had was if he could hit the pot on the CID officer's head. Even if he accomplished the task, the terrorists might kill them anyway. This could just be a bit of sadistic entertainment for Qatrun and his troops. Yet Bolan didn't have any other option.

He gripped the Beretta with both hands in a firm

Weaver's combat stance. Bolan guessed the distance to Ahmed to be roughly eight yards. He had scored bull's-eyes on smaller targets at much greater distances, but the little Beretta was designed for close quarters and wasn't very accurate beyond five or six yards. Worse for Bolan, he had never fired the weapon he held and didn't know if it had any particular characteristics of a barrel pull to one direction or another. It had also been some time since he had practiced with a .380 pistol of any kind on the firing range at Stony Man Farm. The handgun wasn't a proper combat piece, and he seldom carried a weapon not designed for a serious firefight.

The soldier took a deep breath and aimed. He ignored the dull pain in his ribs and the side of his face. He mentally shut out Qatrun and the threat of the Makarov at his own head and tried to concentrate solely on the jug perched on Ahmed's cranium. Bolan's eyes focused on the target, his hands steady as the front sight bisected the pot. He exhaled slowly and squeezed the trigger as the air left his lungs.

Clay exploded with the report of the medium-caliber pistol. Ahmed closed his eyes and ducked in a response that would have been too late if Bolan's marksmanship had failed to score the right target. Several men applauded, impressed by the shot. Qatrun snatched the Beretta from Bolan's grasp and glared at him, perhaps disappointed the .380 round hadn't drilled Ahmed's forehead. Yet Qatrun returned his Makarov to leather.

The captain strolled to the CID officer as he slowly rose. Ahmed's legs shook, as he was understandably rattled by the ordeal. Qatrun drew a knife from a sheath at the small of his back. Bolan glimpsed the long, curved blade as the knife spun from Qatrun's hand. He grasped it in an overhand grip, obviously skilled in the use of cold steel. Qatrun delivered a single stroke with the blade behind Ahmed's back. The ropes fell from the CID man's wrists. Ahmed's arms hung free, his hands trembling slightly.

Qatrun marched from the canvas corridor, apparently no longer interested in the situation. Jinn 2000 members patted Bolan and Ahmed on the back and shoulders.

More than one voice sounded apologetic.

The soldier nodded and remembered to display another simpleminded grin. Ahmed appeared drained by the stress, yet clearly glad he was still alive. Although the danger seemed to have passed for the moment, Bolan noticed their pistols weren't returned to them.

A man approached the pair, an ornate green box in hand. He opened it and produced two copper medallions attached to necklace chains. The gifts were given to Bolan and Ahmed. They nodded and bowed as they thanked the Jinn 2000 follower. Other medallions were presented to the remaining five men who had been singled out by the sect, apparently now accepted and welcomed into the fold.

Bolan glanced at the copper amulet. It contained a crescent moon—symbol of Islam—on one side, and the likeness of a bearded man on the opposite side. Perhaps the Prophet Muhammad, he guessed, or maybe the Jinn 2000 soothsayer, Omar. He slipped the chain over his head as Ahmed also donned his award around his neck. The ordeal seemed to have been some sort of initiation rite, and Bolan hoped this meant they were no longer under suspicion.

Still, something nagged at the Executioner as he glanced down at the medal on his chest. Of course, he couldn't relax in the lair of the enemy, but he felt something else was wrong. The guards ushered them from the corridor to join the congregation for the service that was about to begin.

Ahmed looked at Bolan and smiled, clearly relieved to be out of the figurative frying pan. Yet Bolan was still worried about the fire....

CHAPTER NINETEEN

"Are you Ziyyon?" David McCarter demanded as he hurried down a narrow hallway at the basement level of the Agaf Modiin headquarters building.

The beefy figure, clad in Israeli army fatigues and a red beret of the Israeli Defense Forces, turned to glare at the former British commando. McCarter marched toward the military-intelligence officer, followed by T. J. Hawkins.

"That's *Major* Ziyyon," the Israeli stated. "And this is a restricted area. You are in a high-security military building. No civilians are permitted here, especially foreigners."

The Phoenix Force pair wore civilian attire. As usual, McCarter's slacks and windbreaker seemed wrinkled, as if he had kept them in a duffel bag for days and put them on without bothering to press the clothes, which was exactly what he had done. Hawkins wore a sport coat, blue jeans and boots with a decidedly Western flavor. The steel tips on the collar of his shirt labeled it as purchased in Texas as surely as a price tag with a miniature map of the Lone Star State would have.

"Oh, we have authorization," McCarter assured him. "Don't worry about that. Director Geller himself gave us access to this installation. If you don't believe us, call him."

"I will," Ziyyon replied. "If you're not telling the truth, I'll have you both placed under arrest and charged with suspicion of attempted espionage against the State of Israel."

"Whoa," Hawkins said with a soft whistle. "Now, that sounds like a whole heap of trouble. Is that charge just as serious when an Israeli citizen is guilty of it as a foreigner?"

"What is that supposed to mean?" Ziyyon demanded, his eyes as hard as marbles.

"Just curious," Hawkins replied. "I am a stranger to your country, sir. I want to figure out how customs work and all."

"Who the hell are you and what do you want?" Ziyyon asked in a voice that dripped venom.

"We're using a couple phony names if you want to hear them," McCarter stated. "Don't even feel like wasting time with that. We're interested in the safety and security of the VIPs who will be here for the peace conference."

"The British prime minister isn't scheduled to attend," Ziyyon remarked. "Besides, with that cockney accent, I doubt the United Kingdom would have placed you in charge of a task that required any degree of education beyond the ability to order fish and chips in Soho."

"That's cute," McCarter replied, taking the insult in stride.

"The point is, Major," Hawkins said, "you're under house arrest or restricted to quarters or something like that. Anyway, you're not supposed to be here."

"That situation changed when I received orders to

replace Lieutenant-Colonel Paran for the establish-
ment of special field communications for persons involved with the conference you referred to. Those
orders were hand delivered to me and signed by both
the commanding officer of Agaf Modiin and the director of Mossad.''

"Field communications?" McCarter asked. "You
mean two-way radio communications? They need a
field-grade intelligence officer to handle a job a good
commo NCO could do just as well?''

"They want the most qualified and highest-ranked
personnel on this assignment," Ziyyon replied.
"That's why I'm here. I have a background in this
field. That part of my file isn't classified, so you
might be able to examine that for yourself...except
they are written in Hebrew. I doubt you two can read
my language.''

"You're making me suffer a bloody awful burden
of inferiority in your presence," McCarter said with
a sigh, "but we can send you back to your restricted
quarters, Ziyyon. We're not sure we can trust you,
but my American mate here is trustworthy and he's
also an electronics wizard with qualifications as good
or better than yours. Like it or not, Major, you've
been replaced.''

"I don't think so," Ziyyon stated. "Why don't we
contact Geller and settle this business?''

"Because we already know the answer," Mc-
Carter replied. "But I reckon we can play along.''

Two figures appeared at the end of the hallway.
The Phoenix Force commandos immediately recognized Calvin James and Yakov Katzenelenbogen.

"Shalom," Ziyyon greeted Katz when he approached. "Have you been chatting with your friends in Mossad again?"

"Tell this bloke to move his arse, Yakov," the Briton urged.

"Let the major do his job, gentlemen," Katz replied.

"What the bleedin' hell...?" McCarter began.

"Major Ziyyon has authorization from Mossad and his own military-intelligence organization," Katz explained. "The restrictions against him have been lifted because there is no evidence to support any allegations against the major's loyalty, and his flaws in judgment are regarded as extreme devotion to duty. He has been assigned to supervise the radio communications for security personnel during the conference."

"What do these dumb bastards think they're doing?" Hawkins asked.

"This area is restricted to you gentlemen," Ziyyon declared. "I suggest you get out of here."

"Come on, man," James urged. "We're wasting our time here."

The Phoenix Force commandos and Katz headed for the stairs. McCarter uttered something under his breath. The others couldn't understand his words, but the tone left no doubt he was furious about the turn of events.

They mounted the stairs as Katz explained that the final decision about who handled what for security remained in the hands of the Israeli government. The government associated high rank with top ability. They wanted Major Ziyyon after Lieutenant-Colonel Paran fell ill.

"How sick is he?" Hawkins asked. "Any chance

he'll recover in time to take over the assignment from Ziyyon?''

"Paran has been hospitalized with food poisoning," James explained. "I managed to get a look at a report on his condition. The colonel suffered from amanita poisoning. That's a kind of mushroom."

"Mushroom," McCarter repeated. "Somebody could have fed them to him deliberately. That's possible, right?''

"Almost anything is possible," James replied with a shrug, "but we don't have any proof that happened. Accidental mushroom poisonings happen all the time. Paran will probably recover, but it'll take days."

"I don't like coincidences, and I don't like that smug son of a bitch Ziyyon," McCarter growled. "At best he's an unstable fanatic and at worse he could be working for the enemy."

"We don't have any proof of that, either," Katz reminded the Briton. "For now we have to accept what's happened and make the most of the situation."

"Time's running out," Hawkins remarked. "The conference is tomorrow. Hell, the President is on his way in *Air Force One*."

"And a number of the Arab delegates are already here," James added. "Some of them seem real nervous about being in Israel. A couple of those countries are really sticking their necks out to try to make this peace meeting a success. They have neighbors who aren't going to look kindly on them for this. A lot of Arabs still maintain Israel doesn't have a right to exist. They'd like to see this entire country shut down, all the Jews gone and the whole place turned into Palestine again.''

''Speaking of which,'' McCarter said, ''are the Palestinians sending anybody to this event? The last meeting got a lot of attention, plenty of praise and a couple Nobel Peace Prizes.''

''I'm not sure what they're doing,'' Katz replied, ''but I have to catch a flight to Saudi Arabia to try to get some information about a certain Professor Barrah who seems to be involved in this mess.''

''That means we're on our own?'' McCarter asked.

''You fellows are Phoenix Force now,'' Katz replied. ''I'm retired, remember? Try to keep an eye on Ziyyon. Geller doesn't really trust him. Mossad will cooperate with you.''

''They haven't been so great to work with so far,'' Hawkins complained.

''The Israelis are just defensive about having a bunch of outsiders coming to their country and telling them how to do their job,'' James said. ''When Mossad realizes we're here for the same reason they are and we all need to work together, you'll see how professional they really are.''

''They'd better be,'' McCarter commented. ''We don't have much time to get prepared for the conference, and we still don't know any more about the SHC device or what the terrorists plan to do with it than we did when this began.''

MACK BOLAN KNELT on the prayer rug and faced east, toward the Islamic holy city of Mecca. The medallion dangled from his neck as he placed his forehead to the rug in the Muslim style of prayer. Ahmed knelt on a rug beside him. The other five men, previously herded from the congregation and awarded the Jinn 2000 amulets, surrounded Bolan. The seven-man group remained separated from the others during the services.

The teacher read aloud from the Koran. Bolan understood little of what he said, but the instructor leafed through the book to select different *suras,* chapters written in a poetic style by the Prophet Muhammad.

The Executioner wondered why the group he and Ahmed were part of was still separate from the rest. Perhaps they were to be introduced as new members, officially accepted into the fold. Perhaps they still had more initiation rites to complete for the sect. Whatever the reason, the attention made Bolan uneasy.

They raised their heads and sat on the prayer rugs after the lesson ended. Captain Qatrun emerged from a canvas doorway, still clad in his fatigue uniform, and marched onto the platform before the crowd. Bolan guessed the man wouldn't appear so boldly in front of the recruits unless the occasion was important. Qatrun addressed the congregation in a clear, loud voice. He mentioned *"Hariah Allah"* several times. Perhaps another demonstration of "God's fire" was about to take place.

Two men rolled a two-wheel wagon to the platform. A long metal cylinder jutted from a box-shaped base. Bolan sucked in a tense breath when he recognized the SHC device. The contraption was mounted like a field howitzer. Bolan guessed the barrel to be about a yard in length and the control box no larger than a small suitcase.

Ahmed glanced at Bolan. His eyes revealed amazement and a trace of fear. The Executioner sympathized with the CID officer because the muzzle of the SHC device was pointed in their general direction. Qatrun continued to speak as one of his hardmen moved to the controls and prepared to operate the weapon.

Bolan noticed that two guards armed with AK-47s once more stood watch on the segregated men. Although they carried automatic rifles, they seemed to avoid getting too close to the disarmed group. Why would they be worried? Did they fear the possibility of spontaneous human combustion or being too close to a person who suddenly erupted in blue flame?

Had Qatrun decided to use Bolan, Ahmed and the other five for the demonstration? The captain obviously thought one of them might be a spy. He had even accused Bolan of being a CIA agent in English to see how he would react. Terrorists and fanatics tended to be ruthless. They wouldn't hesitate to kill five or six innocent men to take out one or two enemies. The Executioner realized they were facing a firing squad with a cannonlike device that produced real fire from within the bodies of its victims.

Bolan had to think quickly, yet he had to remain calm. The SHC weapon hadn't affected him at the West Bank. Would he still be immune? What might be different this time compared to the previous incident?

The medallion.

He recalled Congressman Morrow wore a medallion around his neck before his body burst into flames. At the time Bolan had assumed it was a good-luck piece, a trinket or perhaps a religious symbol of a saint or similar emblem. What if the Jinn 2000 terrorists had put it around his neck for a reason? Could there be a connection?

Bolan glanced at the guards. Neither appeared to wear an amulet. He saw no trace of a chain or leather strap at their necks to suggest they had their Jinn 2000 medallions hidden inside their *brussa* shirts.

The Executioner knew it was time to act. He closed a fist around the medal that hung from his neck and yanked hard to break the chain. He tossed it aside and grabbed Ahmed's amulet. The CID agent gasped with surprise when Bolan abruptly ripped the medallion from his neck. Committed to a course of action, the soldier didn't hesitate. He quickly sprang to his feet and charged the closest guard.

Startled, the man tried to swing his Kalashnikov rifle toward Bolan, but the soldier was on him too fast. He grabbed the AK-47 frame with one hand and the barrel with the other. Holding the weapon at bay, he swiftly kicked the guard between the legs. The man rasped in agony and doubled over from the blow. Bolan twisted the rifle from his adversary's grasp and whipped the walnut buttstock in a high sweep. Wood slammed into the guard's skull at the temple, and the man collapsed to the ground.

The second guard advanced toward Bolan and began to raise his weapon. The Executioner suddenly stepped closer and swung the barrel of the confiscated AK-47 into the gunman's weapon before the guy could attempt to use his rifle. The big American brought up the barrel of his weapon in a vicious slash that drove the blade-shaped front sight into the side of the guard's neck. Steel pierced skin, and a hard yank tore a jagged line in the man's flesh. Blood squirted from his carotid artery as the horrified man stumbled backward and dropped his rifle to grasp the terrible wound with both hands.

Ahmed appeared near Bolan, amazed and confused by his companion's actions. Voices cried out in alarm and surprise. Another guard rushed toward Bolan, working the bolt to his AK-47 as he ran. Qatrun shouted something as he drew his Makarov from leather.

Brilliant blue light suddenly exploded among the five remaining members of the seven recruits. Bolan turned his head to avoid looking into the white glare he knew burned at the center of each victim. Fire claimed the men so quickly only one or two managed to scream as they were consumed by flames.

The gunman and the majority of other Jinn 2000 followers covered their eyes with their hands, blinded by the SHC glare. Bolan took advantage of the situation and bolted for the exit. Ahmed stumbled in an awkward run behind him, his vision also hampered by the monstrous, lethal flames.

A pistol shot cracked as the two men reached the threshold. The bullet punched a hole in canvas inches from Bolan's head. He guessed the captain had fired the Makarov at them, but the Executioner didn't look back for confirmation.

The odds were too great to fight the Jinn 2000 gathering. Many of the men were potential recruits, not hard-core members of the terrorist force. They might have extremist viewpoints and a degree of fanaticism, but not all would be willing to obey the sect commander if ordered to risk their lives or kill for the Jinn 2000 cause.

Chances were better outside the canvas mosque.

Bolan anticipated the first obstacle they would encounter the moment they set foot outside. He canted the barrel of the Kalashnikov and took aim at the closer minaret tower. The Executioner was familiar with the Soviet-made assault rifle, and he was confident of his marksmanship at the distance required to pick off the tower sentries.

The first minaret guard didn't even notice Bolan until the AK-47 rattled a short burst of full-auto fury. He had been distracted by the weird glow within the canvas walls of the tent. The salvo of 7.62 mm slugs smashed into the sentry and pitched him headfirst over a handrail to the platform. He uttered a single strangled scream as he plunged to the merciless ground below.

The second tower guard swung his weapon toward Bolan, but the soldier had already trained his AK on the next target. He triggered the weapon, and a trio of Kalashnikov projectiles hit the sentry. Bullets drilled into the man's stomach, liver and spleen. The high-velocity slugs traveled upward to crack two vertebrae and puncture a lung. The sentry slumped on the platform, his rump landing on the floorboards and his back against the rail. The unfired rifle remained in his grasp as he quietly died in a seated position atop the wooden minaret.

Ahmed jogged alongside Bolan as they headed for the Land Rover. The CID officer's eyesight had largely recovered from the glare inside the tent. The Executioner swung the AK-47 toward the mosque and opened fire on half a dozen Jinn 2000 hardmen. One crumpled to the ground, which caused the others to retreat.

"What happened, Ulysses?" Ahmed asked as he

rubbed at his eyes to try to clear the spots before them. "Why didn't we burn with the others?"

"Toss me the keys to the Rover," Bolan said. "I'll drive."

"I can drive," Ahmed assured him. "The medallions? You ripped off the medallions and that saved us."

"Not for long if we don't get the hell out of here," the soldier replied.

Ahmed slid behind the steering wheel and started the engine. Bolan got in the passenger seat and kept his attention on the tent as more figures appeared along the corners of the canvas structure. They had to have slipped out from other exits to avoid the fate of the man who was brought down by the main entrance.

Weapons snarled, rounds from handguns and automatic rifles pelting the parking area. A few bullets hit the reinforced windshield of the Land Rover, but they barely scratched the tough surface. Bolan returned fire as the rig rolled backward, firing the last rounds from the Kalashnikov magazine in a generous volley directed at the tires and gas tanks of four parked vehicles. A hubcap hurled from one tire, convincing evidence of a direct hit.

As the Land Rover headed from the camp, flames ignited the gas in the punctured tank of a small yellow import. Fire spread across the rear of the vehicle, and the tank exploded as if charged by a half stick of dynamite. The blaze reached another vehicle, and a chain of burning vehicles soon appeared in the parking area. Bolan discarded the empty Kalashnikov and slithered to the back of the vehicle for the weapons cache under the seat.

"How long do you think that will slow them down?" Ahmed asked.

"Not long enough," the Executioner replied grimly.

CHAPTER TWENTY

The muzzle-flash of enemy weapons streaked through the night like orange laser beams. Headlights winked on in the remaining cars and trucks as the Land Rover sped from the scene.

As Bolan predicted, the enemy hadn't been slowed very long. Ahmed stamped his foot on the gas pedal, but the armored vehicle wasn't a sports car. They wouldn't be able to outrun their pursuers. The Land Rover might give them an advantage off-road, but the soldier knew they wouldn't gain enough lead to get beyond effective range of the terrorists' gunfire.

The Executioner withdrew his M-16 assault rifle from the compartment in the back seat. A 30-round magazine was already in place, and he pulled the charging handle to chamber the first cartridge. He thumbed the selector switch from safety to full-auto and took aim at the pursuing enemy.

A terrorist bullet whined along the frame of the Land Rover, the ricochet slicing air near Bolan's left earlobe. He instinctively ducked his head and sucked in a tense breath. The Jinn 2000 gunmen fired a lot of ammunition at the fleeing rig, but the majority of rounds missed the target. Shooting accurately from a fast-moving vehicle at another fast-moving vehicle was difficult.

However, Bolan had firsthand experience at this task and appreciated the difficulty of a running gun battle. He didn't attempt any fancy marksmanship. Trying to shoot out a tire would be almost impossible. He couldn't even see any tires due to the darkness and a dust cloud that rose from the unpaved road. The soldier used the enemy headlights to locate targets. Like the eyes of a demented band of mechanical hyenas, the headlights swayed and bounced with the motion of the terrorists' vehicles.

Bolan fired the M-16 at the closest opponent. He aimed between the headlights and allowed the barrel to climb slightly as the 5.56 mm slugs spit out of the muzzle. He hoped to hit the radiator, engine or windshield by this tactic. The car swung in a wide arc in an effort to avoid the gunfire, cutting into the path of a pickup truck that raced along the shoulder of the road to try to catch up with them. Instead, the truck crashed into the rear end of the car.

Sound of metal on metal drew Bolan's attention, and he glimpsed both vehicles at the side of the road. They had come to a halt, damaged enough to terminate their roles in the chase.

Another vehicle gained on the Land Rover, close enough now that it was clearly visible. Bolan fired another salvo between the pursuer's headlights. The vehicle bounced as the barrage of 5.56 mm rounds slammed into the bodywork, and a bullet shattered one of the headlights. A terrorist poked his head and shoulders from the passenger-side window, then extended a pistol, trying to fire at Bolan.

The soldier quickly altered the aim of his M-16

and triggered a 3-round burst. The gunman's torso convulsed from the impact of the multiple bullets, a single shot erupting from the guy's weapon before he tumbled onto the ground, dead or dying. Bolan hit the enemy vehicle with another volley, and the rig backed away, slowing enough to allow others to assume the dangerous position of point for the pursuit.

The terrorist gunfire ebbed long enough for Bolan to grab a 40 mm grenade from the back-seat arsenal. He opened the breech to the M-203 launcher attached to the underside of the M-16 barrel and inserted the big cartridge. He snapped it shut and swung the weapon toward another target.

The Executioner triggered the M-203, and the grenade streaked across the shadows. It crashed into a pickup, exploding on impact, and the blast tore the truck apart. Flaming gasoline, metal chunks, charred upholstery and grisly body parts hurled across the desert road.

"What the hell was that?" Ahmed asked, alarmed by the unexpected explosion. "Did you do that, Ulysses?"

"Just trying to cut down the odds," Bolan replied.

The truck explosion discouraged the other vehicles from getting closer to the Land Rover, but they didn't give up the pursuit. Several weapons sprayed the fleeing vehicle and the road around it with a vicious wave of bullets. Bolan ducked as ricochets whistled above his head. Their vehicle swerved and almost swung off the road as Ahmed hunched behind the steering wheel, turning it to the right in the process.

The Land Rover began to ride with a pronounced

bounce. Bolan realized a rear tire had taken a bullet, and they wouldn't be able to achieve much speed.

The big American returned fire with the M-16, watching as an enemy car swerved off the road, plowed into deep sand and rolled onto its side. The soldier had scored a direct hit on the driver. He didn't have time to celebrate because five more vehicles were in pursuit.

"We're approaching the Roman ruins," Ahmed announced. "Should we use it for shelter and try to make a stand?"

"You're getting the hang of this," Bolan replied. "Get us there as fast as you can. Still have pursuers on our tail determined to kill us."

The Land Rover swung off the road, its headlights illuminating the ancient walls of the ruins. Bolan discarded the spent magazine from the M-16 and ejected the empty shell casing from the M-203 attachment. He reloaded hastily and pulled off his *keffiyeh* and robe. The soldier grabbed a gun belt with a .44 Magnum Desert Eagle in a hip holster and magazine pouches, and slipped the belt onto his shoulder.

Ahmed struggled with the wheel and pumped the pedal as the disabled Land Rover protested the drive across deep sand. The three remaining tires spun in the soft surface, spewing sand. The rear hub and axle of the destroyed fourth tire sank in the mire and threatened to prevent the vehicle from advancing.

The Land Rover pressed on at a crawl to the ruins, finally reaching the ancient brick walls. The shelter seemed feeble against modern weapons. What remained of Roman stones was no higher than two yards at the tallest portion, and most of the crumbled barriers stood less than half that height. Bolan jumped from the vehicle and headed for the wall to assume a stance with the M-16 braced along stone as a bench rest.

"There's an Uzi in the back seat," Bolan reminded Ahmed.

The CID officer found the submachine gun in the hidden compartment and rushed to join Bolan as the Executioner fired the automatic rifle at the enemy. The soldier lined the sights on a target as a terrorist car approached, breathed slowly to control his nerves and steady his hold before he squeezed the trigger with a gentle index finger.

Three rounds sizzled from the M-16 and struck the automobile through the windshield. Bolan watched the car swing and weave out of control, confident he had nailed the driver. The other vehicles came to a halt, and the gunmen emerged to use the cars and trucks for cover. The Executioner tracked one man with the sights of the rifle and scored another hit. Three 5.56 mm slugs between the shoulder blades brought the terrorist down before he could reach shelter.

Ahmed opened fire with the Uzi. He jerked the subgun from side to side to spray bullets in a wild zigzag pattern. Rounds tore into sand more than a yard from the line of enemy vehicles. The terrorists returned fire, bullets chiseling stone from bricks near Ahmed's position. The CID man retreated and ducked for cover.

"What do you think that is," Bolan asked, "a fire extinguisher? Don't spray bullets, Ahmed. You're wasting ammunition, and the muzzle-flash betrays your location to the enemy."

"You might have mentioned that sooner," Ahmed

replied as he gingerly touched a cut on his cheek caused by a flying chunk of stone.

"I thought you'd had some combat training," Bolan answered. "They're too far away for the effective range of a submachine gun. Just hold your fire until they get closer."

"We don't generally use this sort of weapon in the CID," the Egyptian stated, "especially not Israeli-made firearms."

"The Uzi is one of the best SMGs ever made," Bolan replied. "You just need to use it for what it was designed for."

The enemy gunfire subsided. The Jinn 2000 forces were probably running low on ammunition. They had thrown together their posse to chase Bolan and Ahmed, and all they had were the weapons and ammo they carried. Most were probably armed with pistols, and only a few had a rifle. Bolan didn't know how well trained the terrorists might be. Fortunately their marksmanship didn't seem exceptional, but they displayed plenty of determination.

"What are they doing?" Ahmed asked, wondering why the shooting had ceased.

"Trying to figure out how to take us," Bolan replied.

He unslung the gun belt from his shoulder and prepared to buckle it around his waist. One of the enemy vehicles suddenly bolted toward the ruins. Bolan dropped the gun belt to grab his M-16 with both hands. The headlights of the truck grew larger as the rig rushed forward. The Executioner squeezed off a trio of 5.56 mm rounds. He saw bullet holes appear in the windshield above the headlights. Glass cracked and shattered, but no human form sat behind it.

Bolan didn't waste more ammunition on the enemy vehicle, aware the terrorists had to have weighted the gas pedal with a rock, stick or some other object and unleashed the unmanned truck as a battering ram. The two men moved clear of the section of wall targeted by the vehicle, and the truck crashed into brick. Stones that had stood for nearly two thousand years toppled from the impact of the machine, the top of the wall crashing down on the hood and roof of the vehicle. The rig came to a halt, tires and axles jammed on the thicker foundation of the barrier. Bolan glimpsed a cord tied to the steering wheel of the rig, no doubt to keep it on course for its brief journey of destruction.

Ahmed blasted a wild burst of rounds at the truck before he, too, realized no one was in it. Bolan turned his attention to the enemy beyond the walls, aware they had to have launched the truck as a preamble for an attack, perhaps to serve as a distraction. He stayed low and peered over a low portion of the wall.

The enemy advanced. Two cars rolled forward without headlights to try to conceal their approach. Bolan scanned the area and wasn't surprised to see several terrorists on foot. They kept low and favored the darkest shadows in an effort to avoid detection. Others remained by the last two vehicles, probably armed with rifles to provide cover fire for the attackers.

Bolan swung his M-16 toward the closest opponent and fired a short burst. He saw the man convulse from the dose of 5.56 mm death and quickly selected another target, blasting a trio of high-velocity slugs through the windshield of an advancing automobile.

"Ulysses?" Ahmed asked, unsure of what was happening or what he should do.

The Executioner had no time to spare on instructions. He estimated the distance to the vehicles parked farther from the ruins and raised the rifle barrel to calibrate the M-203 beneath it for a long-range shot. He triggered the launcher. The M-16 was thrust into his arms and shoulder by the recoil as a 40 mm projectile sailed high above the heads of the advance terrorist team.

The grenade shell descended upon the Jinn 2000 backup vehicles with a roar, the blast scattering the two machines across the ground in a jagged junk pile. Gasoline caught fire to create a massive blaze around the wreckage. A human shape staggered from the flames, body draped in yellow-and-orange fire. Clothes and hair ablaze, the man shrieked in agony.

Bolan aimed the M-16 and terminated the burning man's suffering along with his life. The Executioner realized this act of mercy cost him precious ammunition and soon the rifle would run dry. Extra magazines, as well as the .44 Magnum pistol, were attached to the gunbelt on the ground near the crumbled wall.

The soldier headed for the belt, but the roar of an engine warned him to go back. A powerful blow knocked loose more ancient bricks from the wall. The terrorists had responded with desperation and rammed the barrier again.

This time the vehicle wasn't unoccupied.

Two terrorists emerged from the back doors of the sedan, pistols in hand. Bolan swiftly snap-aimed his

M-16 and fired a trio of bullets that sliced a line of holes in an adversary's solar plexus, sternum and throat. The gunman dropped his weapon and pawed at the wounds as he wilted to the ground.

Ahmed triggered the Uzi and smashed the second terrorist with a volley of 9 mm slugs. The impact hurled the man across the hood, blood seeping from the bullet-riddled form as a third terrorist kicked open the front door on the passenger side. The guy had to have been under the dashboard to steer the car and work the pedal while low enough to avoid being shot through the windshield.

Bolan aimed the M-16 and clicked the trigger—he was out of ammo. The terrorist swung a revolver toward the Executioner, who ducked behind the wall a moment before the enemy fired two .38 rounds in his direction.

Ahmed prepared to point the Uzi at the gunner, but movement along the end of the wall drew his attention to another threat. A Jinn 2000 killer appeared by the stones, a British Sterling subgun in hand. The CID officer swung the subgun toward the enemy and fired the last two 9 mm rounds. The gunner fell backward from the double parabellum punch to his chest as he triggered the Sterling to blast a useless stream of bullets into the night sky.

A pistol shot erupted as the terrorist tumbled to the ground. Ahmed cried out and stumbled off balance, blood oozing from a bullet hole under his right shoulder blade. He fell to one knee, but turned to try to bring the Uzi into play. He spit pink froth from a punctured lung as he triggered the empty SMG. The bearded face of the terrorist pistol man appeared above a crumbled portion of the wall and smiled at the helpless, wounded Egyptian agent. The hardman aimed his revolver and fired two more .38 slugs into Ahmed's chest.

Bolan was busy staying alive and couldn't help his companion. Another Jinn 2000 assassin emerged from the end of the wall across from the body of the slain figure with the Sterling. Bolan had anticipated such a tactic; a cross fire was a standard attack technique. The gunman at the corner didn't know his partner had already been taken out. He seemed confused as he thrust a Stechkin machine pistol forward like a divining rod.

The Executioner charged with the empty M-16 in his fists, chopping the hard plastic buttstock across the gunman's wrist to strike the Soviet-made Stechkin from his grasp. A backhand sweep slammed the rifle butt into the terrorist's face and knocked him on his rump. He sat on the ground, stunned with glazed eyes and a bloodied and broken nose.

Bolan spotted the fallen Stechkin. A true machine pistol, the weapon was similar to his Beretta 93-R, and he could certainly put it to good use against the enemy. Suddenly another shape rushed from the corner of the wall, the big American glimpsing the flash of steel as the terrorist attacked.

The Executioner raised the empty rifle to block the attack. He didn't have time to speculate why the hardman came at him with a blade instead of a gun. Perhaps the man had exhausted his ammo and drew the knife in desperation, or he might have been a survivor from a blasted vehicle who had lost access to any other weapon. At that instant all that mattered was the terrorist intended to plunge sharp steel into the soldier's heart.

The frame of the M-16 formed a bar and struck the attacker's forearm above his knife hand. Bolan turned to shove with the rifle and push the blade away in the process. He pivoted on his left foot to move behind the terrorist as his right leg executed a back-kick. The heel of his boot slammed into the small of the knife man's spine to send the man hurtling off balance.

The report of a pistol warned of more danger. Bolan turned and saw the knife-wielding terrorist drop to the ground, forehead split open by a .38-caliber bullet. The guy had stumbled into the path of a projectile meant for the Executioner. Enraged by his own error, the bearded killer hopped over the wall, revolver in both hands.

Bolan tossed aside the empty M-16 and looked for the Stechkin. Perhaps he could dive for the Russian machine pistol and try to take down the gunman even if he stopped another bullet himself. With a grin the terrorist pulled the trigger. The hammer fell, and the firing pin landed on a spent shell casing in the cylinder. It clicked twice more before the fanatic accepted the fact he was out of ammo.

The man cursed and hurled the empty revolver at Bolan's head. The soldier dodged the clumsy attack as the terrorist screamed and charged. The man's hands flashed in a flurry in front of his own face, fingers blurred above his head. Bolan recognized this as a distraction effort, and he was ready when the enemy launched the real attack.

A karate side kick streaked for the Executioner's abdomen. Bolan's hands snared the terrorist's ankle before the blow could land. He pulled to keep the enemy off balance, poised on one foot. Swiftly the big American swung his left leg high in a roundhouse motion, sweeping across the captive leg of his opponent. The Executioner turned the ankle to the right as he dropped to his left knee.

The combined weight of Bolan's body on the back of the man's calf and the pressure of his ankle drove the guy to the ground hard. His belly landed in the sand as the Executioner grasped the hardman's foot at the heel and toe. A vicious twist crunched bone at the ankle joint. The Jinn 2000 gunner cried out as pain shot through the nerves of his leg.

The Executioner threw himself onto the fallen man's back, then rapped a sledgehammer blow to his opponent's nape. Bolan wasn't certain if the blow crushed vertebrae. Although the enemy lay still, Bolan chopped the side of his hand across the neck again to be certain it was broken.

He started to rise and inhaled to replenish air in his lungs and attempt to control a racing heart. A bellow of rage announced yet another attack. The terrorist stunned by the rifle butt to the face suddenly rushed Bolan, teeth bared and stained crimson by blood from his smashed nose. A big fist rocketed for the soldier's face as the fanatic swung a wild roundhouse right.

The Executioner stepped to the left to dodge the attack and swept his right forearm across the terrorist's extended limb. The blow knocked the man's arm aside and opened the target for Bolan's next move. He swung the right arm forward and stepped into the move to add power and momentum to the blow. The inside edge of the soldier's forearm struck the terrorist under the jawline with an aikido version of a clothesline maneuver.

The opponent hit the ground hard, dying from the blow across his throat.

Silence seemed to descend upon the scene with oppressive force. Bolan heard fire crackle from the burning debris, wind whispered along stone and his own pulse throbbed behind his ear. He moved to the motionless form of Ahmed. The CID officer had been shot through both lungs and the heart, yet Bolan knelt by him in the slight hope the man might still be alive. He wasn't.

Gentle fingertips closed the slain CID agent's eyes. Bolan rose, alone on the battlefield. He collected his weapons and selected a vehicle that seemed to be in the best condition to continue the journey to Cairo.

CHAPTER TWENTY-ONE

T. J. Hawkins punched the keyboard to the laptop computer on the bench in the back of the van. He accessed the line to Stony Man Farm as Mack Bolan entered the vehicle. The Executioner placed a U.S. Army duffel bag on the floor of the van and closed the door.

Gary Manning and Rafael Encizo sat in the front of the vehicle. The big Canadian started the engine as Bolan took a seat by the computer. Hawkins moved back so the Executioner would have the machine and the screen to himself. Bolan felt the van lurch forward as images appeared on-screen.

Hal Brognola's face registered surprise when he saw Mack Bolan. The big Fed realized the broadcast came from Israel, and he expected the man to still be in Egypt.

"Got bored with Cairo?" Brognola inquired.

"It was exciting enough. I wanted to get to Israel as fast as possible. I just got off a C-130 at Lod Airport, and Phoenix Force met me with the mobile unit. That's where I'm calling from."

"I recognize it," Brognola replied. "Something must have broke big time at Cairo."

"You could say that," Bolan confirmed. "Jinn

2000 had another demonstration of their SHC machine. This time they didn't settle for a pig. Apparently they found the listening-device probe Ahmed lost at the site the other night. The terrorists figured one or more of the new recruits had to be spies."

"That included you and Ahmed," Brognola said. "I'm surprised they didn't feel especially suspicious toward you because you couldn't speak or understand much Arabic."

"Oh, I got some special consideration," Bolan stated. "The captain gave me some personal attention. Didn't get around to introductions, but I'm sure that's who he was. Big guy, about forty. He's strong, hits pretty hard. Speaks at least some English and Hebrew, and he carried a Russian Makarov."

"Sounds like an officer with some education from a country that got a fair amount of military support from the Soviet Union during the cold war," the big Fed speculated. "I don't know if that'll help Aaron get a handle on the son of a bitch."

"Too bad Ahmed couldn't evaluate the captain's dialect to give us an idea what part of the Middle East the guy might be from," Bolan commented. "Ahmed had a good ear for that."

"You mention Ahmed in the past tense," Brognola observed.

"We managed to escape before the enemy could burn us along with five other suspects. We had to shoot our way out and had another firefight...without any SHC devices. Ahmed was KIA. I'm not sure how many terrorists we took out. More than a dozen."

"Anything that lowers the odds," Hawkins remarked.

"There are still enough of them left to be a problem," Bolan said. "This isn't close to being over, T.J. The Jinn 2000 sect at Cairo has already struck camp and fled."

"Aaron picked up a transmission by an Egyptian military-unit computer system in Cairo that concerned an immediate mobilization with the participation of U.S. Marine personnel from the embassy," Brognola remarked. "No other details were available. That happened about two hours ago."

"That was put together on my command," Bolan confirmed. "I was afraid we wouldn't get there in time, and we didn't. It took too long to reach Cairo and hook up with Coburn at the embassy to coordinate the search. We flew over the mosque tent and discovered it was deserted. There were about thirty piles of ashes. Apparently the captain and his comrades decided to get rid of every recruit they didn't think they could trust one hundred percent."

"Ruthless bastards," Hawkins commented, shaking his head.

"Common trait among terrorists," Brognola told him. "The President will arrive in Tel Aviv in a matter of hours. Better assume another gang of those ruthless bastards are already in place and waiting for him."

"Yeah," Bolan said, "but now we have a major clue as to how the SHC weapon works...or at least something required for it to kill. Ahmed and I didn't go up in flames with the other five suspects at the tent because we ripped off a couple medallions given to us by the Jinn 2000. The others still wore their amulets. They burned, and we weren't touched by the fire."

"Medallions?" the big Fed asked with a frown.

"The SHC machine needs the medallion to ignite the fire inside a victim," Bolan explained. "I don't know how it works. Something in the amulets must focus the energy or wavelength transmitted by the device."

"So the target has to be wearing one of these medallions?"

"I guessed it just in time to yank mine off and pull the one from Ahmed's neck before they used the machine to burn the others. I recalled Morrow wore some sort of medallion at the Jinn 2000 setup at the West Bank. That's why I wasn't affected the first time. The terrorist bodies were destroyed because they wore the medallions. Most probably don't even suspect the connection and figured they were just religious symbols of the sect, but it provides the terrorist leaders with a fast and sure way to destroy evidence and prevent anyone from identifying members of the order as a lead to the people in charge of the conspiracy."

"What about all those Israeli paratroopers who burned up during the raid?" Hawkins inquired. "They wouldn't be wearing religious symbols of a fanatic Islamic sect. This SHC stuff work on a Star of David pendant, as well?"

"The symbols aren't important," Bolan said. "The SHC energy must need a certain type of material for a conductor. Like metal for electricity. The composition of the medallions is what acts as a focus. Maybe it works more like a radio receiver. Whatever it is, somebody must have planted the conductors on the Israeli troops at the West Bank raid."

"Somebody who had a chance to tamper with their

gear,'' Hawkins mused. "Somebody would have to plant something on the President and other VIPs at the peace conference for the SHC to work."

"How?" Brognola asked. "Striker said they made a pig go up in flames. Was that animal wearing a medallion, too?"

"Not that I noticed," Bolan answered, "but I really wasn't looking at the time. Could be they had a conductor of some sort clipped to the pig's ear or tail. Maybe it was even introduced to the animal in its food. We don't know how big the conductor is. Can't be very large. Might be the size of a pinhead."

"Does a victim actually have to be wearing it?" Hawkins wondered aloud. "Could it be in the nails or staples used on a platform? Maybe a silicon compound is used instead of metal. They could have the conductor installed in the protective glass of motorcade vehicles."

"Jesus," Brognola muttered. "I thought this would help us if we knew more about this crap."

A small window suddenly appeared in the lower right-hand corner of the screen. The computer transmission had been joined by a link from Kurtzman's center. The man's face and shoulders in the window confirmed they were now on a Stony Man high-tech version of a party line.

"Sorry to butt in," he announced, "but I think this is pretty important. I've got Yakov on line, calling from Saudi Arabia. It's past 3:00 a.m. over there, so I figure it can't wait. About the same time in Israel. You fellas are earning your pay this week."

"None of our usual slacker assignments," Bolan said dryly.

"Things must be getting hairy," Kurtzman commented, "but I'll get the details from Hal that I may have missed. I'll patch through Yakov now."

The face in the computer window changed. Yakov Katzenelenbogen appeared tired. A set of green draperies behind him betrayed little of Katz's location.

"Isn't anyone going to sleep tonight?" he remarked. "Of course, it isn't even night anymore. Striker? You're in Tel Aviv?"

"We'll explain later," Brognola assured him. "What did you find out from the Saudis?"

The Israeli performed a slow shoulder stretch as he spoke. "I discovered they were reluctant to discuss their nuclear-fusion research even when I convinced them this was a matter of international concern that threatened the entire world. I also assured them no one was blaming the Saudi government or the royal family for the SHC technology we suspected came from Professor Barrah's experiments."

"You've always been good at the diplomatic part of the business," Brognola said. "You did manage to get through the red tape at Mecca?"

"Eventually," Katz answered. "I met with Professor Hamad who had worked with Barrah. We already knew Barrah had vanished after an assistant had been killed during an experiment."

"Yeah," Brognola said, "but we didn't have any details about the guy's death. Sure doesn't speak well for the alleged 'safe nature' of nuclear fusion."

"Barrah's experiment was rather unconventional and potentially more dangerous than most efforts at this technology," Katz said. "Hardly a reason to condemn all work in the field. I'm not going to get off the subject. Barrah had worked on a sort of super-microwave machine that transmitted a type of powerful force field that would create a wave layer for a nuclear vessel, a method used to contain the million-degree heat necessary to even attempt nuclear fusion.''

"I remember," Brognola assured him. "Such great heat causes metal of virtually any kind to melt so the microwaves keep the heat from actually reaching the metal with full force, right?"

"But Barrah had tried to alter his microwave system to actually create the enormous pressures necessary to compress light atomic elements and create fusion energy."

"Cold fusion," Hawkins said, his tone almost awestruck by Barrah's ambition. "Nuclear energy without the need for unstable fission techniques or extreme degrees of heat. Sure would be something if somebody could pull that off."

"It took only a few seconds to consume Barrah's technician," Katz continued. "The poor fellow headed over to the vessel to place a special synthetic quartz crystal in the core, which was supposed to cause fusion in a liter of water when the waves were focused on the crystal to start the process with the hydrogen in the water."

"What's that about this crystal being used to focus Barrah's supermicrowaves?" Brognola asked.

"The quartz absorbs the microwaves and concentrates their force in a manner similar to how certain crystals react to vibration and carry sound or a gemstone used to focus light for a laser beam. Hamad said the crystals used were developed by Barrah himself. Synthetic quartz based on the silicon-dioxide type found in nature, but there had been some modifications even Hamad wasn't certain about."

"And what happened to the assistant when he stepped in front of the microwave with one of these quartz crystals?" Bolan asked.

"The same thing you described as spontaneous human combustion at the West Bank Jinn 2000 site," Katz replied. "Hamad described it as a sort of 'human fusion.' Apparently the quartz directed the microwaves to the nearest source of concentrated hydrogen and oxygen heavier than air. The human body is mostly water. They teach that in high-school science."

"Junior high," Brognola remarked. "Hamad and Barrah actually saw this guy burn to ashes? There's no doubt it could be some other type of mishap? A fire by some more conventional source?"

"Hamad didn't actually witness the fire," Katz replied, "but he arrived a few minutes or seconds later to find Barrah standing over the ashes. Part of the assistant's hand was left, enough to get a thumbprint to identify him."

"What did they do then?" the big Fed asked.

"Reported the death and shut down their operation until an investigation could be conducted," Katz answered. "At least, that's what Hamad thought would happen. Barrah virtually took everything and disappeared. The machine, design plans for the device, notes on computer disk and the crystals were all gone. Hamad suspected Barrah might have taken everything to destroy the device to try to prevent anyone else from ever making one again. When he didn't return, Hamad guessed Barrah went into self-imposed exile due to guilt or fear of punishment by the government. Barrah seemed to feel he had been persecuted for being a Shiite Muslim in a country with a Sunni Muslim majority.''

"Did they think he might defect to Iran?'' Brognola asked.

"Yes," Katz said. "Although, they thought Bahrain would be a more likely place for Barrah to flee. It also has a Shiite majority, but Bahrain's government is less repressive and not noted for fanatical behavior. This might have been wishful thinking by the Saudi authorities because they didn't seem eager to admit Barrah might be a fanatic himself. I think they might have hoped he had committed suicide so he wouldn't be an embarrassment for them.''

"No such luck," Bolan said. "We know what happened. He hooked up with Jinn 2000, and they intend to use the SHC device to carry out the prophecies of Omar.''

Katz held a drawing of an object with a cylinder barrel, a cone-shaped muzzle and box-style base for the others to see on the screen.

"This is a sketch Hamad made by memory," he explained.

"That's it," Bolan confirmed. "Did Hamad say how large the quartz crystals are?''

"No bigger than a battery for a quartz wristwatch," the Israeli replied.

"Pretty small," Hawkins commented. "Wouldn't have any trouble putting one of them inside a medallion.''

"Or planting them in the gear of Israeli paratroopers," Bolan added. "Won't be too hard to do the same to the VIP personnel at the conference, either.''

"What about transporting this stuff?" Brognola asked. "It sounds like Hamad was pretty confident

Barrah could manage to move everything by himself. This device can't be too large or heavy.''

"He said the machine can be broken down to basic parts fairly easily," Katz explained. "Disassembled, it could pass for parts to a machine press of some sort or perhaps metal pipes for a large commercial freezer unit. The whole thing weighs about forty or fifty kilos."

"How long ago did all this happen in Saudi Arabia?" Bolan asked.

"About six months ago," the Israeli replied. "Long enough for Barrah to go almost anywhere to join forces with the terrorists."

"Long enough to make more SHC machines?" the soldier asked.

"Sorry. I didn't ask Hamad about that. Better assume they have more than one. After all, Barrah took all the information with him, as well as the only prototype."

"Now we have an idea what to look for," Brognola said. "I suppose everybody knows *Air Force One* has arrived at Lod Airport. The President is there with you guys in Israel, and you've only got a few hours before the conference."

"Thanks for the reminder," Bolan commented. "I brought Coburn with me from Cairo. He can help coordinate security efforts with CIA here. David and Calvin have him in a separate car now. They'll take him straight to the U.S. Embassy. You can make sure the Company cooperates with him, and try to get the Secret Service to do likewise."

"We'll do the best we can," Brognola assured him. "The President himself will back us. Hopefully he can help influence the security personnel for the other heads of state and representatives from other countries involved.''

"Tel Aviv is crawling with cops, spies and security experts," Hawkins remarked. "Problem is, the Arabs and Israelis don't trust each other's people. I don't know how much cooperation we'll get from them. A lot of the Arab nations represented don't get along with each other all that well, either. Hell, Tel Aviv police arrested some guys for having a big fist-fight in front of the art gallery this evening. Turned out to be security men from Jordan and Lebanon. Seems they had an argument about where a new Palestine should be established. A couple of those boys drew guns, but no shots were fired.''

"There are a lot of sensitive issues in the Middle East," Katz said. "They decided to hold the conference in Tel Aviv instead of Jerusalem to try to avoid the debate about the status of the city. Of course, Israel insists Jerusalem is now their capital and they don't want to give up any of it. It is considered a holy city by Christians and Muslims, as well as by Jews, and everyone is determined to claim it.''

"Maybe it would be worse if they tried to hold this wingding in Jerusalem," Hawkins admitted, "but they still have a potential powder keg here. You know, that gallery is only about five hundred yards from the town hall?''

"That's where they finally decided to hold the conference?" Brognola asked with a frown. "Seems like that's a sort of drab spot and one that's bound to annoy the Arabs because it's located in an Israeli seat of authority.''

"Just local authority," Hawkins replied. "But they might not have the conference there. The big speech-making session and photo-op bullshit will be held at the clock tower. They got a real mess here. Everybody wants to make gestures and look good for the media. Nobody wants to lose face. Security is sort of a secondary concern. As if there weren't enough problems, the Israeli government insists on having that Ziyyon in charge of field communications."

"Ziyyon?" Bolan asked with surprise. "I thought Geller had placed him under restriction until an investigation could be conducted about his behavior."

"Yeah," Hawkins said with a sigh. "It's politics. The guy who was supposed to handle the job got sick from eating poison mushrooms, and they wanted Ziyyon because he was supposedly the best-qualified field-grade officer for the job."

"Well," the Executioner stated, "I want to have a little talk with the major."

"I know you're pissed off with the guy," Brognola said, "but you have to remember this is being conducted on Israeli territory and they have final say about which of their own officers they want in charge of various matters."

"I'll be tactful."

"Sure," the big Fed replied. "I bet."

CHAPTER TWENTY-TWO

Major Ziyyon supervised several technicians engaged in the preparation of wireless microphone units and miniature radio receivers. The intelligence officer peered over the shoulder of a man busy with wires and delicate tools.

"Be careful!" he snapped. "That has to fit in a cylinder small enough to be concealed inside a standard fountain pen. We can't have our visiting heads of state carrying anything bulky enough to cause an unsightly bulge in a suit jacket.

"We can't afford any mistakes with this equipment," the major told the crew. "I want our security officers to be in touch with one another at all times during the conference. No suicide truck bombs will reach the site. Such a vehicle will be spotted two kilometers away. That will give us time to get the prime minister and his guests to safety in case the truck manages to get through the first line of defense. I doubt that will happen, because we'll have skilled marksmen in place to take out such an attack."

"And the VIP delegates will also carry receivers?" a young tech inquired.

"They'll be signaled only if anything goes wrong," Ziyyon stated. "We don't want any of them to get killed because some bodyguard failed to reach the man fast enough to push him down to avoid a bullet. These diplomats might be dense, but they should have enough sense to duck if we tell them they might get killed if they don't.''

Pounding at the door interrupted Ziyyon's lecture. He rolled his eyes and crossed the room. The thuds continued. Ziyyon placed a hand on his side arm as he approached the door.

''Just a moment!''

''Come on,'' a voice replied in English. ''Open the bloody door. It's late, and we have to get this over with.''

Ziyyon recognized the cockney accent. That British pest he had encountered earlier was back. The major didn't want to waste time with the man or let him into the workshop area, yet he had been instructed to cooperate with the foreigners. They appeared to be friends with the one-armed retired colonel who had an association with Geller. Reluctantly Ziyyon unlatched the door and opened it.

Mack Bolan stood on the threshold.

Ziyyon's eyes widened with surprise, and his mouth fell open. Bolan's fist suddenly caught him hard on the jaw and slammed his mouth shut. The punch spun Ziyyon, but he kept his balance and started to drag a .357 Desert Eagle from leather.

The Executioner quickly grabbed the major's wrist with his right hand and thrust his left elbow under Ziyyon's arm. He pulled the wrist forcibly as he dug the elbow into a nerve center at the man's armpit. The officer groaned as the pressure forced his arm extended and straight, the pain in his armpit raising him onto his toes. The Israeli commo techs watched in astonishment, uncertain what to do.

McCarter entered the room, accompanied by James and a short, wiry figure dressed in an Israeli military uniform. Three bars on his collar marked his rank as a captain. Some of the communications personnel recognized the lean features and pencil-thin mustache of Captain Lavi, a respected Mossad officer. His presence with the strangers assured the other Israelis that whatever caused the man in black combat fatigues to attack Major Ziyyon had some sort of official sanction. Besides, Ziyyon wasn't popular with most of the men, and no one seemed eager to come to his assistance.

The Executioner shifted his right hand to Ziyyon's fist around the pistol, his elbow still planted firmly in the officer's armpit. Bolan dug his fingernails into the base of his adversary's thumb while he pressed his own thumb into the ulnar nerve at the back of the major's hand. Ziyyon's fist opened to drop the heavy Desert Eagle. Bolan stomped a boot heel to the back of his opponent's ankle. The major groaned from the pain at the Achilles tendon.

"You sent your men to Cairo for me," Bolan remarked. "Here I am, Major."

He turned to McCarter. "Cuff him."

The Briton appeared pleased to produce a pair of handcuffs as he moved behind the major. Lavi addressed Ziyyon in Hebrew while the man's hands were being manacled. They dragged him to his feet. Ziyyon clenched his teeth as pressure on his right leg caused more pain from the injured ankle.

"What the hell do you think you're doing?" he demanded. "Why are you all standing by and allowing this Yankee to attack me and accuse me of treason and sabotage against the state of Israel?''

"That's pretty much what's going on, Major," McCarter said. "What has you confused?"

"You don't have any grounds for this action," Ziyyon insisted. "You can't just take Belasko's word against mine. He's not an Israeli citizen, and that incident at the West Bank must still be considered suspicious."

"That little mystery is about to be solved," Bolan told him.

He moved to a workbench and examined one of the miniature radio-receiver units. Bolan used a screwdriver to pry a knob-shaped speaker from the wiring and popped it open. A small hexagonal crystal fell from it. The Executioner nodded with satisfaction.

"You planted these in all the transmitters and receivers," he said, "just as you put them in the gear of the Israeli paratroopers who accompanied me on that raid of the Jinn 2000 base at the West Bank. You didn't get a chance to touch my gear. That's why I didn't go up in the flames with the others. The SHC device needs these crystals to activate a type of nuclear fusion inside a victim's body."

"That's insane! Those crystals are used for radio transmission and receiving vibrations to produce sound."

"We have other communications experts who will evaluate your work," Lavi said, "and those crystals. Meantime the director has personally instructed me to place you under arrest and assist in your interrogation and the investigation that begins as of this moment, Major."

A senior tech NCO glanced at his co-workers and approached. The man had apparently decided to act as spokesman for the group, and none of the others challenged him for the role. Perhaps he outranked the others or simply had a better command of English.

"Excuse me," he began, "but we have been working at this for several hours. We're not sure what we're supposed to do now."

"You have to remove all the quartz crystals like this one," Bolan instructed. "They're not explosives, poison or anything that can harm anyone without the influence of a type of invisible microwave used by a certain terrorist group."

"Microwaves?" the NCO asked, still puzzled.

"Just do as he says, Sergeant," Lavi urged. "We'll get a qualified commo officer to help supervise. I suspect you really don't need help. You've all made similar devices for field communications before and you can probably do quite well on your own."

"That's true, sir," the sergeant replied.

"Fine," Lavi said. "You carry on here, and we'll take care of Major Ziyyon."

"Absolutely," McCarter commented as he shoved Ziyyon toward the door. "We're looking forward to taking care of this bloke."

THE INTERROGATION ROOM was bleak and cold. White walls and ceiling surrounded Ziyyon as he sat in a straight-backed chair, wrists cuffed to the metal arms. Bolan glanced at a computer printout sheet while James opened a small case that contained three small bottles of amber liquid and a trio of syringes.

"Interesting file, Ziyyon," Bolan commented.

"Your family is listed as Egyptian Jews who moved to Israel in 1958. My guess is they were double agents working for Nasser's government with the intention of getting a sleeper deep within Israeli Intelligence."

"How dare you make such accusations about my family?"

"Nice act," the soldier said, "but I'm sure you're really very proud of your family's devotion to duty. After all, they groomed you since childhood to be an undercover agent against Israel. I wonder if it helped you to pretend to be a Jewish fanatic because you're really a Shiite Muslim fanatic. You played the role very well for a long time. Even after Nasser died and the Egyptian government became a moderate nation that established peaceful relations with Israel, you still continued your mission."

"That's a pack of lies," Ziyyon snapped.

"I suspect you probably continued to work as a double agent for another Arab country," Bolan said. "Khaddafi tried to take Nasser's place as a would-be Genghis Khan in the Middle East. Of course, he didn't get too far, and nobody else has been able to unify Arab nations under a common banner, but you might have worked for his government for a while. Maybe you just hooked up with some extremist group. Probably a Shiite outfit. Whatever it was, it must have fallen apart and whatever was left eventually became part of the Jinn 2000 movement."

"That's the most demented story I've ever heard."

"Well," James began as he approached Ziyyon, "we'll soon know how close Belasko came to guessing the truth about you. I don't have the proper equipment, but your medical records don't indicate any problems with high blood pressure, and I can take your pulse the old-fashioned way.''

He placed two fingers to Ziyyon's inner wrist and looked at his watch as he counted the beats. The major stared at the syringes and bottles on the table.

''What is that?'' he asked. ''Truth serum?''

''Yep,'' James confirmed. ''Scopolamine. We use only the very best. Don't worry. I've used this stuff plenty of times before and never lost a patient. You've got a nice strong heartbeat, so you won't be at any special risk.''

''That's a relief,'' Ziyyon said without enthusiasm. ''How effective is this drug?''

''About eighty percent,'' James answered. ''It won't do any good to try to resist the serum. I'm pretty good at guessing a man's weight and measuring the necessary dose.''

James prepared the injection. Ziyyon recoiled as best he could, trapped to the chair, but he realized there was no point in struggling. James located the cephalic vein in Ziyyon's arm and stuck in the needle.

While the drug took effect, Bolan opened the door and signaled to Captain Lavi. The Israeli Intel officer entered the room and watched Ziyyon sweat in the chair. Lavi spoke Hebrew and Arabic, as well as English. Interrogations, especially under the influence of scopolamine, were best conducted in a subject's own language.

The Executioner left the room. There wasn't much he could do during the interrogation aside from get in the way. Rafael Encizo and David McCarter met him in the corridor. The Cuban commando held a bundle of data sheets. McCarter fired up a Player's cigarette and glanced at the door to the interrogation room.

"Bastard give you a hard time?" he asked.

"He's not in a position to give anyone a hard time now," the soldier replied. "Is T.J. working on the commo part of the operation?"

"Yeah," Encizo answered. "They've located all the crystals. Between the radio-transmitter units for security personnel and receivers intended for the VIPs at the conference, that spontaneous-combustion microwave would have caused almost a thousand people to go up in flames."

"Including the President of the United States, the prime minister of Israel, the president of Egypt and a number of others," McCarter added.

"Glad to hear it," Bolan said, "but the threat isn't over yet. The terrorists almost certainly plan to hit the meeting, and they may have a backup plan of some kind if their original scheme goes sour."

"We've got detailed maps of the city," Encizo stated. "Unfortunately we don't have any idea how far the range is for the enemy SHC device. Maybe Ziyyon will tell us after he starts talking in his sco-polamine sleep."

"I wouldn't count on that," Bolan said. "If the effort to take out the targets fails because of Ziyyon's actions or lack of them, the terrorists probably have another strike in mind. It wouldn't involve Ziyyon, so they'd have no reason to share the information with him."

"Need to know," McCarter commented with a nod. "Don't tell them any more than they need to know. That's one of the ten commandments of clan-destine operations."

"The maps of the city might give us an idea where the enemy might set up the SHC machine if they need a clear view to aim the weapon," Encizo said. "I don't know if those microwaves can flow around buildings in the way, pass through solid objects or how they work."

"I'm not sure, either," Bolan admitted, "but I think they'll want to see the infidels burn before their eyes. That'll be a crowning achievement to these guys. Jinn 2000 is based on the idea of the destruction of their enemies—which they claim are the enemies of God—and the power and conquest that will allegedly follow as their reward. They'll want to witness this fulfillment of one of Omar's prophecies. Maybe they'll want it on videotape."

"Even with a zoom lens they'll need to get fairly close if they want a video," Encizo remarked. "That doesn't mean they'll get that close with the SHC weapon."

"There are hundreds of police, government agents and military Intel people involved in security for this meeting," McCarter stated. "It won't be easy for anyone to get anywhere near the VIPs with anything more lethal than a nail file."

"There's always a way," Bolan commented. "Ziyyon had sabotaged the commo gear with crystals because the terrorists planned to use the SHC device. They must have a plan to get through the security net. Ziyyon was an inside source for them, and he would have given them information to help penetrate the security for the meeting."

They entered a small office at the end of the hallway, which belonged to Captain Lavi. Bolan and Phoenix Force had moved to Mossad headquarters to conduct business with greater privacy. The Executioner placed the data sheets and maps on the top of Lavi's desk as his fellow Stony Man commandos secured the door.

"The meeting is going to be held at the clock tower?" Bolan asked with surprise when he noticed the site on the map had been marked.

"That's where they plan to address the public with a string of speeches, hand-shaking photo-op nonsense and the usual political showmanship," Encizo explained. "It was selected because it's near a couple of large mosques and at least three Christian churches."

"Who would have thought we'd see the day the state of Israel was concerned about looking too Jewish," McCarter commented.

"I think it's an effort to try to present the impression Israel is tolerant of other religions and respects the beliefs of the Arabs visiting Tel Aviv," the Cuban said. "Nice gesture, but they're presenting the terrorists with an ideal chance to take out all the VIPs with one fell swoop."

"So we know where they'll probably strike," Bolan agreed. He glanced at the stack of data sheets. "What's all this, Rafael?"

"We tried to gather as much information as possible because we couldn't be sure what might be useful," Encizo explained. "There's a computer-enhanced photo print from an NSA satellite with an orbit across Tel Aviv. Reports of individuals crossing the borders and activity in the harbors have been included."

"That's covering a lot, and most of it will be completely useless," Bolan commented. "I assume this went through computer evaluation so the most promising material has been separated from the least likely to do us any good.''

"Yeah," the Cuban confirmed. "Maybe the most interesting item is one of the most recent entries."

He scanned the top sheet and easily found the item highlighted with yellow liner. Written in Hebrew with an English translation, Encizo read it aloud.

"'Entry at the border with Gaza,'" he began. "'Zero-one-twenty-four hours. A truck crossed from Egypt to Israel. Vehicle was searched and found to contain machine parts for an air-conditioner unit, supposedly for a large mosque in the Jaffa section of Tel Aviv.'"

"Same area as the clock tower," Bolan remarked. "They rolled across the border only four hours ago? Could have been members of Jinn 2000 from Cairo."

"Why the hell would they wait so long to set up their weapon?" McCarter asked, puzzled by the situation. "The city is swarming with security and bound to be more risky now."

"One can look at that two ways," Bolan mused. "If they brought the device into Israel months ago, there would be the risk of having it discovered, as well. Perhaps they figured this was a bigger problem. Mossad and other intelligence agencies have been preparing for the meeting for some time. They've been searching for bombs, sniper weapons and the usual terrorist and disgruntled-lunatic forms of assassination. The longer the SHC weapon was in Tel Aviv, the more likely it would be spotted by some nosy cop, soldier or potential informer."

"There's also the possibility they only have one weapon," Encizo added. "They needed the SHC device to carry out those demonstrations in Cairo and recruit more members. Pushing it to the wire and racing the clock, but terrorists are all at least a little loco.''

''More than a little in the case of Jinn 2000,'' Bolan said. ''I don't know if they're crazy enough to actually give us the location where they plan to set up.''

''The Jaffa section is a major Arab sector in Tel Aviv,'' McCarter said. ''May have made the border guards suspicious if they had said anything else. Have to have a pretty good reason to order an air-conditioning unit from Egypt instead of having a local system put in. Arabs wanting Arabs to handle everything associated with a mosque wouldn't seem unusual to anyone in the Middle East.''

''Did they record the license-plate number and number of men in the vehicle?'' Bolan asked.

''That's here,'' Encizo answered, nodding. ''Even emphasized their search of the truck. No guns, no explosives, stuff in the back appeared to be hollow tubes, a temperature-control unit and a crate with dry ice.''

''The cone to the muzzle was probably in there,'' Bolan said. ''Any other vehicles cross from Egypt after the truck entered Israel?''

''Yeah,'' Encizo confirmed. ''All searched and let through. A fair number of Egyptians want to witness the event. They've had a peace agreement with Israel for some time now, and the guards don't generally have any reason to be terribly suspicious of Egyptians. Hard to say how many Jinn 2000 members slipped across.''

''Or how many were already here,'' McCarter

added. "Well, we have about six hours to find them before they have their goodwill ceremony at the clock tower. I'm signed up for a Cobra helicopter. I can help scan the area from the air, and we should get cooperation from the Israelis for a manhunt."

"Let's hope we get lucky," Encizo remarked. "A lot of agents, police and troopers are on the streets right now. Maybe some of them saw the terrorists unload their truck."

"Well," Bolan said, "we've got our work cut out for us. When Gary and T.J. finish their jobs with the Israelis, we'll need them to help comb the city. Cal might take longer with the interrogation of Ziyyon. We can't rush him, and he'll need to get a translation from Lavi before he'll know exactly what information Ziyyon has for us."

"Be nice if he told us where the terrorists will set up, how many we can expect to come up against and what kind of weapons they'll have aside from the SHC device," McCarter commented. "At least the SHC microwaves are only dangerous to someone carrying one of those synthetic crystals."

"Maybe not," Bolan said. "We don't know what would happen if they dropped a couple quartz crystals down the drain of a sink and used the device to set off a fusion effect on the hydrogen and oxygen in the water. It might blow out the plumbing of an entire building. Whether that would make the walls cave in is a matter of speculation unless the terrorists actually do it."

"At least we know it doesn't cause oxygen and hydrogen in the air to ignite into flame," Encizo remarked. "It must need to have those elements concentrated in a solid or perhaps liquid form."

"I'm glad to hear some good news," McCarter muttered. "It's not much, but I reckon I'll take what I can get at this point."

CHAPTER TWENTY-THREE

Captain Jadallah al-Qatrun peered from the gap between curtains to gaze out the window. Tel Aviv seemed very different from Tripoli or even Cairo. The buildings appeared more modern, more Western. Not all, of course. Qatrun had studied the capital city of Israel and realized many sites were hundreds of years old.

The monastery of St. Peter in the Jaffa section had been built by Crusaders when the Europeans attempted to claim Palestine in the thirteenth century. The clock tower and Mahmudiye Mosque were remnants of Ottoman rule. Indeed, Qatrun had read that archaeologists had discovered tombs and relics that suggested the area of Tel Aviv had been occupied by prehistoric humans before the Bronze Age. Legend claimed the area had been founded by Japheth, the son of Noah, after the Great Flood. Jonah had been swallowed by the great fish in the Mediterranean and vomited up along the shore by Jaffa.

Yet the Libyan captain saw little evidence the Israelis truly cared about their ancient and varied history of the land they called a Jewish state. He regarded them as Europeans with no more right to claim any territory in the Middle East than the Romans, the British or the French. The Westerners had occupied lands Qatrun believed to be the birthright of the desert people. The Arabs, Berbers and Kurds had lived in the region since the cradle of civilization began along the Tigris and Euphrates rivers.

Qatrun didn't care what claims the Jews made to the land they called Israel. In his opinion they had fled the Middle East to become Europeans. They started to return in large numbers during the twentieth century and finally flooded in after World War II. The Holocaust gave the Jews widespread sympathy, and the Europeans supported their desire for a homeland due to a sense of guilt, in Qatrun's opinion. The British had occupied Palestine and surrendered it to the Jews. The Americans helped the new state of Israel in 1948, and the U.S. continued to support the Jews with economic and military aid.

Infidels helping other infidels conspire against Arab Muslims—that was Qatrun's view of recent history in the Middle East. Yet he believed the Israelis and the Americans served as a test for the strength and spirit of Muslims and the desert people. Just as the Europeans and Turks once ruled their lands, the Arabs needed to endure and hold fast to their faith in God and divine justice.

Most didn't meet this challenge. Arab nations were seduced by the wealth and comforts offered by the Americans and Europeans interested in the oil trade. Others embraced support from the Soviet Union, which brought a godless doctrine of communism along with assistance motivated by a desire to use Arabs as pawns for a cold war.

Only a comparatively small number proved to be true believers, and Qatrun felt certain he was among the elite few. He had remained a devout Shiite although the majority of Libyans were Sunni Muslims. Qatrun believed the incredible spontaneous-combustion weapon would allow the Jinn 2000 followers to finally claim their just reward.

He relished the destruction of his enemies as he stared at the rows of large, box-shaped buildings along the city streets. Qatrun had crossed the border into Israel before, but he had never seen Tel Aviv until that day. It resembled photographs he had seen of European cities, perhaps Rome or Athens. That disgusted him even more because the Jews seemed to emulate a life-style of the former oppressors of the Middle East.

The captain was surprised to see so many vehicles in the street at such a late hour. People owned more cars in Cairo than in Tripoli, and the number seemed even greater in Tel Aviv. He hadn't expected to see so many signs written in Arabic and English, as well as Hebrew.

"Captain Qatrun?" a voice spoke softly. "We have assembled the fire of God, sir."

The Libyan turned to face the other men in the room. They stood by the tube barrel, box controls and cone muzzle of the fantastic device of destruction by glorious flame. Qatrun smiled with approval.

"It is a shame Professor Barrah is not here to see this," a Jinn 2000 hardman remarked.

"Yes," Qatrun agreed. "A shame."

He knew the Saudi scientist didn't belong in the field. Barrah was an intellectual, best suited for laboratories and research libraries. Qatrun admired the man's mind, dedication and Shiite devotion, but the physicist was no soldier.

Qatrun didn't regret the absence of Sabkhat. He neither liked nor trusted the banker from the United Arab Emirates. Sabkhat thought he was so clever the other members of Jinn 2000 couldn't see through his masquerade. Qatrun grudgingly admitted they needed the banker for his ability at finance and organizational skills. Yet Sabkhat had his own agenda and plans for Jinn 2000 that had nothing to do with the sect's effort to fulfill a righteous destiny. Qatrun wasn't certain what the sly bastard's scheme might be, but he suspected when it was discovered, Qatrun would probably decide to put a bullet in the man's head.

"Captain," someone said, "I think you should find a different place to oversee the mission."

"This is where I choose to stay, Amir," he replied. "I am a battlefield commander. I would not ask my men to take risks I myself would be afraid to take. Besides, I want to personally trigger the weapon and strike down the infidels' leaders with the fire of God."

"I appreciate your zeal, sir," Amir began, "but I fear the future if anything happens to you. You are our military commander, our general, despite the rank you hold in the Libyan army. You are too important to risk losing if anything goes wrong."

"If a true Shiite dies in battle against the infidels, he will be delivered to Paradise," Qatrun replied. "There is no reason to fear death. If we die today, we will be with God in his kingdom. We won't even have to wait for Judgment Day."

"Your courage and faith are admirable," another hardman stated, "but you must consider the whole movement and your vital status, Captain."

"We are all expendable. No individual is so important to this cause he cannot be killed today. This movement is to carry out the will of God. That will shall be done. We need only believe in it and do our duty to God and Jinn 2000."

"I wish we were better armed," Amir commented. "We don't even have enough pistols to arm all our men. There were supposed to be more weapons for us."

Qatrun nodded. He felt concern about this fact, as well. Their agent inside Israeli Intelligence was supposed to have planted a cache of assault rifles and grenades for the Jinn 2000 assassination team. Something had to have happened to the undercover agent.

He and the others couldn't bring any weapons across the border from Egypt. Qatrun carried only his dagger when he arrived at Tel Aviv. Fortunately some Jinn 2000 members had already been stationed in Israel and they provided what weapons they could, but their firepower was far less than expected. Qatrun realized that meant the entire mission could be in jeopardy. But he couldn't allow the scarcity of weapons to keep him from carrying out what he believed to be the will of God. The captain hoped the undercover agent had successfully prepared the special quartz crystals necessary for the SHC effect.

If they were discovered by the infidels, it would make little difference if they didn't have automatic weapons and grenades. Tel Aviv was filled with security forces of the Israelis, Americans and various Arab nations. A small army would descend upon the Jinn 2000 operatives if the enemy located them. They would have no chance against such a large number of opponents.

Yet if they died for the sake of their divine mission, Qatrun believed that would also be part of God's cosmic plan. Perhaps a sacrifice would be necessary. The blood of the faithful seemed to be the price sometimes. There had been many great Shiite martyrs in the past, and Qatrun would accept his fate if he was meant to join their ranks.

He looked at the SHC machine. Soon he would have a chance to accomplish the greatest mission of his life. What devout Shiite wouldn't welcome an opportunity to fulfill a prophecy of one of his faith's dervishes? What soldier would not march to war for his God instead of simply serving a government of human frailty?

Qatrun had never been so eager for battle. In a few hours they would strike a blow that would change the world forever.

MAJOR ZIYYON SAT on a cot in a cell. He wore a different uniform than the garb of a military field-grade officer. Dressed in gray prison wear, the man seemed smaller and stripped of his former arrogance. Perhaps it was an aftereffect from the scopolamine, but the major had good reason to feel depressed and defeated.

The cell door was open, and Mack Bolan and Calvin James stood on the threshold. Captain Lavi also waited in the corridor outside the cell. None of them carried weapons, due to prison security regulations. Ziyyon wasn't in good enough shape to try to take on three opponents after his bout with truth serum and an ankle bandaged because of torn tendons. He gazed up at the trio with bloodshot, red-tinted eyes.

"Gamel Jizah," Lavi began. "That is your real

name? You revealed that during interrogation. Actually you conversed mostly in Hebrew. I suppose you have used it far more than your parents' language over the years. Your Arabic even seemed a bit rusty.''

"I doubt a court will accept information acquired through the use of truth serum," Ziyyon commented in a slurred voice. "What you did may not even be legal.''

"You may not see a courtroom, traitor.''

"He's not a traitor," Bolan stated. "He was acting as an agent against the state of Israel, but his allegiance was to another country and eventually a fanatic cause. You can charge him with espionage and conspiracy against the state, but he isn't really a traitor.''

Ziyyon managed a weak smile. "Thank you for that much, Belasko," he said. "I suppose you're very proud of yourself for correctly guessing just about everything about me.''

"It wasn't that hard after I had enough facts to put the puzzle together," Bolan replied.

"Espionage against the state of Israel is also a capital offense," Lavi declared. "You're in a very bad position, Jizah.''

"A trial could be embarrassing for Mossad, as well as Aman," the prisoner remarked. "You Jews like to pretend this government is blessed by God and you never make any mistakes. It would be easier if I 'committed suicide' in my cell.''

"That may be an option," Lavi replied.

"I'd rather not be hanged. Perhaps I could be shot trying to escape instead.''

"Let's change the subject," James suggested.

"We know all about your involvement in the Jinn 2000 conspiracy and how you started out as a sleeper agent for Arab governments and eventually became part of these fanatics. You know we found the crystals, so the SHC microwaves won't make the VIPs go up in a burst of fiery glory to delight your comrades."

"So you came here to gloat?" Ziyyon asked. "Did you enjoy yourselves?"

"We're here to see if you can give us any additional information you didn't include while under the influence of scopolamine," Bolan began. "Memory is a tricky and mysterious matter. The truth drugs can dredge up your deepest secrets and even things you're not aware you know by reaching into the subconscious. Yet some information readily held in your conscious mind can sometimes be bypassed by the drug."

"You expect me to help you willingly?" Ziyyon asked with amusement. "Why should I? This man already wants to see me dead."

"As an enemy of Israel," Lavi said with a nod. "Of course I do."

"I once asked my mother if it was my fate to die as a Shiite agent against the Jews," Ziyyon stated, "but she did not know my destiny."

"To be honest," Bolan told him, "I'm not happy with the idea of making a deal with you. I saw those soldiers at the West Bank burn because you planted those crystals in their gear. I figure you've done enough to deserve to pay with your life, one way or the other. Life in prison would be okay by me. Might be harder for you than to face a firing squad or a hangman's noose."

"Then why would I care if they decide to sentence me to life instead of execution?"

"Because as long as you're alive, there's a chance you'll be set free," Bolan explained. "You know how the world of espionage works. Spies are exchanged like commodities. One country holds another's agent, questions him and gets what information possible, then trades him for another agent, one of their own, who was taken prisoner by the other side. Everybody compares data gathered by their agents to assess damage to national security and to find out how much the spies managed to learn and not share with their captors."

"I know how that game is played," Ziyyon replied. "I also know it doesn't work if your country doesn't want you back. My original homeland was Egypt, but that was when Nasser was president. It is different now. None of the old goals remain. Everything changed under Sadat."

"And it might change again," Bolan said with a shrug. "That's the nature of world politics. If anything, things changed more rapidly and drastically since the end of the cold war. There's also the chance some other country may be willing to trade for you. Maybe Iraq or Iran."

"There's always the chance you might escape," James added.

Lavi cast an angry gaze at the tall African-American.

"Just trying to be helpful," James assured him.

"I haven't heard all of the tape," Ziyyon said, "so I'm not even certain how much I might have told you under the influence of the drug."

"You mentioned the key players in the Jinn 2000

conspiracy are a couple characters named Professor Barrah and Captain Qatrun,'' Bolan replied. ''We knew about both of them before, but we didn't know the captain's name or that he's an officer in the Libyan army. You confirmed they plan to strike at the conference, and they have targeted the VIPs when they gather at the clock tower. We had that much figured out already. We didn't guess you were supposed to deliver a cache of weapons to them.''

''I would have had trouble managing that even if you hadn't arrested me,'' Ziyyon admitted. ''Being forced to put Colonel Paran out of action long enough to personally sabotage the communications gear put me on a rather busy schedule. You see, originally I would have assisted in the chore and would have been able to do it without drawing much attention. Thanks to your friend Katzenelenbogen and those bungling idiots who failed to take you out in Cairo, I was under house arrest or at least restriction. I rather regretted having to poison the colonel. Paran isn't a bad fellow for a Jew.''

''I'm sure he'll be glad to hear that,'' James remarked. ''You may also be glad to hear he's going to recover from those poisonous mushrooms you slipped him.''

''Good,'' Ziyyon said with a shrug, already uninterested. ''It was the only way I could put myself in a position to plant the quartz crystals. We would have succeeded if you hadn't been involved, Belasko.''

''Well, you didn't,'' Bolan replied. ''Where are the Jinn 2000 going to set up their machine, Major?''

''I don't know,'' Ziyyon replied. ''There was no reason for them to tell me.''

"How many weapons did you plan to supply them with?" Bolan asked.

"I don't recall the exact number," Ziyyon said. "Didn't I tell you where I had the weapons stored and where the drop was supposed to be made?"

"You had the weapons hidden at the old cemetery on Pinsker Street," Lavi declared. "Our men found it at a mausoleum under the name Silverstein— thirty-one assault rifles, twenty submachine guns, eighteen pistols and almost four hundred kilos of ammunition, grenades and other explosives."

"If you already knew," Ziyyon stated, "why did you ask?"

"To see how cooperative you'd be," James answered. "You talk more and have a better memory when you're drugged, pal. The drop was supposed to be by the opera house. They found a vehicle that fits the description and license plates of a suspicious rig that crossed the border a few hours ago. We think it brought in the SHC machine and a couple of your terrorist buddies."

"Terrorists?" Ziyyon asked with a smile. "That's the term you use. We consider ourselves soldiers against the Jewish oppressors and their infidel allies."

"Too bad, Major," Bolan began. "It doesn't look like you have much information for us we don't already have. That means you don't have anything to bargain with."

"You can kill me," Ziyyon admitted, "but Jinn 2000 will win eventually because we won't stop until the prophecies of Omar and the will of God have been fulfilled. Kill me and I'll be in Paradise and your souls will be condemned to spend eternity in hell.''

"If you'll excuse us," Bolan said, "we've got a lot of work to do."

CHAPTER TWENTY-FOUR

The photograph of the control box wouldn't have received much attention under ordinary circumstances. However, Mack Bolan was very interested in anything connected with the SHC machine. Katz had faxed the photo from Saudi Arabia.

"The controls on this thing aren't too fancy," Hawkins remarked as he gazed over Bolan's shoulder. "Has a simple on-off button and a light to signal when the power has reached high level to transmit the concentrated microwaves. That dial on the right allows you to adjust the length and width of the waves. Of course, microwaves are comparatively short wave transmissions."

"To be honest," Bolan stated, "I don't know much about microwaves. How short is the wavelength?"

"Generally limited to about one yard," the Phoenix Force electronics whiz replied.

"One yard?" the Executioner said with surprise. "I've seen this SHC weapon in action. It's taken out victims from a distance at least ten times greater."

"Yeah," Hawkins replied. "You've got to give that guy Barrah credit. He came up with a hell of an advanced version of a concept that's been around since about 1931. You might say Barrah made an innovation with the microwave similar to the laser beam with concentrated light. Since the only working model of the device is in the hands of Jinn 2000, we don't know the exact range, but Barrah apparently believed it could transmit up to half a kilometer.''

"It could be worse," the Executioner said with a shrug. "What about the width of these waves? If they're concentrated for greater distance, that would probably limit the span width-wise."

"Only about five yards," Hawkins stated, "but that's small comfort because the machine is built on a pivot base. It can swing across in any direction without a break in the power of the wavelength itself. Sort of like spraying a burning building with a fire-hose in reverse. The SHC microwaves just keep going and trigger any substance with organic hydrogen elements suitable for the fusion process, so long as that substance is equipped with those quartz crystals we pried out of Ziyyon's sabotaged communications gear.''

"You're sure you got them all?" McCarter asked. "Security people from several nations were supposed to be issued those transceivers, as well as the VIP diplomats and heads of state."

"We got all the stuff Ziyyon monkeyed with, David," Hawkins assured him. "The problem is, we don't know if Jinn 2000 has other people already in place in Israel who may have planted more crystals we don't know about. Unfortunately the amount of knowledge about the system is limited to what the other scientists at the Saudi project had observed. Only Barrah really knows what the machine can do."

"Or exactly what 'organic hydrogen' includes,"

Gary Manning added as he joined the conversation. "We know it doesn't cause a fusion reaction with hydrogen found in the air, but that's about all we know for sure. Obviously it works on humans and swine. That means there's a good chance it would cause a sort of atomic spontaneous-combustion effect on anything with an organic composition similar to that of most warm-blooded mammals."

Bolan sighed as he glanced at the grim faces of the three Phoenix Force commandos and Captain Lavi. Once again they had decided to use the Mossad officer's room for the conversation. It wasn't the Stony Man Farm War Room, but it would have to do. Bolan tapped a finger on the photo next to a switch marked by a word written in Arabic.

"What's this?" he asked. "My Arabic is pretty poor, but this looks like the word for 'danger' to me."

"It is," Lavi confirmed. "Perhaps that switch is to shut down power if it reaches a critical level. We know so little about this machine. Perhaps it could blow up somehow."

"There's a note enclosed that explains that," Manning began. "The machine won't blow up exactly. It's powered by a fairly conventional electrical battery and not much chance it will malfunction based on the data we have. However, if that switch is thrown, it will cause the microwaves to remain confined within the machine as the power level rises. The outside hull is metal, and we all know what happens to a microwave oven when metal is cooked in it."

"Sparks ignite and the oven burns itself out,"

McCarter replied. "You mean this machine would burn out its own mechanical guts?"

"On a much higher level," Hawkins stated. "The strength of the microwaves is so great it would vaporize the entire internal portions of the machine. Might even melt the hull. Throw that switch, and in a couple minutes you won't have anything left except a gutted chunk of hot metal or perhaps a pool of molten slop."

"Self-destruct mechanism," Bolan mused. "Barrah must have designed the weapon so it would be destroyed if anything went wrong. He might have done that originally to stop the fusion process if he saw a serious danger occur during the machine transmissions for the experiments in his lab. Probably figures this will keep it from falling into the hands of the infidels in an emergency."

"Fanatics," Lavi said with disgust.

"Is there a photo of the entire device?" Bolan asked.

"Yeah," Hawkins confirmed. "It's pretty much like the sketch you saw before. You'll find it in the stack somewhere."

The soldier shuffled through the pile and soon found the photo. It was a fax copy, but the details were clear enough. Bolan grunted, less than pleased by what he saw.

"This isn't the same machine I saw in Cairo," he announced.

"Bloody hell," McCarter muttered. "I thought you said it was before."

"That was when I saw the sketch. The machine in this photo is silver. The weapon I saw in Cairo is gunmetal gray."

"Maybe they painted it for camouflage," Lavi suggested.

"No," Bolan insisted, "this machine is different. The barrel and control box are larger. It seems longer, as well. Barrah and his Jinn 2000 comrades have at least one more weapon. Probably made a slightly more compact and darker-color model than the prototype."

"So even if we find these bastards and get their machine," McCarter said, "we still have to worry about the terrorists using SHC technology in the future."

"We'll deal with that later," Bolan replied. "We still have the Jinn 2000 hit team here in Tel Aviv to cope with for now. The effective range of the SHC microwave is approximately half a kilometer. Correct?"

"That's what Barrah claimed when he was still working on the project back in Arabia," Hawkins answered with a shrug.

"Let's assume he was probably right about that," the soldier said. "After all, you said the normal range for a microwave is only a yard or so. Considering the limited range, it seems likely the enemy would try to get as close as they dared to be sure the SHC device would be effective."

"That might be pretty close," Lavi remarked. "Shiite fanatics tend to be among the most suicidal. They believe martyrs get a special reward from God if they die while trying to kill infidels."

"Maybe we can help some of them achieve that goal," McCarter commented as he lighted a Player's cigarette.

"We have to find them first," Manning told him.

The big Canadian scanned a wall map of Tel Aviv and used a pen to circle a portion of the southwest coastal region. "This is probably where we'll find the terrorists. That's not a very large area. A house-to-house, building-to-building search ought to locate them."

"There are sure plenty of security forces, cops and soldiers for a search," Hawkins added. "Luckily Ziyyon didn't get to deliver those weapons and explosives to the enemy. He sure had a load of hardware stored away."

"He's probably been preparing for something like this for years," Bolan said. "Don't assume the terrorists won't be heavily armed. Gunrunners in the Middle East are as prolific as carpet merchants. The Jinn 2000 members already in Israel prior to the arrival of Captain Qatrun, and the SHC machine, would have had ample opportunity to assemble quite an arsenal."

"Perhaps," Lavi said, "but we certainly outnumber them. If the terrorists want a fight, there's no doubt who will be the victor."

"Yeah," Bolan agreed, eyes on the map, "but we don't want to have any more bloodshed than necessary. There are some mosques located near the clock tower. Might be a good idea to have Arab agents search them."

"You think the terrorists would launch an attack from a mosque?" Hawkins asked with a frown. "I know these Jinn 2000 loonies are real bad guys, but they're still Muslims. The fact they're fanatics would probably mean they'd be even less likely to do anything in a mosque."

"But," Bolan said, "they consider killing infidels

to be a righteous act, encouraged by their prophets and their dogma in general. Jinn 2000 members figure they're doing God's will, so they won't see anything wrong if they carry out their killing from his house.''

"Belasko is right," Lavi agreed. "He's also right when he suggests it would be best if members of the Arab security personnel check the mosques for terrorists. It would be good public relations for my government, and it demonstrates faith in the Arabs who claim they're interested in peace in the Middle East. If synagogues had to be searched for enemy terrorists, I'd certainly prefer it be done by Jews. The Muslims would probably feel much the same about who searches the mosques."

"Fine," McCarter said as he jammed his cigarette butt into an ashtray. "So what do the rest of us do?"

Bolan traced the circle on the map as he spoke. "We need this ring covered—roadblocks, foot patrols and boats in the harbor. Cut off any escape routes for the terrorists and prevent any reinforcements from coming in to back them up."

"You think that's likely?" Lavi asked with a frown.

"We don't know how many enemies we're dealing with," the Executioner replied. "Better to assume a large number rather than underestimate their strength. Besides, I want to put the various security forces somewhere they might do more good than harm. A lot of those guys are basic bodyguards. I'm sure they're all very brave and very loyal to their leaders, but that doesn't mean they'd know what the hell they need to do for a job like this."

"Yeah," Manning agreed. "There's also the problem about trying to get all those different police, soldiers, bodyguards and government agents to work together. That can be hard enough to do when everybody is working for pretty much the same government. The rivalry between federal agencies and their counterparts in provinces or states is incredible."

"It's worse between different Intel outfits," McCarter added. "Those blokes don't trust anybody. That's the nature of their profession. That situation is even worse when so many governments of Middle Eastern countries are involved. If you just distrust one another in this part of the world, you're doing pretty well. Better than outright hatred."

"I might find that comment offensive if it wasn't true," Lavi said with a sigh. "Nobody in this room is a diplomat, so I won't waste time trying to deny anything. You're probably right. Putting most of the security forces on glorified guard duty might ease possible conflicts within their ranks, but it will also reduce the number of men we can use for searching the area within that circle."

"We don't need a huge number to do that effectively," Bolan told him. "If they see a large group of armed troops, they'll be more apt to start shooting and throwing bombs. An obvious house-to-house search will tip them off. Better if you have enough men out in the streets to get their attention, distract them without triggering an extreme response."

"And what will this accomplish?" the Mossad officer asked.

"It'll give us a chance to hit the enemy more or less off guard," Bolan replied. "My friends and I have a lot of experience at this sort of thing, Captain.''

''Damn right,'' McCarter confirmed. ''Handled dozens of situations like this all over the world. You can see we're good at it because we're still alive.''

''That's very impressive,'' Lavi told him, ''but there is a rather obvious problem. How will you know where the terrorists are located?''

The Executioner shrugged and said, ''We can't tell for sure, but we can select the most likely sites. The SHC microwave is narrow enough it will have to be aimed at the targets to be sure they can try to take out all the intended victims. That means they'll want an elevated position with a clear view of the clock tower.''

''That still includes a number of structures,'' the Israeli said.

''Not as many as you might think at first glance,'' Manning told him. The Canadian studied the map and realized Bolan's logic. ''The Great Mosque and the Siksik Mosque are within the circle, but we already agreed they should be searched by Arab Muslims. Just make sure you've got good people on that job. Most of the other buildings in the area aren't tall enough.''

''There's St. Peter's Church, the archaeological museum and a Greek Orthodox monastery in the Artists' Quarter,'' Hawkins observed. ''All would certainly be tall enough and offer a good view of the tower at right angles.''

''And,'' Bolan added, ''I'm sure security has been beefed up for the conference. A band of terrorists could still manage to sneak into any or all of those sites, but they'd have a tough time smuggling in crates containing the parts to the SHC device. Nobody is going to believe a delivery of machine parts or an air-conditioner system at 0400 hours. Not so soon before a conference that has everyone worried about security."

"The monks would sure be suspicious even if Mossad doesn't have it covered," Manning remarked. "I think Belasko's right. The terrorists have some other site for their attack position."

"That's not to say those places shouldn't be searched, too," Bolan stated. "The coastline needs to be covered, as well. There's a possibility the enemy may use a boat to launch the attack. Personally I think it more likely they'll make their play from a building to the north of the tower."

"Why north?" Lavi asked. "There are a few tall buildings in the Artists' Quarter to the south even if you rule out those already mentioned."

"The Artists' Quarter is also going to be crowded with thousands of people, including hundreds of security and crowd-control officers for the conference," Bolan explained. "They can use a crowd to try to get lost among the startled masses and attempt an escape, but that also raises the risk of being seen and recognized when they attempt it. The crowd to the north will be smaller, and their odds of escape will be greater if they head in that direction."

"And there are two buildings tall enough located on Elat Street," Manning stated. "They both appear to be office buildings of some kind."

"We need as much information on them as possible," Bolan declared. "Time is running out. The conference is scheduled in about three hours."

"Have you considered the possibility you and

your five friends might be seriously outnumbered if you go after these killers?'' Lavi asked.

"Actually," the Executioner replied, "it'll only be three of my friends. The other two are uniquely qualified to join the patrols at sea. We'll worry about the odds when we see what they are. We need that information on the Elat Street buildings.''

CHAPTER TWENTY-FIVE

Sunlight reflected off the surface of the Mediterranean Sea and seemed to cast hundreds of brilliant jewels across the water. Rafael Encizo would have enjoyed the morning boat trip had circumstances been different. The green-blue sea reminded him of the Caribbean. As a boy, he had swum and fished in the sea, where even the tyranny of Castro's Communist government seemed to vanish for a while.

The Phoenix Force commando couldn't spare many thoughts on pleasant reminiscence or gazing at the beauty of nature. The motorboat approached a trawler off the coast of Tel Aviv, between the shore of the Jaffa section and Andromeda Rock. The latter was a large stony fist that jutted above the water about a hundred yards from the shoreline.

The rock owed its name to Greek mythology. According to the colorful tale, Andromeda, daughter of Cepheus the king, was chained to the rock to be sacrificed to a sea monster. Perseus, the hero of Argos and slayer of the dreaded Medusa, arrived in time to save her, mounted on the amazing winged horse, Pegasus. Still a romantic despite years of hardship, loss and the harsh reality of combat, Encizo liked the story.

However, the trawler wasn't a vessel from Greek

mythology, and the men on board might be Jinn 2000 terrorists disguised as fishermen. The boat had approached close to shore, closer than trawl fishing permitted. The craft was within the half-kilometer radius estimated to be effective range for the SHC microwave.

Crowds had already begun to assemble near the clock tower to wait for the historic meeting of heads of state and diplomats. Perhaps the fishing trawler had moved closer to observe the event. Encizo noticed the nets to the boat were out of the water. The crew wasn't fishing, but that didn't mean they were terrorists.

"How many you figure are on board?" James asked as he stepped next to the Cuban.

"The trawler is about ten yards from stem to stern," Encizo replied. "I'm not sure how many cabins it has or if the hull is empty or really contains a catch of fish. Could be any number from eight to twenty...depending on what they're really doing."

Harry Coburn looked at the weapons carried by the Stony Man warriors. Armed with Uzi submachine guns, Walther P-88 pistols in shoulder leather and fighting knives, the pair appeared ready for battle. Half a dozen Israeli paratroopers aboard the patrol boat had also suited up for combat, complete with military hardware. The CIA case officer had been issued a pump-action Remington shotgun in addition to his SIG-Sauer P-226. Yet Coburn felt uncomfortable with the weapons, and the possibility of combat terrified him.

The Company man had never fired his pistol except at a firing range. Like many CIA operatives, he had joined the Central Intelligence Agency when he graduated from college. He had never served in the military, and his background in weapons, martial arts and survival training was minimal. Coburn was accustomed to duty behind a desk at the embassy, not work in the field.

The agent had agreed to join the patrol boat to serve as a representative of the CIA, and he spoke fluent Hebrew, as well as Arabic. He hoped the crew on the trawler would prove to be harmless fishermen so he wouldn't have to participate in any violence.

Several figures appeared along the handrail on the port side of the trawler. They seemed to be young, tough and suspicious. Their Semitic features and dark complexions could have belonged to either Arabs or Jews. An Israeli greeted them in Hebrew. A crew member replied, apparently with some difficulty with the language and not much enthusiasm.

"They agreed to let us on board," Coburn explained, aware James and Encizo didn't understand Hebrew. "I can tell by the accent the guy who spoke is an Arab."

"Lot of Arabs live in Israel," James commented. "It doesn't mean he's not a real fisherman. The fact he doesn't care to have a bunch of Israeli soldiers on his boat doesn't mean anything, either."

"Stay alert just in case," Encizo cautioned.

The patrol boat pulled alongside the trawler, and Encizo and James prepared to climb aboard the other vessel. The men clad in fisherman's gear didn't carry firearms, although they all had sheathed knives on their belts. Faces at the cabin portholes revealed that other men aboard hadn't come on deck.

Three Israelis accompanied the Phoenix Force commandos as they crossed over the space between vessels. One by one they jumped across the gap to the trawler. The fishermen made no attempt to stop them. Coburn and the other troopers remained on the patrol boat.

Encizo landed surefooted on the deck of the fishing vessel. The crew glared at the Uzi that hung from a shoulder strap, the holstered Walther under his left arm and the Tanto fighting knife in a cross-draw position on his belt. A burly figure with a beard and white cap stepped forward to speak to the Israeli lieutenant in the group. Encizo wondered if the guy was really a fishing-boat captain or if he had merely selected the wardrobe for the occasion. His black turtleneck shirt and chino pants seemed too heavy for the hot weather. He spoke briefly with the officer.

"What are you?" the captain suddenly addressed them in heavily accented English. "American CIA? You have no business on my boat."

"Our President is going to be over there in an hour or so," James replied. "Protecting him is our business, Captain. I'm sorry about this disturbance, but we have to make sure this vessel doesn't present any threat to him or the others at the peace conference."

The captain glared at the Americans. Encizo shrugged. He appreciated the man's outrage at their bullying tactics on his craft. Yet they were acting within the legal framework of Israeli law, which allowed emergency search and seizure without a warrant due to an antiterrorist act. The skipper would have to tolerate them until they were satisfied the boat presented no danger.

"We have to check out the boat," Encizo told him. "The sooner we do it, the sooner we'll leave."

The captain muttered something in Arabic and stomped toward the foredeck. Encizo and the Israeli lieutenant followed. James and the remaining soldiers moved aft, in search of the catch hold. They were aware that a number of the crew still watched from portholes.

Encizo and the Israeli officer followed the captain up a short ladder to the fly bridge. A lanky mate stood by the control console, hands loosely gripping the wheel. He glanced at the strangers and turned his attention to the controls. The engines had been shut down, and the boat wasn't moving. Encizo doubted the guy had a special fascination with tachometers and oil gauges. He seemed to be trying too hard to act uninterested with the visitors.

"Will you at least tell me what you're looking for?" the skipper asked gruffly. "Opium? Stolen plutonium? We do have a few guns on board. Sometimes sharks get in our nets and we have to shoot them."

"What kind of guns?" the lieutenant asked, his tone suspicious.

The boat captain explained, shifting into Arabic when he failed to come up with the right terms in English. Encizo glanced about the bridge, his gaze falling upon a canvas tarp draped across a lumpy shape on the floor. He knelt by the tarp and peeled it back to reveal two video cameras and a stack of metal stalks.

"You making a documentary, Captain?" Encizo asked.

The skipper's body became stiff as he watched the Cuban examine the camera gear. Encizo discovered the metal poles were tripods for the video machines. Another stalk held a microphone at one end. The mate looked over his shoulder at Encizo, his eyes wide with surprise or perhaps alarm.

"We make some videotapes occasionally," the captain stated. "That's not against the law."

"You have a boom mike," Encizo remarked. "That's pretty fancy. These are expensive machines, too. Looks like they're brand-new. Plan to film something special today?"

"The peace conference is an interesting event," the captain said with a shrug.

"Long-range lens for the cameras, too," Encizo continued. "I'd say you had to be very interested in the conference. Maybe we should stay here while you film. We can all enjoy the view you have of the clock tower and see what happens. Figure there will be anything special? Something unexpected?"

"Such as murder?" the Israeli added. "Perhaps assassination by fire? *Hariah?*"

The mention of "fire" in Arabic drew an immediate response from the mate. He suddenly abandoned the wheel and control panel to reach for a drawer next to the console. Encizo bolted toward him as the mate produced an old Enfield revolver from the drawer.

The Cuban grabbed the Uzi as he approached and swung the heavy steel frame at the man's forearm and wrist. The blow landed before the mate could aim his antique wheel gun. The revolver roared and blasted a .38 slug into a wood cabinet an instant before it slipped from numb fingers. Encizo pumped a knee into the mate's gut and delivered another swipe with the frame of the SMG. The Uzi struck his opponent in the side of the skull and dropped him to the floor in a senseless heap.

Encizo turned to discover the boat captain rushing toward him. A mass of angry muscle, clenched teeth and furious eyes, the skipper seemed to have swelled into a giant attacker. Light flashed along a blade in his right fist to warn Encizo the man wouldn't rely on size and strength alone.

The captain's left hand grabbed the frame of Encizo's Uzi to shove the barrel toward the ceiling as he plunged the knife toward the Cuban's ribs. Encizo's left hand snared the wrist above the knife fist to prevent the deadly thrust, but the force of the Arab's charge drove both men off balance. Encizo's back connected with the console with his opponent's weight against his chest.

Hot breath assaulted Encizo's face. The captain grunted and snarled like a rabid beast as they struggled.

The little Cuban rammed a knee into his opponent's midsection, but the captain barely reacted. He hit him again, driving the knee under the guy's rib cage. The captain's body shifted from the painful blow and eased the crushing weight from Encizo's chest. He used the console against his back for leverage and shoved a boot into the big man's belly.

The captain staggered backward. More by accident than design, his wrist pushed Encizo's thumb to break the hold, although the Arab still clung to the Uzi. The Cuban was abruptly yanked away from the console and propelled across the bridge, the shoulder strap to the SMG slithering from his arm. As he slammed into a wall, the captain confronted him, knife in one hand and the confiscated Uzi in the other.

Aware he couldn't reverse his grip on the frame to hold the subgun by the pistol grip and use the trigger, the captain tossed the Uzi aside. He seemed confident he didn't need more than the blade to dispatch the Cuban. Encizo drew his Tanto fighting knife, reflexes faster than conscious thought. The captain either failed to notice or didn't care as he advanced.

The big man raised his blade in a quick motion to deliver a short slash at the air. Encizo recognized the action as a feint intended to distract him from the real attack. The captain swung his boot, aiming a kick at the Cuban's groin. Encizo immediately side-stepped the attack and delivered a low sweep with his weapon.

Sharp steel caught his opponent across the ankle before his foot could return to the floor. The captain hissed and attempted a slash with his blade. Encizo's knife rose to meet the attack and sliced the back of the man's fist. Blood spurted from small arteries, and the knife hopped from a hand crippled by severed tendons. The captain screamed in pain and hobbled backward on his damaged leg.

Encizo took advantage of the situation and hooked his left fist to the side of the captain's jaw. The punch spun the guy to present his back to Encizo. The Phoenix Force commando had a number of possible targets. He could have easily killed the captain, but elected to use the copper butt of the knife handle instead of the blade. He hit the guy behind the ear and watched him crash to the floor.

Gunfire sounded outside the bridge. The first shot fired from the old .38 Enfield had signaled the terrorists to take action against the unwanted visitors aboard the trawler. The Israeli lieutenant lay in a corner, a trickle of blood at a split lower lip. The officer stirred and groaned. Apparently the boat captain had slugged him while Encizo had taken out the mate. The lieutenant didn't seem to be seriously hurt.

The Cuban slid his knife into its sheath and looked for his discarded Uzi. Suddenly the door to the bridge burst open. Encizo immediately dropped to one knee and reached for the Walther pistol holstered under his arm. The figure on the threshold wore fishermen's gear and held a British Sten subgun in his fists. The Cuban drew his P-88, clicked off the safety and aimed with a single fluid motion. The terrorist saw him and swung the muzzle of the Sten toward the commando.

Encizo triggered two rounds, both 9 mm parabellum slugs tearing into the enemy gunner's chest just below the sternum. The trajectory drove the projectiles upward to burrow into the gunman's heart and lungs. The impact drove the man backward through the doorway before he could fire his British chopper.

CALVIN JAMES and the paratroopers on the deck of the trawler found themselves under attack the instant the report of the .38 erupted from the bridge. The unarmed terrorist fisherman charged the Phoenix Force commando and the Israeli soldiers.

An enemy hardman lunged forward and grabbed James's slung Uzi, trying to pull it from the Phoenix Force pro's grasp. James didn't attempt to struggle for possession of the subgun. Instead, he moved forward with the pull of his opponent. He shoved upward and glimpsed the startled face of the terrorist an instant before the steel frame smashed into his mouth and jaw.

The man wilted to the deck. Another terrorist rushed James, a knife in hand, raised high in an overhand ice-pick grip. The commando faced his attacker, stepping forward on his left foot and whirling to unleash his right leg in a tae kwon do kick. The edge of his boot slammed into the terrorist like a jackhammer, the kick hurling the guy backward into a handrail. He toppled over the rail and cried out as he plunged into the sea with a dramatic splash.

James headed port side as more terrorists emerged from the cabins, armed with an assortment of firearms. He opened fire on the closest enemy and blasted him onto the deck, body riddled with slugs. A pistol-packing terrorist fired a round at the Phoenix Force commando, the bullet tearing into the edge of the bulkhead and splintering wood above James's head.

"Shit!" The commando ducked and triggered his SMG.

A stream of 9 mm projectiles ripped the pistol man with a diagonal slash of bullet holes from right hip to left armpit. Other terrorists scrambled for cover when they saw another comrade go down. Two bold Jinn 2000 fanatics pointed weapons at James and prepared to open fire.

The Phoenix Force warrior's Uzi spoke again with a metallic rattle of lethal fury. Another salvo of full-auto rounds streaked from the patrol boat as a paratrooper provided backup with a Galil assault rifle. The combination of 9 mm and 5.56 mm slugs chopped into the enemy gunmen before they could trigger their weapons.

Shadows from above warned James of movement by terrorists on the upper deck. He raised the stubby barrel of the Uzi as he turned to see two pairs of legs by the top rail. However, the terrorists above failed to notice James. Their attention was fixed on the men aboard the patrol boat. One man fired a Sten subgun as the other yanked the pin from a hand grenade.

James triggered his Uzi to blast the remaining rounds into the belly of the gunman. A scream of agony escaped the terrorist's throat before he crumpled to the deck.

The man with the hand grenade was startled and distracted by the fate of his companion. He forgot about the live grenade in his hand or that he was no longer protected by his comrade's cover fire. The soldier aboard the patrol vessel took advantage of the reduction of enemy gunfire to aim his Galil and unleashed a short burst. Struck in the torso, the terrorist cried out and toppled backward to the upper deck.

James ducked and covered his head, aware the man had pulled the pin to the grenade before the trooper nailed him with the Galil. The explosion roared above the Phoenix Force commando's position. Part of the handrail, some planks and other debris hurtled from the upper deck. Screams announced the grenade blast had injured two or more Jinn 2000 terrorists, as well.

"Rafael!" James shouted when he recalled Encizo and the Israeli lieutenant were on the upper deck.

He ejected the spent magazine from his Uzi and reached for an ammo pouch. Suddenly a figure charged from the bulkhead. The terrorist rushed toward James with a long wrench held high. He had probably been unarmed and forced to find cover when the firefight erupted. The Jinn 2000 extremist had to have waited for an opportunity to use the tool as an improvised weapon.

James realized he couldn't reload before his attacker could bash in his skull with the wrench. He saw the terrorist swing the metal club and raised the empty Uzi as a shield. Steel clashed against steel as the tool connected with gunmetal. James felt the impact ride into his arms and lashed a karate kick at his adversary's abdomen.

The terrorist groaned from the blow. James swiftly slammed the Uzi along his opponent's forearm to strike the ulnar nerve and jar the wrench from the guy's grasp. The tool dropped from his fingers, but the Jinn 2000 fanatic attempted to seize James's throat with his other hand.

The Phoenix pro blocked the attack with a forearm. He released the Uzi, allowing it to hang by its shoulder strap, and used both hands to quickly grab the terrorist's head. James pumped his knees into the man's already battered belly. The knee kicks hit hard and fast...right, left, right. The enemy convulsed from the punishment to his intestines, stomach and liver.

The guy was finished. He didn't try to fight, and he sagged in the commando's grasp. James swung a right uppercut to the terrorist's jaw to dump him unconscious on the deck. Unsure if the wrench had damaged his Uzi, James discarded the subgun and drew his Walther from shoulder leather.

A muffled explosion and a large gush of water by the bow drew his attention. Water splashed across the deck, propelled by a blast beneath the surface. James guessed another enemy grenade had been pitched into the sea to prevent an explosion aboard the trawler. Since a terrorist would have been more likely to throw it at the patrol boat, James guessed that meant someone on his team had disposed of the grenade.

A familiar figure appeared at the bow to confirm his hypothesis. Rafael Encizo approached slowly, careful not to present a clear target to the enemy or the patrol boat, aware of the risk of friendly fire. However, the fighting appeared to be over. Only four terrorists remained on their feet, hands held high in surrender. The rest were dead, wounded or unconscious.

"I'm glad to see you," James announced. "I wasn't sure what might have happened when that first grenade went off on the upper deck. Thought you might have caught some shrapnel."

"Actually," Encizo began, "I was starboard when that happened. The explosion didn't reach the bridge, so I would have been okay anyway. Hopefully the lieutenant wasn't hurt. The boat captain and one of his mates will need some first aid, but they're probably going to survive."

"At least one Israeli trooper was hurt pretty bad," James commented. "I saw him get a knife in the belly. Our allies get first consideration. Did you find the SHC machine up there?"

"No," Encizo replied. "I'm sorry to say all we found was some fancy camera equipment. I doubt we'll find the device on board. Maybe we'll get lucky, but I think these guys just intended to film the fiery deaths of infidel leaders and maybe provide some backup."

"Great," James muttered. "So we had a shoot-out with a terrorist camera crew, but the guys with the SHC weapon are still out there somewhere."

"Better let Striker and the others know what happened," Encizo said.

CHAPTER TWENTY-SIX

The clock tower stood at the center of the Jaffa section of Tel Aviv. A symbol of the Turkish occupation of Palestine, it had been built in 1906 to honor Sultan Abd ul-Hamit II of the Ottoman Empire. Yet it bore a commemorative plaque in recognition of the Israelis who died in 1948 during the war for independence.

Perhaps the site had been selected for the assembly of VIP government representatives because the clock tower presented images of a nation that had seen many changes, endured foreign rule and numerous conflicts. Mack Bolan wasn't sure what had motivated the organizers of the meeting to choose this site. It was probably as good a spot as any.

The Executioner saw the clock tower as he approached the Mediterranean Horizons Building. A large crowd by the tower voiced concern and curiosity in a dozen languages that reached Bolan's ears as an unintelligible grumble. Onlookers were distressed by the gun battle and explosions among the boats between the harbor and Andromeda Rock.

Bolan knew about the encounter with the terrorist film crew aboard the trawler. Encizo had transmitted a radio report of the incident. Activity at the harbor had immediately erupted when the battle occurred.

Motorboats raced to the scene, and uniformed cops and soldiers restrained the crowd from getting closer to the shore.

Encizo, James and the men with them had discovered a band of Jinn 2000 terrorists, but the SHC machine hadn't been found. Bolan hoped the weapon was located in the Mediterranean Horizons Building. The thirty-story structure seemed the most likely site for the terrorists to launch the deadly flame-producing microwaves.

A computer scan of city records revealed several offices in the building were leased by Arab businessmen and professionals involved in legal and medical occupations. There was nothing sinister about that, especially considering the number of Arabs living in the Jaffa district. However, one office on the twenty-ninth floor belonged to a law firm that specialized in defending the rights of Arabs accused of terrorism and other acts of violence.

Located on the same floor with the lawyers were the offices of an optometrist and a dentist. Both had formerly been clients of the law firm. Though they were suspected of conspiracy in a terrorist bombing in 1994, the charges had been dropped against both men due to lack of evidence. The lawyers and their neighbors all were Shiite Muslims.

That produced enough suspicion under the circumstances for Bolan to feel they had found a likely location for the enemy attack point. He approached the building on foot, accompanied by T. J. Hawkins and a Mossad officer named Zachariah. They wanted to avoid drawing attention from any terrorist lookout who might be posted at a window. All three wore windbreakers and civilian trousers instead of military uniforms.

More than a dozen Israeli soldiers, clad in full uniform and armed with submachine guns or assault rifles, rushed about the immediate area of the Mediterranean Horizons Building. None entered the structure. They were intended to serve as a distraction for any of the enemies in the area. The activity by the clock tower and harbor was also frantic, due to the gunfight close to shore.

Bolan realized that the enemy would change its original scheme. Security forces would naturally prevent the government leaders and diplomats from arriving at the clock tower and the obvious risk presented there. The most logical action would be to scrap the planned assassination and attempt to flee the area before the inevitable dragnet closed in.

The Executioner didn't intend to let them get any farther than possible. He reckoned they wouldn't be willing to abandon or destroy the SHC machine unless there was no other option. They would probably disassemble the weapon and try to escape with it regardless of the risk that involved.

The trio strolled to a door at the rear of the building. Hawkins removed a set of lock picks, inserted two probes in the keyhole and went to work on the lock. A few seconds later the door was open. Bolan entered first and stepped into a narrow corridor surrounded by stone walls. The foot of a flight of metal stairs revealed that the data they had previously studied about the construction of the building was correct.

The Executioner drew his Beretta and made certain the silencer was firmly attached to the threaded barrel. Hawkins produced his micro-Uzi. The Phoenix Force pro didn't have a sound suppressor for his weapon, so Bolan took the lead. They started to climb the stairs, trying to pace themselves. The twenty-ninth floor was a long way up.

DAVID MCCARTER and Gary Manning entered the Mediterranean Horizons Building via the front entrance. As the name suggested, the place had originally been a travel agency that specialized in ocean cruises. Posters in the lobby still advertised luxury tours, and the first level remained devoted to the business.

Few employees appeared on duty that morning. They didn't expect much business when a major peace agreement held the public's attention. Manning crossed the lobby to a pair of elevators while McCarter and Captain Lavi headed toward a startled receptionist. Although they were clad in civilian attire, the bulges of weapons under their jackets told her they weren't customers.

"May I help you?" she asked in uncertain English.

"We need to speak with the building manager," McCarter stated. "Do you know how many offices upstairs are open for business today?"

"Not many," she replied.

"On the twenty-ninth floor?" Lavi asked.

"I don't think any of them are working today."

The receptionist's attention turned to the elevators. Manning had opened the doors to one car, stepped inside and stood on a step ladder to reach the ceiling hatch. A security guard approached the elevator, but a Mossad officer cut him off and waved an ID card in the guy's face.

"Will you call the manager?" the Briton asked.

"What is that man doing?" she countered.

"Checking the elevators to make certain they'll be

safe for the evacuation," McCarter explained. "After we talk to the manager, we'll want everybody out of the building. It really has to be done, okay?"

"The manager only speaks Hebrew and Yiddish."

"I'll talk to him," Lavi assured her.

Manning emerged from the elevator with a small plastic bag taped to a black box with a stubby antenna. He approached the desk, nodded a curt greeting to the woman behind it and showed the discovery to McCarter and Lavi.

"Found this attached to the gears on the roof of the elevator, gentlemen," he announced. "Appears to be a crude compound somebody whipped up in a home workshop. Probably ammonium nitrate or potassium nitrate with a gel pulp."

"A bomb?" the woman asked, her eyes wide with fear.

"Sort of poor-man's gelignite," the Canadian demolitions expert replied with a nod. "Not much of an explosion with this sort of thing unless you use a fair amount of it. Enough to take out the cables and plunge the lift into the basement. Notice the little radio detonator?"

He tossed it to McCarter. The receptionist gasped, and Lavi hissed in a tense breath. The Briton caught the bomb and examined it with only mild interest.

"No doubt the bastards are in the building now," he said. "Rather crude radio receiver, isn't it?"

"Real low-tech," Manning confirmed. "Short range. No more than two hundred yards or so. Let me get the other one before you try to contact Striker by radio. The wrong transmission wavelength might set it off."

"It can still explode?" the woman asked.

"Not this one," Manning assured her. "I disconnected it, so it's harmless now. They probably sabotaged the other elevator, and I have to get that one. I hate it when amateurs do this sort of work. They usually put together something this crude that can be set off too easily.''

''Yeah,'' McCarter said with a shrug, ''but they're usually easier to deactivate.''

''Oh, yeah,'' the Canadian agreed. ''Simple explosives like this just need to have the detonator unhooked from the blasting cap and yank it out.''

''Will you please get the other bomb?'' Lavi asked in an urgent tone.

''I said I was going to,'' Manning replied as if annoyed at being rushed to do his job.

As the Canadian headed for the second elevator, the receptionist quickly dialed the number for the manager.

MACK BOLAN HAD REACHED the landing to the twenty-sixth floor on the fire stairwell when he received the radio message from an earphone to his transceiver. He signaled for Hawkins and Zachariah to stop as he listened to the unmistakable cockney accent in his ear.

''Found two sabotaged elevators,'' McCarter's voice stated. ''We've cleared them, and we've got the evacuation in progress. Not many folks in the building. The manager says there shouldn't be anyone beyond the twentieth floor.''

Bolan spoke into a throat mike. ''How long until the building is cleared of civilians?''

''A few more minutes,'' McCarter answered. ''We'll have the place to ourselves then, and the exclusive use of the elevators, as well. Can work it the way we planned without any alternate version.''

"Nice when things go smoothly," the soldier said. "As often as not, something unexpected happens. Stay alert."

"Right. You, too."

"I'm shutting off the radio now. No more contact until we reach twenty-nine."

The trio continued to mount the stairs. They moved with even greater care than before as they got closer to the suspected terrorist site. Mindful of noise and possible shadows that might betray their presence to an enemy—or vice versa—they climbed riser after riser until they approached the stairs for the twenty-ninth floor.

A figure stood on the landing, a cut-down shotgun in his hands. He saw Bolan at the foot of the stairs, and the muzzle rose as the man reached for the trigger of his scattergun. A 3-round burst of suppressed 9 mm rounds rasped from Bolan's weapon. The sentry fell backward, hit a wall and slid to the landing, his chest stitched by a line of horizontal bullet holes across the heart and lungs. The shotgun rattled on the stairs with enough noise to make the commandos wince.

"Think they heard it?" Hawkins whispered.

The Executioner figured they would find out soon enough and mounted the final stairs to the fire exit. He carefully approached the metal door and peered through the small square window. Two men stood in the hallway on the other side of the door, neither appearing to have heard the shotgun on the stairs. Their attention was fixed on the elevators.

Both men held weapons ready as they watched the light indicator travel along the numbers to the panel. They saw that one of the elevators was headed for the twenty-ninth floor, and they prepared an unpleasant reception for its arrival. Hawkins appeared beside Bolan and examined the door as he reached for his lock picks. He found no keyhole; the door had a locking bar on the other side.

Hawkins reached inside his jacket and withdrew a jimmy.

The Phoenix Force pro looked at the tool with distaste, aware it was about as crude as a stone ax, but still had advantages in circumstances when lock picks wouldn't work. Bolan placed a hand to Hawkins's arm to restrain him from using the crowbar as he watched the men by the elevator.

The doors rolled open, and the terrorists pointed their weapons at the interior of the car. A loud bang and a flash of brilliant white light burst within the elevator. The sentries staggered, stunned and blinded by the unexpected blast. Aware the grenade had been rigged to go off when the doors opened before Manning and McCarter sent the elevator up the shaft, Bolan had waited for this moment.

Hawkins jammed the crowbar into the door, sprung the bolt and pried it open. Bolan and the Phoenix Force fighter charged into the hallway, followed by Zachariah. Hawkins dashed to one of the dazed terrorists and swiftly clubbed him behind the ear with the crowbar.

The second guard swung his pistol toward Hawkins, still half-blind by the flash. Bolan moved beside the gunner and chopped the butt of his Beretta across the man's wrist. As the weapon fell from trembling fingers, the Executioner struck his adversary in the kidney. The Jinn 2000 thug groaned and jackknifed from the blow.

Bolan wrapped his right arm around the man's neck, forearm across his throat. He grabbed the hard-

man's wrist with his left hand to increase the pressure
of the hold and jammed his hip into the small of his
opponent's spine. The man struggled briefly and
raised his hands to try to gouge Bolan's eyes. His
fingers groped, unable to locate the Executioner's
face. He succeeded only at clawing Bolan's hair.

The windpipe and carotid arteries constricted by
the hold, the terrorist went limp in Bolan's grasp seconds later. The Executioner held him a moment
longer to be certain the man was dead, then he allowed the corpse to fall to the floor. Zachariah
watched with amazement, impressed by how quickly
and effectively the two Americans took out the terrorist pair.

A row of office doors faced the elevators. Hawkins
pointed the micro-Uzi at one door, Bolan covered
another with his 93-R and Zachariah drew his .357
Magnum Desert Eagle to guard the third. Lights
flashed along the elevator panel as the second car
rose to the twenty-ninth floor.

McCarter and Manning appeared when the doors
slid open. The British and Canadian commandos
emerged from the elevator, micro-Uzi machine pistols in hand. Bolan barely glanced at the two men,
aware they would know what to do. The doors to the
offices bore legends in five languages, including English. The law firm had the largest office and probably contained the most terrorists. Bolan hoped the
SHC device was there, as well.

The Executioner approached the door and stepped
to one side, near the knob. The others moved clear,
aware those inside the law office would respond with
violence when the big American kicked in the door.
Bolan glanced at his companions to be certain they

were ready for him to make the next move, then took a deep, calming breath.

Suddenly the door to the dentist's office swung open. Two figures charged, weapons in hand. Gary Manning's Uzi immediately sprayed the attackers with a salvo of 9 mm slugs. One enemy gunner fell, his unfired pistol still in hand. The other toppled back through the doorway and triggered his Sten SMG, blasting several rounds into the ceiling. Bullets splintered wood from the top of the frame.

So much for stealth, Bolan thought as he swung a back-kick to the law-office door. His heel struck hard, and the door gave way. Hawkins fired a stream of Uzi rounds through the opening as a volley of enemy gunfire sizzled from inside the room. The door to the optometrist's office opened slightly. McCarter fired into it before the enemies within could attempt an attack.

Manning rushed to the dentist's office and triggered another wave of parabellum rounds into the room as he reached the threshold. The Canadian saw a terrorist convulse from the impact of bullets while he tried to find cover behind the dental chair. Blood oozed from his punctured torso as the man slumped against the sink and saliva ejector. His limp form dropped across the chair's headrest.

A shape rose by a filing cabinet. Manning saw the motion from the corner of an eye and swung to confront the threat. A terrorist gunman triggered a small black pistol with a short barrel before the Canadian could fire his Uzi. A small-caliber bullet struck the frame of the machine pistol, sparking against steel and jarring the weapon from Manning's grasp. He heard the ricochet shriek past his face, inches from the tip of his nose.

The terrorist jerked the trigger to his weapon, muzzle pointed at Manning's chest. The Canadian braced himself for the bullet, but the pistol didn't fire. Manning saw that the slide was drawn back, a copper shell casing stuck in the ejector port. The gun had jammed. The Phoenix Force pro recognized the weapon as an obsolete Portuguese Model 915. The gun was probably more than seventy years old and most likely hadn't received enough care and maintenance. Even if it had fired, the low-power 7.65 mm round wouldn't have pierced Manning's bulletproof vest.

Frustrated and angry, the terrorist hurled the empty pistol at Manning's head. The big Canadian ducked the projectile and reached for his Walther P-88 in shoulder leather. The Jinn 2000 gunner raced forward and lashed a kick for the commando's groin. Manning chopped a fist into the shin above his opponent's boot to block the kick.

The terrorist's teeth clenched in pain, but he responded with his other leg to deliver a high roundhouse kick aimed for Manning's head. The Canadian slammed a forearm to the leg's calf to block the second attack and drove his other fist into the side of his opponent's knee. The man hobbled backward and nearly lost his balance.

Manning stepped forward and jabbed his left fist to his adversary's face. The man's head bounced from the punch, and the Phoenix Force fighter drove his right to the terrorist's liver. With a gasp the man doubled over to receive Manning's knee under his jaw, then he crashed, senseless, to the floor.

MACK BOLAN YANKED the pin from the flash-bang grenade and tossed it into the law office. He heard the device explode and voices cry out with surprise and pain. The Executioner held up a palm to signal Hawkins to hold his fire, then dived across the threshold, his body low and the Beretta 93-R held close to his chest.

At the same moment David McCarter switched the micro-Uzi to his left hand and used the right to draw his Browning Hi-Power from shoulder leather. An adrenaline junkie who loved the thrill of combat despite the fear and stress that accompanied the risk to life and limb, the Briton had to control his bold nature as leader of Phoenix Force. At last he had an opportunity to literally plunge into action.

"Cover me!" he shouted.

"Jesus, David!" Hawkins roared.

The British ace dashed to the optometrist's office, turned in midstride and threw himself backward into the partially opened door. The commando's weight flung the door wide as his body hit the floor. Arms extended like a giant V, McCarter fired both weapons through the open doorway.

McCarter had guessed one or more enemies might be stationed by the doorway. If the tactic wasted a few rounds, he would have accepted the loss, but the sight of the enemy gunman by the wall revealed his hunch to be accurate. The terrorist slid to the floor, eyes and mouth open wide with an expression of astonishment. His lungs perforated by a trio of Uzi slugs, the man seemed to be quite surprised by death.

A second figure fell from behind the door, his upper torso and face punctured by two slugs. The Briton's efforts hadn't been a waste of ammo, but he couldn't spare precious time congratulating himself. Gunfire around him warned there were more terrorists still very much alive.

One enemy positioned by a counter tried to point a Sterling subgun at McCarter, but exposed himself to Hawkins's line of fire. A burst of Uzi slugs nailed the terrorist through the top of his head, his skull exploding in a ghastly blossom of brains, blood and skull fragments. Aware of the risk of friendly fire, McCarter stayed low and crawled to the edge of the counter.

A Jinn 2000 gunman lurked behind the furniture. He knelt low and kept his head down, fearful of the automatic fire from the doorway. The terrorist didn't see McCarter until the Briton's Browning was pointed at his face. The Phoenix commander squeezed the trigger, and a single round punched into the bridge of the man's nose.

McCarter glanced about the optometrist's office. Shards of glass littered the floor behind the counter. Display cases of eyewear had been struck by numerous bullets, which had shattered the window, as well as the lenses inside. A metal tray also lay on the carpet near a chair that appeared to have been moved from a desk for the examination section.

Hinges and slots in the metal revealed the tray was actually a vented lid. McCarter glanced up and saw a square gap in the ceiling above the chair. Someone had removed the vent to climb inside the air-conditioner duct. The missing terrorist could be crawling through the ducts of the cooling system above the Briton's head.

T. J. HAWKINS REMAINED in the hallway to provide cover fire and backup for his three fellow Stony Man commandos. With three offices to watch, he was busy even with Zachariah on hand to help. The Phoenix Force pro's attention was focused on the offices, not the ceiling.

The clash and rattle of a large metal object against the tile floor behind Hawkins startled him. He spun and barely glimpsed the vent cover to an air-conditioner duct. A figure clad in gray work clothes dangled from the gap in the ceiling. Both hands gripped the rim of the duct as the man hung full length from the conditioner unit.

A leg lashed out before Hawkins could respond to the unexpected threat, the boot catching him in the side of the face and staggering him. The terrorist dropped from the ceiling and rushed the stunned warrior. Hands grasped Hawkins's Uzi and a furious face appeared inches from Hawkins's nose, eyes filled with frenzied anger and a bayonet clenched by the blade between the man's teeth.

The terrorist twisted the Uzi and tried to wrench it from Hawkins's grasp. The commando held on to the pistol grip with one hand and grabbed the handle of the bayonet in the guy's teeth with the other. He shoved hard and pulled.

Sharp steel cut into the man's mouth and slit skin at the corners of his lips. Blood flowed like crimson drool as the blade slid free of his abruptly enlarged mouth. Hawkins rammed a knee to his opponent's groin, all the while maintaining his grip on the Uzi.

He pushed the weapon against his adversary's weakened grasp, pointed the muzzle at the guy's leg and squeezed the trigger. A trio of parabellum rounds blasted into the terrorist's thigh, mangling muscle and shattering bone. The man collapsed to the floor and screamed in agony before the shock to his nervous system rendered him unconscious.

Zachariah's .357 Magnum roared in the confines

of the hallway. Hawkins turned to glimpse another figure plunge from the air duct in the ceiling. The second Jinn 2000 tunnel rat dropped gracelessly to the floor and sprawled across the tiles, a scarlet bloom in the center of his chest.

The Mossad agent stared at the corpse, apparently surprised by his own actions. He turned to Hawkins. The Stony Man warrior nodded with approval.

MACK BOLAN HIT THE FLOOR to the law office in a shoulder roll that carried him across the carpet to an armchair in front of a large desk. Sounds of battle bellowed from the hall and other rooms on the twenty-ninth floor, but the terrorists in the law-firm quarters were still stunned and half-blinded by the effects of the flash-bang grenade.

Only one enemy gunner fired his weapon as Bolan dived into the room, and the shots were high and wild. The bullets didn't come close to the Executioner's hurtling form. He rolled to one knee and grasped the Beretta 93-R in a firm two-handed Weaver's grip. He glanced about the room and spotted four terrorists.

Bolan recognized Captain Qatrun although the Libyan officer pawed at his face with one hand as he waved a pistol about with the other. Qatrun attempted to clear his vision enough to see a target and held his fire, aware he might hit one of his own men if he fired in blind panic. The captain remained close to a long gray tube with a clear nozzle at one end and the control box at the other. At last Bolan had found the deadly SHC weapon.

With cool efficiency the Executioner aimed his weapon for the most serious immediate threat. He lined up the Beretta's rear sights with the upper torso of the only gunman who fired a Sten chopper in his direction. Bolan triggered a 3-round burst, the impact of the parabellum shockers hurling the man into a corner to die.

The big American swung the 93-R toward a terrorist positioned by the door to the office. Although the gunner seemed to be as dazed and disoriented as the others, he presented a threat to Bolan's allies in the hallway. Almost blind and deaf from the grenade, the terrorist was unaware Bolan was even in the room or one of his comrades already lay dead. The Executioner didn't dwell on his unfair advantage as he drilled the gunman with another trio of 9 mm slugs. All was fair in war.

The soldier turned his attention to Qatrun and the remaining hardman. The captain still stood by the SHC weapon as if he intended to guard it to the bitter end. The other terrorist had enough sense to use the desk for cover and crouched behind it, a blue-black revolver in one hand as the other tried to wipe the glare from his eyes.

Suddenly a door burst open by the west wall of the office. An armed figure plunged across the threshold and dived to the floor in a tumble, similar to the method Bolan himself had used to enter the office. The Executioner started to point his Beretta at the shape, but his battlefield savvy caused him to turn instead to the entrance used by the new opponent.

Another figure stood by the doorway to the adjacent room, a Czech-made Skorpion machine pistol in his grasp. Standard combat procedure dictated a second gunman would be stationed by the door to cover the guy who had dived into the office. Bolan guessed his opponents would use this tactic.

The silenced Beretta hissed another short burst, and the face behind the Skorpion became a crimson pulp, mangled by 9 mm slugs. Bolan immediately swung the 93-R back to the enemy who tumbled across the floor in a shoulder roll. The terrorist completed the move, landing in a kneeling stance, gun in hand. He did everything correctly, but the Executioner already had him cold. Bolan triggered the Beretta and fired the last rounds from the magazine, and the terrorist dropped to the carpet, his skull smashed open at eyebrow level.

Bolan didn't have time to reload. He discarded the empty 93-R and swiftly drew his Desert Eagle from his belt. The terrorist behind the desk stared at the room with an expression of astonishment and horror. Apparently his vision had finally cleared, and he saw the results of the Executioner's lethal skills. He also saw the big American and tried to point his revolver at the commando.

The Desert Eagle bellowed before the man could trigger his weapon. Bolan shot him once, a .44 Magnum round to the center of the chest. The force of the powerful projectile hurled the guy backward into a window. Glass shattered, and the gunner's body tumbled through the broken pane and over the edge of the sill. His revolver fired a harmless bullet into the sky. A scream announced he was still alive and conscious as he plunged from view.

Qatrun's vision was still blurred, and his hearing was impaired by the grenade blast. Nonetheless, he heard the roar of the big Magnum despite the ringing in his ears. The Libyan wasn't certain which direction the shot came from because the sound echoed within the confines of the office. He thrust his pistol toward the hallway and fired two rounds.

Bolan rushed the captain before the man could alter the aim of his weapon. He slammed the heavy barrel of the Desert Eagle across Qatrun's fist and wrist to strike the pistol from the terrorist leader's grasp. The soldier's left hand drove a hard straight jab to the point of Qatrun's chin, the punch staggering the captain into the control box of the SHC weapon.

Qatrun leaned on the panel with one hand and reached for his sore jaw with the other. His eyes widened as if the punch had suddenly cleared his vision. The captain stared at Bolan and blinked with surprise when he recognized the man who pointed a big steel pistol at his chest.

"You!" he declared. "The CIA spy in Cairo!"

"I'm not CIA," Bolan replied, "but that's not important. You want to surrender or do I have to shoot your kneecaps off and drag you out of here? Either way is okay with me, Captain."

A brilliant blue light suddenly rose behind Qatrun. Bolan turned his head slightly and closed one eye to avoid being blinded by the fierce glare.

Qatrun took advantage of the distraction and pounced. One hand seized Bolan's wrist above the Desert Eagle, and the other lunged for his throat. The Executioner grabbed his opponent's shirtsleeve to stop the strangling fingers, Qatrun's weight and momentum driving him backward.

He didn't resist. The Executioner followed a basic rule of judo and used the attacker's weight and motion against him. Bolan dropped to the floor on his left thigh and buttocks. He pulled his adversary forward as he thrust his right foot into Qatrun's abdomen. Bolan's back rolled on the carpet as he straightened his knee.

Qatrun sailed overhead in a judo circle throw. He crashed to the floor hard, yet managed to hold on to Bolan's wrist. His thumb jammed into the base of the Executioner's palm and forced Bolan to release the pistol. The big American snapped free of Qatrun's grasp and thrust himself from the floor.

The captain also rose quickly, right hand behind his back. Bolan knew he was reaching for a knife, so he grabbed the handle of his Ka-bar combat knife and drew it from the belt sheath as the captain lunged for Bolan's belly.

Qatrun's move was a feint, and he quickly altered the attack for a stab to Bolan's chest. Steel clashed as the two blades met. The big American's free hand grabbed his opponent's wrist above the wicked curved blade, but Qatrun also snared Bolan's wrist before he could counterattack.

They struggled, neither able to use his blade or break free of the other's grasp. Bolan pumped a knee toward Qatrun's groin, but the man blocked it with a leg. Qatrun suddenly twisted his trunk and dropped to one knee, yanking Bolan off balance and hurling him to the carpet. The warrior landed on his back with Qatrun over him. They still held on to each other's wrist to keep the knives at bay, but Qatrun now had a better position to press down with his weight and lunge with his blade.

Bolan bent his left knee, braced himself with his back and right hip. He brought the knee up hard and smashed it into the side of Qatrun's head. The captain groaned from the unexpected blow, but still held on to his adversary's wrist, trying to bring his knife into play. The big American used his knee again and hammered a blow to Qatrun's knife fist. The hand popped open, and the blade fell to the floor.

Aware Qatrun might have another hideout weapon, Bolan struck before his opponent could reach for it. He lunged upward and drove the tip of his blade into the captain's chest, plunging it deep into Qatrun's heart. The terrorist convulsed, blood spewing from his mouth, then collapsed in a heap on the floor and lay motionless.

"Sweet Jesus," Hawkins rasped as he entered the office. "Reckon you don't need my help after all."

"All of our people okay?" Bolan asked as he rose from the floor.

Hawkins gingerly touched the purple bruise on his cheekbone and said, "I think this is the worst any of us got. Sneaky bastard swung down from the ceiling and caught me with a boot. None of them got away. Two are still alive, but I think I might have fractured the skull of the guy who kicked me. He damn near ate his own bayonet, so I don't know how well he can talk anyway."

Bolan approached the SHC machine. The metal glowed as if inside a furnace, and the heat prevented him from moving closer. Parts of the device had melted and fused in the moment of intense heat when the blue flash occurred. Hawkins looked at the twisted metal and whistled softly.

"That's it?" he asked.

"What's left of it," Bolan replied. "Qatrun triggered the self-destruct switch. My guess is the insides of this thing are completely gutted. You can see what happened to the frame. The fusion occurred inside, so it must be at least a hundred times greater."

"At least they didn't get to use it on anybody today," Hawkins remarked.

"Yeah," Bolan agreed, "but there are still more Jinn 2000 out there, and they have another SHC weapon."

CHAPTER TWENTY-SEVEN

Hal Brognola chewed the unlighted cigar as he watched the wall screen. The big Fed had already heard from the Stony Man commandos in Israel and wasn't surprised by the news report on the television broadcast. Footage of the fishing trawler and patrol boat appeared on the screen. Gunfire sounded like firecrackers, and the voices of the crowd expressed alarm and surprise.

A tourist had videotaped the sea battle with a handheld video camera, and the footage was shaky yet still dramatic. Gasps and a few screams erupted when a grenade exploded on the upper deck of the trawler. The voice of a reporter explained the scene. Brognola saw several figures move rapidly on both vessels. He didn't recognize any of his personnel although he knew Calvin James and Rafael Encizo were involved in the conflict. The patrol boat blocked the port-side view of the trawler and reduced any clear image of the firefight, which was fine with Brognola. He didn't want the security of any of his people jeopardized by their faces appearing on international television.

The report stated the incident had occurred less than two hours before the VIP meeting at the clock tower was supposed to take place, which had forced the participants to cancel the original plan. The second gunbattle at an office building in the area was also mentioned, but didn't feature video of the actual incident. No real details were given. Of course, it was obvious the violence was connected to the peace conference.

The news speculated that extremists had attempted to disrupt the conference. Several alleged terrorists had been killed and a number of others captured according to Israeli authorities. The conference would still take place without the public display by the tower.

The prime minister of Israel appeared on-screen to declare fanatics wouldn't destroy the efforts of men of goodwill. He was followed by the president of Egypt and the President of the United States with similar statements. A buzzer sounded and a light flashed to draw Brognola's attention to a row of phones. A special red phone was the cause of the distraction. The big Fed thumbed the volume control to silence the TV as he moved to the hotline.

"I was just watching you on television," he announced when he answered the phone, aware of who had to be on the line.

"Thanks to your people I'm still around to be on TV," the voice of the President of the United States replied.

"How are all the heads of state and diplomats holding up after those fireworks in Tel Aviv?"

"Pretty good," the President replied. "A couple want to call off the conference and head for home, but they're afraid they'll lose face if they look scared. The prime minister here is determined to hold the conference. The Egyptian president doesn't even consider this incident to be a close call. He's had a number of assassination attempts since he took office, and he's not too concerned about a terrorist effort that didn't even fire a shot in his direction. Of course, he doesn't know about the SHC device. Did your men find the machine?"

"What's left of it," Brognola said. "Seems it had a self-destruct mechanism and the insides are virtually vaporized. Unfortunately it's a copy of the original. Jinn 2000 still has at least one more SHC weapon."

"That's not such good news," the President remarked. "Do they know where the enemy headquarters are?"

"They're interrogating the terrorists taken alive during the encounter. A high-ranking member of the Jinn 2000 conspiracy was killed, but even in death he may provide some answers."

"Really?" the President asked with interest. "How's that?"

"We've been able to identify him as Captain Qatrun, an officer in the Libyan army. Of course, Libya is ruled by a guy who calls himself a colonel, so a captain has a hell of a lot more authority there than most parts of the world."

"You think the Libyan government is behind this?" the President asked. "So this is state-sponsored terrorism?"

"Libya has been accused of that before," the big Fed answered, "but we can't assume too much too quickly. Evidence so far suggests Jinn 2000 has been acting on their own. They don't have a large number of members, and their resources seem limited. They've got some finances to help operate their schemes, but they don't appear to have the kind of big-money backing that could be provided by an oil-rich government like Libya or Iraq, Iran or Syria.''

"Syria sent troops to back the Allied forces during the Gulf War against Iraqi occupation of Kuwait. Unlike the other three countries you mentioned, we have diplomatic relations with Syria and they have participated in peace negotiations with Israel since 1994.''

"Yeah," Brognola replied, "but I wouldn't say they're exactly our friends at this point. Syria has been involved in the promotion of international terrorism against both the United States and Israel. I hope Syria has changed and we'll find its government trustworthy in the future, but I think it's too early to say that at this time.''

"But you don't think Jinn 2000 are state-sponsored terrorists?''

"Still can't rule out the possibility, but we don't think so based on what we have so far.''

"You and your Stony Man team saved a lot of lives and kept the hopes for a lasting peace in the Middle East from going down the drain," the President began. "I owe you my personal thanks for probably saving my life.''

"The commandos in the field led by Striker deserve credit for that, Mr. President.''

"Thank them for me and express my regret they'll never get the public recognition they deserve as truly great heroes. It's no exaggeration to say the entire world owes them a debt of thanks.''

"They're not in this for recognition and to be honored in parades," Brognola explained. "They believe in what they do, and the satisfaction of knowing what they've accomplished is enough reward.''

"Well," the Man began, "I have to ask something else of them. From what you've told me about the spontaneous-human-combustion weapon, it's a major breakthrough in the development of nuclear-fusion technology.''

"I don't know if it is exactly a breakthrough in fusion technology,'' the big Fed replied. "We have strong evidence that suggests a Saudi scientist named Barrah discovered the SHC process by accident while working on nuclear fusion. It damn sure destroys human beings and other life-forms under special circumstances. That obviously produces some kind of energy, but I'm not sure that device will help harness fusion for productive purposes.''

"Even if it only functions as a weapon, it's still important the United States has it.''

"A matter of national security, I assume.''

"That's the way the world is, Hal,'' the President stated. "We may not like it, but our country has to maintain a military force and advanced weaponry greater than any nation that may be an enemy to world peace and democracy.''

"So much for the hope of cutting down the size of nuclear arsenals around the world,'' Brognola said. "You want us to find this damn SHC device so our scientists can use it as a prototype to make more weapons? Bigger and better weapons. Maybe some sort of advanced cannon satellite that can vaporize a nation's population without need of quartz crystals to focus on a particular target. Could be better than that neutron bomb they talked about back in the midseventies. That was the one that was supposed to kill people and animals but would leave buildings standing. Don't have to worry about radiation or contamination afterward.''

"We're not going to use our military might to conquer or control other countries, Hal. You understand better than most this nation needs to be prepared to protect itself from all sorts of enemies. Stony Man deals with certain threats our conventional military and intelligence sources can't handle as well, but there are other situations that require massive troop strength and awesome firepower.''

"Yes, sir," Brognola agreed reluctantly. "I just hope the temptation to use some of these monstrous weapons doesn't prove too great one of these days. One of the things we try to do with Stony Man is prevent incidents from blowing up into full-scale war."

"Nobody wants war, and nobody wants mass destruction," the President insisted. "That's why we can't allow a weapon of this sort to be in the hands of terrorists and extremists. If another country has a weapon of this kind, especially a country hostile to the United States and our allies, we have to have firepower equal to or greater than our enemies. I'm repeating myself and I shouldn't have to with you, Hal. You know what I'm saying is true. Maybe we both feel things should be different, but we both know better."

"I'll pass on the instructions to my men in the field," the big Fed assured him. "They'll be thrilled."

"They've done a fine job so far," the President said. "We could turn the mission over to the CIA or NSA now."

"I don't think they'll want to do that," Brognola stated. "The mission isn't finished, and they'll want to see it through to the end."

"Fine," the President agreed. "I trust you not to let ego get in the way of appropriate procedure. Now I have to get ready for some business of my own.

Politics may not be as exciting as tracking down terrorists, but this is where my talents lie. Hopefully we can agree on a lasting peace arrangement in the Middle East.''

"Good luck, Mr. President," Brognola replied.

ABDEL AL-BARRAH KNELT on his prayer mat and faced east. The Jinn 2000 flag hung on the wall above the conference table at the base headquarters. The banner bore the colors and symbols inspired by other Islamic national flags and the cult's own militant version of the Shiite Muslim faith.

The emblem of the gold scimitar represented their devotion to the jihad against the infidels. The crescent and the name of God declared their belief in the Koran and the One God of Islam. Yet their great victory in Israel hadn't occurred. What had gone wrong? How could they fail? Why had God denied them the glory of crushing their enemies in his name?

Barrah didn't understand and prayed for guidance. He placed his forehead to the rug and pleaded for divine revelation to do the bidding of God. Qabus an-Sabkhat barely glanced at the Saudi scientist. The banker hadn't been moved to prayer when he learned their efforts in Tel Aviv ended in disaster. The man had often pretended to share the extremist beliefs of the Jinn 2000 members, but he was in no mood to perform rituals he considered useless nonsense.

Sabkhat wanted a drink. He would have gone to his quarters and gulped down an entire bottle of his forbidden French brandy if he didn't have to worry about the attitudes of the other Jinn 2000 followers at the base. Just as well, he thought as he worked the keyboard to a computer terminal on the table. He needed a clear head and couldn't afford to fog his senses with alcohol.

The screen revealed bank accounts he had established under various false identities. He had two hundred thousand pounds sterling in a bank in Singapore, transferred through a bank in London, England. Other accounts in Switzerland and Panama appeared on the screen, both registering amounts in local currency. Three hundred thousand Swiss francs and five hundred thousand balboas, he noticed. To most, the total would seem a small fortune, but Sabkhat had dreamed of wealth in the billions, and his reserve funds seemed a pittance in comparison.

He could wire most of the money to a bank in Qatar. It did a fair amount of international trade while maintaining a low profile. Qatar was closer to the UAE than he cared to be, but he reckoned he could travel there with a forged Kuwaiti passport. His Arabian Peninsula accent wouldn't be out of place, and he could always smudge a thumbprint and alter his handwriting slightly in case the efforts to track him down for previous violations had extended to Qatar. Sabkhat planned to make a large withdrawal and head for some other country...far from the Middle East.

Despite his ambitions of wealth and power that drove him to the risky schemes of Jinn 2000, Sabkhat remained pragmatic enough to appreciate the reality of their situation. Their plans had gone sour, and the entire conspiracy was doomed. Barrah and the others could pray until they sweated blood, but nothing would help them claim success.

The combined Intelligence networks of the United States, Israel, Egypt and probably a dozen other countries would hunt them down. Only a fool would assume they wouldn't find the base with such a concentrated effort and vast resources. Unfortunately the majority of Jinn 2000 were fools and they would remain at the desert stronghold in Libya, blissfully confident their faith would see them through the crisis and God would watch over them and protect the fanatics from the infidels out for blood.

Sabkhat guessed they might have a week to ten days. Maybe longer if the Libyan government decided to be stubborn, but even then they wouldn't be able to get far after they fled the country. The SHC weapon they regarded as a gift from the almighty would do them little good without the crystals planted on potential victims. More than a hundred hard-core Jinn 2000 fanatics were stationed at the base. The lunatics might go down fighting against superior odds, but there was no doubt they would go down if the other side came for them with the full fury available to the nations offended by the Tel Aviv incident.

"Do you think Captain Qatrun is still alive?" Barrah asked.

Sabkhat was surprised the scientist took time from prayer to direct a question to him. The banker turned to see Barrah still staring at the flag, his eyes glazed as if in a trance.

"I doubt it," Sabkhat replied. "Qatrun would have probably fought to the end and taken his own life rather than be captured. Whatever else could be said about him, Qatrun was no coward."

"He was a very great commander and soldier," Barrah declared.

"He was an idiot," Sabkhat said with disgust. "Qatrun never should have gone to Cairo let alone

Tel Aviv. He wanted to be a hero and he only served to get himself killed.''

"He's a martyr.''

"We have enough of them already,'' the banker scoffed. "We needed a military strategist and commander. We don't have his expertise in that area, Abdel. I doubt anybody here can really replace him.''

"What about your friend Kamel?'' Barrah asked. "He seems to have a lot of authority here, and he's acted as chief of security while Qatrun was gone.''

"Kamel is a good man, but he's not a strategist. It's one thing to protect a stronghold and another to plan actions against enemies in foreign lands.''

"He's loyal,'' Barrah stated. "Loyal to you, as well as the cause. Kamel and many of the others considered you to be the real leader, Qabus. The others looked to the captain as their commander. You have organizational skills, and your mind is better suited for this sort of intrigue. I'm just a scientist.''

"The men think you've been touched by God,'' Sabkhat insisted. "They'll be looking to you as their spiritual leader now. You can take care of things here while I'm gone, Abdel.''

"Where do you plan to go?'' Barrah asked with surprise.

"I'm going to find someone to help us plan our future strategy and establish a network of agents to replace those killed in the field,'' Sabkhat lied. "I know some military officers in Bahrain and Qatar who may be able to help us. Have to meet with them in person, of course. It should take only a few days.''

"Then we'll pray that you'll succeed,'' Barrah stated. "I still don't know what went wrong. I just don't understand.''

"Maybe it was a test of faith,'' Sabkhat said, try-

ing to give him an answer that would appeal to a
fanatic. "Who knows the mind of God? Perhaps if
we achieve something too easily, it will be too
quickly taken for granted. Sacrifices always have to
be made during a jihad."

"Perhaps you're right," Barrah said. "Genuine
faith can only be measured when one faces a situation that seems hopeless and still believes he will
succeed."

A knock at the door interrupted the conversation.
Kamel entered, accompanied by Muda. The burly
henchman turned sideways as he crossed the thresh-
old, his shoulders almost too wide to fit otherwise.
Muda stood a head shorter than Kamel, his physique
thin and wiry. A cruel grin always seemed to play at
Muda's lips, unlike the solemn expression that
Kamel wore.

Barrah found the pair vaguely disturbing. Kamel
was a quiet mountain of muscle, skill and cunning.
He had been Sabkhat's chief enforcer even before
they left the United Arab Emirates. In fact, Kamel
had joined Jinn 2000 before his boss became a leader
in the movement and actually introduced Sabkhat to
the cult. Kamel remained Sabkhat's man, yet sometimes he seemed to be more than a bodyguard. Kamel
behaved as if he had become Sabkhat's spiritual pro-
tector and moral guardian.

Muda was Kamel's familiar. A small man with a
mean streak, he seemed to favor Kamel's company
because the larger man represented physical strength
and commanded respect and fear among the other
followers of Jinn 2000. Muda could bask in the glory
of his association with Kamel.

"We were about to call you in, Kamel," Sabkhat

began. "How would you like a promotion to permanent base security chief and military adviser?"

"Isn't that what I'm doing now?" Kamel replied.

"This will make it official," Sabkhat stated. "We'll also need you to take over Captain Qatrun's position until we can get a qualified military officer to take his place. I'm going to leave tonight and head for the peninsula to see about recruiting a replacement."

"You can't leave tonight," Kamel said. "A sandstorm will make travel too difficult and dangerous."

"Perhaps this is also an omen," Barrah remarked. "You should stay here and join us in ritual prayer. Together our voices can call to God for strength and insight."

Sabkhat didn't relish spending two or three hours of formal prayers, chants and Koran recitals, yet he realized the importance of maintaining the right image among the Jinn 2000 followers. Sabkhat knew many of them regarded him with suspicion. Bankers weren't viewed as particularly religious individuals by virtually any culture. He couldn't afford to feed any doubts among the fanatics.

"Of course," he said with as much conviction as possible. "That would be good for us all."

"I'll start to prepare the mosque and assemble the rest," Barrah declared with approval.

The Saudi left the room. Kamel moved to the table to switch off Sabkhat's computer. The banker opened his mouth to protest only to stare in astonishment as Kamel yanked the terminal cable from the wall.

"What do you think you're doing by this insolence?" Sabkhat demanded, stunned by Kamel's actions.

"We have to consider the danger of communications being monitored and tracked,'' Kamel explained without apology. ''The infidel Americans have access to advanced technology that may allow them to intercept computer transmissions and locate this base.''

''You could have explained that before you disconnected my machine,'' Sabkhat commented. ''I'll need to plug everything back in to try to contact Nadia. I haven't heard from her since she left here after her visit.''

''That woman really isn't a proper Muslim,'' Kamel stated. ''She was a bad influence, and you'd do well to find a better mate.''

Sabkhat clenched a fist in anger but didn't attempt to throw a punch at the big bodyguard. He was no match for Kamel, and he knew it. Kamel's face remained stern and expressionless. Muda glanced down at the floor, uncomfortable with the situation.

''What right do you have to make such judgments about my personal life?'' he asked.

''Your faith is weak, sir,'' Kamel answered, ''but Jinn 2000 needs you to help make the prophecies of Omar become reality. We need your abilities and intelligence. You were delivered to us as surely as Barrah and the SHC weapon.''

''What happened to Nadia?'' Sabkhat asked. ''What did you do to her?''

''Forget about that whore,'' Kamel replied. ''We are going to change the world. You must be strong and rise above the weakness of the flesh. Paradise will be our reward and the power of mighty jinn over lesser souls.''

''I understand,'' Sabkhat began, aware it was pointless to argue with a fanatic. ''You're going to help me be a worthy leader.''

"You will be," Kamel assured him. "When you see the truth and realize this is the path to real glory and salvation. Besides, you really have no choice."

"No," Sabkhat replied, "I guess I don't."

He thought of Nadia, but forced himself not to dwell on her. Sabkhat didn't want them to see how much the woman had meant to him. He could cry for her later, after Kamel was dead. Perhaps he couldn't take Kamel in a fair fight, face-to-face, but eventually he would get his chance to put a bullet in the man's brain.

Indeed, he had no choice now.

CHAPTER TWENTY-EIGHT

Mack Bolan operated the controls and rudders of the Bell helicopter as he scanned the Mediterranean below. Although the flight would be brief from the deck of an Egyptian naval vessel to the oil-derrick platform at Khalij Surt, tension made the journey seem much longer.

Yakov Katzenelenbogen sat in the rear of the chopper, the sole passenger.

The shoreline formed a huge horseshoe formation in the sea as the chopper approached the platform. The chopper had entered Libyan airspace.

"I'm beginning to think being semiretired may not be as restful as I expected," Katz remarked.

"You regret volunteering, Yakov?" Bolan asked. "Coburn or Captain Lavi or someone else who speaks fluent Arabic could have accompanied me."

"I realize that," Katz admitted with a shrug. "I suppose I really wouldn't want anyone else to go with you for this little meeting. After spending hours in Saudi Arabia with scientists discussing nuclear fusion, I was ready to do something a bit more familiar."

"This isn't exactly a familiar job," the Executioner said. "Neither of us has ever met the leader of Libya before."

"No," Katz agreed, "but I doubt he agreed to meet us if he intended to kill us. Hopefully he doesn't know we've ruined a number of terrorist operations that involved agents from Libya."

"Well," Bolan replied, "I won't tell him if you won't."

"Might not be a wise topic of conversation," Katz agreed.

Lights ringed the platform to the derrick. No longer used for offshore drilling, the structure had been converted to a heliport and observation post. Although a chopper occupied part of the platform, Bolan had plenty of area to land the Bell craft. Several figures waited by the port, most armed with AK-47 assault rifles.

"Okay," the Executioner announced, "this is it."

The helicopter descended to the platform. Uniformed men watched with hard expressions and firm grips on their weapons. Yet Bolan noticed none pointed a gun barrel at the Bell. The gunship touched down, and he shut down the engine.

The Executioner and Katz emerged from the aircraft, heads bowed although the rotor blades spun slowly above them with no risk of decapitation. Soldiers seemed concerned as the pair approached. Bolan saw three figures advance, fists on the pistol grips of their Kalashnikovs, although the barrels remained pointed toward the sky. A voice shouted in Arabic.

"They want us to raise our hands and stand very still," Katz translated for the Executioner.

"Probably worried about our pistols," Bolan commented.

"I think that's probable," the Israeli replied.

"Tell them we'll put down our guns if they do likewise," Bolan instructed.

"I don't think we're in a position to dictate terms," Katz warned. "We're on Libyan territory."

"All the more reason we can't look like wimps," Bolan replied. "We're not embassy diplomats or representatives from the State Department. They know it, and there's no point for us to try to pretend to be something we're not."

"American?" a man inquired. "I speak English, American."

He stepped forward as he spoke. He was a young officer with a holstered side arm. His hands were behind his back, away from his pistol...unless he carried a second weapon at the small of his spine.

"You refuse to surrender your weapons?" he asked.

"We didn't come here to surrender," Bolan replied. "We're basically soldiers, not unlike yourself. Your leader is supposed to be here. If he isn't, we'll fly out. Sure would be a shame because we came here to try to save lives, including Libyan lives."

A voice greeted them and a figure emerged from the shadows, his back ramrod straight. Although he didn't wear his familiar military uniform or dark glasses, Bolan and Katz immediately recognized the Libyan leader.

Some had referred to him as a madman. Allegedly Anwar Sadat had once said the Libyan was "possessed by the devil." Indeed, many believed he had arranged the assassination of Sadat and sponsored numerous terrorist actions against the United States, Israel and Egypt.

Most of the world regarded him as one of the most dangerous men in the Middle East. Only Saddam Hussein and the late Ayatollah Khomeini could equal him as a notorious leader of an Islamic nation. Yet his dark eyes seemed intelligent and calm, without the slightest hint of a fanatic zeal. He spoke quietly.

"The colonel welcomes us and assures us we will not be harmed," Katz translated. "He says we have courage to come here and he admires courage, even from his enemies."

"Tonight we're not enemies," Bolan replied. "The colonel certainly knows about the terrorist incident in Tel Aviv today."

The Libyan's translator spoke to the colonel, who frowned and replied with a shrug.

"He says he had nothing to do with it," Katz explained.

"We believe him," Bolan stated, "but we also believe Jinn 2000 has a headquarters in Libya. He can probably tell us where it is because Captain Qatrun was one of his officers. I wouldn't be surprised if he had been assigned to provide protection and security to Professor Barrah after the scientist fled from Saudi Arabia."

"Why would I give protection to a Saudi scientist?" the colonel asked through the translator.

"Barrah is an expert in nuclear fusion," Bolan replied. "You have a great interest in nuclear power and weapons. Of course you'd welcome him despite differences between your country and Saudi Arabia."

"Perhaps. What does the professor have to do with what happened in Tel Aviv?"

"Barrah isn't really working for you," Bolan said. "He's involved with Jinn 2000. Probably one of its leaders. You know about the cult movement, Colonel?"

"Shiite Muslim extremists," the Libyan confirmed through his translator. "I am a Sunni Muslim and so are the vast majority of my people. Jinn 2000 hate us as much as they do you Jews and Christians. I wouldn't give aid and shelter to lunatics as apt to carry out terrorist actions against my government and people as they would against America or Israel.''

''You probably haven't welcomed them or know about their activities in Libya,'' Bolan replied, ''but Jinn 2000 has a base here. Barrah didn't tell you he belonged to the sect, and I'm sure Qatrun didn't mention it.''

''Where is Captain Qatrun?'' the colonel asked through the translator. ''I would like to speak with him myself.''

''He's dead,'' the Executioner replied. ''He's been identified, and we're sure about his involvement. I know about this firsthand when I saw him ruling over cult activities in Cairo. We encountered him again in Tel Aviv in the act of terrorism and attempted assassination.''

''You're sure he's dead?''

''I plunged a knife in his heart,'' Bolan answered. ''That usually does it.''

The Libyan leader considered what he had heard before he spoke to the translator again.

''The colonel says he'll look into this matter, and they'll take care of it,'' Katz explained.

''Please tell the colonel we've got to take care of this ourselves,'' Bolan replied.

The Libyan's eyes hardened when he heard this. He fixed his gaze on Bolan as he spoke.

''If this is a Libyan problem, Libya will take care of it.''

''The threat is international,'' Bolan insisted. ''It extends far beyond Libya and the Middle East. You

wouldn't know anything about this if we hadn't come
to you tonight.''

The colonel shrugged when this was explained to
him by a hesitant translator. The Libyan leader didn't
seem offended by Bolan's remarks.

"We appreciate the information," the colonel
stated in English. "Thank you, and we'll handle the
situation now."

"We have to finish this mission to satisfy the governments of the leaders threatened by the terrorist
actions today," Bolan insisted. "Otherwise, Israel
and Egypt, perhaps others, will believe your country
was involved. We can't even promise the United
States government will be satisfied unless we handle
this personally."

"Just you two?" the colonel asked with amusement.

"There will be a few others with me," Bolan explained. "A small group of special men trained for
this sort of operation will be the best way to handle
it."

"We have commando units here in Libya."

"I'm sure they're very skilled," Bolan assured
him, "but Qatrun was a member of Jinn 2000 and
no one knew it. The terrorists even managed to plant
a spy within the Israeli Intelligence system, and he
wasn't discovered until yesterday. The men in my
outfit have worked with me many times in the past.
None of them are secretly connected with Jinn
2000."

"They're Americans?"

"Exact nationality isn't really important," Bolan
replied. "We don't want to cause a conflict with
Libya, Colonel. Just the opposite. We came to ask
for your help and help you in return."

"Really?" The colonel seemed surprised. "What sort of help do you want from me?"

"We have a pretty good idea where the base is located. The terrorists seem to be able to travel to and from Egypt and their headquarters. That means they're probably based near the eastern border of your country. They'd need to carry out their activities with a low profile and as much privacy as possible. Most likely they've got a base in the Libyan Sahara."

"The Sahara," the colonel mused.

"A recent satellite scan of the region will probably help us select the target," Bolan continued. "You must realize your country is under constant and intense surveillance."

"American technology," the Libyan commented. The expression of contempt on the colonel's face dispelled any notions he spoke with admiration.

"There's also British, Canadian, German and Japanese technology," Bolan said with a shrug. "Hard to tell them apart these days. Still, you can help us get the right target if you have any information that might help. You can also arrange for us to enter Libya without having to sneak past border patrols or radar. Of course, we'll need to get out again, as well."

"You ask me to risk my country's security by allowing agents of an enemy infidel nation to simply stroll in and out freely," the colonel remarked. "And you expect to carry out whatever mission you wish without Libyan involvement?"

"Your soldiers and my people wouldn't trust each other anyway, Colonel," Bolan stated. "Best we do this quietly with as few people aware of what's involved as possible."

"How do you intend to help me?" the Libyan asked.

"If the world in general learns the Jinn 2000 base is in Libya, your country will be subjected to even more isolation and restrictions on international trade," Bolan began. "Libya has already suffered economic problems due to restrictions and sanctions imposed because of accusations of terrorist activity."

"We have endured and will continue to do so," the colonel insisted. "Despite what you Americans might think, I took power in 1969 with the support of my people, and I stay in charge for the same reason."

"I won't argue with you about that," Bolan assured him. "I know the standards of living and education for Libyans have improved during your rule. Of course, you can't maintain good medical care, schools and various goods and services if you can't export your most valuable natural resource."

"The Americans and the British may not trade with my country, but other countries are still willing to do business with us."

"Last I heard, you were selling most of your oil exports to Germany, Italy and Spain," the Executioner remarked. "I also recall you've tried to mend fences with the United States to try to reestablish trade, but you've been turned down every time. It had to have gotten tough after the Soviet Union fell and you no longer received support and military aid from Moscow."

"You're not suggesting America will be more willing to trade with Libya if we cooperate with you?" the colonel asked.

"Of course not," Bolan replied. "We're not politicians. We can tell them back in Washington you cooperated and that may be in your favor, but we don't have any say about national or international policies. No hollow promises and no threats."

"Talk about increased restrictions is not a threat?"

"You know that will happen if you turn us down. That's not a threat, colonel. The U.S. will certainly use its influence to try to get other Western nations to cut off or reduce trade with Libya. You also know how America can respond to terrorism when they decide to take off the gloves."

"You refer to the bombing of Tripoli after your country accused my government of being involved with that business in Germany in 1986. You know my adopted daughter was killed during that attack?"

"Like I said," Bolan replied, "we don't have anything to do with U.S. policy, but you don't want to anger Uncle Sam. We need to shut down Jinn 2000, and it's really in your best interest to let us do it."

"Professor Barrah must be involved with these fanatics for a reason," the Libyan commented. "His work in nuclear fusion is part of it? Terrorists aren't usually interested in a new source of energy unless it means they have a new weapon of some kind."

"Or a money source," Bolan stated. "Barrah's research gets investors to provide funds, but this is used to finance terrorist operations, not to develop fusion power."

The colonel frowned and glanced down at the deck. Bolan wasn't certain if his expression meant he was annoyed by this claim because he knew it wasn't true or because he believed he had been one of the investors suckered by the scheme to provide funds for Jinn 2000.

"Barrah has not had any success developing fusion technology?" he asked.

"I'm a soldier," Bolan replied, "not a scientist. Sometimes they claim they've made progress because they have a new theory or an experiment suggests they're on the path to making a breakthrough. I'm not sure how scientists judge success when they can't really show you anything they've accomplished to prove it."

Katz glanced at the Executioner, aware of the gamble he had made. Bolan guessed the colonel didn't know Jinn 2000 had the spontaneous-human-combustion device. Barrah had probably arrived with impressive credentials to prove his knowledge and background in nuclear research. That would be enough to get a VIP welcome from the Libyan and plenty of support for the Saudi scientist's work in the field.

If Bolan was wrong and the colonel was a sponsor or coconspirator with Jinn 2000, they wouldn't get permission to carry out a raid on the enemy compound. Bolan and Katz probably wouldn't even leave the platform alive. They could go down fighting, perhaps even take the colonel with them, but they were seriously outnumbered and outgunned by the troops on the derrick and those stationed along the shore. Even if they managed to reach the helicopter, they would be blown out of the sky before they could fly clear of Libyan airspace.

"Your group will be permitted to cross the border from Egypt," the colonel announced. "You'll even be provided with a map to avoid land-mine fields and other obstacles, as well as indicating a clear route to Barrah's base. I strongly advise you to follow it exactly. You will be under surveillance. If we have any reason to doubt your motives, we will treat you as enemy invaders. That is understood?"

"Yes," Bolan agreed, "we understand."

"How much time will you require for this mission?"

"That will depend on transportation methods, distance, how long it will take to recon the site and evaluate the target before putting together a strategy to launch the raid. Then we have to get out. Someone may need medical attention. Perhaps more than one member of our unit and prisoners taken alive."

"No prisoners," the colonel insisted. "You either kill them all or leave survivors for us to deal with as enemies of the nation of Libya. You're not taking anyone out of my country who is not a member of the original insertion team."

Bolan considered this demand for a moment. He didn't like the idea of leaving anyone, even a terrorist, to the mercy of a government that authorized the use of torture. Libya had a notorious reputation for such human-rights violations, although several other nations in the Middle East and North Africa were probably much worse.

However, the colonel had two reasons for this demand. One was the obvious desire to maintain conditions and show outsiders they couldn't simply enter his country and do as they pleased without regard for his authority. The other was to have evidence that Libya had cooperated due to the mutual desire to stop extremists who threatened Libya and Sunni Muslims, as well as other countries considered to be infidel nations. If the colonel had enemy terrorists held prisoner and given a public trial, the outsiders couldn't claim full credit for the defeat of Jinn 2000 when and if it became known to the world at large.

"Agreed," the Executioner declared. "I can't

promise how long the entire operation might take,
Colonel. Perhaps eight hours.''

"All right. You'll have eight hours when you enter
Libya at the border. Two battalions will be on
standby alert if you need assistance. They can supply
air support, cover fire, backup units or medical assistance if necessary. They can also help with transportation when you're ready to leave.''

"Very generous, Colonel,'' Bolan replied.

"If you all get killed during the raid,'' the colonel
continued, "my troops will have no option except to
destroy the base with rocket fire and cannon shells.
We could do that rather than let your people in. It
would certainly present less risk.''

"But you wouldn't be sure you got all the terrorists that way, and you'd probably destroy records
they may have which will help track down other terrorists in place outside the base. Some are in other
countries, but some may be in Libya, as well.''

"I'd say we have an agreement,'' the colonel
stated. "You have heard the Arab proverb 'The enemy of my enemy is my friend.' I doubt your country
and mine will ever be friends, but tonight we are
allies.''

"That'll have to do,'' the Executioner said, "for
tonight.''

CHAPTER TWENTY-NINE

The desert-terrain combat vehicle rolled across the sand, its tractor wheels working smoothly in the loose surface. Developed by Egyptian and German military engineers, the DTCV had been specially designed for desert transportation and combat. The engine purred, and the gears made less noise than the grinding sand under the treads.

David McCarter drove the vehicle, seeming to be pleased with its performance. Mack Bolan was also impressed by the desert rig as he sat beside the Phoenix Force commander. The exterior of the vehicle was gray-and-tan desert camouflage, but the interior was black metal and leather. It handled sixty miles per hour without sliding out of control across the dunes, and thanks to a pair of Starlite night-vision goggles, McCarter safely drove the rig in the dark without need for headlights.

Bolan studied the map provided by the Libyans when they crossed the border. He checked a compass to be certain they were on track to the Jinn 2000 headquarters.

"Any idea how many terrorists we can expect to find at the base?" Hawkins asked as he leaned forward in a seat behind the Executioner.

"The place is large enough to house about a hundred and twenty," Gary Manning stated. "We got pretty detailed blueprints from the Libyan Intel department. Let's hope there won't be quite that many men to deal with when we arrive."

"I never cared much for fifty-to-one odds," Rafael Encizo added. "Since there are only six of us, I'd just as soon find the place empty except for a couple sleeping sentries to guard that damn SHC device."

"That would be nice for a change," Calvin James agreed. "I'm still surprised by how much cooperation we got from the man who runs this country."

"The colonel may not have much use for America, Israel, Egypt or a few other countries threatened by Jinn 2000 terrorism," Bolan replied, "but his own country and government are at risk, too. The danger of having Libya bombed or invaded for harboring the fanatics is even greater than that posed by the terrorists themselves. Whatever else can be said about the man, he isn't stupid. This is the best way to deal with Jinn 2000, and he knows it."

"Best for him maybe," McCarter mused. "Not so sure about us. I like a challenge as much as the next bloke, but this one has to rank pretty high on the level of high risk even by our standards."

"I can't believe I'm hearing that from you," Manning commented with surprise.

"It's not just my life at stake," the Briton explained. "Not even the lives of all you, which mean a lot to me. We've got a problem even if we do make it to the base, take out the terrorists and find that SHC device."

"Yeah," Bolan said with a nod. "Getting out of Libya with the weapon in tow. They might have let us in without a problem, but it's not likely they'll let us leave carrying something that's obviously a weapon of some sort.''

"The colonel might have bought that story that Barrah was running a kind of con to get assistance and funds for Jinn 2000,'' Manning began, "but he knows the guy was involved in nuclear-fusion technology, and any large item we try to take out of here is going to raise suspicion damn quick.''

"If we knew more about the device, we could probably break it down and try to smuggle out the essential parts,'' Hawkins remarked. "Sure wasn't enough left of that gizmo back in Tel Aviv to teach us anything. The way all the metal had been fused together after Qatrun triggered the self-destruct button...hell, I can't even tell you how we could begin to disassemble the thing if we get a chance to grab the one at their head shed.''

"At least we know the one they have there is the original smuggled out by Barrah,'' James commented. "Some of the terrorists interrogated back at Israel told us there were only two SHC microwave cannons. One is a piece of melted junk, and the other is at the base.''

"They planned to build some more weapons, but they won't get a chance to now,'' Hawkins commented. "That might not be much comfort if the Libyans get their hands on the original and use it for a prototype to build more for their own use.''

"I'm not too happy about delivering the SHC technology to the U.S. government,'' Encizo admitted, "let alone having it fall into Libyan hands.''

"Hopefully it will be put to good use for productive fusion energy instead of the manufacture of more weapons,'' Manning said. "I wish I felt more confident that would happen.''

"Empirical evidence from the study of history isn't very encouraging," James added. "Well, I guess we just do our job and hope the leaders of our government show more wisdom than we usually give them credit for."

"First we have to stay alive long enough to make that delivery," McCarter said. "How much farther until we reach the base, Mack?"

"About twenty klicks," Bolan answered. "Better slow down and stay alert. We can't be sure if they have motion detectors or other surveillance gear set up in the area."

Manning glanced up at the dark, cloudy sky. A storm predicted to reach the Mediterranean had shifted north to Europe. Turbulent winds wouldn't create a massive sandstorm across the desert, but the cloud cover suggested a change in the weather would occur. A chill gripped the commandos as they traveled the Sahara.

The clouds favored their mission by blotting out light from the moon and stars. Their night-vision gear prevented this from being a problem for the Executioner and Phoenix Force. Of course, Jinn 2000 could have similar equipment.

The DTCV approached a row of sand dunes, and McCarter began to drive between two mounds. He suddenly stopped the vehicle when he saw the large dark structure on the western horizon. Surrounded by sand drifts, the building stood like a mirage in the desert.

Bolan raised a pair of night-scope binoculars to observe the site. A rectangular structure, it featured a roof with a curved dome at the east wing and a box-shaped object at the south wing. McCarter shifted gears to back the rig between the dunes. The other members of Phoenix Force weren't certain what happened.

"We found the base," Bolan explained. "About four or five klicks right in front of us. They seem to have an observation post on the roof that looks like a kind of elevated guard house."

"That dome has a cupola with something on the top," James stated as he peered through a pair of binoculars. "It's kind of hard to tell from here, but I think it's a crescent. Must be a mosque built inside the building."

"Yeah," Bolan agreed. "Its position at the wing supports that theory. They must have a sort of Islamic indoor chapel. Gary, you're more familiar with the construction of the site. What can you tell us about strengths and weaknesses according to the blueprints?"

"It was built on the site of an ancient ruins," Manning answered. "Nobody is quite sure how old it was or what purpose the site once served. Probably was an obscure military outpost built sometime during the Ottoman occupation. Archaeologists weren't too interested in whatever function it once had. Only unusual features worth mentioning are some old tunnels under the site. The Libyan Intel officer who provided the data speculated the terrorists might not even know about the tunnels."

"That might be the best way to enter the place," Hawkins suggested. "We could crawl through and enter at the basement level before they know what happened."

"Sure wouldn't count on that," McCarter said, shaking his head. "It's hard for me to believe those blokes wouldn't have discovered the tunnels. After all, they don't have all that much to do out here.

Somebody would be bound to search the remains just out of boredom.''

"I have to agree," Manning said. "The tunnels would be easy to guard. A motion detector would be almost impossible to avoid in a tunnel. Explosives could easily be set in the tunnels to blow the hell out of them if they suspected anyone tried to enter that way. We wouldn't have a chance if we were inside a tunnel and somebody launched a rocket from the other end. Or a flamethrower."

"We can't go in that way," Bolan told them, "but they may use the tunnels for an escape route. Think you can find the openings?"

"Probably," Manning confirmed. "The blueprints show where they are, and there can't be much else out here except sand."

"So find them and set explosives to blow the tunnels to prevent the enemy from using them. Might serve as a good distraction, especially if the effects of the blast travel all the way to the base to make them think someone is trying to attack from the tunnels at basement level."

"A shaped charge with enough shrapnel ought to do it," the Canadian demolitions expert mused. "There are some steel pipes in the storage compartment of this vehicle. It's part of the camp gear, designed for chimney stacks for field stoves and adjustable center poles for tents. I can use them as improvised gun barrels, and they ought to increase the range and trajectory of shrapnel. Same principle as a bazooka."

"Rafael and T.J. can help you," Bolan stated. "The rest of us will investigate the area around the base for detectors, land mines and other types of booby traps. We'll determine the best route to approach the base, making the most of shadows and cover for concealment.''

"Right," Manning agreed.

"Make it quick as you can," the Executioner suggested. "We need to be at full strength when we hit the place."

THE SIX STONY MAN commandos slowly crept toward the enemy base, with Mack Bolan leading McCarter and Hawkins to the south end of the structure. Dressed in black, they blended with the shadows around the building.

The three men carried Uzi submachine guns, favored pistols, knives, garrotes and hand grenades. McCarter also held his Barnett Commando crossbow, equipped with a special night scope. A bolt was set in the Barnett, notched to the bowstring. They approached a pair of thick, rubber-coated cables that extended from the base of the building to the lip of the roof. Cords branched from the main lines to plug into the wall at different levels.

Electrical lines, Bolan realized. Jinn 2000 appeared to have a set of generators in the basement level to supply power to the building. The exposed cables were an obvious flaw because the lines could easily be cut. Bolan intended to take advantage of another opportunity offered by the cables. He adjusted the Uzi, pushing it in well behind the holstered .44 Magnum to be certain it wouldn't scrape or clatter along the stone surface.

He gripped the cables with both hands and pulled hard. They held fast. Bolan placed a boot on the wall and raised the other off the ground. He was a big man, and he wanted to be sure the cables would hold his weight before he tried to climb.

The Executioner grabbed the cable and worked the soles of his feet along the wall. He walked up the surface with ease, experienced in mountaineering and other climbing skills. Bolan gazed up at the rim of the roof as he moved higher and higher along the wall.

A figure appeared above him. The big American leaned close to the wall and clung to the cords. He tried to become part of the stone. Perhaps the sentry on the roof had heard something amid the wind or noticed movement in the shadows. Maybe he had just approached the edge of the roof to relieve himself.

However, a sharp hiss announced he wasn't the only one to notice the enemy on the roof. Bolan heard a thud as a projectile struck flesh. A soft moan with an ugly choked sound was all the sentry could utter.

The Executioner glanced up and saw the shape topple from the edge, then glimpsed the crossbow bolt jammed in the center of the sentry's chest. Bolan knew McCarter's Barnett fired steel-tipped lances, the shaft filled with cyanide. Death was almost instantaneous, the poison gripping nerves and muscles to all but silence the victim.

The body plunged to the ground. Bolan wasted no time and quickly scaled the cords to the roof. The Briton's crossbow was a quiet killer and made less noise than a silenced firearm, but he assumed there was probably at least one more guard at the rooftop station. He also had to assume the guy would have seen the sentry fall from the edge.

Bolan gripped the lip of the roof and hauled himself onto the top. He propped himself up with his left elbow, and drew the silenced Beretta 93-R from shoulder leather with his right hand, then pointed the pistol at the guard shack.

A figure emerged, an assault rifle in hand. Bolan triggered the Beretta, and a 3-round burst rasped from the weapon. The second guard groaned, dropped his rifle and fell backward into the open doorway. His body slumped into a seated position, twitched slightly and lay still in death. Bolan got to his feet, cautiously moved to the shed and peered inside.

He discovered a small desk, two chairs and a stairwell that descended to the interior of the building. A two-way radio transceiver sat on the desktop, but it was switched to a broadcast of music sung in Arabic. The microphone for transmitting remained hooked to the set. The guard hadn't reported his suspicions before he left the shack to investigate his comrade's swan dive.

Bolan emerged from the shed. Hawkins had already climbed to the roof and stood by the edge, Uzi held at hip level. McCarter's hand appeared with the Barnett. Hawkins took the crossbow and helped his partner onto the roof. The Executioner glanced at his wristwatch. The others should be in position and ready for their cue to begin the raid.

"I found a way downstairs," he announced. "T.J. cut the cables and the wires. We'll put the enemy inside in the dark. That'll give us an obvious advantage with our night goggles."

"Probably won't shut off power for the whole building," Hawkins replied. "The cables seem to have limited capacity. There's probably another set over by the north wing."

"The others should be in position there," Bolan

said. "When they realize half the lights have gone out in the windows, they'll cut the rest. They're all smart enough to don their goggles before they go in."

"Would have liked a little more recon to get an idea of the enemy strength," McCarter admitted, "but what the hell. Let's do it."

Hawkins extracted a pair of rubber-handled clippers from his gear and knelt by the edge of the roof. Sparks ignited as he snipped through the cables, followed by shouts of alarm that echoed from the staircase inside the guard shack. Bolan headed for the stairs, followed by the Phoenix Force commandos.

A thunderous explosion boomed outside the compound. The building trembled in response. Gary Manning had recognized the signal and triggered a radio transmitter to set off the detonators to the charges by the tunnels. Shrapnel had clearly bombarded the shafts to tear into the basement level of the structures. The ancient ruins were certainly ruined now.

Bolan held the Beretta forward as he descended the iron staircase. The Starlite goggles used special optics to increase reflected light. Even in the pitch darkness within the building, Bolan saw clearly, although images appeared ghostly yellow and sickly green.

He reached the bottom riser and discovered a supply room. Rows of canned goods, bags of flour and rice, boxes of food and other items lined wall shelves. Two terrorists were already busy at a table, their backs turned to the stairwell. One man held a flashlight for the other, who had dragged a long wooden box from under the furniture. A third terrorist located some cardboard boxes from a shelf that contained more flashlights.

Bolan hurried toward the pair with the crate, which he guessed held a packed weapon of some sort. They would never get to claim the prize. The situation called for ruthless tactics, and the Executioner didn't hesitate. He raised his pistol and shot the first man at the base of the skull. The flashlight fell to the floor and rolled to cast a wild streak of light low across the room.

The slain Jinn 2000 hardman collapsed across the tabletop. His companion looked up, unsure of what had happened in the dark. He had probably heard the muffled report of Bolan's Beretta, but didn't fully comprehend what it meant. The big American shot him between the eyes before he could figure it out.

David McCarter attacked the third man from behind and swiftly swung a wire garrote over the terrorist's head, yanking the handles to tighten the steel noose around his adversary's neck. The SAS veteran stomped the back of the man's knee to buckle his leg and bring him down as he expertly twisted the wire to hasten his victim's death.

Twin beams of light appeared from the entrance to the room. Two more Jinn 2000 members had entered with flashlights. If the three Stony Man commandos had worn the old infrared night-vision gear, they would have been blinded by the sudden glare, but the Starlite system simply produced a bright blob of yellow with greenish humanoid shapes around it.

Hawkins nailed the closest opponent with the stubby barrel of his Uzi subgun. He struck it across the man's wrist to knock the flashlight from the guy's grasp, then rammed the metal buttstock into the terrorist's solar plexus. The man gasped, winded and stunned by the blow. Hawkins hooked his ankle behind the guy's leg and pushed with the frame of the SMG. The combination tripped the man and dumped him on his back. Hawkins followed him to the floor, hammered his skull with the Uzi to render the terrorist unconscious.

McCarter pounced on the second terrorist, then grabbed the man's arms as he pumped a knee to his groin. He followed through by snapping his head forward to butt his frontal bone into the bridge of his adversary's nose. He shoved the stunned man into a wall and picked his next target.

The Briton's arms shot out like pistons, hands clenched in fists, but the index fingers bent at the center knuckle, reinforced by the thumb. In Chinese kung fu this technique was known as a "phoenix head," and McCarter was very skilled in that lethal hand formation. Each knuckle struck like a blunted spearhead. One blow caught the terrorist in the windpipe, and the other hit the sphenoid at the side of the guy's head. Either blow could be fatal. When the man slid to the floor, McCarter had no doubt he would never get up again.

They had no time to spare congratulating themselves. Mack Bolan strode from the supply room, Beretta held ready. Hawkins and McCarter followed. Voices within the compound warned there were still many more Jinn 2000 terrorists to confront.

Their job had just begun.

CHAPTER THIRTY

When the lights went out at the windows and voices cried out within the building, Gary Manning switched the radio detonator to set off the charges by the tunnels. The Canadian demolitions expert knelt by the north wing of the base as he triggered the long-range blast, then immediately set off another detonator attached to a special blasting cap inserted in a strip of CV-38 plastic explosive placed by the electrical cables near his position.

A low-level explosive, the CV-38 ignited to blast apart the cables while barely scorching stone. James and Encizo were also at the north wing, but their attention was fixed on two terrorist sentries positioned by the west-wing entrance. The guards were distracted and disoriented by the sudden blackout, explosions and general confusion.

The African-American and Cuban warriors were ready for that moment. The sentries had turned to face the building, trying to determine what had happened. Their backs toward the Phoenix Force pair, neither man realized the danger until the commandos charged. James galloped forward, judged the distance and leaped toward the closer opponent.

One leg extended, he sailed into the terrorist with a classic tae kwon do flying kick. His boot slammed

between the man's shoulder blades and propelled the
sentry facefirst into the wall. Encizo rushed past the
dazed thug to attack the second man.

James landed surefooted behind his target and continued his assault on the stunned guard. He drove a
fist to the guy's kidney and lashed a karate chop to
the man's nape, then wrapped his arm around the
sentry's throat and slid the other under the guy's arm
to place the palm on the back of his head in a half
nelson. He secured the hold in a viselike manner before he turned hard. The final twist caused a crunch
of vertebrae. The body went limp, and James allowed
it to fall.

Encizo grabbed the frame of the second sentry's
AK-47 as the man turned to face him. The Cuban
shoved to prevent his opponent from bringing the
barrel into position as he struck with the Tanto fighting knife in his other fist. Sharp steel pierced the
terrorist under the rib cage to puncture his liver.
Blood splashed the Phoenix Force commando's wrist
as he worked the blade from the man's flesh.

A moan of pain escaped from the terrorist's throat
as he convulsed in Encizo's grasp. The Cuban delivered a rapid diagonal slash to the side of the man's
neck, the edge slitting the carotid artery. Crimson
splashed from the terrible wound, and the man's
body sagged to the ground. Encizo wiped the blade
on the dead man's clothing before he returned it to
the belt sheath.

Manning approached, barely glancing at the slain
sentries. He reached for another packet of CV-38 to
blast the door. Encizo and James stepped away from
the opening and gripped their Uzi subguns as Manning prepared to set the charge by the lock.

Suddenly the door swung open, and the startled

face of a young Arab stared at Manning, his eyes wide and jaw dropped in an openmouthed gasp. The Canadian was vaguely aware of the heads and shoulders of more terrorists behind the first, but he didn't hesitate, instead swiftly charging across the threshold.

The brawny demolitions pro plowed a muscular shoulder into the chest of the first Jinn 2000 hardman. The force of the blow lifted the guy off his feet and drove him backward into two of his comrades. Manning and the terrorist trio crashed to the floor in a thrashing mass of arms and legs.

Other terrorists stared down at the struggling group and started to move their weapons, unsure if they should open fire or use the buttstocks as clubs to avoid hitting their comrades. James and Encizo spared them of the need to decide. The Phoenix Force pair fired their Uzis in unison, twin streams of 9 mm slugs tearing into the skulls and upper torsos of several Jinn 2000 gunmen.

Manning continued to struggle with his three adversaries as bullets sizzled above them. He grabbed one man by the forelock of his hair and rammed his head backward to hammer it into the face of another terrorist. The third opponent threw a short, awkward punch to Manning's head, the big Canadian barely grunting from the blow.

The terrorist attempted another punch as Manning raised his Uzi with one hand, continuing to use the other to punch his other two foes. The fist intended for Manning's head crashed into the steel frame of the submachine gun, the attacker yelping in pain.

James arrived, slamming a hard kick to the temple of a terrorist's skull to take the guy out of play, repeating the maneuver to take out a second gunner.

Manning finished off the last man with a fist to the jaw and another blow to the mastoid bone.

Two more Jinn 2000 followers rushed from a corridor to investigate the cause of gunfire, uncertain as to what had happened. Encizo didn't give them a chance to find out and hosed the pair with a volley of Uzi slugs. Manning started to rise while James lobbed a grenade into the corridor as light beams danced along the walls.

The explosion roared in the hall, and chunks of human debris, pieces of a wall and a battered flashlight hurled through the air. The three commandos headed for the south wing, gunfire from above revealing that Bolan, McCarter and Hawkins continued the battle with the enemy upstairs.

They encountered a few terrorists, fumbling about in the dark without benefit of flashlights. The Phoenix Force trio couldn't hesitate just because the situation appeared to be unfair. This was war, not a sporting event. The Uzis opened fire and cut down the Jinn 2000 hardmen. Only one managed to point his weapon at the muzzle-flash of their subguns before 9 mm parabellum shockers blasted off the top of his skull.

A row of doors lined the hallway. Encizo watched the corridor as James approached a door by the lock, Manning taking a position parallel to the African-American. They stood clear as James kicked the door in. The big Canadian fired a short burst while James yanked the pin from a grenade. He tossed the explosive egg inside while Manning triggered another volley to discourage anyone from trying to scoop it up and throw it from the room.

The grenade erupted with a monstrous bellow. They glanced inside and spotted bloodied, mangled figures among the wreckage within. An arm moved, perhaps only a twitch of a fresh corpse, but James sprayed the fallen enemies with Uzi fire to be sure. Manning took advantage of the moment to reload his SMG.

They repeated the process and swapped positions so no member of the team would exhaust his supply of ammo or grenades. They hit room after room. Enemies returned fire, but none scored a hit. The Jinn 2000 terrorists lacked the Phoenix Force trio's experience and training, which cost them their lives as the one-sided battle continued.

THE EXECUTIONER, MCCARTER and Hawkins conducted a similar program of enemy destruction on the second floor of the building. Terrorists had flooded the hallway in response to the blackout and the sound of combat downstairs, but three Uzis had quickly brought down several hardmen and drove the rest to cover in the rooms.

The Stony Man team made its way from the south wing to the north, taking out dozens of opponents in the process. The terrorists seemed even more confused, startled and disoriented than circumstances justified. Perhaps they believed so strongly they were the true believers and soldiers of God that they couldn't conceive how infidels were able to invade their stronghold.

If their inability to grasp reality worked in Bolan's favor, this was fine with the Executioner. His first concern was to stop the terrorists and keep the SHC device from being used by ruthless killers. His second goal was to try to get Phoenix Force and himself out of the compound and Libya alive and as healthy as possible.

Only two rooms remained on the second-story level as Bolan assumed the chore of lookout for his companions. He held his Uzi ready while McCarter and Hawkins moved to the first door. The Briton kicked it in, then Hawkins fired into the room and McCarter lobbed the grenade.

The explosion ripped the support beam from the doorframe and propelled large chunks of the wall into the startled commandos. A second blast hurled more debris, dust and grisly remains into the hallway. Bolan saw McCarter and Hawkins had been knocked to the floor and were half-buried by the rubble, but his first concern had to be a possible threat from the enemy.

The big American rushed to the enlarged opening and sprayed the room with a sustained burst. But no one had survived. The damage was greater than one would expect from a single grenade blast. Bolan guessed one of the terrorists had to have pulled the pin from a grenade when Hawkins first opened fire. Bullets had claimed the man, but the explosive had already been unleashed. It apparently blew near the threshold to hammer the Phoenix Force pair to the floor.

Hawkins and McCarter stirred beneath the wreckage. They were alive, but Bolan didn't know how badly they might have been injured. Movement by the last door forced him to concentrate on the danger that remained. The warrior whirled, glimpsed a figure and triggered his SMG.

The last three rounds from the Uzi tore a jagged line of bullet holes in the upper torso of an enemy gunman. The guy fell backward into a corner and slid lifeless to the floor, a Russian-made Stechkin machine pistol still gripped in his fist. Bolan dis-

carded the empty subgun and unleathered the Desert
Eagle as he moved to the door.

He realized the terrorists inside the last room had
to feel trapped and desperate. Unless they were total
fools, they realized virtually all their comrades were
gone. Bolan guessed they listened to the pattern of
automatic fire, explosives and more automatic fire.

However, the Executioner couldn't use the same
method alone. Two men could fire at the enemy to
keep them busy while a grenade was tossed and prevent them from throwing or kicking it back into the
hallway. Chances of success with this method were
slim if Bolan was alone.

The soldier moved to the open door, back against
the wall and pistol pointed at the threshold. He
switched the big .44 pistol to his left hand and
plucked a grenade from his belt. He didn't remove
the pin from the M-26 fragger as he canted the barrel
of the big steel gun toward the doorway.

He triggered the weapon twice, then hurled the
grenade. Bolan deliberately tossed it high enough to
allow anyone inside to see the M-26. He hoped they
didn't observe it well enough to notice the spoon and
pin were still in place. Startled voices shouted something in Arabic that suggested they recognized the
threat.

Bolan's right hand streaked for the Beretta under
his arm as he dived through the doorway. He fired
both pistols while in midair and glimpsed a figure a
moment before a Magnum slug slammed the enemy
gunner backward. The big American hit the floor and
continued to trigger the handguns, firing more for
effect and to hold them at bay than to hit a particular
target.

A Jinn 2000 hardman seemed frozen in place, like

a deer caught in the headlights of a car on a lonely
stretch of road. He bent at the waist, one hand near
the M-26 and the other clutching the grips of a
Kalashnikov assault rifle. The terrorist seemed to realize the pin was still in the grenade and a human
tornado, spitting bullets, had suddenly materialized
in the room. He appeared too baffled to know what
to do. Bolan split his skull with a trio of 9 mm rounds
to end the burden within the man's baffled brain.

Bolan pivoted on the small of his back as his left
hand triggered the big Desert Eagle. The shots went
high, but he saw figures scramble, alarmed by the
thunderous report of the Magnum as much as the
threat of .44 projectiles. A big hardman dived for
cover by a large metal desk, accompanied by a
smaller bearded terrorist who sprayed a hasty salvo
of rounds from a Skorpion machine pistol into a wall
well above Bolan's position.

Two other shapes cowered in a corner near a long
silver metal tube with a clear muzzle. Bolan was surprised to see the original SHC device. The pair near
the weapon didn't appear to be armed or even to
possess enough battle savvy to seek adequate cover
in a gunfight. Civilians, Bolan realized, probably Professor Barrah and someone else better suited for research work or paper plots than actual combat.

The Executioner rose from the floor and crossed
his wrists to get better control of the pistols. The four
men he had located seemed to be all that remained
of Jinn 2000. He swung the guns toward the guy with
the Skorpion as the big man appeared behind the
desk.

Bolan's weapons boomed. A big .44 slug struck
Muda in the upper lip. The Magnum round shattered

the maxilla bone, pierced the palate and burrowed into the terrorist's brain. Bone fragments contributed to the damage, but Muda was already dead before his body collapsed by the desk.

Three Beretta rounds slashed near Kamel's position, two barely missing. The third tore into the big henchman's left arm to puncture the brachial muscle and exit at the triceps. Kamel cried out as the wounded limb swung out of control. He lost his grip on his Makarov pistol, and the handgun skidded across the desktop to fall on the floor, well beyond his reach.

"Please!" Sabkhat shouted. "We surrender!"

The banker raised his hands as he stepped next to the SHC machine. Professor Barrah stared at Sabkhat, startled by his actions. Although the scientist didn't raise his hands, his palms were open and held in front of his chest in a pleading gesture. Bolan saw the scientist didn't hold a weapon.

"Don't shoot," Sabkhat urged. He turned to the desk and addressed Kamel in Arabic. "No need to kill us. Agreed?"

Kamel shuffled from the desk, his right hand clutched to his wounded left arm. He glared at Bolan but made no threatening gesture as he approached.

"What do you mean?" Barrah demanded.

"It means we quit this whole stupid business," Sabkhat snapped at the scientist. "And speak English so this man will understand. You are an American, sir? Yes?"

Bolan's Desert Eagle was empty. He dropped it to grip the Beretta 93-R with both hands. Kamel shuffled closer. The Executioner was suspicious of the big man, but he also didn't trust the other two.

"That spontaneous-human-combustion device or

fusion microwave or whatever the hell you call it,"
Bolan stated. "Are there any more of them we don't
know about?"

"They built only one other like it," Sabkhat replied, eager to be helpful and divorce himself from
the terrorist activities. "I assume you got it or someone has it now. Captain Qatrun took it to Tel Aviv."

"You traitor!" Barrah snarled. "You betray the
jihad!"

"It failed, Professor," Sabkhat replied. "Time to
accept that and make a deal with Uncle Sam and the
CIA."

"Deal with infidels?" Barrah seemed stunned.

"He invented the machine," Sabkhat told Bolan.
"You'll need him and me, but the big man is just a
stupid fanatic. I suggest you kill him now."

"Kill him?" Barrah asked with astonishment.

Kamel didn't understand English, but he obviously
realized by the tone of Barrah's voice and gestures
of outrage Sabkhat had said something to upset him.

"Don't be foolish," Sabkhat told Barrah.
"There's nothing else we can do now."

"Yes," Barrah insisted. "There is one other
choice."

The scientist reached for something by the base of
the SHC machine. Bolan swung his Beretta toward
the Saudi, but saw the zealot had grabbed a thin
chain. Barrah suddenly lunged at Sabkhat. He
brought the chain around the banker's head as the
impact of the unexpected charge drove both men off
balance to stagger into a wall.

Bolan was distracted by this display. He turned his
attention toward Kamel, but the big man had already
seen his chance and made his move. The karate-
calloused edge of the bodyguard's hand struck the Ex-

ecutioner's forearm above the wrist. The blow jarred the ulnar nerve and forced him to drop the 93-R.

Kamel shoved his good right arm across Bolan's chest and swept a foot to the soldier's ankle. A fundamental judo move, the trip threw Bolan off balance and dumped him on his back. No stranger to martial arts, he automatically broke his fall with a forearm slap to the floor and landed on his left thigh and buttocks. He instantly lashed out a leg in a fast arc and sunk the steel toe of his boot between Kamel's legs. The big Arab gasped in pain as Bolan braced his back to the floor and launched another kick.

His leg rose high and slammed a boot heel into Kamel's mouth. The kick staggered the big man and sent him back several steps, blood oozing from split lips. Bolan rose swiftly and prepared to square off with Kamel. The report of a small-caliber pistol suddenly drew his attention once more to Sabkhat and Barrah.

The Saudi scientist slumped along the wall, crimson dots on his white shirt. Sabkhat had drawn a diminutive chrome pistol from a pocket or ankle holster, probably a .32 caliber. It had little stopping power, but was lethal at close quarters. The banker turned toward Bolan. He saw the Executioner didn't have a gun and his expression suggested he was no longer interested in surrender.

"You seem too hardheaded to deal with," Sabkhat announced as he pointed the pistol at Bolan. "Nothing personal..."

The Executioner saw that a copper amulet dangled at Sabkhat's chest, and he realized Barrah had slipped it around the banker's neck before the man shot him. The soldier glanced at the SHC machine and reckoned he could reach it with two long strides.

Kamel stood in place and waited for Sabkhat to kill the American.

Sabkhat's pistol barked. The bullet struck Bolan in the center of the chest. The impact felt similar to a hard poke by a metal rod and threatened to push him off his feet. The soldier weaved with the motion and used the shove to propel himself to the control panel of the SHC machine. Sabkhat stepped closer and aimed his weapon.

Bolan had seen the photo of the controls and recalled which button activated the intense microwave. He punched it before Sabkhat could trigger the pistol again, the man's eyes widening as he seemed to realize what was about to happen.

The banker burst into blue flame when the wavelength hit the crystal amplifier in the amulet. Bolan turned away to avoid looking at the white core he knew would be at the center of Sabkhat's fiery form.

Kamel bellowed with rage and charged Bolan. His vision seemed affected by witnessing the glare of the lethal blaze, but he swung a vicious cross-body karate stroke at the Executioner. Bolan thrust his arms forward to chop the sides of both hands into Kamel's forearm to block the attack. He quickly hooked his left fist to the side of the big man's jaw.

Before Kamel could attempt another move, Bolan grabbed his wrist with his right hand. The soldier pulled hard and thrust his left hand under his adversary's hand. Bolan suddenly pivoted and raised the captive arm to twist at the wrist and elbow. He stepped forward and swung both arms down. The leverage on Kamel's arm threw the big man to the floor.

Bolan held his opponent's wrist and hand as he rammed a heel into the nerve center at the terrorist's armpit. Kamel flopped onto his back, dazed by the painful blow. The Executioner swiftly dropped to the floor, slid one leg under Kamel's head and pressed the other across his throat. Still holding Kamel's arm firmly, he locked his ankles together to apply pressure with his legs around his adversary's neck.

Kamel struggled weakly, already battered and stunned by Bolan's tactics. His wounded left arm prevented him from trying to pull Bolan's legs apart as they constricted his windpipe and carotid artery. Kamel's boots kicked the floor in a wild spasm before his body went limp. Bolan continued to apply pressure until he was certain the man was dead.

"Doesn't look like you need any help," Rafael Encizo remarked as he entered the room. "You okay?"

"Yeah," Bolan answered as he rose from the floor, "but I probably wouldn't be if I hadn't worn my Kevlar."

He tapped his chest near the tear in his shirt caused by Sabkhat's .32 bullet. The slug hadn't even dented the dense weave of the bullet-resistant vest under the cloth. Encizo nodded and turned to stare at the SHC device.

"That's the thing?" he asked. "They didn't get a chance to fry the guts out of this one?"

"No," Bolan replied, "it still works. There's a pile of ash on the floor to prove it. David and T.J. were hurt."

"They're okay," the Cuban assured him. "Cal is looking after them now. Looks like a wall fell on them. They're a little bruised, but nothing seems to be broken. Probably the worst injury will be McCarter's wounded pride."

"That'll pass soon enough," the soldier commented. "You guys sure all the terrorists are taken care of?"

"Positive," Encizo confirmed. "Jinn 2000 will find out how accurate their notions were about life after death. Bet they'll be surprised."

Bolan approached the SHC machine. He placed his hands on the controls and glanced at the corpse of Barrah and the cremated remains of Sabkhat. Gary Manning appeared at the doorway and joined Encizo.

"Oh, shit," the Canadian remarked. "I sort of hoped we wouldn't find that thing. David and T.J. are fit to travel. I guess we can leave, but I don't know how we'll get that SHC weapon past the Libyans at the border."

"That won't be a problem," Bolan told him. "Better look the other way, fellas."

Bolan hit the destruct switch on the panel. He turned and headed for the doorway as the machine glowed from the fusion process within. Encizo uttered a low whistle, while Manning gave a thumbs-up in approval of Bolan's decision.

James, McCarter and Hawkins met them in the hallway.

"You burned the machine," James said, "didn't you?"

Bolan nodded. "Yeah. Nobody gets it. No terrorists, no Libyan colonels and no U.S. government."

"The President won't be very happy," Hawkins remarked.

"The terrorist threat is over," Bolan stated. "That's what we do. Helping to make or supply the military with more weapons of mass destruction isn't our job. Enough people work on those sort of projects already."

"I reckon they would be inclined to use it for that

purpose rather than constructive power sources," McCarter said with a sigh. "That's how things always seem to turn out."

"Eventually someone else will come across the same microwave fusion process or something like it," Bolan remarked. "Maybe when it's 'rediscovered' it will happen in a world more interested in developing fusion energy for all the right reasons instead of just another way to kill."

"Think that world will ever exist?" Manning asked.

"Maybe if enough people want it to," the Executioner replied. "Let's get the hell out of here. We've got a long ride home."

From the creator of Deathlands
comes...

OUTLANDERS™

An all-new series by James Axler!

Enter the future—a postholocaust world where
the struggle between the classes takes on a
whole new reality...where the misery of the
final conflagration gives way to a promise of a
new beginning...and where the inhabitants of
the entire planet find themselves facing a new,
all-powerful and alien enemy....

Available this June
wherever Gold Eagle books are sold.

OUT-G

TAKE 'EM FREE
4 action-packed novels plus a mystery bonus
NO RISK
NO OBLIGATION TO BUY

SPECIAL LIMITED-TIME OFFER

Mail to: Gold Eagle Reader Service
3010 Walden Ave.
P.O. Box 1394
Buffalo, NY 14240-1394

YEAH! Rush me 4 FREE Gold Eagle novels and my FREE mystery gift. Then send me 4 brand-new novels every other month as they come off the presses. Bill me at the low price of just $15.80* for each shipment—a saving of 15% off the cover prices for all four books! There is NO extra charge for postage and handling! There is no minimum number of books I must buy. I can always cancel at any time simply by returning a shipment at your cost or by returning any shipping statement marked "cancel." Even if I never buy another book from Gold Eagle, the 4 free books and surprise gift are mine to keep forever.   164 BPM A3U4

Name	(PLEASE PRINT)	
Address		Apt. No.
City	State	Zip

Signature (if under 18, parent or guardian must sign)

* Terms and prices subject to change without notice. Sales tax applicable in NY. This offer is limited to one order per household and not valid to present subscribers. Offer not available in Canada.   GE-96

When terrorism strikes too close
to home...

DON PENDLETON'S

THE EXECUTIONER®

THE
AMERICAN
TRILOGY

An ultraright-wing militia force is using acts of
terrorism to splinter American society. But a greater
conspiracy is at the heart of the violence on U.S. soil
as a foreign enemy seizes the chance for revenge
against a nation in turmoil. It's up to Mack Bolan to
infiltrate the group and bring it to its knees—before
it's too late.

Available this June, July and August
wherever Gold Eagle books are sold.

GOLD
EAGLE®

AT-G